MW01240612

KASIM THE KOMEDIAN

Meja Mwangi

HMBOOKS

1st Edition 2023

Cover by George Abuga

Contact: info@mejamwangi.com
www.mejamwangi.com

For Alex Kamau a onetime comedian

BOOK 1
How do you tell a Kuyu is dead?

Chapter 1

The roosters overslept. She would have overslept too but for the cold. It was the cold that woke her.

She thought to get up and start on his early morning tea, for he liked a cup in bed before rising to face the day. But it was still too dark and cold outside. She gathered the bed cover around her and tried to go back to sleep. An hour later, she was still awake. The neighbours' dogs were howling and there was not a hint of dawn in the air.

She rose twice in the night to peer round the curtains expecting to see a big, yellow moon in the sky. Dogs did not bark madly unless there was a full moon, or the chicken and mango thieves were about. They had grown daring, stealing in broad daylight when she was home, and he was dozing in his rocking chair on the back patio.

Thinking of thieves, she felt on the table for the matchbox. The match was unnaturally loud when she struck it, but it flared and caught. A second later, it flattered and died though there was no draft in the room.

It must be the cold, she thought, taking out a second match. She struck it, cupped it in her hands until it caught, then held it to the clock tick-ticking loudly on the bedside table. It was five o'clock.

As she marveled at how so quickly the night had passed, the match burned down to her fingers. She dropped it and lay in the dark thinking of the day ahead.

She bathed him every morning before breakfast, then she shaved him, combed his hair, the little that was left of it, and parted it in the middle like that of his heroes Lumumba and Mandela. Then she dressed him in one of his custom-tailored suits that he bought while on official visits abroad. Beautiful, dark grey suits, with lighter grey pinstripes, that he had worn them with a white carnation on

1

his lapel when he received foreign dignitaries at government house. The suits did not fit so well anymore, but he felt good in them, for they made him look distinguished.

Today she would dress him in one of his slant-striped neckties, the one with which he taught her how to knot a tie. He never went anywhere, not even to inspect his fruit trees, without suit and tie.

For lunch, she would serve chicken soup, with potatoes, carrots, leeks, tomatoes, and spinach. She learned to make chicken soup from Eva, who learned it from her mother. It revived his stamina and made him stronger, made him speak loudly, with authority as he did when he was somebody.

He would then sit in the shade of his tree and talk of pruning the old mango and avocado trees and planting pear trees and plum trees, and apples trees. Everyone told him plums, pears and apples would not grow, but he was adamant they would. His garden would be the garden of Eden full of calm, sweetness, fragrance, and peace. A place birds, and bees, and children would feel safe and welcome.

When she reminded him he was not strong enough for it anymore, that he could no longer shelter orphans and runaways, and neither could she, that they were both past running after grandchildren to see that all was well, he got a faraway look in his eyes, smiled, nodded, and kept on smiling.

Today her neighbour's son, would catch and slaughter the chickens for her. Other than old memories, chicken soup was the only thing he still relished.

The barking intensified outside. She felt on the table by the bed for the matchbox. She struck a match, and lit the kerosene lamp. On the table lay a dog-eared bible with a black leather cover and gold lettering. Next to the table was a metal lampstand with an electric bulb inside a blue-flowered lampshade.

She threw back the covers. She could not remember another July night so cold she thought, as her feet felt for her slippers on the cold floor. Hugging her gown for warmth, she picked up the lamp and shuffled out into a cold, drafty corridor. The house was dead silent. There were six doors in the corridor, three on each side. Hers was the farthest from the exit.

Kerosene lamp in hand, she hobbled along to the first door on the right.

"Are you awake?" she called out softly.

Not a sound from within. She tapped on the door and raised her voice.

"Caesar?" she called, "Are you awake?"

She waited to hear him clear his throat, meaning he was awake and ready for his early morning cup. Hearing no sound, she shuffled back to her room, closed her door, and got back in bed.

She took the Bible and started to read, speaking the words out softly to herself. She read for half an hour every morning, the same verses of the Psalms she felt gave her strength to carry on. Then she put the book back on the table and closed her eyes to pray.

"The Lord is my shepherd I shall lack nothing," she prayed. "He makes me to die ... to lie ... down in green pastures. He leads me beside the still waters. He protects me."

Then she lay in contemplation a while before rising to go make his tea.

The embers from the night before were still warm inside the wood-burning stove in the kitchen. Caesar had the stove imported from England for the wonderful kitchen he was building for his foreign wife. A kitchen fit for a palace; it was large enough to cater for an entire clan. But the soaring ceilings and the walls, once ivory and full of light, were now black with soot. The large, glass windows were opaque from smoke. Two panes had long been replaced with pieces of cardboard.

The kitchen was planned with electrical appliances in mind, things never seen in Kathiani before. A six-burner electric oven, to one side of the sink, a dishwasher to the other side. The counter held high-capacity microwave oven, toaster, mixer, and a deep-fryer. At the end were a large freezer and a refrigerator.

The house was built long before anyone could believe electricity coming, but electricity did come, at the right time and in the right amount, and stay long enough for his wife to learn to use the electrical appliances that came with the house, and get used to a brightly lit, smoke-free kitchen.

Then, just as everyone started taking it for granted that it would always be there, it disappeared. Not just from Caesar's palace but from all over. People blamed Caesar for offending the President by declining to join in the abuse of power and the looting of national resources.

Electricity was gone for so long everyone forgot about it. They turned back to the old ways of lighting their lives. When decades later electricity returned, not even Caesar could afford paying for it. His wife's magnificent kitchen and its awe-inspiring apparatus remained to collect dust, cobwebs, and rust, long after her death. Gone too were his big cars, his friends, and all the trappings that came with the illusionary power of a high public office, which could not survive a fall from grace.

The fridge was a dry foods cupboard, the oven a ready food storage. The freezer was a safe for important family documents. The mixer, the blender, the fryer, and the microwave waited for someone who knew what to do with them to come and take them away. Of all the appliances Caesar bought to honour his wife, only the woodburning stove still did what it was meant to do.

"Thank God," she said, as she stirred the ashes and added wood.

The fire caught and the wood crackled. She filled the kettle, added a generous spoonful of tea leaves, and placed it on the stove. It was still dark, and unnaturally cold, but it would be soon light and warm when the sun rose over the hills.

Her hands shook slightly as she laid the breakfast table on the veranda. Beige tablecloth, white serviettes, old, slightly cracked china, and silver cutlery. Real silver service used when he entertained big, important men.

Back in the kitchen, tea was ready. She poured one-cup in his special teapot and placed it on a tray. She fetched his favorite cup, the one Eva brought from America for his seventieth birthday, and placed it on the tray. Two ginger biscuits went on a white saucer.

She carried the tray carefully back down the corridor to his door and placed it on the small mahogany table by the door. In the old days, she would knock twice and walk away. Now she knocked twice, and waited to hear him clear his throat announcing he was awake and ready for his tea. Getting no sound from within, she knocked again.

"Caesar," she called.

She softly opened the bedroom door and stuck her head inside. It was dark inside the room, with the curtains drawn and the light from the corridor reaching no farther than a foot or two.

"Are you awake?" she asked softly from the doorway.

There was no response. The room was dead still. Leaving the door open, and careful not to bump into his reading chair and startle him, she felt her way to the window. She was reaching up for the curtains when the silence penetrated her mind. Caesar was a loud sleeper, so loud she could hear him from her room at the end of the passage. Now from a few feet away, she did not hear him breathe. A chill descended on her, as she drew the curtains.

Caesar lay on his back, mouth slightly open and not a sound of air going in or coming out of it. She stepped closer, slowly reached out and touched him. His forehead was cold. She grabbed the bedstead to stop from falling, and stood trembling, staring at the stone-cold face, the thin, grey hair, and the head that had once held the wisdom of the clan and the politics of a nation. It was shrunken and dry, devoid of an expression. She could not find the tears.

She stumbled out of the room with her mind numb. She softly shut the door, picked up the tray and took it back to the kitchen. She placed it by the sink and leaned on the table, staring out of the window, at the orchard and the old place under the mango tree where he loved to sit. His old chair was there, waiting. On the hills beyond, tiny metal-roofs clung to mud brick houses like ticks on an old cow. Caesar had paid for most of those metal roofs.

She had never seen the hills in such a light before. Now she understood what he meant when he said to her at bedtime, "Sleep with peace, my child, and rise with hope, for no day dawns like the other."

She sighed wearily, picked up the tray and carried it out to the veranda where she had laid out his breakfast table. She placed the tray at his place on the table and sat down. She sat for a long moment, still on the inside and on the outside, as the sun rose over the hills and school children passed noisily by the gate on their way to school.

Her eyes misted over, and she saw a girl, seven years old, step off the veranda in a green and orange uniform, and run to the gate. At the gate she, stopped to look back and wave. And Caesar, tall, lean, and grey limped out of the house and hobbled to the middle of the yard holding out a blue lunchbox. The girl ran back for it, hugged him, and ran to catch up with the other children.

The old man walked slowly to the gate, looked the way the girl had gone, then the other way, then turned and smiled at the old woman and waved. She smiled and waved back. Then he turned away and was gone.

Finally, she rose, supporting herself on the table, and walked round it to sit in his chair.

She had tears in her eyes as she filled his teacup.

Chapter 2

They said it would never happen, but it did. The old normal came back, with fury and fire, and reckless abandon. It had reopened the floodgates for everything that was familiar, and a lot that was not, the good, the bad, and everything in between, and left them wide open for joy and laughter to return. Throughout the city, the living had come back to life and resumed interrupted life's journeys.

Haalloo!' the comedian shielded his eyes from the glare of the spotlight and peered in the gloom. "Remember me?"

"We know you, Kasim," said an irritated woman with pink hair. "Up here every night, telling jokes and, when we have time, we laugh to make your life less miserable."

"You know me too much, my sister," the comedian said with a laugh.

"I am not your sister," she said. "And you are not funny."

She was a professional hunter-gatherer, a veteran wallet inspector decked out in fluorescent pink wig, pink lipstick, and finger nails to match. Her hands were all over the intoxicated man slumped over the table by her side, ransacking his pockets for a wallet.

The old normal came back burdened with a foreign spirit drape in an aura of uncertainty and fear like a haunted animal. Hard-life men, the men who pushed pull carts and pulled push carts, and whistled as they did so, were back hustling a living, but they did not whistle as much as before. The hard-life women, the women who rose at dawn and walked miles to sell them breakfast wrapped in old newspapers, on the streets where they worked and lived, were also back at work, but they did not trust as before.

All over the city, restaurants and meat-roasting dens were sizzling, bars popping, clubs hopping, but everyone was struggling to catch up with lost time and past lives.

Muggers were back at work in their dark alleys behind River Road, and the street girls were back at their street corners around town, as thin as gazelles in a draught, and full of the old, invincible spirit. The old normal was back. Those that saw it for what it was, a second chance at life, escaped the confines of their imagination and crossed the invisible social divide to the upper side of town where grass was always green.

For resourceful street women, there was no greener pasture to migrate to than *Uncle Dave's Curry and Comedy House*. The place was full of fat, old men with bundles of money to burn, and pretty, young women to light it for them. The wheelers and dealers, the landlords and politicians, were out enjoying their right to happiness and pursuit of happiness, and it was a sight no one thought they would ever see again.

Everyone was welcome at *Uncle Dave's*. Black, white, rich, poor, man, woman, or whatever, were received with open arms, so long as they had money to spend, they paid their bills in full, and kept their club demons on short leashes.

No one knew club demons better than the proprietor, Mr Dave, as he sat in his place at the quiet end of the bar observing the comedian on stage sweat to persuade the audience to love him.

"*Jaamboo* again," he yelled in the microphone.

Drawing out his *aas* and *oos* in a cranked-up microphone was his way of starting another session of disdainful exchange with a scornful audience. But, apart from pink hair, who was always bored and annoying, few seemed to have noticed or wondered what he was doing on stage.

"Kasim the Komedian," he said to them. "*Triple K* for Kuyu, Kamba and Kisii."

"*Booring*," said the pink wig.

"Remember me?" the comedian said, ignoring her. "The nuisance up here every night toiling to help you find meaning in your lives? *Haa-haa*, as if you had any?"

The only other person who heard him yelled from the back of the club telling him to shut up and go home.

"Not before you tell me how you know a Kuyu is dead."

The question made Mr Dave cringe. This would have been a suitable time to forget laughter, and run the club without comedy. But the comedian had months of contract left, and sacking him now could cost more than keeping him on the payroll, and, besides, short of hiring scantily clad women in short reed skirts to flaunt their assets on stage, there was no other way to keep the patrons distracted, and spending, when the club band took a break.

His club band, the legendary *Black Survivors*, was in recess by the open-air urinals at the back of the club smoking weed, drinking from clear liquor bottles, and discussing politics.

Weed, unlabeled concoctions and politics were forbidden at the club, but the band could ignore the rules quietly, and peacefully, out by the men's toilets.

"They are good boys," Mr Dave had assured to calm Kasim's jitters about sharing a stage with a gang of *khat*-chewing, weed-happy rebels.

Then Kasim had leapt on to the stage bouncing with wild enthusiasm, only to have it quickly doused by the patrons' indifference.

"Kasim," Mr Dave called from the bar.

"I will be right back," Kasim said to the audience, hopping off the stage and rushing over to the bar.

"What is the matter?" asked Mr Dave. "You seem to struggle too much?"

"Where did you get this lot, Uncle Dave?" Kasim asked. "All they want to do is sleep."

"Hard working men tend to do that this time of night," said Mr Dave. "But that is not why I summoned you."

"Club policies again?"

"Just to remind you."

"No tribal, racial, or political jokes? I remember all that."

"Then go wake them up, and keep them drinking so they can pay your salary."

It was the wishing hour at *Uncle Dave's*. Any man not dead drunk, sleeping with his face buried in the bosom of a pretty, young woman, was wishing he were home sleeping next to someone who would not be gone with his wallet when he woke up. And any woman not on wallet-inspection duty wished she were somewhere else, with a younger companion who did something more exciting than snore in her bosom.

Left to their devices, women inspected sleeping men's wallets, ordered expensive drinks, and kept the change. On occasion, they returned the wallets after they had reordered the contents, thinned it appropriately, and stuffed the extra money inside their bras. Sometimes they were still around when the men woke up.

"Tell me, my sister," Kasim said to the only person who noticed him. "You are so clever. How do you know when a Kuyu is really dead?

"If it is dry, it is dead," she said.

"A Kuyu is not a tree."

"It is."

"It is not."

"It is."

He hopped down from the stage, approached her table and lowered his voice.

"Go back to school," he said.

"I am a Member of County Assembly," she said.

"Was," he reminded.

She lowered her voice too.

"Elected not nominated," she said. "You can't be elected without University degree,"

"The whole country knows all about those degrees, and how you lost that job?"

Her appearance suddenly changed, her eyes got inflamed and her hair seemed to glow. He stepped back fearing she was about to spit in his face.

"You are a bad comedian. Why do you talk to me when I am working?"

"Because I understand you, sister," he said. "You have children at home and a husband who lost his businesses to lockups, lockdowns, curfews, and all that mayhem, and you have rent and school fees to pay and relatives who believe you are still a county big man."

"You understand," she said.

"But have you ordered your mosquito suit?"

"Mosquitos wear suits? Where do you come from?" she said to him. "Half Kikuyu, half Kamba, half Kisii? What sort of tribe is that?"

"What sort of tribe wears red hair?" he asked her.

"Pink," she raised her voice. "My hair is pink."

"Why?"

"I said I was busy."

"And I asked why. You would hear me, if you took your fingers out of the man's wallet for a moment."

Men jerked awake and felt for their wallets. Some wallets had gone missing, along with the girlfriends sitting next to them. Coats, phones, car keys, and house keys were also missing. Wallet inspectors swore innocence, and the men turned on one another with accusations of stealing, money, phones, drinks, and girlfriends.

"Stop," Kasim ordered through the cranked-up microphone.

The fracas stopped, startling Mr Dave as much as it did Kasim.

"Sit down all of you," he ordered. "I said sit down or I have you kicked out and barred from returning ever. I said sit!"

Some sat, others demanded to know who he thought he was to order them about.

"Kasim the Komedian," he said. "I have an important announcement from the manager."

Everyone sat down. The last time they heard a special announcement from the management was on New Year's day when Mr Dave offered free drinks from five-thirty to six in the morning, and they tried to drink his week's stock in half an hour. Kasim turned to the bar and smiled at Mr Dave. Mr Dave shook his head, raised a finger in warning. Kasim turned to the house, lowered his voice to a reconciliatory level.

"We have all been here before," he said. "We know what goes on here. You buy her a drink, she slips you something, you fall asleep and wake up a little later, a little poorer and a little wiser. Remember? That is all there is to it. So let us all grow up and be men. Be more careful with your money next time."

They looked at one another. Was that all the management had to say?

"Go home and die," someone called out.

"No, no," said the woman sitting next to him rifling his wallet, "Go home, eat *githeri* and die."

"No, no, no," said a happy wallet inspector. "Go home, eat *githeri,* get corona, get cholera and die."

They finally had something to laugh at, and Kasim had his audience back.

"All in due time," he said to them. "But first, I must tell you this joke."

The room was about to allow him his last wish. At the bar, Mr Dave shook his head and left through the door to his office at the back. Then the *Black Survivors* stormed back and announced Kasim's time was up. Some people cheered.

"Not before you hear this one," Kasim told them.

"It is not funny," said the band leader, grabbing the mike from him. "Go home, Kasim."

"I must sing my closing number."

"The big, fat policeman song? I will sing it for you."

"Go home, Kasim," yelled pink lips.

A half-full bottle landed by his feet. Watching him wipe his shoes, the audience finally laughed. Someone tossed another bottle at him. He ducked. The bottle struck the drummer, and he hurled back. The audience went wild pelting Kasim with bottles, glasses, ashtrays, and shoes borrowed from sleeping companions.

Mr Dave peeked round the office door, saw what was happening, and shut it again. The band carried Kasim to the stage exit and tossed him out back of the club. A moment later, he stuck his head through the door.

"My guitar?" he yelled.

The band leader threw it after him, slammed, and bolted the stage door.

"I will be back," Kasim yelled through the closed door.

Then he stopped to reorientate himself. *Uncle Dave's Curry and Comedy House* was an old colonial government residence set in sprawling gardens with blooming jacarandas and flame trees and overrun with flowering tropical bushes. The house was renovated and extended to accommodate the bar and the night club, and there was talk of it one day becoming another Panafric Hotel.

He turned left through fragrant kiss-me-quick bushes, picked his way through the dark and round to the well-lit front of the club. The parking was full as usual for the time of month. He made his way past Mr Dave's black Mercedes and proceeded to a battered, orange Beetle parked three spaces away. He tossed his guitar in the back seat through the open window, opened the door and crawled in the driver's seat.

He paused to reflect on the night's events and wonder how life would have been, had he turned left, instead of right, at the point of no return. Realising that his life would probably have been the same unpredictable maze of challenges, he reached down and felt under the seat for the car key. He often dreamed of reaching under the seat and finding the key gone, but this time it was there.

He inserted it in the ignition and turned. Not a whimper from the engine. He turned the key again with the same result. He crawled out of the car, went to the back, and opened the engine cover.

He knew a lot about car engines, having spent two years as a student at *Uncle Tivo's College of Motor Engineering*, but he did not know what to do when a car had fuel and the engine would not start. He did what stranded motorists did on Ngong Road. He tap-tapped on the engine cover, massaged the wires, pulled, and pushed, touched this and that, all to no avail. Then he took out his screwdriver and looked for screws to tighten or loosen, as he had seen roadside mechanics do, but again to no avail.

"*Ero!*" a voice called behind him.

He jerked up startled and banged his head on the engine cover. A security guard stood behind him, wielding a *rungu* and looking aggrieved.

"Oh, it is you," Kasim said rubbing his head. "I have no cigarettes today."

He turned back to his repair work.

"Why do you tell bad jokes about Kikuyu?" the guard asked him.

Kasim stopped startled. The guard was still there behind him, still armed and still aggrieved. He hardly ever spoke to Kasim except to ask for a cigarette. Kasim could not imagine how a man guarding cars for what he imagined was a pittance would know what he did in the club.

"You have heard my comedy standup?" he asked him.

"Stand up how?" said the guard.

Men with less stressful jobs than guarding sleeping cars, men with university degrees in something or other, men who had doctorates earned in record time, had trouble too understanding what Kasim really did.

"Stand up?" they asked. "Stand up how?"

"Comedy stand-up."

"How do you make it stand up?"

14

Kasim's own Uncle Richard who had been round the world, and brought home a load of degrees and a woman from Scotland, had Kasim explain exactly what he did for a living. Then he had refused to understand or accept it as a legitimate way of making a living. Who would pay to hear Kasim speak once he opened his mouth?

But a carpark watchman had risked his stress-free job sneaking backstage to hear him make people laugh. It warmed Kasim's heart.

"*Ero*," he said, to the man he now suspected was a distant relative. "Just as you watch cars sleep, I tell jokes."

"Why?"

"Are you a Kuyu man?"

"No."

"Then let me finish fixing this engine and I will tell you why."

He went back to tinkering with the engine. The guard watched him tight wires, and probed with his screwdriver looking for something to loosen or tighten.

At *Uncle Tivo's College of Motor Engineering* he would have had the use of a pick axe, and an array of spanners, hammers, and monkey wrenches to choose from. All he had now was a pocket screwdriver and a vague recollection of what he was supposed to do..

"*Ero*," he said to the guard, taking a break to rest his knees. "I like people. Thin people, fat people, ugly people, short people, tall people. Kuyu people, Kalenjin, Kamba, Luo people, Mzungu people, Chinese people … green coloured people, blue coloured people, and all shapes, sizes and colours of people. That is why I tell jokes about people. Would you like to hear one about Martian people?"

The man had started walking away the moment he heard mention of blue coloured people.

"*Ero*, don't go yet, I need a push."

The man disappeared back in the shadows without a break in his stride. Kasim exhausted all his remaining mechanical knowledge and skills trying to reconnect the wires he had disconnected from the engine. He had no money for a taxi home. He considered calling Cousin Salim, but he remembered Salim had money problems of his own and kept calling to ask when Kasim would pay for the Beetle.

He was half-asleep, slumped over the driving wheel, contemplating the meaning of life without money, when Mr Dave found him after the club closed in the early hours of the dawn, and banged on the roof. He sat up startled.

"Just resting my eyes, Uncle Dave," he said, getting out of the car.

"Go do that at home," said Mr Dave. "We can't have you sleeping here like a homeless person."

"My most understanding landlord locked me out."

"Again unpaid rent? Didn't I pay your salary just last week?"

"You know how it is with money," said Kasim with a shrug. "In through one pocket and out of the other."

"So, what are you going to do now? Move into this parking?"

"May I?"

"No."

"I will just sit here and work on my jokes until opening time."

"Your jokes need a lot of work. Your jokes need jokes."

"I'm on it, Uncle Dave."

"I know you are on it, Kasim, that is what worries me."

"I told you not to worry, I'll get there."

"Get to a real job."

"This job is to me real," Kasim said. "As real as rain. Rain may make us wet, cold, and uncomfortable, but there are no pickings, no harvests, without rain."

"Uncertain dreams, like political promises, are washed away by the slightest drizzle."

"Not mine, Uncle Dave," said Kasim. "I will be the greatest comedian in the world, if it kills me."

"But it need not come to that," said Mr Dave. "You are an intelligent man, Kasim. You can do better than simply be. You can make things happen."

"Now you have lost me, Uncle Dave," said Kasim

Mr Dave considered, placed a hand on Kasim's shoulder and lowered his voice.

"I will take another chance on you, son. I will make you my assistant."

"Assistant club owner?" asked Kasim.

"Don't push it."

Kasim paused and thought about it.

"Uncle Dave," he said, "I have trouble managing my own life."

Between morning clubs, afternoon clubs and night clubs, there was little left of his life to manage, and even that was a challenge. He had no bank account, no wife, no girlfriend no budget, and still could not manage. Comedy was all he could manage.

"It is the only thing I know."

"Now may be the time to know something different," Mr Dave tried, with a fatherly pat on the shoulder. "To start in a new direction; learn something new."

He stopped just short of saying *be a useful member of society*. He knew where that would lead.

"You could start by learning to play that thing," he pointed in the back seat.

"My guitar?"

"They can see you do not play it."

Kasim knew it too, and often wished he could learn to play the guitar for real, read and write music, and be a composer all in one day. And have his own music label and recording studio and comedy club where he could make them laugh any time of day or night. With a day job at *Uncle Dave's*, he could do all that and more.

"Will I still entertain here?" he asked Mr Dave.

"Entertain?" Mr Dave let out a sad laugh. "My customers are deserting because of you and your jokes, and the band just quit ...

"Quit? They say you fired them."

"I gave them conditions."

"Uncle Dave, poets don't understand conditions."

"They are reggae boys."

"Poets."

"Are you a poet too?"

"So that you na fire me? Let's not make it personal."

"I could not pay them more, because my customers are deserting me, because of you and your jokes. And you want to still entertain here? Entertain whom? Invisible people?"

"Uncle Dave, I will get your people back. I will bring all your customers back, I promise. The reggae boys too. I know they will. Where else is there for them to go play? The Hard Life Club? Even cockroaches don't go there to dance."

"You really are a comedian," Mr Dave started off laughing and shaking his head.

"See you tonight then," Kasim called after him.

"Tonight is Monday."

Kasim had not realised it was no longer Sunday night.

"Uncle Dave," he called, "is it true you are joining the political cartels?"

"Go home, Kasim," said Mr Dave.

Kasim crawled back inside his Beetle, curled up in the driver's seat and closed his eyes. He instantly fell asleep and dreamed of gunshots and AK 47 bullets coming through the doors and windows looking for him.

The sun was up, when he next opened his eyes, and his phone was ringing, echoing round the car. He found it wedged between the seat and the backrest of the driver's seat. It was Salim.

"Why do you wake me up before I have slept?" Kasim asked him.

"Caesar is dead," said Salim.

"Again?"

"Caesar is dead."

"I heard you the first time. Caesar died again?"

Caesars had been reported dead numerous times before. Since he acrimoniously quit his Government job, and retired to tend to his pigeon peas in the hills of Kambaland, rumours of Caesar's death had become regular. He died whenever tabloids had nothing more shocking to trumpet, and whenever Aunty Charity mistook the old man's deep sleep for death and phoned Salim. Salim phoned other family members and the panic spread. This time, Salim had to call three of his aunts to confirm it.

"Arrangements at Uncle Sam's house as usual," he said to Kasim.

"Not again," Kasim groaned. "They will send me for Uncle Richard's pickup."

"Uncle Sam's house," Salim said and hung up.

Kasim stepped out of the car to stretch. The watchmen were smoking by the gate.

"*Ero*," he called.

They glanced his way, continued talking.

"Give us a push."

They took their time finishing their cigarettes.

"Ero," he called again.

They walked over laughing, no doubt about him and his car. One of them went round the car inspecting it before leaning in at the window.

"*Ero*, why don't you buy a new car?" he asked.

"All in due time," said Kasim. "For now, I would appreciate a push."

They were tired of pushing him every morning. No one else ever asked them for a push. That was not why they were there. That was not their job.

"I know," Kasim said. "You are paid to watch sleeping cars sleep. I just need a little push tonight. I promise, with my next pay cheque, I will buy a Mercedes."

They laughed at him, but put their shoulders to the car. The car rolled forward leaving a trail of engine oil.

Chapter 3

Cousin Salim reclined in his executive chair waiting for someone to call. He had been waiting since the break of day hoping for a call from a client, a friend, a fairy godmother, a rich uncle, anyone but a creditor, to ease his pain. It was the end of the month, a time to deal with financial woes. The time debtors came out of the woodwork to remind him how bad the economy was, and especially in the real estate business.

Now and then, he buzzed his secretary in the front office asking whether anyone had called. No one had called. Not even the creditors he did not want to hear from. It was nerve-wracking.

"Call them," he said to his secretary.

"I have called and called, Mister King'oo," she informed him. "They do not take my calls anymore."

He knew which ones those were, and how to deal with them next time they came begging for his services. Charge them twice as much and take a big retainer.

"Call again," he said. "You know what to say to them."

"Mister King'oo," the secretary pleaded, "Why don't you call them yourself? You are a man; they will respect you."

"They must learn to respect you too, Mrs Kilonzo," he said and hung up.

He leaned back in his executive chair, an extravagance from the old days before corona made everyone poor and unhappy. He closed his eyes and dozed off.

He had slept little in the last few weeks for thinking about money. Many of his clients claimed to have lost everything to corona. Government closedowns, the lockdowns and the enforced social distancing had left them broken and disoriented. Businesses, from street corner food kiosks to bars to factories and offices, had gone under.

Creditors could not pay him, and he could not pay salaries; and Mrs Kilonzo could not pay her house girl or the rent.

And Salim had the office and house rents to pay, car payments, utilities and Mrs Kilonzo's salary. More than enough worries to keep him awake all night long. Then Aunt Charity had called to add to his woes with news of Caesar's death. He had not slept a wink after that.

Caesar was the reason Salim had his law office ten floors up one of the most desirable locations in the city. He was at first skeptical when, straight out of college, Salim approached him for an introduction to *Douglas and Duncan*, a British law firm.

"Why Douglas and Duncan?" asked Caesar.

It was the oldest established law firm in the country.

"A British colonial establishment," reminded Caesar. "Why?"

"I could learn a lot from them," said Salim.

Caesar was silent, expecting more. But that was all Salim had at the time.

"What can you teach them?" Caesar asked.

Salim's thoughts stumbled. What could he teach a hundred-years old law firm with offices all over the world and in China? He expected to learn not teach.

Caesar seemed disappointed, as Salim's well-prepared presentation faltered. He had to stop thinking like a King'oo man and start thinking like a man. Think like Caesar. Which was hard to do with Caesar frowning at him, reading him like a badly forged report card.

"Must go think again," Salim said rising.

"That is best," said Caesar.

Six months later Salim was working for *Douglas and Duncan Law Office*. His peers, the ones with whom he had made pledged of starting own law practices, and never working for a white man, were still filling out applications forms and wading through swamps of nepotism, corruption, and bureaucratic protocol to register their own law firms. They heaped scorn on him for lack of solidarity, called him a sellout, a colonial lackey, office tea boy and white man's footstool. All for not remaining a rebel, shunning employment, and struggling with the herd.

Salim was the sole proprietor of his own law offices ten floors up a prestigious building in the city. Out of one window he had unobstructed view of the city all the way to the airport, to the cement factories and beyond. Another wall-to-wall window offered a panorama view of green uptown suburbs, and, on clear days, he could see the Kilimanjaro.

He was owner, director, and manager of *King'oo and King'oo Law Offices*. He had added an extra King'oo in the name to give it weight and inspire his clients' confidence. The only person to ever wonder was his secretary, who on her first day at work wanted to know where to find the other King'oo.

Mrs Kilonzo was a career secretary and came to him from an even older law firm, *Smith and Bentley*, when it relocated to Lusaka and Salim was just setting up his office. Efficient, organised, and knowledgeable, she run the office by herself, updating client's files, scheduling meetings, and keeping Salim's diary up to date.

When his phone rang again, it was Mrs Kilonzo with more unwelcome news. The street carwash man was at the reception asking if he should wash the car?

"What do I tell him?" said Mrs Kilonzo.

Salim had to weigh the question. He owed the man for a month of car washing. Should his answer be come back tomorrow? End of next month? End of year? Or never?

"How much do we owe him?" he asked her.

The secretary added it up, hesitated before answering.

"A lot," she said.

"Tell him to come back tomorrow."

He was about to hang up then remembered.

"Mrs Kilonzo, put all my calls through from now on."

"All of them?"

"Banks and pests too," he said.

Bank managers, the friendly ones, called about loan arrears, while unfriendly ones sent demand letters, and family and friends called to borrow money from him. He could appease some with his own corona story, for everyone knew how corona had closed government offices, the land registry, the banks, and devastated businesses like his. Most did not believe him, just as he did not believe all his debtors, but they got the message. He no longer had money to pay, give, lend, or donate to anyone. Banks and creditors got a highly modified version of his corona story, and they did not believe it either.

Mrs Kilonzo walked in with a pile of files and dropped them on his desk. Someone had called six times.

"He sounded unhappy," she said.

"Everyone is unhappy these days," he said. "Did he leave a name?"

"He would not leave his name."

Creditor, Salim thought, or pest. Most of such callers were burdened small businesses, friends, and friends of friends, and struggling relatives who should not have had his phone number.

"The landlord called."

"He already agreed to give us time till mid-month?"

"Not the office landlord," she said.

"Don't worry about him. Who else?"

"Someone who said he was your *jua kali* mechanic."

"Kajicho? He should be talking to Kasim. Has Kasim called?"

Secretary shook her head.

"Did anyone call who did not want money from us?"

"One," she said. "The client, Riara Road, will be coming for his title at six."

"You told him I would be here at six?"

"You are always here at six."

But the title in question was still at the land's office awaiting palm-greasing.

"Hezron?" he asked.

The office messenger knew the ins and out of the corridors of titles. Sometimes he could persuade a clerk to defer or waive the palm-greasing.

"Hezron has been off sick for the last three days," Mrs Kilonzo said. "I informed you."

"Go to the Lands Office," Salim said. "First thing tomorrow morning. See Mister Munene. I will call him beforehand. That will be all for now."

He turned his attention to the files on the desk. Realizing she was still there, he looked up.

"What is the matter, Catherine?"

She did not reprimand him this time for calling her by her first name. She took it as her mission to make King'oo and King'oo as serious and professional a law firm as the ones she had worked for before.

"Mister King'oo," she now said, her voice level but strict. "I understand the situation we are in financially, and I hate to pressure you at a time like this, but my husband lost his job eight months ago and has not found another one, and our landlord is trying to evict us and … I had to borrow money for bus fare to come to work this morning."

She paused, swallowed back the feelings.

"This whole week, I had to borrow money from neighbours to come to work."

A sharp pain stabbed Salim's stomach. His worry ulcers, under control for months had returned with corona. He pressed on his belly and groaned.

"I am sorry," she said.

"No, Mrs Kilonzo, it is not your fault."

She started to leave.

"Wait," he pressed his stomach to hold down the pain. "Mrs Kilonzo, you have heard from my landlord and from everyone I owe money. It is not that I do not want to pay them, or you, or the man who washes my car. You are the bookkeeper; you know our financial situation."

"I am sorry," she said again.

"Not your fault," he said again. "No one could have seen this coming."

The phone rang. He pounced on it.

"Hallo? Yes, this is King'oo and King'oo Law Office," he said. "What do you want? Salim King'oo speaking. You are cousin who? Yes, this is Salim King'oo. Was it you who called six times today? Why didn't you leave a message? So, what do you want? I have no money to buy your daughter schoolbooks. I know Caesar did that, but I am not Caesar. And Caesar is dead. I will be there at the meeting too. Yes, at Uncle Sam's house, but do not ask me for money there, here, or ever again. You understand?"

He slammed the phone down. Mrs Kilonzo quietly withdrew.

Chapter 4

Uncle Sam's house was an old colonial government mansion, a solid, two-storey building resembling a castle. It was built in the early years of British colonial rule, on two acres of an old garden blooming with flowers from over the British Empire, interspersed with manicured lawns, and sheltered by Nandi flame trees, jacarandas, and Asian flamboyant.

Kasim was an hour late when he arrived with his car smoking like the engine was on fire, and spewing out black smoke that his mechanic had said would stop before he got where he was going in such a hurry. But the car was still smoking when he got to Uncle Sam's house, and parked out on the street behind Salim's Mercedes.

There was ample parking for any number of cars inside the compound, but funeral meetings rarely ended on time. They were hard to escape from when one's car was boxed in by cars whose owners were in no hurry to leave. Having his car blocked in by mourners who were not ready to go home meant enduring endless, often banal, conversation with distant relatives, some barely remembered, and a long night of flat reminiscences, false eulogies, and small, small talk that left him drained of patience and humour. And, if by a stroke of bad luck, there happened to be a rare evangelist or an old politician, or both, the night turned to a crusade and lasted until the next Sunday.

He was about to pass the Mercedes when the door sprang open, and Salim popped out saying,

"You are late."

"Your fault," said Kasim. "Your mechanic kept me."

"Why?"

"I had no money."

"I am not paying for it, okay?"

"Don't worry," said Kasim. "I will take care of the repairs. Why are you sitting out here?"

"I was not about to go in there on my own."

He yawned and stretched.

"Can't wait to go home sleep," he said.

He was dressed in his lawyer's suit, dark grey with lighter pinstripes and beige tie. With his hair was well-groomed and parted on the right side, he looked like he had stepped out of a meeting for a cigarette break.

"How do you dress like that every day and not feel ridiculous?" Kasim asked.

"You would not understand," he said. "It is called class."

"I have been to class too."

"And left before this lesson," Salim said seriously. "You must dress the part, so people believe, respect, accept and trust you."

"Would you lend me this one for a night?" he said, examining Salim's suit. "I need respect at work."

Believe and respect were things Kasim needed a lot of in his job. He often wondered what would happen if he turned up to work in a business suit. Mr Dave would probably have a stroke, clients freak out and flee, and pink lips would likely laugh at him and ask who he hoped to impress with a recycled monkey suit.

He was about the same size as Salim, the same height and build, so matched the aunties called them pigeon peas in a pod. Twins who were not twins. But one was always elegant in suits and ties, wore real Italian shoes, and real gold watches, while the other looked like a quarry miner after work.

Uncle Tivo, in one of his chang'aa inspired trances, discerned they were twins of different mothers, one Abyssinian and the other King'oo. That did not make normal sense to most people, but King'oo relations were so wild and crazy that nothing was impossible. It would also explain why no King'oo thought, or acted, like the other no matter how simple the task. Kasim chose to believe Uncle Tivo's version of his bond with Salim, until then day a young man stopped him on River Road and asked him if he was Kisii.

"Kisii?" he asked startled.

"You walk like Uncle Mogaka," said the young man.

That day Kasim became half Kisii, half Kuyu, and half Kamba.

"Where do you get all this craziness?" Salim asked him, as they stood outside Uncle Sam's gate about to go join the clan in the campaign to bury Caesar.

He laughed, clapped a hand on Salim's shoulder.

"Come," he said. "Let us get this over with and go back where we belong."

As they approached the palatial mansion, with windows a horse and carriage could have driven through in the old days, they could tell by the rabble of conversation the meeting had not begun. The front entrance was fit for a castle, and led to what was once the ballroom. Uncle Sam, with only one wife and three grown children always away in India studying, had no idea what to do with the stately room until King'oo clan discovered it and made it an assembly hall for clan functions such as fund-raisers, and funeral arrangements.

Kasim led Salim through the garden and round the house, along the old servants' footpath, to the kitchen entrance at the back. The kitchen was Kasim's first call whenever he went to Uncle Sam's for clan gatherings. Aunt Kamene was always there supervising the party of women cooking for the mob of hungry visitors. It was his routine since the first day he and Salim entered through the back entrance by mistake and found the kitchen full of food and cooking women. Aunt Kamene was always there ready to fatten them.

"Don't you boys eat?" she asked always.

"Too busy, Aunty Kamene," Salim said, walking through.

"And you?" she asked Kasim.

"You know me, Aunty," he said with a laugh. "Always hungry, and hungry."

Salim only went through the kitchen to avoid shaking dozens of hands from the hall entrance, through the vast room to the back of the crowd.

Aunt Kamene handed Kasim a bowl of *muthokoi*.

"Eat it here," she said.

She did not want everyone crying for food before the meeting. Some would eat and go without contributing for Caesar's funeral..

"Stand there in the corner," she ordered.

"Like at school?"

"You were better fed then," she said. "Does Salim ever eat? He looks the same scrawny boy he was then."

Salim was by the open door, surveying the mob in the living room, plotting a path with the least handshakes to where there was room to sit or stand. Hearing her, he turned.

"I am fine, Aunt Kamene," he said. "I eat three times a day. He is the one that does not eat or sleep."

"Making people laugh?" she could not believe it.

"It is harder than making them cry," Kasim said.

She understood that even less.

"All I hear is how you go from bar to bar making people laugh. How can you make enough to eat doing that?"

"They laugh, they pay," he said. "But not enough for me to eat enough."

Salim finally made up his mind and stepped out of the kitchen. The meeting room was crammed with men, women, old and young, close cousins and distant relations, their friends, and their friends' friends. It appeared the whole tribe and not just the clan was there. A restless mix of humanity that made the stately room small and cramped.

Traditionally, men sat on one side, silently absorbing it all, in stoic silence and, when unavoidable, expressing their thoughts and feelings in monosyllabic utterance that needed one to have been present for a while to understand.

The women sat on the opposite side of the room, in a tight, protective herd round Aunt Charity, all with downcast faces lined with worry and the weariness of the night vigils. They had been with her from the moment they learned of Caesar's death, sat with her by day, sat in her living room by night, cleaned the house, cooked, and encouraged her to eat, when they saw she was about to fall from hunger, and to sleep when sadness wore her out.

Aunt Charity sat between two of her sisters, each of them twice her size, looking older and frailer than Salim remembered her. She was his favorite aunt, and he was her most successful pupil. She often told of her disappointment when he chose law instead of medicine. He was such a good soul, she said, he would have served the clan and humanity better as a medicine man. As a lawyer, the only clan business that came his way was that of feuding families suing one another for goats and pigeon peas and both sides expecting him to win their cases for them. All without payment, because he was family.

"Son of King'oo," they argued, when they received his bills, "if you were a mango tree farmer, and we stole your ripe mangoes when we were dying from hunger, would you ask us to pay for your mangoes?"

Neither Salim nor the judge could see any relevance to the case in court, and he gave up trying. Mangoes, oranges, bananas, pigeon peas and goats were the clan's reference points. Anything that did not tally at that level was not King'oo and was, therefore, not relevant. But when used by more than one side in a disagreement they often left everyone confused as to what the dispute was all about.

"You would have served the clan better as a brain surgeon," Aunt Charity often said.

"I know, Aunt Charity, I know," he said with a wry smile. "Free lobotomy for everyone."

31

Now she sat eyes downcast, hands in her lap, occasionally wringing them helplessly and, from time to time, raising the handkerchief to her eyes. She looked up when he reached down and clasped her hands in his.

"Salim?" she said, startled to see him.

"Yes, Aunt Charity," he said, holding and pressing gently on her hands. "I am here too."

Then he let go and went down the line shaking aunts' hands and mumbling words of sympathy. Moving on, he shook hands with people he did not recognize, until he crossed to the men's side and stopped. There were too many hands to shake, too many faces to recognise.. They sat on heavy sofas, on dining room chairs, on stools and coffee tables, and on anything that could be sat on, their eyes on the silent images on the television to avoid looking at other sad faces.

Looking right ahead, Salim made his way to the two faces that stood in the crowd. Unlike most King'oo young men, who were always dubious and always shifty, the Chinese boys were always puzzled and disoriented at clan gatherings. Puzzled because they never really understood anything that took place at King'oo gatherings, and disoriented because that was the normal appearance of strangers trying to navigate King'oo intrigues. But the boys were not strangers, and that made them intriguing.

"Who is who?" Salim asked, when he got to them.

"Cousin Salim," one said in a voice too level to be serious, "you ask the same question every time we meet."

"And we give you the same answer," said the other.

"Which is?" he asked them.

"Karate," said the one, with a big, amused smile.

"Kung Fu," said the other, with an identical, bemused smile.

They were Aunt Charity's boys. Most people knew them since they were babies crawling in Caesar's yard with the chickens and the kid goats, but apart from Aunt Charity and her sisters, hardly anyone spoke to them. One assumption was they were deaf and dumb since they did not speak unless spoken to. The other was they did not understand Kikamba, a language they had spoken since they could say *nau*, dad, and *mwaitu*, mama. It was the only vernacular they knew but, no one spoke to them.

Aunt Charity had fostered cats, dogs, babies, and children of all ages that turned up at Caesar's gate in need of food, shelter, or care. She had received them with open arms, washed and dressed them, fed them, and provided for them a place to sleep. Most of them went back home, when their wounds were healed or their parents came to reclaim them, or when whatever crises had driven them to Caesar's house was over. Others stayed so long that they and everyone else forgot where they came from. Those became Caesar's family. They became Charity's children.

"So, how have you been?" Salim asked Charity's boys.

"Okay," they said together.

"Good," he said.

That was the long and the short of their conversation at every gathering. They did not talk much, and he did not know how to make them. It made him uneasy. He looked round the room for someone to escape to.

"Cousin Salim," Kung Fu said, startling him, "Do you always wear a tie?"

"Yes," he said.

"See," Kung Fu said to his brother.

Salim informed them he needed to look sharp for business. He surveyed the room for someone to go to.

Uncle Tivo sat like royalty, front-centre of the men's side of the room, with the rest of the menfolk in rows left, right and behind him. He was on a three-seater sofa between two equally bored old faces with tobacco-stained moustaches and tangled beards. Uncle Tivo was easy-going, he liked his honey beer strong, and he distrusted politicians, preachers and anyone who did not drink beer. He was someone Salim could talk to sometimes.

He was about to go join him, then he saw Kasim enter through the kitchen door ready for anything. The Chinese cousins saw him too and suddenly perked up.

"Cousin Kasim," Karate said, nudging Kung Fu.

They watched him go round the room shaking hands, mumbling greetings, and words of sympathy, joking with some, and making some smile. When he came to the woman the boys called mother, but only in Chinese and only between the two of them, he stopped speechless, took both her hands in his and held them so she could feel the pain in his own heart. Swallowing back sobs, he told her how sad he was. He made her smile when, with such sincerity as she would never have expected of him, he said they were all in it together, as one family, and together would see it through. He silently shook the other aunts' hands before joining Salim and the Chinese cousins.

"Karate and Kung Fu," he said faking a kick and a punch. "*Hoo-haaa.*"

"That is old now, Cousin Kasim," Kung Fu said.

"How old are you?" Kasim asked him.

"Twenty-two."

"And you?" Kasim asked the other.

"We are twins."

"So how old are you together?"

They looked at each other, and he guessed they said in Chinese, *see, joker cannot count.*

"You always do that *hoo-haaa* thing," Karate said to him. "Why?"

"You only remember me when someone dies," he said. "Why? You will be investigated for dubious far eastern connections."

"By a big, fat corrupt detective?" Kung Fu asked.

"You see this scar?" he said to them, "One of them tried to mug me. He did not get very much, and you know why?"

"You did not have very much," said Karate.

"You boys know me too well," Kasim laughed with them.

Only he could make them laugh aloud at functions. Unlike disgruntled King'oo boys, the two had not forgotten their roots. They appeared at clan meetings every time to baffle some supposed relatives with their purpose.

"When was the last one?" Kasim asked them.

"Grandpa Chalo's funeral," said Kung Fu.

"No, Aunt Kalo's," said Karate.

"Grandpa Chalo," Salim said from the sidelines, where he remained ignored by the three of them. "I remember that funeral.".

He would remember any clan event that cost him so much time and money that it fired up his ulcers as well. He valued time and hated losing money.

"What took you so long?" he now asked Kasim. "I waited in the office until six o'clock."

He had planned to come in Kasim's Beetle to temper clan expectations. He had found out that arriving at clan fundraisers in his Mercedes had everyone assuming he could be the solution to all their money problems.

"Engine oil leak," Kasim said.

"With old cars you top up every morning. I told you all the time."

"I know."

"You also know you will have to pay me for it, whether it moves or not."

"I know."

"When?"

"When I make money."

"What you said before corona."

"And now it is after corona. Life is coming back to life."

He looked round.

"Or not. Did someone else die here? Why is it suddenly so quiet?"

"Waiting for Uncle Sam," said Kung Fu.

Uncle Sam arrived late from work and went upstairs to shower and change. His wife was in the kitchen supervising refreshments and everyone else was a guest. Tired of making small talk, they were waiting for someone to tell them what to do.

"I could tell them a joke," Kasim offered. "Did I tell you the one about a drunk who gatecrashed a wedding party at a funeral?"

"Stop it," said Salim.

"In that case," Kasim said to his Chinese cousins, "Sayonara."

"That is Japanese," they said together.

"I go tell that to Uncle Tivo."

Uncle Tivo sat sulking in his seat, sighing repeatedly and about to rise and leave the meeting. He looked up when Kasim stepped in front of him, regarded him for a moment.

"Is this you?" he asked.

"Me, myself and I," Kasim said. "Now all the clan is here, Uncle Tivo."

Uncle Tivo shoved the old man to his left off the seat.

"Sit down," he said to Kasim.

Kasim took the place, and Uncle Tivo leaned over. He had been waiting for someone he could talk to.

"Do you know where they hide their beer?" he asked Kasim.

Uncle Tivo hated clan meetings without beer. It was like being naked at a friend's funeral.

"They are religious here," Kasim said to him.

"I am religious too," said the old man, striking the floor emphatically with his stick. "A clan meeting without beer is against all religion. It is an abomination. Go tell them that."

"I am a guest, Tivo," Kasim pleaded.

The old man shoved him off the seat.

"Go," he said. "Get me someone who is not a guest. Go."

Kasim looked round. Everyone, including the women serving, was a guest he did not recognise.

"Go look in the kitchen," the old man said.

"Uncle Tivo," he said, "you taught me the kitchen was for women."

"You went there first. Now go back and get me someone who knows where Sam hides his beer."

He had not had a drink since leaving home early in the morning, and he had been festering since Sam's wife bluntly informed him there was no beer in the house.

"Such a big house?" he had said. "A man cannot live in such a house without beer. Go bring me your husband's beer."

Her husband did not smoke or drink, and she did not allow such things inside her house.

Her house? Uncle Tivo was ready to leave in protest, but he could not get enough old men to join in his protest. He had skulked in his seat ever since, talking to himself, striking the carpet with his cane, and swearing to never again set foot in Sam's house. Then Kasim turned up and landed the problem.

He was about to go find an aunt to pass it to when Uncle Sam came down to start the meeting. Dressed in casual, khaki trousers, a brown long-sleeved shirt rolled up to his elbows, he looked like the gardener not the master of the house.

He took out a pair of reading glasses from his shirt pocket, as he walked to the front of the gathering.

"Right," he said, reading from the clipboard in his hand.

"Lets us get this show on the road."

He stopped abruptly, looked up at the eyes fixed on him and seemed embarrassed.

"I meant to say let us get the train moving."

The gathering stopped talking over him and tried to understand the train he was talking about. He explained it was a metaphor train, not the SGR for which the government made them pay money they did not have.

"Why?" someone asked him.

He was about to respond. Then he remembered King'oo men had an uncanny gift for switching tracks between stations, and the question may not have had anything to do with anything he had said so far.

"Right," he said, returning to his clipboard. "The First order of business is …"

"Greetings," said a woman next to Aunt Charity.

"Sorry," he said. "I had a long day. This is the busiest time of year for the company, and I have a meeting after this so we must move faster."

"Greetings," Aunt Kamene reminded from the kitchen door.

She had a tea kettle in one hand and a tray of cups in the other.

"Greetings," he said, waving at the guests. "Greetings to you all."

"Greetings to you too," said Aunt Kamene.

Others had their eyes on the tray in the hands of the woman next to her.

"Our second order of business is …"

"Prayer," said Aunt Kamene.

"Of course," he said, with rising discomfort. "Is there someone here to lead us in prayer?"

He looked round.

"You know who always leads us in prayer," Aunt Kamene again.

"Where is he?" he asked. "Pastor Kioko?"

The Pastor rose from the back of the room and waved. He was a small man in his seventies, dressed in a well-pressed black suit, a pastor's black shirt and white collar, his large ears jutting out under the brim of his black hat. He made his way through to the front and stood next to Uncle Sam. He waited to be told what to do.

He was expected to officiate at every clan function, but was often reduced to a silent observer after the opening prayer. Sam introduced him to the gathering, one that he knew and that knew him well.

"Pastor Kioko," he said, "Start us off with a prayer."

Pastor Kioko waved at the gathering.

"I greet you all in the name of the Father and of the …" he started.

"Make it quick," Aunt Kamene called from the kitchen door. "This tray is killing me."

Her sharp tongue was rumoured to have driven a few men to suicide, and others to leave Kathiani never to return.

She was the most formidable King'oo woman when Eva was not present. Everyone knew she did not fear or respected men who did not fear and respect women. She was a single mother of grown children, all from different fathers, the first of whom made her drop out of school at sixteen. As a result, some women said with malice, Kamene had whipped all her children through high school, and forced her daughters to marry non-King'oo and move as far away from the clan as they could.

The Pastor smiled tolerantly at her jibes, and tried to keep his discomfort hidden. Their paths had crossed often when she helped Charity take care of Caesar and the Pastor went to comfort him. But for his love for Charity, and his respect for Caesar, Kioko would long have moved away from the clan.

"Greetings," he said again.

"Greetings," they said impatient.

"Let us bow our heads."

He made it brief, as ordered, but the woman started serving before he finished, and he retreated to the back of the room with overwhelmed non-King'oo guests. From there he saw them scramble for the *mandazi* and worried it would be another long night of unproductive exchanges.

Then he saw Uncle Sam glance at his watch and was glad he was not alone in his worries.

Uncle Sam called for everyone's attention and reminded them the meeting had to start right away, or they would be there all night.

"The first order of business," he said. "Volunteers."

"Uncle Sam?" Kasim raised his hand.

"Thank you, Kasim," said Uncle Sam. "Radio and newspaper obituaries, as always."

"I was not volunteering," Kasim said.

"You have now," he looked around. "Anyone else."

"Uncle Sam," said Kasim. "I was going to say that Uncle Tivo had a concern."

"What is it, Mzee Mativo?" Sam asked the old man.

Uncle Tivo hesitated. Kasim nudged him, whispered in his ear. This was his chance to ask where they hid their beer."

"Where is Eva?" the old man asked instead.

Kasim sat back defeated.

"Eva is in America," Uncle Sam said to Kasim. "Can you explain that to him?"

"I know where she is," said the old man. "Why is she not here?

"We only just informed her this morning."

"Why?"

Sam did not have time or energy to explain distances and time differences, and he left it to Kasim.

"We only learned of Caesar's death this morning," he said. "Will you explain that too, Kasim. And, please no more interruptions. We have many items today's agenda."

"Uncle Tivo," Kasim lowered his voice. "California is not Kathiani. It will take a long time for her to be here."

The old man cleared his throat loudly, struck the floor hard with his cane and wagged the stick at Uncle Sam.

"No more talking before Eva comes," he said aloud. "You will not bury Caesar without Eva. Go now, everyone go home."

The room fell silent. Guests looked at one another, at the old man and back at Sam. They waited for him to speak.

"We are not burying Caesar today, Mzee Mativo," said Uncle Sam. "This is a planning meeting. We can't wait for her to be here before we start."

"We don't have to wait for Eva for anything," Aunt Kamene said to Uncle Tivo. "We can bury Caesar without her."

"Eva will not like that," he said.

"Is that what she told you?" she asked him.

Uncle Tivo did not argue with her when he was sober. Any man who tried ended up looking and feeling foolish. He withdrew in his shell and festered.

"Someone, please, talk to Mzee Mativo," Aunt Kamene said. "Salim?"

Salim reluctantly left the calm surrounding the Chinese cousins and joined Kasim and the old man on the sofa.

"It is all right, Uncle Tivo," he said sitting on the other side of him. "Nothing will happen before Eva comes home. Uncle Sam is preparing so she does not have too much to do when she gets here. Eva would like it that way. We can't bury Caesar without her."

The old man thought quietly, then nodded at Sam to continue. He leaned over to whisper to Kasim.

"Let us go," he said. "You will buy me beer."

"I have no money," Kasim whispered back.

"You are a liar," said Uncle Tivo and left it at that.

They listened to Uncle Sam read a list of things and processes that had to start right away. His duties were clear, inherited the day he married in the clan. His responsibilities were to preside over the mayhem that was every clan function, damage-control family brawls, shepherd funerals to the gravesides, wherever that turned out to be, and, while at it, cover the funeral costs. His attempts to coax the clan out of his house and his life, to encourage them to meet in churches or bars, like other clans, were ignored. His only recourse was to urge them to fundraise and reach their budgets as quickly as possible, and get out of his house to go bury their dead. Again, without success.

"Salim," he called, eyes on his clipboard. "You have also volunteered for obituary notices. You and Kasim go work it out. The whole country must be informed of Caesar's death."

"Whole page notices," said Aunt Kamene.

"Whole page?" cried Kasim.

"Do you know what that will cost?" asked Salim.

"Less than it cost Caesar to educate you."

"Caesar had many friends in the government," Uncle Sam said to them. "They will help pay for his funeral. See that they know he has passed on. Details of funeral arrangements to follow. You know what to do and how to word it. You have done this before."

Salim had drafted, booked, and paid for the clan's funeral announcements often before, but that was before corona, back when he had money to spare.

"Promise me this will come from the budget," he said to Uncle Sam.

"We will see," said Uncle Sam.

They both knew what that meant. They were the last to be refunded in case of any savings.

Salim's phone rang.

"Leave it be," Aunt Kamene ordered.

He put it on mute.

"Treasurer?" she said to Uncle Sam.

He looked round the room at people who did not want to be volunteered for committee duties.

"Kitheka," he said to one of them. "You work at a bank. We need an account for donations."

"We also need an account for telephone payments," said Aunt Kamene.

"Kitheka can do that too," said Sam.

Salim's phone rang again. Thinking it was his own phone ringing, Uncle Tivo took it out and started talking.

While they listened to him reprimand someone on his phone, Salim slipped outside to answer his.

"Hallo," he said. "I'm in a meeting. My grandfather died. I left you a message."

"I am sorry," said the voice on the phone. "Afterwards?"

"It will be late," he said. "I'm sorry, I can't. I must be here every night until the funeral."

"When is that?"

"We have not set the date," he said. "I will see you tomorrow lunch."

There was an uncertain silence.

"Have you told them?" she asked.

"Told them what?"

"About us?"

He hesitated.

"Yes," he lied. "I have told them."

"And?"

"They are okay with it."

"When do I get to see them?"

"After the funeral," he said.

The meeting was breaking up when he went back in the house. Six men had been picked for interim committee members and handed their first assignments, and Kasim had volunteered him for the thankless task of informing Uncle Richard about Caesar's death.

Chapter 5

Salim's worst day started with calls from creditors demanding payment, while his calls to his debtors went unanswered. There were also calls from former clients with poor credit trawling for free legal advice with ill-disguised hypothetical questions.

It was a clear sunny day, so hot the street below shimmered from the heat, and beggars and the jobless walked like zombies about to fall dead from sunstroke.

His eyes dropped to the street below. At the car park, a tow truck backed up to a black Mercedes and men in overalls alighted and started hooking it up to the tow truck. When he realised it was his car, he yelled and frantically tried to open the window. Then he remembered all windows above the fifth floor did not open wider than enough for fresh.

"Stop," he yelled through the crack. "Stop."

They could not hear him from so high up. He dashed out of the office, jumped in the express elevator, swearing, and mumbling to himself. The elevator took forever to get to the ground floor. He shoved people out of his way, as he ran out of the building and across the street narrowly escaping a speeding motorcycle.

They were hooking the car to the tow truck when he reached them. A third man, a big round man in a suit and tie and wearing fancy sunglasses was supervising.

"This is my car," Salim yelled at them.

The big man looked at him, took off his glasses and had a better look, glanced at his clipboard.

"Salim King'oo?" he asked.

"Of King'oo and King'oo law offices," Salim said. "I own this car," Salim said.

"Not anymore," the big man held out the clipboard.

The documents authorised him to repossess the car that now belonged to the bank. The same Finance Bank that Salim had spent half a morning begging to give him time.

"I just spoke to this man," he said, waving at the clipboard.

"So?" said the big man.

"So, you can't take my car," Salim said. "Hang on just a second; no, don't hook it up. Wait!"

The man signaled the tow truck crew to pause, while Salim called the finance company.

"I'm sorry Mr Gitu is on another line," said the secretary. "Would you like to hold?"

"No," he yelled. "I would not like to hold. Tell him this is Salim. King'oo and King'oo law offices. It is urgent."

"One moment please," she said.

They waited. The man in the suit wiped sweat from his neck, looked at his watch. The secretary came back on the phone, offered the finance manager to Salim to speak to instead.

"Hallo," Salim said in the phone. "No, I don't want to speak to you. I want Mr Gitu himself. No, I will not hold anymore!"

The finance company man signaled the tow truck crew to go ahead. They hooked the Mercedes to the truck.

"Wait," said Salim. "Mr Gitu? Salim here. We spoke less than an hour ago. You promised a month for the outstanding payments. You remember? Good. So, what is this tow truck doing here?"

"What tow truck?" asked Mr Gitu.

"You don't know anything about it?"

Salim turned to the suit. The man waved the authorisation papers.

"They have papers," Salim said on the phone.

"Just a moment," said Mr Gitu.

Salim held up his hand. The men waited. Then Mr Gitu was back on the phone apologizing.

"I am sorry, my friend," he said, "The authorisation was issued two days ago, without my knowledge. The crew was on its way as we spoke."

The crew was waiting for orders.

"Unhook it," Salim said to them.

The clipboard man reached for Salim's phone.

"Mr Gitu," he said in the phone. "This is Kharisa. We have hooked it up."

He listened for a moment, handed back the phone.

"Salim here," Salim said.

"Sorry about the mess," Mr Gitu said to him, "but once they hook it up, it passes out of my hands."

"Meaning?"

"You have to deal with them now," he said and hung up.

"What sort of a Kikuyu are you?" Salim yelled in the phone. "I will sue you for incompetence."

He turned to find the crew impatient. He did not know what to say to them. He was about to walk back to his office, when the big man took his elbow and guided him away from the crew.

"Bwana Salim," he said, wiping sweat from his face and neck, "I can see that you are a reasonable man. How can I help you?"

"Leave my car with me."

"Not so easy, Bwana Salim," he said. "Once a tow is hooked, the computer in the office knows. The computer records time and place, begins to calculate mileage."

"Rubbish," said Salim.

The man laughed.

"Okay," he said. "But since your friend, Mr Gitu, agrees to wait for the payment, there will be new paperwork and new instructions somewhere in the computer."

"Meaning?"

"There is something I can do for you. I can authorise a temporary stay of repossession, pending new instructions."

"Then do it."

"The tow truck fees must be paid, though. And the overtime for the driver and assistant."

"How much?"

"Twenty for the tow truck and ten for the boys."

"Twenty cows, goats, or chickens?"

The man laughed.

"Are you Kikuyu?" Salim asked him.

"Giriama."

"Then you can understand how I don't have that kind of money on me," Salim said.

"Perfectly," the man laughed. "Corona ate everything."

Creditors would be laughing at that excuse for a long time to come. Sadly, banks, needy relatives and repo agents did not believe it or find it funny.

"I will pay you next Monday," he said.

The repo man had heard that promise too. He shook his head and turned to his crew.

"Let us go boys."

Driver and his man hopped in the truck.

"Please, have a heart," Salim pleaded. "I have to go to a funeral."

"Take a *matatu*," said the man. "Sort it out with your bank. They know where the car will be."

He squeezed in his car and drove after the tow truck.

"This is the end," Salim said to himself.

He went back across the road, stared at nothing as the elevator whisked him up back to the tenth floor, walked through the outer office without a word to his secretary, and went to his office and shut the door. He sat for a while dazed, trying to think straight. He could not see how he would survive without his car. Kasim was unreachable on the phone.

He rose and returned to the window to watch planes land and take off miles away at the international airport, glad that the windows opened just wide enough for air to get in and out.

Chapter 6

The car windows were open as far as they would go and still it was hot inside the Beetle. And Salim in the passenger seat was sweating and festering.

"Why do you always take so long to answer my calls?" he raged.

"Work pressure," Kasim said.

"We all work."

"I know," Kasim said, keeping calm.

He had been late to pick Salim from his office, failed to beat the rush hour and now they sat in the thick of it, and Salim was angry. He left him to work out whatever it was that was eating him, and concentrated on driving.

Salim loosened his tie, took out a clean white handkerchief and wiped sweat from his face and neck. He scowled at the dirt smear from invisible dust that rose from the road with the sweltering afternoon air. He had already commented on the Beetle being filthy inside and out and ordered Kasim to have it washed before picking him up next time.

Kasim had nodded and refrained asking who would pay for the car wash. He did not sweat a drop, as he was used to crawling along city streets at an old donkey's pace, and sitting for hours in an old car without air-conditioner, in mammoth traffic jams orchestrated by big, fat, corrupt, traffic policemen.

They sat forever at Haile Selassie roundabout where the traffic lights worked perfectly, but not perfectly enough for the half a dozen policemen watching the flow and deciding who should go next. The result was a gridlock that extended three counties out of the city. When they eventually cleared that jam, they got stuck for another forty-five minutes at the next roundabout a few hundred meters farther on.

Salim slept through the next roundabout and lost it when he woke up to find they had covered less than half a kilometre. He yelled at the newspaper and water venders telling them to go find their Governor and tell him to come clear the mess he had made of their city.

"If we had taken your Mercedes …" Kasim started.

"Shut up, Kasim," he said.

"You would have been cooler," Kasim said.

They had been through that already in the half hour it took to crawl the short distance from the major chaos on Uhuru Highway to a minor one along University Way.

A water seller leaned in at the Beetle's window. Salim barked at him to *potea*, get lost. The man jumped back startled. Kasim called him to his window and bought two bottles of water. He offered one to Salim. Salim declined and continued to fan himself with a newspaper, his face a mask of anger.

He had spent the afternoon with bank managers he thought understood well the economic situation in the country. He had come out of the meetings swearing never to trust what bank managers said when approving a loan. The handshake was a nail in the coffin.

The traffic inched forward. The smell of hot engine oil filled the car. Salim turned to Kasim worried.

"I topped up this morning," Kasim said.

Salim took one of the water bottles and read the label carefully. It had the seal of the bureau of standards.

"Did you know they tinted the bottle to make the water look like fresh water?" asked Kasim.

Salim regarded him doubtfully, opened the bottle and took a mouthful. He suddenly spat it out of the window.

"Rainwater," Kasim said. "Harvested from asbestos roofs in Athi River."

Salim read the label again. He was about to toss the bottle out of the window then saw the look that the white driver of the black Prado in the next lane gave him. He tossed the bottle in the back seat and spat out of the window.

"I buy it for the radiator," Kasim said. "A litre a day keeps *jua kali* away."

"What radiator?" Salim sat up alarmed.

"Relax," Kasim laughed. "Beetle engine is air-cooled; even I know that. Nothing wrong with the water. The traffic cops drink it all the time."

Salim spat out of the window again. Then he leaned back and fell asleep. After Riverside Drive the jam eased, and they drove at a steady speed until they turned into Riverside Lane. Kasim woke Salim to ask if they were heading in the right direction.

"I don't remember any of this," Salim said.

He looked around uncertainly until he noticed a name sign peeking out of the lush bougainvillea overhanging a stone wall.

"Keep driving," he said.

"Are you sure?"

"I remember that name plate. Take the third lane to the left."

The third lane left took them down a slight drop then right to a big, steel gate with a sign warning of fierce dogs. They drove up to the gate and stopped.

"I remember that."

"So do I," said Kasim. "But this is such a bad idea."

"Your mother's idea, so shut up."

"My mother did not say a word at the meeting."

"Oh, really? And who was it said Mophat's boys had no balls?"

"My mother would never say balls."

"She did not protest."

"Leave my mother out of it, okay?"

He leaned on the horn impatiently. The Beetle made a bleating sound. Salim pressed it again just for annoyance. Then they waited for the gate to open.

A side door opened. The guard peered out, glared at the car for a moment, then disappeared back inside and closed the door. They waited. Salim was about to press the horn again, when the small door opened, and the guard stepped out with his hat on his head and a guard's club in his right hand. He appeared ready for battle as he approached the passenger window and leaned down.

"What?" he asked.

"Mzee Kitheka," said Kasim.

"You want to see who?"

"Mister Kitheka," Salim said impatiently. "We want to see your boss?"

"He is not in," said the guard.

"Who is in?"

The man looked from one to the other, tempted to believe they were robbers, then he checked out the car and decided they could not be.

"Who do you want to see, again?" he asked the driver.

"Are you deaf?" Salim asked him.

"I just told you he is not in."

"What about Mama Kitheka?"

"Who?"

"His wife."

The guard looked to see if they had guns in their jacket pockets, looked in the back seat for machetes.

"Do you want to see mama or mzee?"

"Mzee," said Salim.

"Mama," said Kasim.

The guard hesitated then made up his mind. They could see Mama, but not Mzee. He would not let them in if Mzee were at home.

"Only because I have seen you here before," he said to Kasim. "I didn't recognise you without your Mercedes."

"Open the gate," Salim said calmly.

"Where is your Mercedes?" the guard asked Kasim.

"Just open the gate," Salim yelled.

The guard glanced at Kasim, then walked back inside and shut the side door. They waited. Kasim honked. They laughed at the bleating sound. Then the gate opened and

Kasim drove through. As they passed, the guard stopped them with a menacing wave of his bat.

"Don't stay long," he warned. "Mzee does not like visitors."

"We know," said Kasim.

They drove through a magnificent flower garden, to a formidable three-story mansion that rivaled Uncle Sam's castle for splendor. Four luxury vehicles sat in the shade of an open garage at the end of the driveway.

Two Rottweilers charged at the Beetle when it arrived.

"I told you it was a bad idea," Kasim quickly rolled up his window.

"Okay, you were right," Salim rolled up his too.

They waited for someone to come rescue them. No one came. The dogs circled the car, marked the tyres, then lay down and waited. Kasim pressed the horn. Not a beep.

"I drove us here," said Kasim.

"I'll drive us back," Salim said.

"Toss for it?"

"My own coin," said Salim.

As he took out a coin, the front door opened and an old, white woman came out.

"I'll go," Kasim stepped out.

The dogs glanced at the woman and stayed put.

"Hello, you two," she said cheerfully. "Thank God, someone remembers the way. I haven't seen any of you since when."

"Housewarming?" said Salim, with a knowing smile.

"My goodness, the fiasco with the shoes," she laughed remembering. "Richard did overdo it that time. Come in, come in."

"Actually, Aunt Gwyneth," said Kasim, "we came to see Mzee."

"I'm sorry, Mzee is not here," she said.

Mzee spent most of his time at the club practicing for a tournament.

"But do come inside," she said. "I have baked a most wonderful fruitcake."

"I'm sorry," Salim said from the car, "But we are in a big hurry. You know Caesar, grandfather Mophat, died?"

"Someone phoned," she said. "I presume you'd like to borrow Mzee's pickup."

"We need to formally beg for it."

"He does believe in protocol," she nodded, smiling sadly. "Now you know where he is, but I doubt he will have time for you."

"We'll try," Salim said, "Kasim?"

Kasim lingered.

"Aunt Gwyneth," he said, "I would not mind a piece of your fruitcake."

"Come with me," she said.

He followed her as far as the front door, then waited nervously.

Aunt Gwyneth was a sweet and generous woman, but the women of the clan would not accept it. Her attempts to reach out to them were frustrated by lack of someone to let her in their circle, as the closest she got was Aunt Charity, who was too busy taking care of Caesar to have time to socialise.

"Proceed with caution, my daughter," Caesar warned her when she went for advice. "You give them a hand they will return for the arm."

King'oo men, on the other hand, treated her with the respect reserved for women of ability, diligent women, women who kept off men's affairs. They pitied her for marrying a mean, arrogant and unfriendly scoundrel. Uncle Tivo had said that to her when she confessed being tired of constantly inventing excuses for her husband not taking her to clan functions. Fortunately, most functions were fundraisers for weddings, hospital bills and funerals, and she made sure to take enough money to deflect criticism. Sometimes she secretly supplemented her husband's donation from her own savings to avoid embarrassment.

The women were harder to pacify. They could not understand why, of all the men in the world, she had settled for Richard. Only a King'oo woman could manage a King'oo man, and she had to work hard at it.

"Is he impotent?" Aunt Kamene asked, during a fundraiser to pay someone's hospital bills.

"Richard is not impotent," she had said. "Not as far as I know."

"Then you are infertile," Aunt Kamene said.

If there was one thing King'oo men knew how to, it is to make women pregnant.

"I am not barren," she said.

"Why don't you have children?"

"With a King'oo man?" She was a fast learner too.

They had a good laugh and, from then on, she was a special King'oo sister or widow, whichever they chose, and was constantly invited to women's gatherings to plot against men, and to church gatherings to raise funds, and to baby showers, to bring gifts. She rarely went. When she invited them to her house no one dared come. Only the two young men, Salim and Kasim, and always looking for Richard.

She brought Kasim two large slices of cake. He promised to visit again, and walked carefully back to the car so as not to excite the dogs.

"You know where to find Richard," she called after him.

Salim did not care for fruitcake. All he wanted was to find Uncle Richard, say what he had to say, and be done with.

Chapter 7

Uncle Richard's driver was dozing in the car when they arrived at the club.

"Still a bad idea," Kasim said as they walked past the Mercedes to the club house.

"Your mother's idea," Salim reminded him. "So, shut up."

They rounded the corner just as Uncle Richard was putting the ninth hole and they stopped to watch him lose his temper after missing it and hurl his club away. The golf practice was not going well. He headed for the club house, then changed his mind and went to the first tee with his hand held out at the caddy. Salim started out to intercept him.

"I don't care whose idea this is, it stinks," Kasim said following him.

"Uncle Richard," Salim called waving.

Uncle Richard was hunched over the ball waggling the club, swaying his behind and muttering to himself. He was about to take a swing.

"Uncle Richard," Kasim called, louder.

He stopped abruptly, slowly turned and watched Salim approach, with Kasim a cautious step behind.

"Who let you two in here?" he asked them.

He was a big man with a big voice, and a bigger temper. Salim fought the urge to turn round and leave.

"The gate was open," he said.

"So, we just …" Kasim started.

"… just wandered into a members-only club without anyone's permission."

"There was no one to ask."

"I will have a word with the Club Secretary," he said. "What do you want?"

"Caesar is dead," Salim said, deciding to keep it short.

"Someone phoned my wife," he said, his attention back on the ball.

"He has really kicked it this time, Uncle Rich," said Kasim.

Uncle Richard stopped his addressing the ball, glared at him.

"Uncle Richard," Kasim corrected himself.

Uncle Richard turned his attention back to the ball, dug his heels in, leaned forward and swayed his hips again.

"What happened to your Mercedes?" he asked, still addressing the ball.

"At home," Salim said.

"I wondered how long it would take you to realise you could not afford to fuel it."

Kasim spun at Salim with an unspoken … 'So!'

"That is not why we are here," Salim said.

Uncle Richard turned, the golf club over his shoulder, and scowled.

"Again, why are you here?"

"We are here to inform you that we are meeting at Uncle Sam's house."

"Who is we?"

"Family, friends, you know, the clan," said Salim.

"The funeral routine," said Kasim. "Meetings, plannings, and fundraisings. They would like you to participate this time."

He lowered the club, leaned it on his leg, took off his glove and reached in his back pocket for his wallet.

"How much?" he asked, exposing a wallet full of cash.

Salim and Kasim looked at each other. Kasim was about to speak. Salim held him back and spoke instead.

"This is not about money, Uncle Richard," he said.

Uncle Richard returned his wallet in his pocket and pulled his golfing glove back on his left hand. He recommenced his dance with the ball.

"So, what is it about?" he asked over his shoulder.

"Burying Caesar," Salim said.

"With dignity," Kasim added.

Uncle Richard stopped his dance, turned, and leaned on the club. Bushy eyebrows twitched when he squinted.

"What do you do?" he asked Kasim.

"Make people laugh. I am a comedian."

"In other words, nothing," he said, and turned to Salim. "What about you? What do you do, again?"

"You know what I do, Uncle Richard," said Salim.

"Then stop preaching and say how much money you people want from me."

They looked at each other. They had been here before. So, why were they back tilling the same rocky patch, when they knew how it would all end?

Salim was tempted to give a sum, a crazy number like one million, and see what would happen. But, he guessed, Uncle Richard would hand them everything in his wallet, say that was all he had on hand, and buy his way out of the night meetings and the funeral. It had happened before.

"Uncle Richard," he said instead. "The aunts respect you more than anyone else. Aunt Charity regards you as the son she never had. You are a man of integrity, she says, and a charismatic, self-made man, second only to Caesar himself."

He paused to see how that would work. Uncle Richard relaxed the grip on his club. His eyes thoughtfully wondered down the fairway after memories of his mentorship under Caesar. Just a fleeting moment of distraction, then he was back with Salim.

"Go on," he said.

"She would be touched and very honoured if you attended at least one of the meetings," Salim said.

He was touched by Salim's words. Again, his mind wandered back to memories of Aunt Charity taking his hand as he was about to leave for the airport and warning him, half-in jest he assumed, against bringing back a foreign wife, as there were enough Kamba girls in Kathiani waiting for him. She never commented about his foreign wife, since his return, and he did not believe he owed her or the clan any explanation.

"How many night meetings do you plan to hold before the funeral?" he asked Salim.

Salim knew him too well to hope he would be attending any of them. They had been there before too.

"Not many," he said.

Uncle Richard squinted at him.

"Until we bury Caesar," Kasim said. "You know how it works, Uncle Rich. I mean Uncle Richard. We keep at it until every Kamba who profited, in whatever way, from Caesar's generosity has paid back. Then we continue until we have enough for a royal funeral. Caesar was not little, you know."

Uncle Richard frowned at him, grip tightening on the club.

"Has any one of you ever wondered why I don't come to your meetings?" he asked them.

Everyone in the clan knew why he did not turn up to clan meetings. Uncle Tivo said it all the time. He was 'a mean, arrogant and anti-social scoundrel'.

They could not tell him that, so they looked at each other and shook their heads.

"All you people do is talk, talk, talk," he said to Salim. "You don't listen, and you don't think. I ask you a simple question, like when you intend to bury Caesar, and you give me a lecture on how you bury your dead?"

Kasim turned to Salim. Salim shook his head at him.

"As soon as we have raised enough money," said Salim.

"How much is enough?" asked Uncle Richard.

"It is best that everyone is present when the budget is discussed."

"That is how we always do it," Kasim added.

But that was not the way Uncle Richard did it.

"Call my wife when you know how much money you want from me," he said to them. "My wife, you understand, not myself. And do not show your faces here again. This is a members' club. Now, bugger off."

"As usual, a disaster," Kasim said, as they walked back to the car. "We should have accepted the bundle in his wallet and left."

"Remember what happened last time," Salim said.

Uncle Richard gave a different story to Uncle Sam months after the funeral of an aunt, telling his own version of events that left Salim sounding like an utter fool.

"All Salim said was you needed money for the funeral," he said to Uncle Sam. "He did not tell me you expected me to cancel my engagements, close my office and drive to Ukambani every evening to attend night meetings."

Uncle Sam was yet to forgive Salim for it. And, as everyone knew, the budget would be decided by the amount the clan raised. That was the way of the clan.

Chapter 8

The clan eagerly awaited Uncle Richard's response to their pleas for help. Uncle Tivo, reclining on his throne sofa, watched Salim and Kasim shake hands through the women's side of the room to the men's side, and when they got to him, he withheld his hand.

"I waited for you all day," he said to them. "Where were you?"

"At work," said Kasim.

"I wasn't talking to you," Uncle Tivo said. "I know you don't work."

"I was busy," said Salim.

"Doing what?"

Any of the old men around could have told him what Salim did. Some of them had been to his office about suing one another and insisting he work pro bono because he was King'oo. But this was not the time or place to explain that to Uncle Tivo.

"I had a meeting," he said. "And don't ask with whom; you don't know him."

He sat on one side of Tivo and Kasim on the other. Uncle Sam was already at his place in front waiting for everyone to settle down.

"Now that we are all here," he said, finally, "Let us get the train moving."

"We are not all here," said Uncle Tivo.

Uncle Sam looked around. Everyone looked around. There was no way of telling whether everyone was there, but they all seemed to be present, and eager to get it over with and go home.

Aunt Charity was in her place surrounded by an impenetrable wall of sisters. In their youth they ganged up to scare off bullies and suitors. Boys went mad trying to date them. For a schoolboy to be recognized and greeted by one of Mophat's girl on the way to, or from, Kathiani market on weekends and school holidays, was something to crow about for months after. A date was an impossible dream. Mophat's girls went everywhere and did everything together. They took care of one another, defended themselves against the world. Now old and weary, all they could do to support one another was huddle together and watch men make fools of themselves.

"Where is Eva?" asked Uncle Tivo.

Uncle Sam's shoulders sagged. It was hard enough for him to leave work to come chair an ungrateful gathering without having to deal with an obstinate old fool.

"Eva is in America, Uncle Tivo," Kasim stepped in to save him.

"I told him already," Salim said impatiently. "Tivo, just be silent and let the meeting continue."

Uncle Tivo shot him a warning look, but he was tired, and it was getting late. His phone rang. He started to answer it. Aunt Kamene ordered him to leave it be.

"Where is Richard?" Uncle Tivo asked.

Everyone groaned. Did he have to keep asking time-wasting questions?

"Uncle Tivo," Kasim said to the old man. "When was the last time you saw Richard?"

"The day his wife made me take off my shoes," Uncle Tivo said.

That put a smile on some old faces.

"Uncle Richard has been informed," Uncle Sam said, perusing his papers. "Formally, I believe?"

"Short of sending him a registered letter," Salim nodded, hopefully putting the matter to rest.

Sam looked up sharply. Salim was studying his shoes.

"We all know he would not read it anyway," said Kasim. "So we went to his house, found only his wife, she gave us cake and sent us to the golf club, we went, we found him, gave him the message and he told us to bugger off. And then we came back here. That was what happened, in short, Except that ..."

"Shut up, Kasim," Salim said to him.

"Just trying to explain *short of sending a registered letter.*"

"Is golf more important than this?" asked Aunt Kamene.

"You ask him that, when he comes," said Sam.

"You don't talk to me like that, Sam," she said to him.

"I apologise, but why are we even talking about him? Uncle Richard will turn up in his own time as always."

"Always?" Uncle Tivo missed the sarcasm.

Hardly anyone remembered the last time they saw Uncle Richard at a clan meeting. Some did know what he looked like, having barely glimpsed him at his palatial house the day he made them take off their shoes and wash their feet before stepping inside. Some, like Uncle Tivo, lived for the day they would be able return the insult.

"To continue," Uncle Sam said to the gathering, "We still do not have a funeral committee. We need a chairman, a treasurer, a secretary …"

"Stop," Aunt Kamene interrupted him. "Men like to make everything complicated."

The men's side groaned as she stepped out to stand next to Sam. It would be another long evening.

"For those who do not know me," she said to the room, "I run my business by myself, and it is harder than what we are doing here. Sam, you stand there in the center. This is your house, so you will be chairman, headman, president or whatever you like to call yourself. Salim, you will be his vice-chairman, his deputy or whatever you like. And these two boys here will be your assistants and do whatever you tell them."

She dragged the Chinese cousins from their safe corner and, speaking to them in Chinese, showed them where to stand. They were not concerned she spoke Chinese to them, but like Salim, they were dumbfounded by the sudden turn of events; at how fast they had been volunteered. But there was no arguing with Aunt Kamene.

When the baby bundle was place at Mzee Caesar's gate early one morning, someone swore she saw Kamene speed away from the scene on a boda-boda driven by a Chinese man. Even Caesar was ready to believe that version of the story, until Kamene came to visit from Sultan Hamud, where she sold fruit to Chinese rail builders, and finding the boys crawling in the dusty yard with chickens and puppies asked Caesar what they were.

Now grown to men, they stood next to Salim and waited for him to tell them what to do. But Salim did not want assistants any more than he wanted to be Uncle Sam's assistant. What he needed was to wind up the meeting and go deal with his problems.

Sam stepped in the center of the room, as ordered, and waited uncertainly.

"What about me?" asked Kasim.

"You can take my place," Salim said.

"You keep quiet," Aunt Kamene ordered. "Kasim, you make announcements. Now start your meeting."

"Since this is our first real meeting," Uncle Sam said, "let us start by confirming duties and responsibilities. Kasim has announcements, the most urgent task right now. Who will take care of the hearse?"

"I'll take care of that," said Salim.

Aunt Charity opened her eyes and looked at Salim gratefully. She knew she could count on him.

"Who will take care of the casket?" Uncle Sam turned to the others. "You, Cousin Mutisia, you are a carpenter."

That provoked gasps of astonishment from some people.

"Mutisia made funeral crates, not caskets," Aunt Kamene reminded. "Why he went out of business."

"He knows coffin makers, though" Uncle Sam agreed. "He can get us a good deal. And do not look so terrified, Mutisia, we are not asking you to pay for it. Cousin Ndekei, the gravediggers. Flowers? Aunt Mueni."

"And you?" asked Mzee Tivo. "What will you do other than talking, talking, talking, talking?"

"This is my house."

"Our house," said his wife. "We take care of the food and drinks. That does not mean we pay for it all."

That cleared and out of the way, Sam again welcomed everyone to his, and his wife's house, and thanked them for coming to honour Caesar, a man of many achievements.

"For those of our guests who did not have the honour and the privilege of knowing him, I have prepared a brief introduction to the great man's life."

He put on his reading glasses, cleared his throat and begun reading.

"Caesar was the eldest great-grandson of Chief Makau wa Kingo'oo. He was educated at the mission school in Tala and later in Machakos and at Alliance High School in Nairobi."

"Keep it short," said Aunt Kamene.

"He joined government service as a District Officer, worked his way up to Provincial Commissioner, then Permanent Secretary in several ministries before ending up at the State House as special adviser to the president."

"Make it shorter," Aunt Kamene ordered.

Realising it was going to be another long night, Salim returned to his place by Uncle Tivo as Uncle Sam in his own words said how much Caesar regretted having to withdraw his services from the administration, from his people and his country. He could not continue serving under the cartel of corrupt lawmakers who declared themselves above the law, awarded themselves titles and honors, and scandalous amounts of salaries while their people waste away in poverty.

"How do you live with yourselves?" he asked them. "How do you sleep at night, when your countrymen have no work, when their women and children sleep in the street. When children go to schools that have no books or desks, when hospitals have no beds or drugs, and their houses have no light, water, or food? How do you call yourselves leaders? What right do you have to call yourselves men?"

Never had anyone walked out on a government appointment under such a dark cloud. Politicians vilified him left and right, called him a slum dog and hurled worse insults at him. People he considered friends, independent thinkers, wise enough to realise they were captaining a doomed ship, called him a traitor, and howled for his blood. They demanded he apologise to the head of state, who had been so generous as to give him a prominent position in the government that he did not deserve, and go back to work rubber-stamping their corrupt international loan agreements. Caesar in turn demanded they resign and apologise to their families and the country for selling them to the devil and the white man.

They paid demonstrators to stir anti-Caesar feelings and held frenzied public rallies across the country calling for Caesar's arrest, trial, and imprisonment for his disrespect to them and to the head of state. But many who heard them rant against Caesar pointed at schools, clinics, roads, and bridges that, but for Caesar, would never have been built. Caesar had put brakes on blatant theft of public funds by politicians who ganged up with contractors who received payment from the government for public projects they had no intention of completing. He repeatedly called for the prosecution of the corrupt officials, and the contractors who abandoned public projects, but the culprits were never prosecuted.

Caesar saw through the fraud they called leadership and resisted the temptation to join them and grow fat, to be elevated to demi-god status, have the government pay him rent to live in his own mansion, pay for his four official cars with drivers and bodyguards, and pay him a salary so large it made a mockery of the fiscal austerity he was supposed to enforce as finance minister. He stopped attending national day parties at State House, the orgy of drinking, goat-eating and self-congratulatory speeches, parties, protesting the waste of scarce finances. That was how he came to be known as Fiscal Caesar.

Failing to make him one of their kind, they banned mention of his name on radio, television, and newspapers. There were rumours of a poisoning, and an attempted assassination, where his official car collided with a military lorry. Official inquiries found no evidence of any attempt on Caesar's life.

Chapter 9

They sat at the bar drinking what his Samburu host said was an alcohol-free rum punch made for the women guests. The women were wives of the men they came with, and their husbands needed someone to carry them home at the end of the evening.

Kasim was in *Club Bombay* as a guest of his River Road fan, a Samburu man who sang Indian songs at Indian clubs around the city; at clubs where men came with their real wives to have a Samburu man serenade them in their own tongue. And there was not a single wallet inspector in sight. It was too strange to be real. There had to be wallet inspectors in the house, Kasim insisted. How could there not be, with so many men flaunting their stuffed wallets? He could smell wallet inspectors too, but it was hard to spot them behind the saris.

"What do you sing about?" he asked his host.

"About love," said his friend.

"Is it hard?".

"I studied in India."

"Singing?"

"Accountancy."

Kasim was about to make a joke of it, then saw the man was serious. His wife was from India, a place with a complicated name, and that was where he met her as a student, fell madly in love, married her in a traditional Indian wedding and brought her home as his wife. That was how he came to be singing love songs at an Indian club.

He saw the skeptical look and decided to explain. He was a serious student, stayed the course, got his degree, came back, but could not find any kind of work. And now he entertained Indian diners for a living. They did not seem to mind that he was not a real Indian, nor should Kasim.

"I still don't get it," said Kasim.

"It is easy."

He learned the songs watching Indian films, and practiced singing them to his future wife as he courted her. Now he made his living singing in the clubs around town. That simple. And with every song he serenaded his wife.

He ordered another round of the rum punch with an Indian name. The air in the club had a romantic fragrance Kasim assumed unique to clubs in India, and he could not tell whether it was the air, the punch or the evening that made him light-headed.

"Are you sure this thing is alcohol-free?"

"It says so on the drinks card," said his host.

Kasim signaled the barman.

"No point asking him," his friend said. "Half the time, he has no idea what he puts in the cocktails. Ancient eastern recipes."

"Are you sure you are not King'oo?" Kasim asked him.

"I am Samburu."

Samburu or not, the man had to be King'oo. He had a foreign wife, a university degree he could not use, and he made a living singing Indian love songs in Indian night clubs. All of those were the attributes of a free-thinking King'oo man.

Then the Parklands Pair, the club comedians, stormed in with a flourish and regulars applauded. They looked like twins in their sequin-studded jackets, somewhere between circus announcers and stage magicians. They were both of average height, well rounded, sleeked black hair, and matching moustaches. They rushed round the room shaking hands, and joking with patrons before going to the bar.

"Why are you here?" they asked Kasim.

"Doing what you do when you crash my River Road gigs," Kasim said to them. "To heckle and steal your acts."

They laughed and spoke to the Samburu singer in Hindi.

"What are you drinking?" one of them asked Kasim.

The singer told them the name of the drink.

"Did he tell you it was alcohol-free?" one said to Kasim.

"Suits me?"

"Then have another one on us," they said. "Barman, Kasim is our special guest tonight. Give him whatever he is drinking."

For themselves they ordered *chang'aa* neat, from an unlabeled bottle the barman fished from the back of the drinks' cooler. Then they pulled out a roll of weed each and proceed to the urinals at the back of the club.

By the time they took to the stage they were clowning and laughing at their own jokes and Kasim was starting to laugh with the audience too, without knowing why they laughed. Then they invited him on stage, and it was all downhill from there on. He told a few good jokes and, though the audience understood him, the Pair insisted on translating and got bigger laughs. They knew most of his jokes anyway, and made Kasim look like the imposter.

"You wait," he said to them," I am going to learn Indian."

"Learn Indian?"

The audience roared with laughter. One of the comedians beckoned Kasim whispered in his ear.

"*Rafiki*," he said, "There is no such language. Ask them."

"Then I will go learn whatever you speak and come back here and put you out of business."

Back at the bar, the singer informed him the Pair spoke ten languages, most of them Indian, and he spoke two of them.

"Would you teach me?"

"You don't need it," the man advised. "You do well in River Road. Stick to your kind."

"My kind? And whose kind are you?"

"Your kind, but also their kind. My wife is Indian, my children are … Samburu and Indian and … let us just have a drink and go home."

They were having that last drink before home, when an elderly man in a white suit and tie joined them at the bar. The singer introduced him as Mr Singh the owner of the *Laugh With Singh* comedy club, a club so unique it defied description.

Mr Singh offered them a round and said he had stopped by to see how the opposition was doing and have a drink. He had never heard of, or seen, a River Road comedian at work but he admired how Kasim had deflected the obnoxious Parklands Pair, and smiled and laughed as he plowed his way through a thoroughly indifferent audience to deliver such a disastrous performance.

"Takes guts," he said.

"Talent," said Kasim.

"Guts and … okay, talent."

He was looking for a diehard comedian, someone who could wake the dead, and turn indifferent strangers to friends or foes, into an engaged audience and repeat customers. A comedian who could make them come back to heckle and drink a lot of whisky, if not to laugh and drink a lot of whisky.

"Can you sing?" he asked Kasim.

"Depends on who you ask."

"Great; they can't sing either."

"I own a guitar," Kasim admitted.

"Which, I assume, you can also play?"

"What sort of comedy club are we talking about, Mr Singh?"

"A gentlemen's club," said Mr Singh. "Where respectable, old gentlemen, working and retired, meet to let their beards down."

The Laughing Singh was an exclusive club of men who loved to laugh. They met Thursday nights at the club, laughed for an hour without provocation, then drunk for an hour without laughing and then went home rejuvenated.

Mr Singh was fine with that for a while, but then he had begun to miss the comedy side of the club. He loved to laugh, as much as they did, but he needed a better reason than togetherness. He needed something or someone to make him laugh.

He proposed stand-up comedians to spice Thursday's manly laugh-ins. The old gentlemen were fine with it, so long as it did not involve half-naked women, and cost more money, or interfere with their rituals.

They kept to their one-hour of manly laughter routine, topped it up with an hour of stand-up comedy during which they laughed, talked and drunk whisky, and they left the club refreshed and happy. That slight adjustment to Thursday night's ritual raised the bar sales so high Mr Singh started importing Indian and Pakistani comedians from London and Manchester. The imported comics promptly raised Mr Singh's club to international status. It was still small, still exclusive, and still mostly turbaned and mostly grey-bearded, but it was now international.

With the fame came demand. Customers who did not understand Indian lined up outside the club nightly, except Thursday night, to hear the same artists tell the same jokes in a language they all understood. Thursday night remained for Laugh-in Club members only.

Laugh With Singh was soon the talk of the town, with customers lining up for admission. It was the place to be for laughs and whisky every night except Thursday night. The reputation eventually reached the sleeping ears of the city government, who promptly sent their team of toilet inspectors, kitchen inspectors and fire hazard inspectors, all of them with their hands out for handouts. The city was already collecting fees for a multitude of licenses, but they fangled several more including a foreign artists' engagement license just for good measure.

The tax authorities were next in line, demanding to see the club's audited accounts for the past fifty years. Then came the immigration authorities to inspect the work permits and investigate the immigration status of everyone working at the club. Starting with the toilet cleaner, they interrogated everyone all the way up to Mr Sing himself.

Mr Singh, too busy managing the business, had left all the bureaucratic mumbo-jumbo to his able secretary, and the accountant. The accountant had receipts and records of every artist that ever appeared at the club, but the secretary admitted she did know she was supposed to apply for work permits every time the same comics returned for short their engagements. Suddenly the foreign comedians were too expensive and complicated to import.

Thursday Laugh-in reverted to its old routine of laugh, drink, and go. Business went down, the management adjusted its expectations, down-grading to a point where Laugh *With Singh* was in danger of becoming another watering hole for old men with young women.

Then Mr Singh stopped by *Club Bombay* for a drink and found a River Road comedian braving an indifferent audience with a disastrous performance, and invited him for a drink at the bar.

Out of the drink, Kasim got an audition at the *Laugh With Singh* club to perform for an audience that had never encountered his brand of River Road stand-up. Mr Singh engaged the Parklands Pair, a pair of middle-of-the-road Indian comics, from time to time and even they struggled to find the greybeards' funny bone.

On his audition night, Mr Singh sat Kasim at the bar before his act, bought him a morale booster.

 and explained what was expected of him.."

"Laughter is the best medicine," he said. "That and a shot of whisky. You make them laugh, I sell them whisky, and you make money"

He signaled the barman to bring Kasim a second booster.

"Your Indian jokes at the *Club Bombay*," he said. "Not very funny. Not funny at all. Keep away from such jokes here. No Indian or Pakistani jokes. Your friends from Parklands tell them better."

They would be standing by in case Kasim needed to be rescued.

Thursday Laugh-in was a group of serious men, professional men whose lives and careers left little time for fun or laughter. They needed their laughter served strong and fast.

"If they don't laugh in the first two minutes, you are out of here."

"Got you," said Kasim. "I deal with grumpy, old men all the time."

"You have five minutes to prepare," Mr Singh said to him.

"Do they speak Kiswahili?" he asked.

"I guess more than you speak Indian."

"Kikamba?"

"Why don't you ask them?"

They were old timers, native born and bred. Between them, they spoke all the languages of the city and dozens from the country. Looking at the greybeards, and the sea of turbans, he wished he had come better prepared.

The five minutes vanished faster than a misplaced wallet at *Uncle Dave's Curry and Comedy House*. Kasim nodded at Mr Sing, took a deep breath, and stepped up to face his audience. One of the Parklands Pair stepped up to introduce him then withdrew. Two dozen heads, grey beards down to the chest, hard, dark eyes, and turbans suddenly huge and tight they looked like helmets turned and pointed Kasim's way. Not one smile among them.

"*Haalloo*," he hailed, flashing the mile-wide smile he had practiced with his Fahari hosts in the desert, while bullets whistled over his head, the smile that eventually made one old man crack up. "Is it hot in here, or what? I bet you all have tiny cooling units humming away under those turbans. You know, a tiny icemaker to keep brains from boiling over."

Two dozen pairs of eyes stared at him from two dozen faces curved out of bone. Sweat broke out under his armpit. There was no way he could have prepared for this, he said to himself.

He leaned over to speak to the closest one.

"*Rafiki*, I'm burning up here," he said. "Can I borrow the upside-down ice bucket from your head for a minute?"

Not a smile. The clock was ticking. In another minute, he would be out of there never to return. He went for broke. Let us see how hard you are, he said to himself.

"Again, *haalloo*," he said to them. "I am Kasim the Komedian, with three Ks for Kuyu, Kisii and Kamba. In River Road they call me the Joker. Remember River Road, where we all started out? The mile-long stream of haphazard love and hate, life and death?"

He laughed alone.

"You," he pointed in the audience. "Yes, you with cement dust in the beard. When is a Singh not a Sikh?"

The room, cold and silent before, was suddenly dead still. Twenty-four serious faces stared at him.

"Come on, old boys," he said. "You are used to laughing at nothing. When is a Singh not Sikh? You work with them all day long."

There was a flicker of curiosity.

"As masons," he said. "As carpenters, cement mixers and artisans?"

The flicker was gone, replaced by a vacant stare.

"Come on, guys, help me out here," he pleaded. "I was informed you were native born and bred."

From the corner of his eye, he saw the next act, the Parklands Pair, start for the stage. His two minutes were over.

"I'll tell you," he said quickly. "A Singh is not a Sikh when he is …"

"Kamau Singh," said one of the rescuers. "Your minute is up."

Kasim snatched his guitar from his chair.

"Not before I sing my big, fat, corrupt policeman song."

"Out!"

"Let him sing," one of the beards suddenly said.

"No, Kasim," Mr Singh rushed to the stage. "Not that song."

He apologised to the audience, grabbed Kasim by the arm and hauled him off the stage.

"You promised no Indian jokes," he said, back at the bar.

"That was not an Indian joke," Kasim protested. "Where do you live? That was a Kuyu joke from Elburgon, honest. Haven't you people heard of *mukurinu*? Kuyu man with a turban. Don't you get it? Kamau Singh? The clown from Parklands has heard it before. Ask him."

"We had an agreement," Mr Singh reminded, escorting him to the exit. "No Kikuyu jokes, no Kamba jokes, no people jokes and no sick, fat, corrupt traffic policeman jokes; although, come to think of it, it might have made them smile. Some of those turbans are senior police officers."

"Really?" Kasim was genuinely surprised. "Policemen in turbans? You should have told me before. Big, fat, corrupt policeman in a big, fat turban."

The possibilities were endless.

"Very senior officers," said Mr Singh. "They can lock you up, throw away the key and close my club."

"I would hate to see you lose your license, Mr Singh," he tried to push his way back inside. "I must go apologise."

"Forget it."

"I will tell them it was not your fault. Then I'll tell them a funny Chinese joke and they'll forgive you."

"Go home, Kasim," Mr Sing said and shut the door.

Kasim got as far as the car park, then a dark figure leaped out of the shadows, *rungu* in hand and demanded to know why he made stupid jokes about Kikuyu.

Kasim was about to tell him to go to hell, then remembered the bat in the man's hand.

"No ill meant," he said. "I'm half Kikuyu myself and I find Kikuyu men hilarious. I really do, but that is not why I make stupid jokes about them."

"Why?"

Kasim looked round in the shadows under the trees and bushes, then lowered his voice.

"Come," he took him by the shoulder and walked him to the Beetle, sat him down on the front bumper.

The guard sat patiently while Kasim stowed his guitar in the car and came back.

"What are you first?" he asked. "A son, a brother, an uncle, a father, a husband, a Kikuyu, or a man?"

"A man, of course," the man said.

"Exactly why they call you a watch man," Kasim said. "Not a watch son, watch brother, watch father, watch husband, or watch Kikuyu. You are a watch man. A man."

Kasim sat down beside him.

"Women," he said. "That is the problem. Women."

"How?" the man asked.

"Women have it in for you long before you are born. They work it all out while you suck your thumb in your mother's womb. Before you are born, they have you all figured out and have a plan for your life. A program for who you will be, what you will do and what you will be, who you will marry and how happy you will be. You are a *mama's boy*. Have you ever heard anyone talk of a *mama's girl*? It is always a mama's boy. They got your whole number, brother. Then they hand you over to your wife, in a secret ceremony the day after your wedding, and that is that. Your fate is sealed."

He thought he heard the man's ego break his confidence falter. He laid a hand on his shoulder.

"What has she done to you?" he asked.

The man shook his head. He could not speak about it.

"Not to worry, man," Kasim said to him. "Whatever it is she will fix it at the proper time. Women have it all in hand; marriages, breakups, and reconciliations, they have it all figured. Just continue being a man. She will deal with the rest. Be the man."

The guard heaved a sigh and nodded. He could do that.

"And, by the way," Kasim said to him, "You are a Kuyu man, not a Kikuyu man. Have you ever heard of a Kiluo man, or Kiswahili man? You are a Kuyu man. You speak Kikuyu and have Kikuyu habits. I speak Kikamba, and have Kamba traditions. Which reminds me I have a funeral harambee. Any amount donation will do."

The man rose and walked away.

"Note to self," Kasim said. "Which is the fastest way to get rid of a Kuyu man? Ask him for *harambee* donation."

It was just after ten. Too early to go home pick the landlord's double locks. He drove to *Comrades Comedy Club* to pass the time and check out the competition. He slipped in through the back door, courtesy of a Kamba security guard, a brother hustler who liked his Kuyu jokes, and he took a seat at the dark end of the bar.

In the three hours he spent there, no one had a joke that could make him smile. They were all kids' jokes, blown up college boy jokes about women that only dropouts understood. They had the advantage of having stayed longer, gone farther in school before dropping out, otherwise they could not touch Kasim. Kasim had the advantage of having once made a Fahari sage who did not understand the language smile at his jokes. He still needed to figure a way to a greybeard's funny bone, but he could teach the college boys the basics of comedy.

Chapter 10

Uncle Tivo was out by the gate enticing Uncle Sam's security guard to abandon his post for a few minutes and show him to the nearest beer shop. Kasim and Salim passed silently behind them and went on to the meeting. Uncle Sam's train was about to start on the third leg of the journey having safely crossed the first two major hurdles to Caesar's funeral.

The first clan meeting was traditionally for hugging and weeping in family arms, mumbling the sorrow, real or not, and for remembering the good that the departed did to the clan. Wealthier clans hired poorer clans to wail and roll in the mud and show their grief for them, but not the King'oo clan.

King'oo frowned on uncontrolled show of grief. Instead, the time was used as Caesar would have it, coming to terms with the inconvenience of another burial in the clan, uniting in facing the loss, not wallowing in despair and self-pity. Not to sit in Uncle Sam's great hall with blank faces, sharing small talk and empty words waiting for Sam to speak.

The first meeting of Caesar's funeral arrangements had exceeded everyone's expectation in simplicity. Aunt Kamene steered the committee away from useless speeches and ritual mourning to planning how, where, and when they would bury Caesar. She avoided talk of the cost or contributions. Such talk would discourage and scare some people away.

King'oo knew they could bury their dead without help from outside the clan. They always had, always did, and always would. But Caesar's funeral was different. Caesar was larger than life, a national hero, a man held in high regard through the world. He was the greatest King'oo that ever was born. Caesar's funeral would cost an unthinkable amount of money.

The nightly meetings got tense, nerves strained, and Uncle Sam's train slowed down to a crawl, as progress reports trickled in, along with messages of condolence, pledges of support and wild suggestions on how to bury Caesar. A former colleague in government who studied with him at Lenin University in Moscow suggested a mausoleum at Kathiani market so tourists would line up and pay to see Caesar's dead body. He had seen such a thing done in Russia. In time the suggestion evolved to having the mausoleum at Parliament buildings in Nairobi, so that Caesar could lie side by side with the founding father of the nation.

The meetings got harder to manage, as egos flared and clashed, and tempers rose, and it became clear that, regardless of the input from rational minds, Caesar's funeral would turn out to be like no other ever seen or heard of in Kathiani, and cost more than anyone dared put in words. The estimated cost, calculated with zeal and optimism and goodwill and the generosity of an entire clan and nation, was mind boggling. So preposterous that Uncle Sam had to say it in dollars to cushion the clan from shock.

"How much money is that?" Uncle Tivo asked Kasim in a whisper.

"A lot of money," said Kasim.

"How much money have we raised?" Aunt Kamene asked everyone.

"Very little," Uncle Sam revealed.

"Then stop whispering and start donating," she ordered.

There was sudden silence in the room. A chilly wind blew in through the open door and hovered in the air over the gathering. Promises had been made. Enough pledges of goods, services, and money to bury an emperor. Clansmen had talked of a military parade, the gun carriage that bore dead presidents, streets lined with soldiers in mourning and a twenty-one-gun salute. Then flags at half-mast throughout the country for thirty days of mourning. Uncle Sam had a hard job dragging the clan back to earth.

"Forget not what Fiscal Caesar stood for," he reminded them.

The *Nation* named him Fiscal Caesar when, as the head of fiscal planning, he faced off shameless lawmakers trying to award themselves higher salaries than those paid to parliamentarians in the countries that loaned the money from which their salaries were paid. He enforced unpopular austerity measures to curb spending in a government choking on unjustifiable debt, insane expenditure, rampant greed, and corruption.

It remained to be seen how many of Caesar's former colleagues would honour their pledges of contributing for his funeral.

"Has anyone informed Richard?" Aunt Kamene asked. "We need money from him too?"

Uncle Sam turned to Salim. Salim pointed at Kasim.

"He told us to bugger off," Kasim informed her.

"To do what?"

"Go away," Uncle Sam translated.

"He wants to see the budget," Salim added.

"Well then, take it to him," she said. "Treasurer?"

"I don't have a budget," said the man they had conscripted for the job.

He was hunkered inside a pack of anonymous, old faces that never volunteered for committees.

"Who has it?" Aunt Kamene asked the room.

"We are yet to make one," said Sam.

"Then make it," she said. "What are you waiting for?"

"Aunt Eva," he said. "I gather she will undo anything we do without her."

"And you gather that from whose garden?" she asked.

Uncle Sam was familiar with King'oo women's lack of decorum, being married to one of them, but he had to constantly work to keep calm.

"I got it on authority from Uncle Tivo," he said.

"Why is Eva not here?" Uncle Tivo asked. "Eva would have handled it like a man."

They ignored him, though there was no doubt in anyone's mind she would have done it differently. Eva would have whipped them in line, extracted their donations and buried Caesar by sunset.

"We waste our time planning without her," Salim said to Aunt Kamene.

Uncle Sam sent him a look of gratitude.

"Why are we here then?" Aunt Kamene asked them. "I have things to do and so does everyone here."

The aunts looked at one another and wondered what would happen when Eva arrived. Others looked at one another and wondered what would happen if she did not come at all.

Aunt Kamene's resentment of Aunt Eva was not a secret. Their egos, opponents from childhood, were never comfortable in each other's presence.

Uncle Sam's train was derailing before leaving the station, and his passengers were ready to bail out and walk home. The clan was for easing the tension by moving to plan B. But there was no plan B. No one thought they would need it. They had all believed the government would give money to bury one of its own, or Uncle Richard would go against the grain and pay for his mentor's funeral, or something would happen so that was Caesar was soon buried and they could all go back to their other worries.

Uncle Sam, who knew better than to expect any help from State House, had hoped Richard would take care of half of the budget, after all the things Mzee Mophat had done for him, and the clan could scrape together the rest of it. With those fantasies now out of the window, and no plan B of any sort, desperation was slowly creeping on people of good will, and despair was not far behind. He was perusing his notes looking for inspiration when Aunt Kamene charged back in. After a quick discussion with her sisters, they had decided to wait for Eva to come home.

"We can't stop the meetings now," Uncle Sam said to her. "You know what happens when we lose momentum."

When a juggernaut like a clan head's funeral stopped moving forward, usually due to squabbles over inheritance or succession, it was so hard to restart it that some litigants were dead and buried long before their cases were buried by the courts. Besides, Uncle Sam knew they would blame it all on him once Eva demanded to know who had interrupted Caesar's journey to the grave.

"I suggest we stop for today," he said it slowly, so as not to be misunderstood. "We resume tomorrow with clearer minds. Tomorrow, not the day after tomorrow, we meet here as usual. Are we all clear?"

The men's side was all clear, and ready to eat and go, but not everyone on women's side was happy.

"I have not heard radio announcement," said Aunt Nyiva.

"Salim?" Aunt Kamene called.

"Kasim," said Salim.

"Where is Kasim?" she yelled. "Kasim?"

Kasim appeared from the kitchen gnawing on a bone.

"Put that down," she ordered him.

He handed it to a man who handed it to a boy.

"Radio announcements," Aunt Kamene said to him.

"I have an invoice," he said, dipping in his pocket.

"Never mind your receipts," she said. "Is it on air?"

"It will cost …."

"You did not book the whole week?" asked Aunt Kamene.

"Must be paid to be on air. You did not give me money."

"Salim?" she asked.

"No money either," he said.

The aunts looked at one another, turned to Uncle Sam. He looked down at his clipboard. He knew what they were thinking. He was a wealthy man, with his own company, a big car, a big house, and a big wife. He should pay for everything and save them time and embarrassment. He had done it once before, under duress, paid for everything with promises of a full refund after the funeral, after the accounts were reconciled, and the pledges made good. His wife never forgave him for being so gullible.

Salim looked down in embarrassment as he heard Uncle Sam start on his corona story, a desperate plea, like everyone made, blaming it all on an impotent government that, succumbing to neocolonial blackmail, abdicated its responsibilities and left its citizens at the mercy of international drug cartels.

The sudden silence, and the bewildered looks on the aunts' faces, said he was not making any sense to anyone but Salim, and possibly Kasim. He had to explain it differently.

While the government imposed total lockdowns and curfews were inconvenient for everyone, they were death blows to an already struggling economy, and a death sentence to small businesses and personal enterprises like his own. The government still demanded revenue from closed and dying businesses and, with everyone wearing masks, no one could tell who was collecting tax or for whom. Uncle Sam had had to lay off staff and now made hardly enough money to feed his family. He would be a poor man too if the clan did not stop coming to his house for meetings.

He looked up from his clipboard, waited for someone to say something sympathetic. There was a chillier, more uncomfortable silence while they digested what he had said. They had been through it all too, the lockups, lock-ins, lockdowns, and lockouts, and the whole gamut of cooked-up protocols, but they did not believe him, especially not the part about being a poor man.

Finally, with skeptical King'oo eyes staring at him, he gave in. He cleared his throat, and announced he would pay for three more days of radio announcements and two more newspaper notices and nothing more.

There was an audible sigh of relief from the aunts. Then he saw Kasim standing next to him, and he could not remember why, and ordered him to sit down.

Kasim wedged himself between Uncle Tivo and a stranger on the sofa.

"Did you hear that, Uncle Tivo," he whispered to the old man. "Eva is coming home."

"Where is the food?" Uncle Tivo had moved on to more immediate concerns. "We are hungry."

There were snickers from the youth camp in the corner. Everyone else chose to ignore him. His peers, old men who had not met since the last clan funeral, continued their conversation without him.

"Who next?" asked Aunt Kamene.

"Casket," said Uncle Sam.

"Salim?"

Salim was now perched on the sofa's armrest next to Uncle Tivo.

"I know where to get one," he said.

"How much?"

The aunts looked at one another, a little skeptical, when he told them the cost.

"Salim," Aunt Kamene said, "If we wanted a wooden crate, we would have asked Mutisia to make one."

"You want expensive?" he asked her. "I can also find expensive."

"You are an educated man," she told him. "Use your head."

Everyone gasped when he told them the highest price he had seen posted on a casket. It was enough money to build a house.

Aunt Charity continued looking down at her hands in her lap. She seemed on the verge of saying or doing something she knew would be as catastrophic as jumping in crocodile infested Masinga Dam. The look on her face worried those who knew her as always calm and clear-headed under stress and as solid as a rock. Someone they could depend on.

"Now we know how much money it will cost," Aunt Kamene said, to banish uncertainty. "Can we raise it?"

There was the usual dead moment, the silence that followed whenever they were challenged to show their grief by giving unto Caesar what respect to Caesar was due. She looked round the room to the men's corner.

Many would have stayed home, and blamed lack of transport, but Uncle Sam hired a *matatu* bus to pick them from home and return them at the end of the meetings. A good few had had sacrificed time and money to travel to Nairobi, hand in the little they could afford, and were waiting for transport home.

They sat hunched over, their heads buried in their shoulders to avoid being noticed and called out again for more money. Less than half of them would have stayed if she had placed the donations basket at the gate. Now they were stuck in the middle of the depressing situation even before the cost of the hearse, the mortuary and other bills had been tabled.

"If the worst comes to the worst," Uncle Sam said to lighten the mood. "Kasim will fetch the pickup."

Kasim sat up alarmed.

"The pickup?" he said, "Why the pickup, and why does it always have to be me who fetches the pickup?"

"Uncle Richard gives it to you," Uncle Sam said calmly. "Me, he would tell, as in your own words, to bugger off and go buy my own pickup."

Sam had sent the elders, the aunts, and all kinds of clan emissaries to plead with Uncle Richard, only to have them report back disheartened and angry at him for sending them to be humiliated by *that man*. He was worse than a policeman, they said. Only someone with a skin as hard as that of a warthog, and no self-respect, could survive the tongue-lashing they got from him. Someone like Kasim.

"Take Salim with you," Uncle Sam said to Kasim.

"What?" Salim came to with a jolt. "Am I now Kasim's assistant?"

Uncle Sam beckoned, laid a hand on his shoulder, and took him outside.

"Salim," he said. "In this family, apart from Aunt Charity, you are the only person I understand that understands me. I need you to stay sane for my own sanity. Uncle Richard respects you more than he respects me."

"You should hear the things he calls me."

"Calls us," said Uncle Sam. "Let us see this thing through together, you and me. Okay? We need Uncle Richard's money for this to succeed."

"His pocket change? What you ask me to do is impossible."

"Well then," Uncle Sam said, giving up. "If you are that afraid of your Uncle Rich, do what Aunt Kamene says. Go rent a hearse and pay for it."

"Me?"

"And Kasim."

"To pay how?" asked Kasim, who had followed them outside and walked up unnoticed.

"You two work it out," said Uncle Sam.

"We two? I don't have a job."

"About time you got one," said Aunt Kamene, also walking up unnoticed.

"Aunt Kamene," Kasim said, thoughtlessly, "Have you ever wondered why your grown-up sons live in your goathouse?"

"Too lazy to find jobs and wives," she said.

"There are no jobs to find," Kasim said to her. "No job, no wife. Ask anyone."

"Then let them go down to Sultan Hamud," she said. "Work for the Indians, work for the Chinese, work for anyone who will hire them. Go with them and get yourself a real job too. Kung Fu and Karate will show you how."

"We are wasting time here," Aunt Wavinya said, also coming up unnoticed.

"I have to go cook for my grandchildren," Aunt Kamene said. "Salim, do what your uncle says. Find a hearse and pay for it. Anything else?"

Salim was already walking away.

"Where are you going?" she asked him.

"Transport."

"Not yet," she said. "You will eat here today. Wavinya, serve Salim the first plate. I want to see how much he eats."

Uncle Sam realised the whole clan would follow outside if he did not move them back inside. He herded them back inside and found everyone ready to wind up, eat and go home.

"Pastor Kioko?" Aunt Kamene asked.

"He is not here."

"I will pray," Aunt Wavinya offered to save time.

She said a fast prayer and Aunt Kamene started serving.

"Does anyone tell us why the pastor is not here today?" Sam's wife asked.

They shook their heads at her. Sam knew the reason, but it was a long story, and everyone was hungry, so he decided to keep it to himself.

Pastor Kioko kept the lowest profile possible by not showing up every night for meetings where his presence went largely unnoticed, and his opinion was rarely thought relevant. He evaded them as much as he could, in and out of church, and anywhere their paths might cross, but it was impossible to get away from the plague. He was their pastor. They were his flock, though he did not dare use such words as shepherd and flock regarding King'oo men. They were King'oo. He was only a pastor.

At weddings, baptisms, funerals, and anywhere the Pastor had to officiate, they commandeered his duties, took over his church, and overturned his programs. They reduced him to an observer while drunken masters of ceremonies rumbled on about nothing to do with the ceremony or the occasion.

Caesar built the church for worship, not a social hall, and entrusted it to Pastor Kioko, but the clan saw it differently. It was their church, built on clan land like the primary school, the clinic, and the courthouse, and built for them by Caesar. Once or twice, he had to send for the chief and his henchmen to evict everyone and lock the church and that did not help their relationship. The plague his father warned him about.

"Closing prayer," Sam's wife called when everyone had eaten and were ready to go.

"Kasim?" Aunt Kamene called.

Someone guffawed. Kasim looked up alarmed.

"Pray for us," she said.

"Me?"

And she was not joking. She expected Kasim to say a prayer. Everyone sat with heads bowed, some to hide the brewing laughter. Salim was smiling too, certain of the disaster that would follow. Kasim swallowed the panic. Stage fright, he said to himself, and I can do this. He squared his shoulders, bowed his head, and mumbled the first thing that came to mind, something he had picked up at Caesar's house when he was a boy and went for evening tuition. Everyone said 'Amen' and rushed to get away.

"Kasim," Aunt Kamene said harshly. "That prayer was for before not after eating."

"Thank you, Aunt Kamene" he said and hurried out.

Salim was waiting by the Beetle.

Chapter 11

The security guard had the gate open the moment he heard the Beetle's approach as it came clattering down the road. Their last visit, and the reception they got from *mama*, had convinced him they were family. He flagged them down to inform them that *Mzee* had given him a telling when he heard about their last visit, but he had not said anything about not letting them in again. Then he stepped back, saluted, and waved them on.

The dogs accepted them too, and they watched from the garage as Kasim drove up to the front of the house. Uncle Richard's black Prado with oversize tyres was not in its parking spot.

"Waste of time," said Salim. "Turn around; no need to bother Aunt Gwyneth."

"We should have asked the guard whether *mzee* was in," Kasim started to turn the car.

Then the front door opened.

"Too late," he said, as Aunt Gwyneth approach.

"There you are again," she said. "Looking for Richard, I presume."

"Your husband is very hard to find," Kasim said.

"You must tell him, when you see him," she said.

"Golf club again?" Salim asked.

"He lives there now," she said, with a laugh. "Only comes home to eat, sleep a little and change his shirt. But do not tell him I said that."

"We won't," Kasim laughing with her.

"Wait here, I have something for you," she said to him.

She went back in the house.

"Such a sweet lady," Kasim said to Salim. "We should visit her more often. And not just for the cake. Seriously."

"You do that," Salim said. "You have the time."

He was turning the car when she brought them two slices of cake.

"Thanks, Aunt Gwyneth," Salim said. "We know where to find him."

Uncle Richard was arguing with another golfer when they turned the corner of the club house. They stopped and waited for him to notice them. He was mid-sentence when he finally did and promptly sent a waiter.

"He will call for you," the waiter said, ushering them back. "Wait in your car."

"He did not say to bugger off," Kasim observed.

"He will," Salim assured.

He called his office, while they waited. Kasim went to the security guard to tell him Luo jokes. The man had heard Kasim's jokes told better by Luo comedians, before he left Kisumu to work in Nairobi.

"Would you like to hear a Kamba joke then?" Kasim asked him.

Before the guard could decide, Uncle Richard appeared at the corner of the clubhouse, and he scuttled back to his post. Salim and Kasim hurried to Uncle Richard.

"Tell me you have not been to bother my wife again," he said to them.

"We haven't," Kasim said. "Honestly."

"Who told you I was here?"

"You are always here, Uncle Richard."

"Says who?"

Salim had accepted that Kasim do all the talking, since Uncle Richard did not expect much logic from him and was more likely to forgive him. But Uncle Richard was glaring at Salim not at Kasim.

"Common sense," Salim said.

"If you had common sense you would have found out who your fathers were," he said to them.

"We are almost there, Uncle Richard," Kasim said. "But you know how slippery King'oo men are. We think it is this one, it turns out he was in Uganda on some dubious business, then we think it is that one, it turns out he is neither Kuyu, Kisii, or Kamba, and was in prison when we were conceived, and then we think ..."

"Stop thinking," Uncle Richard interrupted. "What do you want from me? And fast, I have no time to waste."

"We know who our fathers are," Salim took over. "We just don't know where they are."

"And you want me to go find them for you?"

There was a time Salim believed Uncle Richard's hostility was a deliberate attempt to discourage family from feeling entitled to his person, his time, his property, or his empathy. Now he suspected the unpleasantness was a genetic flaw that compelled most King'oo to see meanness as justifiable self-preservation.

"The pickup," he said. "That is all we want from you."

"My pickup?" Uncle Richard corrected. "Why don't I just let you people keep my pickup for all your funerals?"

"May we?" Kasim asked.

Uncle Richard glowered at him.

"Who is your mother?" he asked.

"Syombua."

"Which Syombua?"

"Aunt Syombua."

"I don't know any Aunt Syombua."

"She claims to be your *sisitar*."

Uncle Richard's eyes narrowed. Kasim tried to soften them with a clowning smile. It did not work.

"Again, who sent you?" Uncle Richard turned to Salim.

"Aunt Kamene," he said. "You remember her."

He remembered her, from past encounters, as the woman who spoke the loudest, disagreed with everything he said, and had opinions contradicting his own. An annoying King'oo woman. And he respected her for what she stood for, what she had done with her life.

"A four-bedroom house with water and electricity?" he said to Salim. "A hardware store in Kathiani, a shop and bar complex, and rental apartments at Sultan Hamud. And all that by a woman without education or husband. Do you even know where Sultan Hamud is?"

"We all envy her, Uncle Richard," said Kasim.

"You should admire, not envy her," Uncle Richard told him.

There was more than enough to admire in Aunt Kamene, Uncle Richard said to them. She, of all the clan's men and women understood the meaning of self-sufficiency, of standing alone from the herd, how to safeguard her time and her money from pests and predators. A woman of substance.

Uncle Richard turned to Salim.

"What have you done for yourself?"

When Salim declined to be drawn, he turned to Kasim and repeated the question.

"The pickup," said Salim. "We just came for the pickup."

"She said, if we don't get it, she will come get it herself," Kasim chipped in.

"Why is she the one who always sends you for my pickup?"

"The others are afraid of you."

Uncle Richard looked from one to the other.

"I am holding you responsible," he said to Salim. "I want it back at my house by sunset, in one piece. Understood?"

"With a full tank of gas," Salim said, wearily. "I know the routine, Uncle Richard. A full tank of gas, however little gas there was in the tank when we got it."

"Come for the pickup on the day of the funeral."

"Thanks, Uncle Rich ... Richard," Kasim said.

"Which is when?" he asked.

"We don't know yet, Uncle Richard."

"Go find out," Uncle Richard said to him.

"May we have it today?" asked Kasim.

Uncle Richard looked him in the eye.

"So that you can use it to ferry stolen goods?"

"That's a good one, Uncle Rich." Kasim laughed.

Uncle Richard glared at him, turned to Salim.

"You get it for a day, on the day," he said walking away. "Now, go away. This is a members' club."

"Thanks again, Uncle Rich," Kasim called.

"Bugger off," he said over his shoulder.

Kasim laughed aloud.

"What is wrong with you?" Salim asked, when they got to the car. "He insults you, and you laugh?"

"He is funny," said Kasim.

"You find being labeled illegitimate funny?"

"Lighten up, man. Life is a play - a comedy to those who think, and a tragedy to those who feel."

"And you have read that book too?"

Kasim laughed.

"Where?" Salim asked him. "When?"

"There is a time and a place for everything," he said. "Now it is almost time for my appointment in River Road with a bunch of hard-life, handcart drivers who do not care for degrees or diplomas, or whether anyone can read."

But first he had to drop Salim off at the office.

BOOK 2
How many civil servants does it take to change a nappy?

Chapter 12

Uncle Sam's train was back on the rails. The great hall overflowed out of the majestic French windows to the lawn where his men were erecting white marquees among red, yellow, and pink flowering hibiscus bushes, and arranging party chairs. Attendance had exploded, since the obituaries started appearing in newspapers and on the radio, and there was subdued excitement, vibrations of hushed conversation and suppressed laughter, as old friends who had not met since the last clan funeral caught up with one another's news.

Many faces were familiar, distant cousins one met on such occasions, and forgotten relatives who, on hearing transport would be provided and *muthokoi* served after the meetings, decided there was no better place to be after work than Uncle Sam's.

They came from town, and from out of town and from Athi River, where many of them worked for flower farms and cement factories. Some had paid fares they could not afford to travel from Voi and Mtito Andei when they heard Caesar was dead.

They sat on every piece of furniture available, and on one another, and on the carpet, and leaned on the walls between paintings.

Salim recognised faces from other family gatherings, but there were also strangers, friends-of-friends, and people who happened to be passing by Sam's gate and saw the vehicles parked on the street and followed the smell of cooking. Funeral fundraisers were not a place to ask anyone who he was, or why he was there. King'oo clan ran into the hundreds if not thousands, so no one knew them all, and all donations were equally welcome.

Uncle Sam was in his place at the center of the room, his clipboard in hand, reading reports. Kasim stood by the kitchen door gnawing on something Aunt Kamene gave him on the way in, and Salim sat next to the Chinese twins trying not to ask which was which.

"Kung Fu," one said, to help him out.

"Karate," said the other.

They looked at each other and laughed.

"Okay," he said. "You laugh, but one day I will figure you out."

He was not the only family member who could not tell them apart. People had been puzzling over them since they were left at Caesar's gate early on a cold July morning when they were just days old. Caesar adopted them and Charity took care of them and taught them to read and write and not to call her mother or call Caesar dad.

They grew up healthy and happy in Caesar's compound, playing in the yard dust with chickens and kid goats, and for a while were a curiosity to school children who did not know what they were and stopped by to and from school to peer through the fence trying to catch sight of them. Grownups peeked through the fence too, when they thought Charity was not there to chase them away like children.

"What do you do these days?" Salim asked them.

The smiles faded, the eyes narrowed in thought and worry was not far behind. They looked at each other wondering who should tell.

"Uncle Salim," said Kung Fu, "You never asked us that before."

"I assume, like other King'oo boys, you just exist. Do no more than be. Do you?"

They looked at each other again. Kung Fu decided to tell more. They worked for the Chinese railway. He said it hesitantly, like something he was ashamed of, something he could not understand. Kung Fu was a cook's assistant, and his brother was a dishwasher.

"I am proud of you guys," Salim said to them. "Only stones serve a purpose sitting still."

His words reassured them enough to want to open up more. They had taken a strict one week's leave to attend Caesar's funeral, Karate added. If Caesar was not buried by the end of the week, they would lose their jobs.

"How many King'oo burials have you seen concluded on time?" he asked them.

They could not remember any.

"Better start looking for new jobs then," he told them.

Their eyes narrowed, and again they consulted with their minds and nodded.

"That is right," he said to them. "I am just another crazy, old King'oo, but I am different from other crazy old King'oo. To me, you are real, you are family. How many King'oo have said that to you?"

"So, you will get us real jobs, when we are fired?" asked Karate.

Salim saw the trap he had talked himself into, the burden he was about to shoulder.

"On second thoughts," he said, "You better sneak out of here right now and go save your jobs. I assure you no one will realise you have left."

"Aunt Charity," said Kung Fu.

That jolted Salim back to reality. This was not a clan party but Caesar's funeral.

"On second, second thoughts," he said to them, "stay and see this thing through. Worry about your jobs after we bury Caesar."

He added under his breath - *if we ever do.*

Then Uncle Sam called for attention to announce he had big and important news. This far, he had only called attention to ask for more donation.

"I have good news for all of us tonight," he said. "Eva is home."

He paused and looked round, expecting a response, an excited applause or something. Not even Uncle Tivo had anything for him. He had overheard old people say Eva died in America without a husband or a child, and what a waste that was. But now she was back.

"Yes," he said, trying to sound excited. "Aunt Eva is back."

He paused, still hoping for a sign of enthusiasm. Getting non, he went back to his clipboard.

"I remember someone asking why she has not been back for such a long time," he said. "Today you can ask her yourself."

Everyone remembered Aunt Eva from different, mostly personal, perspectives. Many remembered her from school, trying to teach them something now long forgotten, while others recalled her from Kathiani market haggling market women to exhaustion, and from the church urging the Pastor to speed it up before Sunday lunch got burned. But the clan's most common and significant recollections of Eva were her Christmases. Like Richard's house warming party, Eva's Christmas feasts were burned in their memory.

Before she gave up on the King'oo and stopped coming, Eva visited every year at Christmas and threw a party for Caesar fit for a president. Clan women cooked for a day and a night under her severe directions to feed the entire clan. Then long tables were set up under the mango trees and loaded with enough food and drinks to feed a whole county.

Caesar stood on a podium in his smart pinstripe suit and tie, just as he had done when she was a girl and he was the President's chief minister, and made his end-of-year speech. He reviewed the clan's journey through the year, highlighted issues of pride and those of shame, and said what needed doing next. But, highly aware of King'oo aversion to criticism, sermons, and lengthy speeches before a feast, and to avoid hurt feelings, he kept it short, and general. When he finished, Eva and her sisters took over and served the food.

Along with the inevitable and strict scrutiny, and related discomfort, Eva served hotdogs, hamburgers, grilled pork sausages and potato salad and green salads and puddings. She also served roast meat, and introduced the clan to raw onions, raw carrots, tomatoes, and strange sauces that tasted fire and honey. The clan talked about it for days afterward. It was the only time the clan feasted on anything other than *muthokoi* at Christmas.

Then one Christmas Aunt Eva collided with Aunt Kamene, a loud, heated exchange ensued, she decided she had enough of trying to lift the King'oo from the stone age, and did not come again for years.

Now she was back, and it was possible she had mellowed out. The clan she had sworn never to come back to had grown in numbers, and in ages, if not in knowledge or wisdom. Most of the old men and women who drove her away with their stubborn old ways had passed on handing the baton to a generation that remembered her from its school years. She would hopefully find the younger, educated, now also old, King'oo easier to manage.

Uncle Sam smiled inwardly thinking about it. He knew, from own experiences, that nearly everyone present was dreaming how Aunt Eva would bail them out of their financial and other difficulties. But the few old, old timers like Uncle Tivo, those who could see beyond yesterday, knew that hurricanes did not get old or mellow out with time. They got bigger, angrier, more hazardous.

"She will be down in a moment," he said, glancing in the direction of the door to the staircase. "In the meantime, allow me to introduce her husband, Roger Culpepper. I am certain you have not forgotten Roger."

Another wasted attempt at humor. Roger was not easy to forget, even for King'oo men who had no time for non-King'oo men. Small Smiles, they called him in Kikamba, and they remembered him as a walking telephone pole, with long hands, claw-like fingers, a ring in one ear whose meaning and purpose he did not explain, and a bony face that was always smiling.

When Roger last visited, Aunt Eva wasted a lot of hers and their time telling off people who would not believe he was not a reincarnation of a legendary Kitui seer, and shielding him from Kasim and Salim who she feared would infect him with King'oo futility.

Now Roger sat with his small smile squashed between two old men who smelled of alcohol, wood smoke and goat manure. Last time, it was Kasim who had insulated him from it, but Kasim was in the kitchen being fattened by Aunt Kamene, and Salim was a poor stand-in.

"Uncle Roger," he tried, walking up and offering his hand.

Roger looked up startled. Then the angular face broke in a bigger smile.

"Kasim?" he asked.

"Salim," said Salim.

"Salim," the small smile blossomed into a sunflower face. "I remember you. You are Kasim's cousin. Finally, someone I can understand. Good to see you, Salim. How have you been?"

"Great. You?"

"Never been better. How's Kasim? Still the comedian?"

"He says so," Salim laughed with him. "There he is now charming the ladies as usual."

Kasim was at the women's corner working to make them smile.

"Kasim?" Salim called out.

Kasim turned, saw Roger, excused himself to the women, and rushed over.

"Roger, my man!" he hailed.

He gave Roger a cheerful handshake and a hug. Uncle Tivo evicted one of the old men to make room for him.

"You aged, my man," he said to Roger. "What happened to you?"

"Time my intrepid, young friend," said Roger.

Kasim lowered his voice.

"Nothing to do with a certain Kamba old battle-axe?"

Roger laughed aloud and they touched palms again. Watching them, Salim wished he could exchange lives with Kasim for a moment, but only for a moment. He was positive he could not manage the whole of Kasim's life for longer than a moment.

"How is the grand plan shaping up?" Roger was asking Kasim. "Are we the world's greatest comedian yet?"

"Depends on who you ask," Kasim said. "We have gigs all over the city now. You must see us perform."

"You reckon she would okay it?"

"Don't sweat it, Salim and me will find a way round the old battle-axe."

They turned to Salim. He shrugged.

"Listen," Kasim said to Roger. "I have a new one about a great American gentleman married to a troublesome King'oo woman"

"Go on," said Roger.

"It is not about anyone we know. Would you like to hear it?"

"Later," Roger said, pointing.

The room had fallen silent. All eyes were on the entrance where Eva stood filling the doorway side to side, her enormous hat touching the top frame. She looked formidable in her light blue dress-suite with wide, white-edged lapels and a silver brooch on the left one. On her head was an enormous black hat as wide as an umbrella.

Eva's presence induced all manner of emotions from the clan. Her name had struck terror in her students' minds from the first to the last day of the school term, a fear so profound their grades went up when she left for America. Pupils formerly too scared to understand anything she taught suddenly understood it all after she left. They would forget it all again when she came for visits, fearing she would stay to teach them again. But it got better when they heard she had no intention of staying or returning to their school

A wave of awe wafted through the ballroom as she entered, gliding in with the dignity of a royal. Instantly ordinary conversation ceased, and was replaced by purposeful attention.

Salim heard a school bell in his head, and felt the cold chill he had felt every Monday morning when she walked into class with her books under her left arm and a cane in her right hand. He suddenly had the same urge he had then, to leap out of the window and flee before she called out the names of those who had failed Friday's math test.

Kasim let go of Roger's hand and stared close to terror. He had imagined Aunt Eva would have grown old, grey, shorter, and shrivelled, and frail, like King'oo women when they got to be a certain age. But she seemed to have become taller, and wider and larger and more woeful than was imaginable. He thought he felt the floor shake when she walked up to Sam, turned to face the room, and waited to be received.

Uncle Sam was no less awed by the transformation. He cleared his throat, and glanced at the first item on his clipboard. It said introduce Aunt Eva. He looked up and cleared his throat again.

"Aunt Eva needs no introduction," he said to the gathering. "But, for the sake of those who never went to school …"

He paused for the laughter. There was none. Most had forgotten school after the last bell rang decades ago. He cleared his throat again.

"For those who went to school late," he said, continuing the introduction, "Eva was head teacher and education board chairman for many years."

He turned a page on his clipboard and continued the introduction.

In keeping with a trend started by his great-grandfather, Caesar, Eva's father, married a woman from

Puntland, a royal princess so tall and lean and elegant. Envious King'oo women said she was as tall as a snake and as arrogant as a pigeon pea. Her hair, black as night, was down to her waist, and her eyes, large and black, were so sharp they seemed to see more than she observed, so that people suspected she was also a sorceress. She was a good wife to Caesar and bore him six daughters, one as beautiful as the next, but died giving birth to the seventh. Aunt Eva was the eldest of the daughters.

Uncle Sam was reading from a welcoming speech prepared for him by Pastor Kioko, who had known Caesar's family more than most. Among the facts Kioko found too controversial to include was the fact that Caesar's Punt wife was Muslim. She considered King'oo a backward and primitive clan. She would not integrate with them, and died without having spoken a single word of their language. How was that for spirit? Those were among Kioko's most private thoughts regarding Caesar's people.

It had taken them long to accept his authority as their shepherd, and to get used to the fact that *'little'* Kioko of baby elephant ears was their pastor. They let him do his pastoral duties, so long as the words shepherd and flock did not come into it, and they treated him with indifference the rest of the time. And when they had a wedding, a baptism or a funeral, the only events that needed the use of his church and the presence of a pastor, they invaded his church, took over his pulpit, usurped his role and reduced him to a spectator in his own church.

Halfway through Sam's reading, the gathering became restless. Aunt Eva was showing signs of simmering impatience. Aunt Kamene marched up to Sam, took the clipboard from his hands, counted the remaining pages, looked up at him incredulous.

"Really?" she said, giving it back.

"I will keep it short," he promised.

"And make it quick," she said to him. "We know who Eva is, and it is getting late."

Everyone seemed to agree, nodding quietly hoping that would be the end of that. Eva weathered the irrelevant introduction, and the short exchange between Sam and Aunt Kamene, with regal majesty. Then she spoke up.

"Were there no King'oo men who could introduce me to the rest?" she asked.

"No," Aunt Kamene said bluntly.

Uncle Sam asked himself the same question every time he had to host one of their unruly gatherings, stand in front of them and tell them things they all knew. He was not a King'oo man, he was not even Caesar's son-in-law by blood. His wife was an adopted daughter, taken in when she was ten to save her from an arranged marriage with a man her grandfather's age. But that did not deter them from imposing on him clan burdens that had nothing to do with him. As with other funerals before, the clan did not ask his consent prior to invading his house and taking over his living room and garden to plan Caesar's funeral. They did not bother to find out his willingness, or availability to chair their nightly meetings. His wife had volunteered him and his house without consulting him, the clan had accepted his services without hesitation, so, why was he explaining himself to Hurricane Eva?

"Sam is one of us," Aunt Kamene said.

"I am happy to help out, Aunt Eva," he added.

He turned to his wife. She smiled encouragingly.

"To continue," he said, turning to the room, "I have briefed Aunt Eva on progress so far. So, unless there is a question, we shall proceed with tonight's program as planned."

He glanced at the paper in his hand.

"Uncle Tivo has a question," Kasim said.

"Speak, Uncle Tivo," he said.

Then Uncle Tivo asked the question that many had been itching to ask her since they heard Eva had arrived from America.

"What did you bring me?" he asked her.

There was sudden silence. All eyes were on Eva. If she had something for Tivo, she would have something for everyone, they reasoned. Uncle Sam turned to Eva, embarrassed on behalf of everyone but Tivo and his cohorts. To them, it was a valid and important question.

"Nothing," she answered bluntly. "Next question?"

Only Tivo dared, and his next question was as startling as her response to the first.

"Nothing?" he said, visibly agitated. "Then why did you come?"

They had buried people before Caesar without her interference. Why was she here? Why without the gifts and the things she brought at Christmas? Old heads bobbed in agreement. Those too were logical and important questions to ask her.

"Have you learned to say thank you?" she asked them.

They looked at one another. Thank you? They asked themselves. But she is family? They waited for her truthful answer.

"I told you people before I left," she reminded them, scowling at Uncle Sam. "You will learn to say thank you, before you get any more Christmas presents from me."

Before she left, she had warned there would be no more gifts until they learned the meaning of gratitude. She had come hoping they could work together to bury Caesar without the usual King'oo male futility, and it infuriated her that they did not see the difference between Christmas and a funeral visit when even goats and children could.

She spared Sam more agony by turning to the men's side, and scanning their faces for one man she could talk to. She was taller than most men, including Uncle Sam who was Maasai, and her school-head harshness intimidated them.

"Richard," she said suddenly. "Where is Richard?"

There was uncomfortable silence. Everyone knew she had issues with Richard ever since he laughed at her when she threatened to have him expelled from school for disobeying her and promised he would pass high school, go to college and be a space engineer without doing a stich of her homework or her extra weekend tutorials. And he would do it all without any help from a teacher. No amount of caning would correct his attitude.

"Salim?" she called.

"Yes, Aunt Eva," Salim said.

"Where is Richard?"

Salim stumbled on his thoughts. How and why should he know where Richard was?

"I don't know, Aunt Eva," he said.

"Stand up, when you talk to me," she said to him.

Salim glance at Kasim. Here we go again look, then he stood up.

"I don't know, Aunt Eva," he said again.

"Golf," Kasim volunteered.

Then he remembered and stood up too.

"Uncle Richard plays golf," he said.

"What else does he do?" she asked him.

"Nothing?" Kasim offered.

"Retired," Salim said to help.

"Retired from what?"

As far as anyone understood him, Uncle Richard had been so many things and done so many things and made so much money, it did not matter what he did. Those who had been to his palace for the infamous house-warming party knew it really did not matter how badly he did at Kathiani primary school. Only a teacher would care about such irrelevance.

"Call him," she ordered Kasim.

"Uncle Richard does not take my calls," he said.

"Why not?"

"I don't know."

"Salim?"

"Mine neither."

"I said, call him," her voice hard and teacher-like.

Salim hesitated. She waited. He made a show of searching in his pockets, then realising she would not let it go, started for the door.

"Where are you going?" she demanded.

"To get my phone," he said. "Left it in the car."

Kasim saw he was about to be abandoned, and left to deal with Aunt Eva on his own, and quickly fished out his phone.

"You can use my phone," he said to Kasim.

"He does not take your calls, remember?" Salim said.

"He knows your voice."

Eva shook her head in disbelief and asked whether there was any other man in the room who finished school. No one dared look her in the eye. Salim took the phone from Kasim and dialed. With any luck Uncle Richard would recognize Kasim's number and ignore the call. The phone rang five times before going dead.

"He cannot be reached," Salim said.

"Call again," Aunt Eva ordered.

"Uncle Richard will never take Kasim's call," Salim said.

"I told you," said Kasim.

"Sit down," she said harshly.

Kasim sat down and Uncle Tivo patted his knee sympathetically.

"Is this why you call me from America to bury your grandfather?" Aunt Eva asked Salim.

Salim dared not meet her eyes.

"King'oo men are useless," she said talking to herself.

She rummaged in her bag talking to herself, raising the suspense, and increasing the uncertainty. Salim could not remember her ever being this this furious. But then he kept out of her way as much as he could.

"Totally useless," she repeated. "Useless, useless."

The last 'useless' was directed at the men's corner that included Uncle Tivo, her husband Roger and the men of the clan. She found her phone and turned to Salim.

"Number?" she asked.

Salim read it out of Kasim's phone. She dialed. While waiting, she turned to Uncle Tivo. He had his eyes glued on her as a lion to a buffalo, while he tapped with his stick. He was furious too, in his own way, and for his own reasons.

"To answer your question," she said to him, "I come to bury your brother, not to bring gifts. The least you could do for Caesar is order this chaos."

Uncle Tivo nodded, appearing to understand and accept her reply, but he was not at all happy. He had expected a new hat, a watch, a phone, or a pair of shoes. At least a pair of socks. Things he could convert to beer when going got hard. He turned to her husband seated by his side.

"And you?" he asked Roger in Kikamba, "why are you here?"

Roger stared at him bewildered.

"Why you come?" Uncle Tivo asked in English.

For some years, Uncle Tivo was head mechanic for the American company building the Nairobi–Mombasa highway between Sultan Hamud and Voi. Along the way he amassed enough words to awe young King'oo school dropouts in market bars at Kathiani. The full extent of his knowledge of the language was most evident when he was drunk and in good humour, but he was not at his best at Sam's house.

"Why you come?" he asked Roger.

Roger pointed at the one person who could best answer that question, but his wife was waiting for Uncle Richard to answer her call.

"Just ignore him," Kasim said to Roger.

Aunt Eva gave up waiting for Richard to pick up the phone and tossed it in her bag.

"Totally useless," she said to Aunt Charity and the aunts.

Judging it safe to resume the meeting, Uncle Sam cleared his throat.

"Before we begin today's meeting," he announced, "our dear Aunt Eva has informed me that she must be back home in nine days' time. That is by the end of next week."

The women around Aunt Charity sighed in resignation. Everyone who understood what that really meant stared at her. Home? Was she not home already? In nine days? What did she think she could accomplish in nine days? Who had ever heard of a King'oo funeral, or marriage or divorce, or any ritual for that matter, taking less than forever to complete? Feeling the sudden discomfort, and the rising impatience with his wife, Roger turned to Salim for help.

"She wants to go back in nine days," he said.

"And?"

"Can't rush a King'oo funeral," Salim said.

The cordon of aunts round Aunt Charity sighed in resignation. Only Uncle Tivo dared speak.

"Home?" He was addressing Uncle Sam. "Home where?"

"America," said Uncle Sam.

"Home?" Uncle Tivo asked again.

"Where she lives," said Uncle Sam. "She has a job and a home there."

"Home?"

"Will someone explain to him?" Uncle Sam looked round. "No, not you, Kasim. Salim."

Salim shook his head, hands raised in submission. He was no good at talking to Uncle Tivo. He was no good at talking to, or understanding, any of the old men around him. Whenever he tried, they misunderstood and raised issues that had nothing to do with why he was talking to them.

Like Uncle Sam, he too had a plan 'B' of his own, for what to do when the clan went barking mad and his sanity was in danger of following. He would move to a place where he was the only King'oo for a thousand miles round.

Chapter 13

Mzee Mativo was well-known in Kathiani for his loud, unpredictable, but easy-going personality. He walked with enough dignity and confidence to be mistaken for an old soldier, or a chief. Children ran to greet him when they saw him coming, and to ask about stories they heard about him that fascinated them. They heard that he had travelled more than Caesar, and seen and done more daring things than Caesar ever did.

The truth was, the farthest he had travelled from Kathiani was Machakos, where he got a job with a road construction company that took him down to Mazeras as head mechanic. The truth did not matter to those who liked to hear him tell one story after another about his travels. Young men fascinated by his imaginary adventures saw him as one of their own.

When the meeting got too long and boring, Uncle Tivo took a decrepit, old phone from his inside coat pocket. Watching him unwrap the protective cloth rag and start making calls, Aunt Eva could not hide her disgust.

"Leave him be," Aunt Kamene advised. "We can proceed without him. Sam?"

They sat on either side of Aunt Charity at the women's corner surrounded by closest relatives.

"Right," Sam consulted his notes. "Let us get this train moving. Kasim?"

"Wait," Aunt Eva said from where she sat. "Before you start off, I want to know at which station your train is standing. What have you accomplished so far with your night meetings?"

Sam was alone in the arena, but that did not mean he was in control. He searched for his wife. She was his compass in King'oo matters, guiding him through a wilderness of likes and dislikes, steering him away from taboos pitfalls, and nasty mind games known to have caused non-King'oo husbands to abandon their wives,

109

children, and homes. But, this time, his wife was of no help. She had given up and retreated to the kitchen the moment she realised Aunt Eva was girding herself to wrestle the controls from Aunt Kamene's hands.

"In just a moment Aunt Eva,," he said returning to his clipboard. "Reports will tell where we are."

"Report, report, report," Uncle Tivo said loudly. "Don't you people get tired of talking? If I had two donkeys and a cart Caesar would sleep in the ground tonight."

There were gasps of shock from the women's corner. Aunt Charity was still, as still, as she had been through all the meetings, her hands in her lap, eyes fixed in space.

King'oo women suffered the most grief, grieving through the wake to the burial, and long after. The burials of husbands, of parent, or of sibling, and at times of good neighbors and extended family members. But the worst of all was of someone they birthed, nursed, and nurtured through childhood to adulthood. Someone to whom they gave love and hope, and from whom they received love and hope in return. Someone they saw through sickness and watched die.

Aunt Charity had been through most of the emotion and all she could do now was stare at nothingness and hope to see Caesar's burial to the end without too much disruption from King'oo absurdity.

Uncle Sam, disregarding Tivo like everyone else did, looked at his notes, looked round the room, and back at his notes. His wife had warned him to come expecting everything and nothing. There could be no age, gender, family, or intellectual solidarity with Eva. He could not answer Aunt Eva's question truthfully, if he wanted to, without burying himself deeper in the King'oo swamp.

"We started fund-raising," Aunt Kamene said, to help.

"How much have you raised?" asked Aunt Eva.

Embarrassed silence from the committee. Aunt Kamene gestured Sam to continue.

"Aunt Eva," he said, lowering his voice politely, "We have been waiting for you."

"Waiting for me to do what?" she asked the room. "To dig the grave? Bury Caesar? What were you waiting for me to do?"

"Uncle Tivo insisted we wait for you."

"Why?" the question was directed at the old man.

Uncle Tivo was busy talking on the phone.

"As his eldest," Sam continued. "We could not plan Caesar's burial without you. But we have started raising funds."

Aunt Eva turned to the women to confirm or deny it. Women traditionally avoided having to explain anything their men said or did, but this time they nodded. Roger leaned over to Salim.

"What is this about?"

"The most fun part of being King'oo," Kasim answered for Salim. "We think it is very rude to pay children's school fees, bride prices, hospital bills, divorce, alimonies, or burial costs without inviting the clan to join in the fun. It is considered arrogant for a man, no matter how wealthy, to not ask for financial assistance. But, as you see, it is a gathering of want."

"All these people?" Roger said unbelieving.

"Do you see them collecting enough to bury Caesar?" Salim asked him.

Most of them looked like they needed donations themselves. The bright-eyed, well-fed lot appeared better off, but that did not mean they could afford to give money to bury Caesar. It would have been simpler if Caesar were not a legend.

"So, what do you to do now?" Roger asked them.

"Bury Caesar," said Kasim. "With or without her help."

"Roger," Salim had an idea. "Can't you talk to her on our behalf? Ask her to ease the pressure on Sam?"

"And pay for her father's funeral," added Kasim. "We worked hard to get to where we are but, as you can see, we are far from the end."

Roger was at a loss. They watched Eva dwarf her sisters and prominent clan ladies around Aunt Charity, a mountain among the hills, a chief among Caesar's women. She was leaning, talking to Aunt Charity.

"Did you marry the fawning, young fool who followed you everywhere like a puppy?" she asked Aunt Charity.

Charity now had her eyes closed and was rocking gently in her seat, and did not see that the question was directed at her, but the silence that followed the question penetrated her peaceful place, and she opened her eyes to find that, not only was the question hers to answer, but all eyes were on her waiting for her answer. She could not remember what the question was.

"She did not," Aunt Kamene answered for her.

"What happened?" Eva asked, again at Charity.

"She just did not," Kamene said irritated.

"Did I ask you?" Eva turned to her. "Let her speak for herself."

"Why?" Kamene's voice hardened too. "Is it your business what happened in her life?"

"It is not yours either, so why are you sour?"

"Leave her alone," said Aunt Kamene.

Eva heaved a sigh, turned to Aunt Kaluki. They were talking loud now, so loud others could hear what was said.

"What happened to him?" she asked.

"Who?" asked Kaluki, so nervous it took a moment to realise Eva was talking to her now. She shook her head.

"What was his name?" Eva asked.

"He was here yesterday," another woman relative said. "He leads us in prayer."

"Pastor Kioko?" said Kaluki.

"He lives in Kathiani."

"Pastor?" Eva said startled. "Baby elephant ears? I knew he would find something useless to do with his life, but a pastor? Is he married?"

Pastor Kioko was in love with Charity from their first day in primary school. But she was a Mophat girl and Mophat girls were special. Their sister Eva had a reputation for beating up boys she did not like, and that meant any boy hanging round her sisters. A smallish, stuttering, timid boy with extra-large ears, one who came from a socially insignificant clan over the hills, was easy to scare away. He had to wait until they were older to confess his affections to Charity.

"Still in love with our Charity after all these years."

"Our charity?" Eva glanced at Charity. "Does she see him?"

"He is our pastor; everyone sees him."

"You know what I mean," Eva said harshly.

"He comes to tea Sunday afternoons," said Aunt Kamene. "And it is still not your business, you two."

"Why are you sour at me?" Aunt Eva raised her voice to match hers. "Because I took your boyfriend Ndambuki in high school?"

"You can have Ndambuki and all his brothers and his cousins," said Aunt Kamene. "Your boyfriend Ndambuki now walks naked at Kathiani market."

Aunt Kamene hardened her heart and sharpened her tongue, at the roadside market in Sultan Hamud where, for a long time, she sold fruit and vegetables to rude, long-distance truck drivers. It was rumoured that she had also befriended the Chinese railway builders, learned their language, become the spokesman for the market women, and made a lot of money. Aunt Eva did not know any of that yet, but it was doubtful she would have treated her differently.

"All I asked was whether she married him," Aunt Eva said.

"What do you care whether she married him or not?" said Aunt Kamene.

"She is my sister."

"And that gives you the right to scoff at her life? Why do you always poke your nose in everyone's life when you come here?"

"Life?" she looked round the room. "You call this life?"

"Ladies, please ..." Sam tried to intervene.

"What?" she barked at him.

He went back to his notes. Aunt Kamene turned to Eva.

"Can't you see how Caesar's death has broken her?"

"Who is not broken by Caesar's death?" again she looked round challenging anyone to disagree with her. "My father carried this clan on his back until he died. You all are the burden that killed Caesar?"

Caesar had fed the clan's hungry, helped their poor, educated their children, found employment for the unemployed and taken in orphans when he could not afford to. No one argued with that but ...

"What did any of you do for him or his children?" she asked them.

They shifted in their seats, looked at their shoes and wished they could get up and leave. Some of them had walked an hour to catch a bus to the meeting and there was still the journey back and the meeting had not even started.

"It is getting late," Sam's wife said. "Sam?"

Uncle Sam quickly bent down to his list aware all eyes were on him, begging him to forget the women and get his train moving.

"Where were we?" he said shuffling papers. "Reports?"

"What reports?" Aunt Eva wanted to know.

"Feedback," said Sam. "We have allocated some chores to make it easier."

"All right then," she said, rising wearily to stand by his side.

She towered over him, making him uncomfortable. He dared not ask her to rest and let him direct the meeting as was customary. His offer of a seat in the arena by his side had elicited a severe retort.

"All right then," she said again. "Who will be first?"

It sounded like a challenge no one dared. He took a step back and sideways, hoping she would not notice or follow him.

"There were no radio announcements last night," said one of the aunts.

"Kasim?" Sam called.

"Where is Kasim?" Aunt Eva asked. "Kasim?"

Kasim had taken advantage of the acrimonious exchange between the women to slip away to the kitchen and get something to eat. With everyone yelling for him, he returned with a plate of food.

"Put that down," Aunt Kamene ordered.

He handed the plate to Kung Fu. Kung Fu handed it to Karate who went ahead to eat the rest.

"Radio announcements," Aunt Kamene said to him.

"I have a receipt," he said, searching in his pocket.

"Is it on air?" asked Aunt Eva.

"It was for three nights from day before yesterday."

"Just three nights?"

"All the money I received from Uncle Sam."

She glanced at Uncle Sam. He kept his eyes on the clipboard.

"Salim?" she called.

Salim had moved to a safer place at the back on the sofa armrest next to the Chinese cousins. He was determined to hunker down until Hurricane Eva blew over. It had been his tactic from primary school to high school, to the last time she came for Christmas with presents expecting the clan to bow and scrape.

"No money," he said.

"See?" she said to all. "King'oo men can't do a thing without women."

"Or money," Kasim added.

"Sit down," she ordered.

He went back to sit between Uncle Tivo and her husband. It was Kasim who branded her Hurricane Eva when, one tumultuous Christmas visit, she tossed the clan into a blender of activity, scrutiny and indoctrination that turned men upside down and inside out, and when she left hardly anyone remembered anything beyond a Christmas full of dreadful stress and uncertainty, excitement, and fear.

"What next?" she asked the room. "The hearse?"

"Salim," said Uncle Sam.

"I know where to get a hearse," he said.

"Speak louder," she ordered. "And stand up."

He rose, as she taught him to do when speaking to her, and stood arms crossed, just as he had done in primary school, and waited to be told.

"We also know where to get a hearse," she told him. "Have you booked yours?"

"Uncle Richard will loan us his pickup," he said.

Her face fell. The other aunts looked at one another startled. Aunt Charity broke out in sobs, the heart-rending sobs of an old woman who has lost all hope. The room was suddenly uncomfortably quiet. Aunt Kamene tried to calm Aunt Charity, told her all would be well, they would find a proper hearse for Caesar.

"A pickup?" Aunt Eva struggled to control her voice. "Salim, you, of all people, would transport your Caesar to his final rest on a pickup?"

"It was not my idea, Aunt Eva," he said. "I was just ...."

"Whose idea was it?" she demanded.

Salim avoided looking at Sam. She saw and turned against him drilling him with her eyes. Sam was about to own up, then Aunt Kamene stepped in.

"It was everyone's idea," she said. "We could not raise enough for a hearse. There, I have said it."

Aunt Eva turned to Salim.

"What do you do?"

"You know what I do, Aunt Eva."

"Still chasing ambulances," she said.

"I have never chased ambulances. Ask anyone. I am a respectable attorney."

"How much does it pay?" she asked.

Salim was already angry from the constant belittling. What he made or did not make was his business. He had never asked for help or borrowed money from relatives for precisely that reason. Not even his aunts had any right to question or denigrate him like this. He was about to explode, blurt out something he would regret for the rest of his life, then Kasim came to the rescue.

"Pay for what?" he asked.

"What?" Aunt Eva asked him.

"It depends," he said.

Everyone was now confused, about hearses and about payments and, especially, about why Aunt Eva seemed to be now chairing the meeting instead of Uncle Sam, whose house this was.

She turned to Uncle Sam.

"What is Kasim talking about?"

"The hearse," he said, diplomatically. "How much it would cost."

"How much would it cost, Salim?"

"Depends on the budget."

"How much is the budget?"

They were still waiting for donations, Uncle Sam revealed. They were in touch with distant friends and relatives, who were responding with donations and pledges. He had opened a bank account for the donations and a pay bill account for telephone remittances.

"So, now you just sit and wait for other people to send you their money to bury your dead?"

"Aunt Eva," Uncle Sam's voice was strained, "we are all donating. I pay their transport here every day. Ask them.

I pay for food and drinks consumed here every day. From my own pocket."

She looked round the room to confirm what he had said was true. No one dared acknowledge.

"So, what happens if no one sends you money?" she asked him.

"They have and continue to send money. It is just that the times are hard, and they don't have much to send."

It had happened before and, while they waited for pledges the mortuary bills rose higher than the entire budget leaving him to plug the holes. But the clan, taking it in its stride, had buried its dead, albeit not exactly according to the original plan, and moved on.

"We'll bury Caesar," Aunt Kamene said, pointedly looking at Eva. "With or without outside help."

"That's right," Aunt Eva said. "And Salim will pay for the hearse. What next?"

Uncle Sam stared down at his clipboard. That was all there was. He could not find the words to admit it to her. That was all they had achieved. Salim slunk away to perch on Uncle Tivo's armrest and brood.

"I want to see Caesar tomorrow morning," Aunt Eva announced.

There was dead silence. She had wanted to go to the mortuary immediately after arrival, but Sam had explained Caesar's remains were preserved at a private funeral home forty miles away in Machakos, which was closer to home for ease of transport. Who will take me to him?" she asked.

Sam cleared his throat.

"As I said earlier …" he started.

"Board meetings," she said to him. "Salim?"

He thought to mention he too had an office to run and business meetings to deal with, and volunteer Kasim for the journey, but he knew it would be a waste of breath.

Chapter 14

It was fascinating, for those with no sense for foreboding, to watch Aunt Eva get in the Beetle with her sisters pushing her from behind, laughing at how big her behind had grown since she stopped eating *muthokoi*. It was said with sisterly love, and prickly King'oo bluntness that she put down to lack of refinement and let pass.

They succeeded in getting all of her inside the front passenger seat, huffing and puffing, and laughing a little too, and handed her the enormous black hat.

Then she nearly exploded out of the car when she heard who was to drive it. It was bad enough that it was such a crappy car, she said furious, but she would never ride in anything Kasim was driving.

"Salim's car," said Kasim gesturing behind him.

She had not seen Salim squeezed in the back with Roger worrying about how they would ever get her out again. She glanced at them.

"Your car?" she asked him.

"Used to be," Salim said, quietly. "It is Kasim's now."

"I want to go in your car," she said. "Where is your car?"

"Garage," he said.

Kasim slid the driver's seat forward for Salim to squeeze out and took his place next to Roger. Salim was seething as he got behind the wheel.

"What is wrong with it?" Aunt Eva asked him.

"Gas," Kasim said.

"You shut up," Aunt Kamene said, through the driver's window. "It is all right Eva; Salim is a responsible man."

"When will your car be ready?" Aunt Eva asked.

"Soon," he said.

He saw her consider postponing her mortuary visit until his car was ready and added it might take longer than a week. She sighed and settled back in the passenger seat, spilling over to the driver's seat so Salim had to sit sideways, and with half his back to the door, to make room. Her hat did not fit on her head and had to sit in her lap all the way to the mortuary.

Salim had called ahead, and the mortuary attendant was expecting them. He showed them to the waiting room, where they sat nervously on a hard wooden bench, silently trying to ignore the overpowering smell of air freshener used to hide the smell of bodies rotting on metal trays in the next room. Then the door swung open, and the attendant wheeled out a trolley with Caesar's body covered with a white sheet. He brought it close to where they sat, and motioned them forward. Three of them went forward.

Aunt Eva stopped and looked back at Salim, still on the bench about to be sick.

"Salim?" she asked.

He shook his head.

"What kind of man are you?" she asked. "Come over here. Right now."

Salim stayed put. He was terrified of dead bodies ever since he found his father dead in his bed early one morning, as he was readying to go face teacher Eva at school.

She took Roger's hand for support as the three of them stepped up to the trolley.

"Ready?" the attendant asked her.

Aunt Eva nodded. He lifted the sheet, pulled it back exposing Caesar's head and upper torso, and left them. Aunt Eva let out a moan and swayed, and would have fallen but for Kasim grabbing one arm and Roger the other and holding her up. She resisted when they tried to take her back to sit down, shook off their arms and stood looking at Caesars's upper torso, old and shrunken, eyes and cheeks hollow, ears and nostrils stuffed with cotton wool. She stood there with them, sighing repeatedly, and swallowing tortured sobs, until the attendant came back and announced viewing time was over and covered the body. Then he waited.

"Aunt Eva," Kasim said discreetly. "We have to give him something."

"Why?" she asked.

"To thank him for the extra effort," said Kasim. "It is customary."

Otherwise, Caesar would be stashed at the bottom of a freezer and, when they fetched him for burial, they would be invited to watch the attendants remove body after body to get to Caesar's.

"Is that how you work here, Salim?" she asked. "Bribe people to do their jobs?"

Salim was still light-headed and stayed out of it.

"No wonder they call you a shithole African country."

"Not his fault," Kasim said.

"Then I will have a word with his boss," she said. "Take me to your boss right now."

The man was terrified. He had not requested a bribe, he reminded, and it was Kasim's suggestion not his. He would never ask for an inducement to do his job. He would lose his job if his boss as much as suspected he had done so. He was an honest man, a family man with a wife and children.

"You should have thought of that before expecting gratitude for doing your job," she said to him.

"Eva?" Roger tried.

"Stay out of this, Roger," she ordered. "You don't know these people. Caesar would have been terribly angry with them."

Now fully recovered, she turned and strode out of the viewing room. Roger reached in his pocket and discreetly handed Kasim money before following her.

Salim had left the moment he heard the viewing was over and had the car engine running when they got to the parking. He tried not to look at her as she forced her bulk back in the car after Roger and Kasim.

"Where to next?" he asked when she was all inside.

"Take me to where you buy caskets."

121

"I don't buy caskets, Aunt Eva," he said.

She shot him a teacher's look to be certain he was not being cheeky.

"They send the old guys," Kasim volunteered. "And the whole burial committee to make sure there are no side deals and kickbacks. They don't trust us, Aunt Eva."

"Is it a wonder, when you bribe attendants to do their jobs?" she said to him. "Take me where they make caskets."

Salim turned to Kasim, Kasim nodded, and they were off. The mortuary neighborhood was full of open-air timber yards, furniture merchants and *jua kali* coffin makers. Caskets were on display by the roadside, placed in rows in front of the workshops. One shop had an open casket up an acacia tree with more positioned around the tree, leaning on it.

Aunt Eva stopped, intrigued by the one up the tree, and stared at it for a minute or so looking for the meaning. When Salim suggested it had no meaning beyond itself, she turned to a carpenter who had also stopped work to stare at her.

"Why do you display caskets like bananas on a tree?"

The man stared at her.

"Speak," she ordered.

She was speaking Kikamba, and it was clear he did not understand it. He looked for someone to tell him what the huge woman with a hat as wide as the roof of his chief's hut in Busia was looking for. Kasim came forward.

"Let me try, Aunt Eva," he said.

Speaking hard-life, the preferred business language on River Road, he asked the man how business was doing.

"Doing," the man said, eyes glued on Eva. "What do you mean doing?"

"How many of these have you sold today?"

"None," the man said.

"And how many do you sell in a day?"

"None."

He turned from Aunt Eva to Kasim and lowered his voice.

"What is her problem?" he asked. "Why is she angry?"

Kasim lowered his voice too.

"She is King'oo."

"Oh," said the man.

"You know King'oo?"

"No," he admitted, but he guessed it meant woman king.

"Close enough," Kasim said. "How much do you sell your coffins?"

"Which one?"

Kasim thumbed up the tree.

"That one is for show," the man said. "To attract customers."

Aunt Eva asked to know what sort of Kiswahili they were speaking. Kasim had to explained it was business shorthand for industrious men and women who found that grammar interfered with commerce.

She seemed startled to hear Kasim utter such words as industrious and commerce, then snorted and walked away with Roger and Salim at her heels. When she was out of earshot, the coffin salesman offered to sell Kasim a slightly used casket at a reduced price.

"Slightly used how?" Kasim asked.

"You know how," said the man with a sly smile.

In the ground by sunset, back at the workshop by midnight, a wash, and a shine, and back on display by sunrise.

"No one will know it has been used," he added.

"I will think about it," Kasim said. "But I would not tell the big king mama about it."

"Just between you and me," said the seller. "And a generous commission for you too."

Kasim could not hide his smile as he followed to the next yard where Aunt Eva was about to assault the salesman for offering her a casket not fit to bury a dog.

"What are you smiling at?" she demanded.

"That man offered a commission for the casket on the tree."

"Is there one honest man in this country?" she asked.

"Salim," said Kasim.

"Leave me out of it," said Salim.

By the time they got to the fourth coffin yard, Hurricane Eva had so much pent-up rage she was about to burst. Salim was yet to recover from the mortuary visit. He was leading from the back, which was his preferred position when dealing with the clan. He was hoping Kasim, who relished following from the front, could manage Aunt Eva by himself.

"Caesar cannot lie in any of these boxes," she said, when they got to the last yard. "Don't they make real caskets anymore?"

"Real people cannot afford them," Kasim told her.

"Salim?" she looked round. "Why are you standing back there?"

"Just thinking, Aunt Eva," Salim said, walking up to her. "Most people prefer these coffins, so the workshops make more of them. These caskets are real for the purpose, Aunt Eva."

"I will not pay for these," she said walking on.

The next three yards leased funeral transport and were full of decrepit pickup trucks, mini-buses and lorries modified to transport entire funeral parties. Aunt Eva returned to Uncle Sam's house in despair.

Reporting on her mortuary visit at the evening meeting, she made such a big issue of the attendant's corruption that the old men feared she would order them to go lynch him. Then she told them about the hearses and made them all feel like they had never seen a real hearse.

"Caesar will not travell in such obscenity," she said harshly. "So, what are you going to do about it?"

The question was directed at the men's end of the great hall, as usual, and they looked at one another, as usual, then down, then up like they were in great thought, as usual, then everywhere but at her.

"Well," Uncle Sam cleared his throat, "Uncle Richard did offer his pickup."

"His pickup?" she asked, exasperated. "What do you normally use?"

"Uncle Richard's pickup," the men's side said.

"Get it then and let us be done with this running about."

"Kasim," Uncle Sam said, relieved, "you know what to do."

Uncle Sam tried to hide his elation. His resources were diminishing, quietly and steadily, consumed by lavish but futile fundraisers that left him settling the bills. His earlier attempts to get the clan to finance the budget on its own, leave his house and go bury Caesar, had been met with indifference and, at times, hostility.

"Are you King'oo or not?" they had asked him.

Everyone knew he was not King'oo, but it was best to pretend he was. Just as King'oo women loathed foreign women who married their men, King'oo men had no reason to like outsiders who married their women. But Sam's was a special case. He offered his hospitality on demand, threw open his gates and paid for food and transport as required. Sam was almost one of them.

He had failed to get them to donate towards the large amount of food and drinks consumed nightly at the meetings. His wife had grumbled she had never seen people eat so much at one seating, and they were her own people. He warned them he would be moneyless, and homeless, if they did not stop eating so much at the meetings.

How could he ever be poor, they had asked, when he had a twenty-story office hotel coming up in Machakos Town? He would own the City of Machakos when the building was completed. He would be richer than Uncle Richard, bury him in his dust. He would take over the county government and run it like he ran his business. He would become Governor

Sam did not want to eclipse or even bury Uncle Richard in his dust. He had no desire to overthrow Machakos Governor or run any sort of government. All he wished was for Caesar's funeral to be over soon so he could go back to living his simple life.

But, as the funeral arrangements dragged on, and the nightly attendance rose, and more relatives and friends turned up with grand ideas on how to bury Caesar with majesty, but none on how to pay for it. The traditional King'oo way of doing it, with everyone contributing only what they could spare, was not going to do it. It would need sacrifices, with everyone selling his laying chicken and milk goats, if necessary, and Uncle Sam did not know how to put that in words that would not cause a rebellion. They would demand he first sell his house and his cars to prove his sincerity, then they might consider whether to sell their laying chickens or not.

He saw himself sink deeper in the King'oo dung pool that his father had warned about. They would eat everything he owned, then demand he stand in for the gravediggers' fees and for the funeral feast too. His wife had tried to calm his fears, reminded him Eva was on her way home. Eva would take control of the process and he would have nothing to worry about after that. Then Eva had come home and doubled his pain.

His wife the said not to worry, Uncle Richard would turn up at the right moment to shoulder his part of the burden, or be cursed to die alone and never know the comfort of a family grave.

That was supposed to put his mind at ease, but Sam shared Uncle Richard's views, if not all the contempt, for scrounging relations and other human pests. But, while Uncle Richard could tell off the clan to their faces, Sam's position was precarious. He was an honorary King'oo, a useful appendage with no rights or privileges.

"They need you," his wife said whenever she sensed his will start to wilt. "You are the only one who can do what you do."

What he did, apart from hosting all manner of clan functions, was chair committees to which he was appointed without consultation and mediate between feuding parties that did not honour his mediation.

"Get Salim," he said to them. "Salim is a lawyer. He can help you."

Salim could give reliable advice as he was a lawyer and true King'oo blood.

"Salim is a boy," they said. "Salim does not understand how things work."

Besides, Salim demanded payment for his time, made them pay to stand in court and repeat to the judge, word for word, what they dictated to him. What sort of kinship was that?

"Uncle Richard," Sam suggested. "He is not a boy."

Uncle Richard would not do, they said. He was a white man in black skin, they said, who could not understand their language anymore and did not know how to speak to clan elders. Uncle Richard was better off left out of clan matters.

"It is you we need," they insisted. "It is you the clan wants. That was why we made you one of us."

Sam was also the only learned man, outside of Caesar who was now dead, that was mature and wise, and stable and honest enough to be trusted to chair their meetings. To order their chaos and find solutions. They had, therefore, voted him the clan spokesman, again without consultation, to articulate King'oo stand on social, religious, and political issues. They planned to register a political party to elect one of their own to county government and there was no reason Sam could not be their candidate for Governor.

In time, Governor Sam became President Sam, and his responsibilities grew to include hosting clan meetings, haggling bride prices for people he hardly knew and officiating at hospital bill fundraisers and funerals; again, for relatives he hardly knew, and was expected to cover arising budget shortfalls. All clan-related problem came to him before going where they belonged. Anyone who had anything to say to the clan, or to another member of the clan, and no courage to do so, came to Sam. They told him what to say at meetings, and exactly how to say it, whether or not it was on the day's agenda.

"We can't raise this issue today," he said to them. "It is not appropriate to demand his father's grave-digging debt at his son's wedding."

"It was his grandmother's grave," the man said. "His father promised to pay and left by the back door."

"I will speak to him afterwards," said Sam.

"No, you speak to him now. You speak better than all of us. That is why we let you speak. Go tell him now."

Uncle Sam regretted having started building *Sam's Plaza* in Machakos. He would have gone down to Mombasa and erected it in the Indian ocean after Caesar's funeral.

Chapter 15

If Uncle Richard had a life outside of golf, it did not take him too far, or too long, away from the golf club. They did not need to go bother Aunt Gwyneth asking where he was anymore.

He was there when they went looking for him, doing the now familiar dance with the ball. He paused to watch them come, holding his golf club in a menacing way. They stopped out of reach of his club and greeted him.

"What are you doing here?" he asked them.

"About the funeral," Salim said.

"Didn't I say you could have the pickup?"

"You did, Uncle Rich," said Kasim.

"Then go back and don't bother me again."

He started his practice swing, realised he was about to use the wrong club and tossed it at the caddy. The caddy carefully handed him the right one. He squared up to the ball, remembered they were still there and looked up.

"I said to bugger off!"

"Uncle Rich ...," Kasim stepped closer.

"Uncle Rich?" he turned, livid.

"Richard," Kasim corrected himself. "Uncle Richard, Aunt Eva has arrived from America."

"So?"

"She brought her husband."

"So, now I don my reed skirt, pick up my drum and go dance the welcome dance?"

Kasim laughed. Salim understood it was not meant to be funny.

"They would like to meet you," he said.

Uncle Richard turned his attention to the ball.

"Go tell them I'm busy."

Kasim leaped back, just as the club whipped back nearly taking off his head. Uncle Richard did not seem to notice or care, as he watched his ball sail out of bounds and over the trees to the right of the fairway. He called for another ball and started his ritual dance. Realising it could take a while, Salim cleared his throat.

"Uncle Richard," he said, "Aunt Charity is in a bad way. The aunts are worried for her health."

"Have they taken her to a doctor?" asked Uncle Richard.

"No, but ..."

"Am I a doctor?"

Salim hesitated.

"Did I say you could have my pickup?"

"Your pickup won't do," Salim said. "We need to hire a descent hearse. Aunt Charity wants her dad to go to his final resting place in comfort."

"Comfort?" he gave them both a penetrating look. "Is he going to a party six feet under?"

Kasim snickered. They frowned at him.

"The man is dead, or isn't he?" Uncle Richard said to Salim. "He is going to lie under six feet of dirt for the rest of eternity. Where is the comfort in that?"

"You know how close he and Aunt Charity were," Salim said. "Caesar brought them up alone after their mother died."

"Not alone," Uncle Richard said. "My mother took care of them too. Your aunts are very selfish women."

"They are your sisters too," said Kasim.

Uncle Richard squinted at him.

"Have they found out who your fathers were?"

"Don't start with that again, Uncle Richard," Salim said. "I am just as fed up with this family as you are."

"Go tell them that. Tell them to grow up and go to a bank. That is where money comes from."

Keeping his distance, Kasim tried.

"Uncle Rich ..."

Uncle Richard turned on him.

"Who are you?"

"Kasim," said thoughtlessly. "You know me, Uncle Richard. Kasim the comedian."

"I thought so," he turned back to his game. "Now go tell you mothers and your aunts a joke from me. Tell them to sober up."

Seeing him get so frustrated with his golf ball, Kasim turned to Salim.

"We must help him," he said.

"Uncle Richard?" said Salim. "Why would we want to do that?"

"He needs help with his balls."

"Do that on your own time. For now …"

Kasim shushed him and stepped up to Uncle Richard.

"Uncle Richard," he said. "Will you lend us money?"

Uncle Richard lowered his club, turned, and leaned on the club. He looked from one to the other.

"Why would I want to do that?" he asked Kasim.

"We need to pay for a hearse, a real hearse not a pickup."

"Why we need to borrow from you," said Salim. "Till the end of the month."

"Which month?" he asked Kasim.

"This month," said Kasim.

Uncle Rich turned to Salim.

"You owe me money from last Christmas. How many months are those?"

"I'm working on it."

"You have not paid for my wife's Beetle, which you were to pay for at the end of … which month was it? Last year, the year before? What are you supposed to do at the end of this month, of this year, so you can pay back any loan? Win a lottery? Rob a bank?"

Kasim guffawed.

"What?" Uncle Richard turned on him. "You don't think I know how you people waste your money?"

"We people don't have any money to waste, Uncle Rich … Richard."

"Then get a job," Uncle Richard said to him.

Kasim shrugged. Uncle Richard returned to tormenting Salim.

"Do you own a shop?"

Salim shook his head.

"Collect rent?"

Salim shook his head.

"What do you do, anyway?"

Salim did not bother answering that one. It would all be fine, if at the end of the derision and the abuse he got the loan he had come for. He watched Uncle Richard address the golf ball.

"Borrow money for a real hearse?" Uncle Richard said, moving his hips with the practice swing. "To pay how? When? And with … what?"

He whipped back the club, and with 'what?' brought it down hard, whacking the ball so hard Salim thought he heard it explode. They watched it soar in the air, sail over the distant trees along the perimeter fence and drop out of sight. There was a loud, metallic thump, followed by the screeching of car tyres, a loud bang, and the grinding of metal on metal.

"Oh, bugger!" Uncle Richard swore.

He motioned the terrified caddy for another ball. He teed it up, then, club in hand, approached Salim and Kasim. One look at his face and they fled.

"What did I tell you?" Aunt Eva said, at the meeting when she heard what happened. "No men in King'oo clan."

"And we all know what that means," said Aunt Kamene.

Everyone had to dig deeper in pockets that were empty ten times over and drop something in the basket.

"*Atsi!*" Uncle Tivo cried out. "Dig deeper where? Inside rock pockets?"

He pointed at Eva, then at her husband, and changed to Kikamba.

"*Ekani maive! Kwani iko mzungu masikini?*" he said.

"Let them pay," Kasim translated to Roger. "No white man is poor."

Uncle Tivo's attitude had changed since the gate guard opened a private *chang'aa* bar for him behind the gatehouse.

"Uncle Tivo," Kasim whispered. "Roje is not a white man."

Uncle Tivo took a closer look at Roger.

"*Atsi*," he said.

It seemed he was seeing Roger for the first time. Roger was not a white man, but he was from America and did not speak Kikamba, so he had to be a white man.

"He speaks like a *mzungu*," he whispered back.

"What did he say?" Roger asked Kasim.

"He said *Atsi*!"

Kasim explained that *Atsi* was Kikamba for *hey!* The ultimate expression of astonishment.

"As in hey! Let them pay. Meaning you and the battle axe. Let them pay for everything. There is no poor *mzungu*."

"*Mzungu* is a white man," Salim added.

"Meaning me?" Roger asked startled.

"And the battle axe."

Uncle Tivo rose, turned his pockets inside out, and showed them to Roger.

"*Roje!*" he said in Kamba. "See, me I have nothing. If you want to bury your Caesar, pay! Pay! *Toeni mali.* Pay!"

"I am sure you got that one," Kasim said to Roger.

"I think we all got that," said Uncle Sam.

Roger nodded, worried, and Uncle Tivo sat back down, took out his phone and made calls.

Eva raised the collections basket for all to see causing more despair. They had donated more than they could donate. They continued attending the meetings only to show solidarity. Seeing the beaten look on the old men, the harassed and fatigue-lined faces, she dropped the collections basket back on the table.

"Roger," she said. "You and I will pay half."

And that was that. Roger did not have to say a word. There were sighs of relief all round.

"They will raise the rest," Aunt Eva said, meaning the rubble.

She expected an ovation, or at the very least smiles of gratitude, but there were none. They looked down to avoid meeting her eyes.

"Money comes from America," Uncle Tivo said in Kikamba for all of them.

Even the government knew that. Americans paid for the roads, for the schools, hospitals and for the big cars that big people drove. They paid salaries for the politicians and their wives. They paid for their children's education and for the big houses too.

The old men were nodding, eyes on the ground, as Tivo revealed things Americans gave to the big people that the small people did not get.

"Caesar was a big man," he said, turning to Roger. "Pay for him."

All eyes were on Roger, expecting a response. Kasim did not wait for Roger to ask for a translation.

"He says you are the richest man in America," he whispered, aware Aunt Eva was watching. "You must pay for everything."

"Who is this guy?" asked Roger.

"Caesar's brother," said Kasim. "He is your father-in-law now."

Which was all for the good, Kasim explained, because Tivo would inherit Caesar's kingdom and what was Caesar's would be his. He was duty bound to pay Caesar's debts and collect whatever was due to Caesar.

Salim saw the uncertain look on Roger's face, nudged him.

"Why do you listen to him," he said. "You know Kasim is full of it. Just ignore him and the old guy like we all do."

Roger worried still.

Chapter 16

Uncle Sam's train was yet to leave the station. The driver was the personification of futility, standing before selectively deaf passengers with his equally irrelevant timetable on a clipboard, saying the same things over and over. He had travelled the same clan line before with other fundraisers, and he knew when the journey was hopeless, but now Eva was back. Eva was back in charge, and he was just a weary engineer with a travel-weary herd.

The meetings had assumed a typically King'oo trajectory despite Eva's best effort, and only a blind and deaf person would expect it to land any different from others in the past. Women kept to themselves, children played outside, youngsters at the back and men to their side of the hall, leaving Sam the floor. The groupings kept to themselves, paying attention only to parts of the discussions they thought affected them but coming together when Eva ordered everyone to show his love for Caesar by contributing more generously.

"Before I continue," Sam said. "I would like to make an important announcement."

He did not call for order anymore. It was a waste of breath for King'oo seemed to hear without listening.

"After consulting with Aunt Eva," he said, raising his voice, "she has decided that we … that the best place to meet is at Caesar's house, which is also Aunt Charity's house."

"Why?" someone asked at once.

"Because it is," said Aunt Eva.

"Why?" asked a new face unfamiliar with Aunt Eva.

"Because I say so," she said to him.

That was the end of that revolt. The troops had grown soft-bellied and feeble-minded in her absence, spoilt by the free rides to Sam's house and the free food and drinks. The businessmen among them spent the days on River Road in Nairobi buying merchandise for their shops and market stalls back home. Nicknamed *Uncle Sam's Express*, the buses that brought them to Nairobi were loaded high with merchandise when they took them back home after the meetings.

"That being the case," Uncle Sam went on, "tonight we start thinking of a realistic timeline, beginning with the burial date and working backwards to this date."

"Not so fast," Aunt Eva shot to her feet, her necklaces and bracelets clanging like battle axes. "I still have not heard of anything worthwhile that you have accomplished with your night meetings."

There was an uncomfortable silence. Sam looked from his clipboard to the committee. They avoided having to take over and admit that they too had no progress to report. It was easier to measure success cent by cent, before Eva came, admit their failures, and move on. But now that Eva was back nothing was so cut and dried anymore.

"Why?" she asked them. "Why meet at all, if all you do is compare hopelessness?"

It exasperated her how little they gave; how little they understood of what she was trying to do for them. All she asked of the clan was to try and fill the baskets with money.

"Starting with the so-called elders," she told them.

Normally the elders would sit outside to decide how much to give together. That way they saved the financially embarrassment from being seen as paupers. Now Aunt Eva was about to destroy that hallowed tradition too. Where did she get the idea that she could force anyone to give?

"You are not the government," they grumbled. "You cannot make us give what we do not have."

Aunt Eva could, she informed them, and would do more than that. She would make them pay back every cent they ever got from Caesar. They owed Caesar more than a burial.

They would not pay back Caesar's loans, they swore. Caesar knew they could not pay back when he lent them money.

Sam wedged himself in the exchange to stop it escalating into a standoff, which would benefit no one. He tried to divert minds from thoughts of money back to the program.

Salim arrived amid the unhappiness after another wasted day trying to find a way to appease Aunt Eva. He had spent the day searching funeral homes for a hearse he could afford, and the only ones he could afford were of the kind Aunt Eva had declared not fit to bury a dog. Aunt Charity was inconsolable.

"I keep looking," he said in her direction. "I will find a decent hearse."

"And pay for it," said Aunt Eva.

"Why?" Aunt Kamene asked. "Why Salim? Why, always, Salim?"

"He is educated."

"So is Richard. Why don't you ask Richard?"

"Why don't you ask him yourself?"

"You are the one who knows everything."

"And you know nothing," said Aunt Eva. "Did you even go to high school?"

And just like that, Caesar's women were at it again. Old rivalries were revived, old grudges revisited, long-buried slights and gripes brought to the surface and expanded. Sisters, women cousins, and in-laws joined in, old bones were exhumed, fuel added to fire, and the guests learned who among the sisters caused Caesar the most heartache, how he had wished they were boys instead of whining and bickering girls, always feuding, and fighting and causing him heartaches.

The men's side lapsed in embarrassed silence watching the feud proceeds down a slippery slope to irreparable harm. They turned to Uncle Sam demanded he put out the fires and restore order.

"'This is your house," they said. "You are the man here. Act like it; do something."

Sam was uncertain what they expected him to do, but he was sure Caesar's women would turn on him if he tried to intervene, and order him to shut up. He chose to address himself to the whole room.

"Ladies, please," he pleaded. "We are here to bury Caesar."

Aunt Eva ordered him to shut up and sit down.

"Caesar never liked you, anyway" one of the others said to him.

"What are you?" another asked. "A bookkeeper?"

"Chattered Accountant," Sam's wife rose to his defense. "What does your husband do? A traffic policeman?"

"Police inspector."

"Why is he not here? And you, your husband is a barman."

"His own bar."

"Ladies, please," said Sam tried.

"Sit down," they said.

"This is my house," he warned.

"Your house?" Aunt Eva said to him. "We know you, Sam; you married in this house for Caesar's property. You can now forget it, no one outside the family gets a bean."

"Get out now," he said. "All of you, out."

There was sudden and uncertain silence, and a sigh of relief from the men's side. The man of the house had finally spoken. They had never heard Sam speak so decisively. Now they looked at one another unsure whether to get up and go or sit and see what he would do if they did not. It was Hurricane Eva that, spinning out of control, put an end to it all.

"Does your wife know you asked me to marry you first?" she asked Sam.

The meeting went suddenly dead. Sam gave up and joined Uncle Tivo and Roger on the sofa where he sat with his face buried in his hands. Roger, who up to then had been following the proceedings with fascination, also buried his face in his hands.

Uncle Tivo patted Uncle Sam's knee in sympathy, said he had picked the right one from Caesar's stable..

"You made the right choice," Uncle Tivo said to him in Kikamba. "She would have made you a black, white man like Roje. Right, Roje?"

Roger uncovered his face, shrugged, and smiled. Sam looked from him to Tivo and back intrigued. Then he leaned over.

"What do you two talk about all the time?" he asked Roger

"I don't know," said Roger.

Most of the time he had no clue what the old man said, but he found him amusingly refreshing.

"*Roje* is a good man," Uncle Tivo said in Kikamba. "But this time he is not leaving without paying the bride price."

"Leave my husband alone," Sam's wife said to all of them. "Or get out of my house."

Men looked at one another and wondered what she meant by her house. Pastor Kioko, unable to restrain himself any longer, rose from the safety of the back of the room and walked slowly to the front. Alone and vulnerable in the arena that Sam had abandoned, he made his plea for calm. He reminded them they had strayed from considering how they would finance Caesar's funeral to other shameful and irrelevant matters.

"Caesar will not bury himself," he said to the daughters. "Hold hands and do it together."

Everyone expected Caesar would be buried in a fitting and agreed manner, on the appointed day, even after the funeral committee said not to count on Uncle Richard's help.

Uncle Tivo asked him how much Pastor Kioko and his church had donated. When the Pastor reminded everyone that he had waived the burial fees, Aunt Eva advised him to deduct his burial fees from the thousands of mangoes, and bananas, and the buckets of pigeon peas the clan had tithed since Caesar gave him the church to manage, and bring the rest.

The pastor skulked to his seat at the back and sat down. Men looked at one another, waited for Eva to lead the way. Tivo was not having any of it. He nudged Sam to stand up.

"This is your house," he said aloud for all to hear. "Now stand up and speak."

Sam rose and Kasim took his place.

"Before you go ..." he said, avoiding looking at the women.

"Go where?" said Uncle Tivo. "We have not eaten."

"You will eat," he said. "As soon as I close the meeting. When do we get a draft of the eulogy? Salim?"

Salim was on an island far away, where there was not a single King'oo for thousands of miles round, when he heard his name.

"When do we get Caesar's life history?" Uncle Sam asked him.

"From whom?" he asked puzzled.

"Kasim volunteered to write it with you. Kasim?

Kasim was starting to explain to Uncle Tivo how the phone that Salim gave him worked without batteries or airtime credit. Salim decided it was in his interest not to interrupt them.

"But, Uncle Sam," he said, "Caesar was old when I was born."

"Caesar was old before most of us were born," said Uncle Sam, "but there are people here who knew him all his life. No one knew him better than his brother Uncle Tivo sitting next to you."

Everyone who heard him sat up.

"Stop right there," Aunt Kamene said to them. "You want Tivo to tell you Caesar's life history? To reveal his opinion of his big brother Mophat?"

The question was for Sam, but everyone who understood it shook his head.

"Tivo is my father," said one of the aunts, "and I say never."

They turned to see how Tivo would take that, but Tivo was busy learning from Kasim how sound travelled through the air into houses without colliding with people coming out.

"We'll find you someone," Uncle Sam said to Salim. "There are other old men ..."

"And women," said his wife.

"And women here who can tell you a lot about Caesar."

Salim knew the King'oo enough not to hold any such hope. The helpers would bury him under a mountain of real and fictitious accounts of Caesar's life he could make neither head nor tail of. And then, and then they would declare Salim a liar and hang him for it when the eulogy was read.

At times like these, Salim understood Uncle Richard's decision to stay off all clan affairs leaving them to find their own solutions. One day he too would be wise enough to walk away and never look back. Relocate to Mombasa ... or to the Seychelles, or to a desert island on the moon.

"Uncle Sam," Kasim rose to the rescue. "What about the life story you read to us the other day?"

"That was not his life story," Sam admitted. "Just something I compiled from old newspaper reports on Caesar."

"Salim and me can work around that," Kasim said.

"All right," said Uncle Sam. "I will give you a copy, but remember no false claims, exaggerations, cooked-up anecdotes, or accolades. Okay?"

"We know all that," said Kasim. "Salim is a lawyer."

"Good," said Aunt Kamene. "Now we can eat."

Salim rose to protest, saw the hunger-fueled impatience on everyone's face and sat back down.

Chapter 17

Sam's train chugged from Nairobi to Kathiani the next day, as scheduled by Aunt Eva, and was shunted to the back of Caesar's house and parked by a rusted Japanese pickup under the mango and avocado trees.

The house sat on fifty acres of fertile King'oo land that stretched from the gate, down a gentle slope to a rocky stream that was a raging river in the rainy season. A three-car garage that had once housed big government cars was now a goat and chicken house.

Caesar had built his house when he was a district officer earning a measly civil servant salary, long before lawmakers got the right to dictate their own salaries.

Caesar's palace was a six-bedroom bungalow, with three bathrooms, a kitchen large enough to cook for a clan, and enough living room for a family of eight and whoever came unannounced. When Caesar was a government man, family and clan gatherings took place in the two-acre garden under the mango and avocado trees. But, compared to Uncle Sam's mansion, Caesar's house was a cowshed.

The slightly raised back patio became Aunt Eva's dais and Sam's new arena. He was still chairman of the burial committee, but, with Aunt Eva taking over the controls he was demoted from engineer to stoker and ticket collector.

"Where is Richard?" Aunt Eva demanded the first evening she stepped on her new dais.

Sam had answered that question before, but he again informed her Uncle Richard did not attend funeral gatherings or burials.

"Why?"

Uncle Sam suspected she had that answer too, but she would not understand his version and would end up making a long evening longer.

"I don't know why," he said to her.

No burial event had demanded Richard's personal appearance until now and, apart from what the boys told him, Sam had no idea what Richard did or where, how, or why. He had not seen or spoken to Richard since the last funeral.

Why did he have to answer these questions, anyway? Richard was her relation. She could call and ask him herself. But Sam lacked the energy, the courage, and the legitimacy to say it to her face.

Kasim cleared his throat, then remembered and scrambled to his feet.

"Golf club," he said, answering her original question. "Where we saw him last time. He said to call his wife when we know the budget."

"Why his wife?" she asked.

"Uncle Rich does not explain."

"Uncle Rich?" Aunt Eva turned to Sam. "Uncle Rich?"

"What they call him," he explained.

"Why his wife?" she asked him.

"He doesn't like to be bothered with fundraisers," said Uncle Sam.

"We'll see about that." She said aloud. "Uncle Rich, is he now?"

She rummaged in her bag, again mumbling to herself in mounting fury. She found her phone.

"His number," she ordered.

"Never had any reason to call him," Uncle Sam admitted.

She turned to Kasim. Kasim turned to Salim.

"Number?" he said.

"Uncle Richard's, not his wife's number?" she said to them.

They were the only relatives who ever had any reason to phone Uncle Richard. They looked at each other, silently wondered whether they had a disclaimer, could beg her not to reveal who gave her the number.

"The number?" she said, with rising impatience.

She had it on her phone, having called him last time, but Kasim dug in his pocket, took out his phone and read it to her. She dialed, waited impatiently for Uncle Richard to pick it up. The old men looked at one another, wondered how long it would take her to give up. She waited. They waited. She looked round agitated. She was about to hang up, when Uncle Richard's voice thundered out of the phone's speaker, so loud people ducked.

"Speak," said the voice.

"Why are you not here?" she asked.

"Who in hell is this?" he asked her.

"I hear you call yourself Uncle Rich," she said to him. "Come show us how rich you are."

There was ominous silence, while he, Salim guessed, tried to place the voice.

"Who is this?" he asked.

"Kimeu son of Kalekie wa King'oo," she said to him. "Come find out who I am."

In all the clan, there was no voice to match Aunt Eva's, especially when, in the classroom, she called out the full names of those who had failed the weekly test.

Salim could guess what Uncle Richard was thinking. Aunt Eva had migrated to America promising never to return to the land that she described as a nation of *corrupt and incompetent politicians leading a nation of blind, deaf, and dumb fools*. He had never imagined anything bringing her back to Kathiani. He was so confounded he was tempted to hang up.

"Listen, you, whoever you are," he said, to be certain. "I am with very important people here."

"I am with very important people here too," she said looking round, daring anyone to have a differing opinion.

"Then state your business," Uncle Richard said. "And make it quick or hang up."

"Richard," Aunt Eva yelled. "Do you know who you are talking to?"

"I ask your name, you will not give it, so I must assume you are either a fool or a joker."

"This is Aunt Eva," she said.

He was silent for a moment.

"American Aunt Eva?"

"How many Aunt Evas do you have?"

"Caesar's Aunt Eva?"

"The one who taught you to wipe your nose and respect your teachers."

"The one who said she would never set foot in Kathiani unless King'oo men matured?"

She looked round the room, oozing fury. They avoided her eyes.

"Have they?" Uncle Richard asked her.

"Have they what?"

"Grown up?"

"You tell me," she said. "You are one of them!"

"Please, stop shouting," he said.

"You stop shouting," she said.

Uncle Richard lowered his voice. Salim had to strain to hear him.

"Are you still teaching?" he asked.

"Confusing and misleading children?" she said. "Isn't that what you said the last time I saw you, you pompous fool?"

"I apologise for that, Aunt Eva, but not for the other things," he said. "I still stand by my words that King'oo men are born with millstones around their necks, and you know what the millstones are. Their women. That was why most never made it to the high school Caesar built for them. Stay long enough and you will see I was right."

"What about you?" she asked. "Did you go to Caesar's high school?"

"Haven't they told you?" he said. "Contrary to your predictions, yes, I made it to Caesar's high school. I went to University too. First, to Mountain View University, then to …."

"It was a village polytechnic when I knew it," she said. "Is that goat yard now a University? Mountain View University? That dunghill is a mountain too?"

He was quiet, staggered by the sarcasm.

"I went to Edinburgh University too," he said. "That is in Scotland."

She was quiet, Salim guessed, confounded.

"What did you do there?" she asked.

"Come to dinner at my house and we'll talk about it," he said, sounding relieved. "Bring your husband George."

"Roger," she said.

"Does Roger play golf?"

"No," she nearly yelled it. "He does not drink or smoke either."

There was an uncertain silence. It was clear Uncle Richard was reconsidering the invitation.

"Bring him over, anyway," he said. "My wife and I are curious to meet him."

"Curious?"

"Eager."

"Why?"

"Eager to meet him."

"Why?"

"My wife is a good cook."

"Where is she from?"

"Scotland."

"Why?"

"She is Scottish."

"You know why I ask why," her voice shot up.

"Aunt Eva," he lowered his. "I am at a club function. I can't discuss that now."

"You are where?"

"Club night at my club."

"You own a club?"

"Golf club. I am a member."

"Why are you not here burying your grandfather?"

"I have an important golf tournament coming up."

"Ah, you have an important golf tournament. Hold on for a second. I said to hold. I want everyone to hear you say it."

She fiddled with the phone, dropped it, picked it up and handed it to one of the young men cowering beside her.

"Make it work," she ordered. "Loud, so everyone can hear."

"But Aunt Eva …"

"I said make it work!"

The young man confirmed it was on full volume, shrugged, fiddled with it, and handed it back. She put it to her ear, pointed at the phone and, not realising they had heard it all, invited the meeting to listen.

"Richard," she said, harshly. "Now tell me why you are not here. And speak up, so everyone hears you lie to me."

"Everyone?" he sounded confused.

"We are all here."

"Here where?"

"Here here."

"Why do you use your American phone here? This is an awfully expensive call."

"It is, and you will pay for it," said Aunt Eva. "When are you coming?"

There was deep silence on the phone.

"Where are you meeting? Uncle Sam's?"

"So, you know all about it?" she said.

"The boys came to see me."

"When do you come to see me?"

The room was attentive, itching for his response. Kasim leaned over to whisper in Roger's ear.

"How do you two talk in America?"

"Same way," said Roger, with a dry smile. "Loud."

"So, Caesar really died," they heard Uncle Richard say to Aunt Eva.

"I did not fly from California to eat *muthokoi*," she said.

"I thought the boys were pulling my leg," he said. "They tried it before, you know. Made me drive to Kathiani only to find Caesar picking mangoes. Those boys are badly educated. By their mothers, I mean. In school you did your best. They will both end up in prison, you will see."

"I am sure their mothers would like to hear you tell them where they went wrong," said Aunt Eva. "When are you coming?"

"Can I call you later?"

"I want to know when you are coming."

"I am busy right now and ..."

"And we have nothing better to do than bury your grandfather."

"Caesar is not in a hurry. I'll call after the game."

"Kimeu wa King'oo," Aunt Eva said harshly. "Stop talking like a politician with voters burning tyres up his rectum. I want you at tomorrow's meeting without fail or I'll come to that golf club you call yours and drag you by the ear."

"But Aunt Eva ..."

"Don't talk back," she said. "I taught you to blow your nose."

"What has that got to do with Caesar's funeral?"

"I taught you everything you know."

"Don't exaggerate."

"Without my teaching, you would have been illiterate like your uncles."

"Aunt Eva, you taught me for three years and left for America," they heard Uncle Richard say. "And I failed in every subject you taught."

He could have also added that the school was so relieved to see her go, that her class suffered amnesia concerning everything she had taught."

"Richard," she said, lowering her voice.

"Yes, Aunt Eva?"

"Be here at five."

She hung up.

It was awfully quiet in the room. All eyes were on Aunt Charity. She had her eyes closed between her living pillars, the women on either side of her whose job it was to prop her up.

When her sisters were growing up fast, and they were busy discovering boys and the world, little Charity was house housekeeping. Cleaning and cooking, and receiving her father's visitors. She supervised the workers hired by Caesar to till, plant, and harvest pigeon peas, and sat with Caesar under the mango tree, to hear of a time when wildlife roamed the hills, and no child went to sleep hungry.

She saw how it made him sad to see her struggle with the responsibilities of attending school and running the house. To ease his mind, she reminded him of how, when he was a government minister with a big Mercedes he drove them out to the countryside to 'see the world'. Sometimes sitting under his mango tree, he would laugh, and then his eyes would cloud, and he would say, "Were they not good days those?"

"Yes, they were," she would say laughing with him.

Then she watched Caesar fade in sickness and the loneliness of being without his wife and children. He remembered with emotions about his adventures in the corridors of power, and about the good friends who had given him the strength to stand firm against sycophancy and the pressure to join in the conspiracy of looters and pillagers that drove the country to its grave.

Charity stood by him throughout the tumultuous seasons of political uncertainty, government upheavals, social unrest, and rumoured assassinations, and learned from Caesar how to keep calm and maintain inner peace whatever happened to the world around her.

Her mother's death at childbirth left a special bond Caesar and his newborn daughter. A bond so strong that, when she graduated from college and could have pursued further education, as her older sisters had done, she chose to teach at the school that he built and take care of him.

He rejoiced with her when she took over Kathiani High School and assumed his mantle of ensuring no

King'oo child was left out of good education due to lack of school fees. He taught her to fundraise, taught her how to squeeze funds and resources from reluctant bureaucrats, to persist until she got what she needed.

It was a sad day when she retired from teaching, turning down pleas and offers from the county to run special education programs on contract. She chose to spend the rest of her days looking after Caesar.

Chapter 18

Aunt Eva's takeover of the funeral process was complete. Resistance, the little there could have been, had evaporated, disgruntled male obstinacy retreated to passive participation or hostile indifference, and Aunt Kamene was back in the kitchen. Uncle Sam, still the chairman of the funeral committee, but reduced to Eva's messenger, smirked watching her try to change the clan.

She imposed women on the funeral committee, forced time and purpose in the meetings and declared she would not let King'oo male obstinacy turn Caesar's funeral into a *jua kali* burial, slap-dash interment for a man who could have been President.

She told men what to think and do, ordering them with no regard to age, gender, or ability. The rebelled. They did not need a woman from America to tell them how to bury their own. They knew what to do. They had done it all before. They pleaded with Sam to control her, but Sam was outnumbered. The best he could do was promise them to repair the damage once she was out of the way.

Salim and Kasim had their problems with Aunt Eva too. She had ordered them to find a proper hearse and pay for radio and newspaper announcements. When Sam informed her they needed money in hand to do that, she ordered him to keep quiet or give them the money. The old men protested. They were not used to being ordered to keep quiet by a woman. The clan functioned by consensus. A slow but democratic process that left everyone happy.

"I did not come to make anyone happy," she said. "I came to bury Caesar, and that is what we do now."

Then she saw Kasim and Salim still there waiting for a chance to speak.

"What are you waiting for?" she said to them. "I want a hearse by the end of the day tomorrow. We'll bury Caesar on Wednesday."

The room was suddenly dead still. Wednesday? The question floated around in silent whispers, numbing minds and freezing tongues.

"Wednesday?" Only Uncle Tivo dared put it in words.

The woman was so far out of order not even he knew where to begin trying to set her right. His peers, old men whose wisdom and guidance were no longer consulted, buried their faces in their hands, shook their heads and would have sobbed.

Then Aunt Charity spoke. She had a staggering confession to make. With a voice so tortured it was barely audible, she told them about a promise she had made to Caesar

"A what?" Aunt Eva exploded when she heard it.

A wave of uneasiness rippled through the gathering. There was confusion in men's corner. A sigh of despair escaped women who had known about it all along, but had hoped she would come to her senses before Eva came home.

"A what?" she asked again, this time to Sam.

Sam explained it, as gently as he could, without offering his opinion. He too had heard about it from his wife and dismissed it as gossip. Eva listened, eyes fixed on her sister, as Sam struggled to defuse the situation. There was no mistaking the thoughts that went through her mind, the sad pity, the disappointment, the suppressed anger. She burst out in dead laughter when Sam finished. Then she went and sat down next to her sister and tried to look her in the eyes.

"You promised Caesar what?" she asked with strained calm.

Attendance had tripled now that there was no bus travell involved. The nightly crowd spilt out onto the lawn and garden on chairs that Uncle Sam brought from Nairobi. Now men who thought they served a purpose by coming to mourn with Aunt Charity sat on the rented chairs pitying her and wishing they could sneak away unnoticed. Aunt Charity had her head bowed. Her eyes were closed as in prayer.

When they were young, the sisters had burdened little Charity with the guilt of their mother's death. She tried to make up for it by doing everything they ordered her to do. She washed and ironed their clothes, tidied their rooms, cooked, and did all the things their mother would have done for them had she not died giving birth to her.

"Look at me, Charity," Eva now said to her. "Tell me what you just told everyone."

Aunt Charity stared at the floor, just as she had when she was a small girl and Eva reprimanded her for being sloppy ironing her school uniform. Eva had pinched her ear every time she got it wrong, and now she had the same fear of Eva pinching her ear as she did then.

"A Mercedes funeral?" Eva lowered her voice, tried to be gentle.

Aunt Charity gave a hesitant nod, eyes still on the floor.

"What is that?" Aunt Eva pressed. "What is a Mercedes funeral?"

Aunt Charity remained silent.

"How much money do you have to even say the word Mercedes?" Aunt Eva asked her, her voice rising.

Aunt Charity, her face wracked with pain, kept her eyes on the floor. She would never have peace if she did not keep her promise to Caesar.

"Auntie Eva," Salim suddenly spoke up, startling everyone.

He could not stand to see Aunt Charity so sad and helpless.

"What Aunt Charity means is a hearse. A Mercedes hearse."

"And you think I don't know what a Mercedes funeral is?" asked Aunt Eva.

"Just a hearse," he said. "Mercedes hearse. We can get one."

"Can you?" she said. "How much money do you have?"

He hesitated, Aunt Eva's eyes on him, intense with anger. Kasim cleared his throat.

"What?" she turned on him.

"We shall all contribute," he said. "That is how we do it."

"Show me your contributions now?" she rose and went back to stand by Sam.

"I will get it," said Kasim.

"So, we now wait for you to get a job so we can bury Caesar? In a Mercedes hearse? A Mercedes funeral with a donkey cart budget? Where do you people get such absurd ideas?"

The old men looked at one another. Did she expect them to answer that? Younger men avoided her eyes exactly as they had done when she taught math and no one in the class had a clue how many eggs the farmer's wife got, if the farmer's eight hens laid eight eggs each and he gave her a third of them before taking the rest to the market. Such days were hard to forget. Teacher Eva standing in front of the class drilling inside their skulls with her terrible eyes and, finding not a clue there, dismissing them with knuckle rapping. Some of them were old men and women now, with children and grandchildren at the same school learning the same futile things. Some were clan elders too with a voice in the community. Their silence, and affected insignificance, were the only skills learned in her classroom that were useful here.

"Mercedes funeral," her chuckle was worse than her scowl. "For a man who lived like a pauper so that you and your children had a school to go to? Shame on you all."

They turned to Uncle Tivo for guidance, but Tivo had descended in an unpredictable sulk and lost enthusiasm for her leadership since she said she brought him nothing.

"How many of you finished primary school?" she asked them. "Hands up those who did not waste Caesar's time and money."

A few old hands rose hesitantly, tentatively hung in the air then fell heavily on burdened laps. It was an admission of futility not a declaration of achievement.

"How many of you dropped out in high school?" she asked them.

There were fewer hands than before. It was safe to assume most had no idea what a Mercedes funeral would mean to their own resources.

"Kasim?" she called searching the room with her eyes.

Kasim rose, his most tolerant smile on his face, and informed her he did not.

"I hate to disappoint you, Aunt Eva," he said. "but no, I did not drop out of high school."

"You graduated high school?"

"Yes, Aunt Eva."

"Grades?"

"Grades?"

"Sit down and keep quiet."

"I did graduate," he protested. "Ask anyone."

"I said sit."

"I almost went to University," he pleaded.

"I know you, Kasim," she said. "You failed in every subject I taught. Sit down and shut up."

Kasim was already sitting. He turned to her husband.

"Does she do that to you? Ask a question she won't let you answer?"

Roger just smiled. He was not a greater talker, and now Kasim understood why.

"We shall bury Caesar," she declared, "the way we always have. In the ground."

"Hopefully alone," Kasim whispered to her husband.

They saw stump back to her seat next to Aunt Charity in the women's corner leaving an air of foreboding. Uncle Sam had to play his diplomatic roll again, try to calm the old men without promising a solution or antagonising Eva. He dared not look anyone in the eye in case their hate for Eva transferred to him.

"Now," he said to his clipboard. "You heard what is required."

He looked up. It was their turn to avoid his eyes.

"Where is the basket?" he asked.

Aunt Kamene brought the basket and dumped it by his feet.

"Who will be first?" she asked.

There were no volunteers.

Chapter 19

Salim drove with his jaws clenched, expecting the Beetle's suspensions to break at any moment and leave them stranded by the roadside. The passenger side hang so low it was about to scrape the road surface. Kasim and Roger in the back sat leaning to the right to counterbalance Aunt Eva's massive weight in the front passenger seat.

It was getting to midafternoon, the sun blazing down and dust blowing from unpaved car rental yards and parking lots. They were tired and hungry, having driven around the city all morning searching, and asking the same question, and getting the same answer.

"Mercedes what?" the lot owners asked.

"Hearse," Salim said, to make it quick and move on.

"Why Mercedes hearse?" the sellers asked.

"Because," Kasim said exasperated, "because Aunt Charity promised Caesar."

"Who?"

"Aunt Charity."

It had taken a night of cajoling for her sisters to see she would not come to her senses, no matter how much pressure Eva put on her. Families were about to break up, clan about to disintegrate, forget Caesar's burial and go mind other important businesses. Then Aunt Eva surprised everyone by coming to her senses, accepting the challenge and, making it her decision to get Caesar a Mercedes hearse, took charge.

At the *Final Rest Funeral Rentals*, Salim let Kasim and Roger out of the driver's door, then together they extracted Aunt Eva from the passenger seat.

"Aunt Eva," Salim said to her. "This is a waste of time."

"I know you King'oo men," she said readjusting her clothes. "Follow me."

The sales manager leaped to his feet, when she stormed through the door of the reception office driving the hot afternoon air ahead of her.

"Good afternoon, Madam," he said. "That is a beautiful hat you have."

"Did you go to school?" she asked him.

"School?" he asked lost.

"Then I don't need your flattery, young man," she said looking about. "Where is the manager?"

"I am the manager," he said. "Manager, accountant, salesman, and owner. I own this place and everything in it. What can I do for you, Madam?"

"Show me what you have."

"Budget?"

"Budget?"

"Aunt Eva," Kasim said, "He wants to know how much you would like to spend."

"What is wrong with you people?" she asked the manager. "Can't you do anything without thinking of money?"

"How it works here," he said with a smile. "I pay rent, need money."

"Nothing," she said to him. "I want to spend nothing. Now show me the ones that cost nothing."

She was serious. The man laughed nervously.

"They all cost something, Madam," he said. "Come, I'll show you the cheapest."

"Cheapest?" she roared.

All the driving around crammed in the Beetle like a sack of pigeon peas had her wound up and ready to explode

"I meant to say the best we have that cost almost nothing," said the salesman. "This way, please, Madam."

He led her out of the office and took her on a tour of the lot, with Salim, Kasim and Roger following at a safe distance, careful not to crowd her decision-making and be invited to shoulder the cost.

It was a large yard with an impressive array of hearses. From station wagons to minibuses to especially made double-decker pickups for transporting multiple caskets to mass burials, they had it all.

"As you can see, Madam," said the salesman, "we have a wide range of affordable funeral transport here."

"Where is the Mercedes?" she asked him.

"Mercedes?"

"Do you have a Mercedes?"

"Look, Madam," he said. "That Volvo is as big as a Mercedes."

She stabbed him with the look she reserved for King'oo men who thought they could outwit her. The man turned to her bodyguard confounded.

"It has to be a Mercedes," Salim said.

"Why?" he asked Aunt Eva.

"It is complicated," Kasim quickly said.

"Are you burying a big man?" Still talking to Eva.

"Very big," said Salim.

"I haven't heard any big man died."

"You will," sad Aunt Eva. "Where is the Mercedes?"

"Mercedes?" he laughed nervously, "Gas guzzling Mercedes? As you can see, we have a lot of fine funeral cars here. Take this one, for example. This car is as big as a Mercedes without guzzling as much gas. I'll give you a fine rate for it."

"Are you Kamba?" she asked him.

"Yes, Madam, why?"

"I can tell by your slyness," she said. "Are you King'oo?"

"What is King'oo?" he asked her.

"A Kamba who does not hear very well," she said to him. "Now listen and listen carefully. I want to see your Mercedes hearse. Now."

"Madam, I don't have Mercedes."

"Why didn't you say so when I walked in?" she demanded.

"I did, Madam," he said helplessly.

He saw the fierce look on her face.

"I think I did," he said, turning to her entourage. "Didn't I? Gentlemen?"

The gentlemen were already following her back to their crappy, old Beetle. He watched as they squeezed her back in the Beetle. Even then he did not believe it was possible.

Most hearse rental salesmen had never heard of a Mercedes hearse and did not believe there was such a thing in existence. At the last yard they went to before despairing, they were presented with a coffin-shaped trailer with glass sides and a white casket inside, with red plastic flowers on top, which the salesman said was better than any Mercedes. He showed how a casket rolled in and out of the trailer on its own without making the slightest sound.

"Deluxe model," he said.

Aunt Eva walked round the trailer, inspected it minutely giving Salim reason to hope. Then she stopped and looked the man in the eye.

"Have you ever been inside it?"

"No, Madam," he said. "But we have had no complaints from those who have."

"Are you sure you are not King'oo?" she asked again.

He had already confessed he was not Kamba.

Certain not," he now said.

"It has to be a real Mercedes," Salim said to save time. "Do you know where we can get one?"

"You are the third person asking that question today," the man said.

"Really?" Kasim was startled.

"Really."

"You know what that means?" Kasim said to Aunt Eva. "Aunt Charity is not so crazy after all."

"I'll tell you what?" said the salesman. "If you find one, I'll give you ten percent commission. Let me know where it is, so I can buy it for here. There are enough crazy people in this town willing to hire it."

He walked them back to the Beetle, offering all sorts of alternative deals that landed on deaf ears. They squeeze back in the Beetle.

"Back to Kathiani?" Salim asked, hopefully.

Aunt Eva was silent. Roger had not uttered two words since leaving Kathiani. Salim was impatient to wind up the day's search and go back to his office. He had appointments and business meetings that were more promising than a search for an improbable hearse.

"We have to find Charity's hearse," Aunt Eva said to him.

"I told you I looked everywhere," he said.

"Drive," she said.

He turned the ignition, angrily shoved the car in gear and pressed on the accelerator. There was a grinding sound, and the smell of burning rubber, as the car lurched out of the parking. Just short of the exit, there was a loud explosion and the car jerked violently, emitting a cloud of dark smoke, and stopped. There was total silence inside. Salim dropped his head on the steering wheel and groaned.

"What?" Aunt Eva asked him.

He turned to Kasim.

"Is there petrol in this thing?"

"You are driving," said Kasim.

"I told you the gauge did not work. You are supposed to fill up every day."

"When I drive," said Kasim.

"Imbeciles," Aunt Eva screamed. "You, no-good, useless morons. How can you drive around all day without once checking you have enough gas in the tank? Where do you all come from?"

She swung at him with her bag. Salim ducked and jumped out of the driver's door, closely followed by Kasim and Roger. Aunt Eva fought to extricate herself from the car. Realising it was a real problem, they tried to help her get out. People stopped to watch. A passer-by suggested she lie back across both front seats and let them drag her out by the ankles.

"Get your filthy hands off me," she yelled at them all. "You and you and you, go away. There is no show here."

The would-be Samaritans walked away embarrassed. Salim, Kasim and Roger watched helplessly as she braced herself with her hands on the roof of the car, twisted, and turned and finally heaved herself out of the door. Once she was out of the car, she straightened her clothes, swung her handbag at Kasim. She missed and hit Roger instead. Without apologising to him, she took Roger's hand and led him away. They stopped by the roadside, looking one way, then the other as cars and *matatu*s buses hurtled by at dangerous speeds. Kasim walked up to them, stood a couple of paces away.

"Aunt Eva," he said, "It was not the gas."

She looked past him to the Beetle. The engine cover was up, and Salim was back there out of sight.

"Just a small engine problem," he said. "Salim is working on it. The car will be fine in a moment."

"I am never getting in that thing again," she said. "Get me a taxi."

"Salim will call you an Uber," Kasim said to her.

"You have Uber here?"

"Salim has it on his phone."

"Come, Roger," she said, walking back to the car.

Salim rose, when he felt her presence behind him, and turned to her.

"It is nearly ready, Aunt Eva," he said.

"You have Uber on your phone?" she asked him.

"Yes, of course," he said.

"Of course," she whacked him with her bag, catching him off-guard and nearly knocking him down.

"Uber?" she yelled at him. "You had me sitting in this shit of a car all day, when you could have called Uber?"

"I had no money for Uber," he pleaded.

She whacked him again with the bag.

"Call uber now," she ordered.

Salim's hands were covered with engine oil. He indicated his pocket. Kasim took out the phone, tapped out their location then turned to Aunt Eva.

"Destination?"

"Home," she said.

"Kathiani?" Salim exclaimed. "It will cost the earth."

"You should have thought of that before bringing us here," she said.

She was still berating him when the taxi came. They watched her and Roger leave.

"You have made her very angry," Kasim said.

"It was her idea to go hunting for a hearse?" said Salim. "Why did you tell her about Uber? Now the bill will kill us."

"You and who else?"

"You."

Kasim slammed the lid shut and got behind the wheel. The guard showed Salim the waterspout in the garden, to wash his hands.

"Where to next?" Kasim asked when he got in the car.

"Anywhere I can die in peace."

"May I come too?" Kasim said. "After we bury Caesar?"

"Don't you understand anything?" Salim turned on him. "At this rate, we'll never bury Caesar."

Everyone was so preoccupied with procedures, appearances, and rituals they did not want to bury Caesar, rest they be left with nothing to do. Even Caesar, it seemed, did not to want to be buried.

"We'll bury him," Kasim said with conviction.

"With a Mercedes hearse?" Salim scoffed.

"We'll find one," Kasim said.

He owed Caesar and Aunt Charity more than a hearse.

Chapter 20

Mr Dave listened, nodding quietly, while Kasim explained that King'oo funerals, like King'oo weddings, divorces, and everything in between, were a communal undertaking. No matter how wealthy or arrogant, a man could not bury himself. The entire clan had to be involved.

Sadly, most of the clan was poorer than the club mice, and they had to fundraise to bury Caesar.

"Caesar? asked Mr Dave. "Fiscal Caesar?"

"He died."

"But he must have stashed a fortune?"

"He was too honest."

"An honest politician?" He could not help the irony.

"Uncle Dave," Kasim was a little riled. "All I am asking for is a small loan from the club. To be recovered from my pay."

Mr Dave thought about it. Kasim waited. From the sounds penetrating Mr Dave's closed office door, the band was still out on its second break, and Kasim was supposed to be out on stage keeping the patrons happy.

Mr Dave glanced at his grandfather's portrait on the opposite wall of the office, thought for a moment longer, then turned to Kasim.

"Kasim," he said. "You are like a son to me. So, I will now tell you what my grandfather, who was richer than God, as you would say, told me when I asked to borrow money for my first newspaper stand."

He cleared his throat, put on an old Indian man's accent.

"Dave," he said to me. "Eat one, keep one. Rain come, umbrella."

"What did he mean by that?" asked Kasim.

"I did not get it either, but it has helped me."

"So, no loan?" asked Kasim.

Mr Dave raised his shoulders and hands in a gesture of helplessness. They had a lot in common, Kasim and he. He too had nothing but guts going for him when he started. He believed Kasim too would succeed in the end. It would not be easy, but the best he could do for Kasim was leave him to his own devices.

"All right then," Kasim rose. "Back to the job."

"And remember, your job is to make them laugh."

"You cannot make a donkey neigh, Uncle Dave," Kasim said.

He had gathered that wisdom as a customs officer up north. Some of his acquaintances smuggled horses stolen from their neighbours farther north and tried to sell them to their neighbours in the south who were contented with donkeys and camels.

"This audience has no heart or mind," he said. "They have not laughed since they were born."

"Since they are here," Mr Dave said. "Just make them laugh."

Kasim had already explained his views. Laughter was an acquired habit. Babies, born crying, learned to grin, smile, and laugh out loud. In time they came to love the sensation of laughter, and laughed at everything funny, even in the presence of fear, pain, or hunger.

He had read a lot about laughter in the books he unearthed under the customs desk sheltering from gunfire. He had started out terrified of death, as bullets flew in through one window and out the other, and ended up laughing at it when bullets missed their exits and got stuck in the wall. After months of the experience, he realised his laughter shielded him from stark terror. Fear was nothing against humour. He made it his mission to spread the message of laughter as a deterrence against despair.

Mr Dave had nodded quietly the first time he heard it at their first of many job interviews. It did not explain anything.

"The job is yours," he had said in the end. "As long as you make them laugh and keep them laughing."

He was still trying to justify it to himself why he took a chance on a self-declared comedian who had nothing but conviction and enthusiasm in his favour. Watching Kasim on stage, he feared for the future of standup comedy.

"*Haalloo,*" Kasim yelled in the microphone. "I am back. No, my name is not Back. I am back on stage to shake your brain, and make you face the reality of your miserable life. To start with, you are neither the richest man in the world, nor the world's greatest lover. So, get that out of your head, drink your beer peacefully, keep your zipper zipped, your demons leashed and watch your wallet."

The audience tried to understand what the fool on stage was talking about.

"Think," he said. "What is red and green spinning at a hundred miles per hour?"

Conversation resumed, a grumble, a growl, a howl of laughter here and there that had nothing to do with his presence on stage.

"*Jaamboo,*" he yelled in the mike. "For those with mosquito memories, I am Kasim the Komedian, or triple K for Kuyu, Kisii and Kamba."

"*Booring,*" said pink lips.

She was in better humor having found and redistributed more of her sleeping man's money, some of it snugly inside her bra. Kasim run into her so often in clubs some audiences believed she was part of his act. He did not denounce her, but he tried to ignore her most of the time.

"Do you ever wonder why there are always old men here with young women?" he asked her. "Never old women with young men?"

"Why ask me?" she said, with a mischievous smile. "Ask him."

She was pointing at the man dead asleep with his arm round her shoulder. Kasim turned to someone who was awake, a man three times older and heavier than the young woman perched on his lap handfeeding him finger-food.

"Have you ever wondered?" Kasim asked him. "What your old woman is doing when you are doing this?"

The man's face suddenly turned ugly. He lifted her off his lap, dropped her on her own seat and started to rise.

"No, don't get up," Kasim said quickly. "I will tell you why, just sit down I tell you."

The man hesitated, sat back down. Kasim turned to the room, pointed.

"You, no not you, you," he said. "You with the ugliest date."

Men suddenly woke up, squinted at their companions in the sleepy club light, decided they looked okay for bar women, then looked at other men's women, and they too seemed fine for bar women. So, at whom was the fool on stage pointing?

"You," Kasim was still pointing. "Stop messing with your friend's young woman. He is not asleep; he can see you. And you, yes, you give back the man's wallet. What is wrong with you people?"

"Why can't you mind your own business?" pink lips asked him.

"If you interrupt me one more time," he said to her, "I will have you banned."

She glanced at Mr Dave at the bar.

"By him?"

"And me."

She made a face at Mr Dave. He sipped his fruit drink. She showed him her tongue, made a face at Kasim, and continued searching the sleeping man for more money.

"Kasim," Mr Dave beckoned.

Kasim hopped off the stage and made his way to the bar. Mr Dave placed his hand on his shoulder, spoke to him discreetly.

"You seem out of sorts tonight, Kasim," he said. "Why don't you come back after Caesar's funeral."

"That could take weeks, Mr Dave."

"Then go home and rest."

"Sleep?"

"That would be one idea," said Mr Dave.

"Uncle Dave," Kasim also lowered his voice. "How can I sleep when the devil is on the prowl and the world is going to hell."

"Are you now the world's greatest redeemer too?"

"I hear voices."

"Is this a joke?"

"Serious," he said. "When I close my eyes to sleep I hear voices."

"You see, Kasim, that would be a joke if you told us funny things your demons whisper in the dark."

"Kasim, Kasim, they say to me, rise and clean the filth and rot that has overwhelmed your land and its people. Gird thyself and go forth to face the big ones."

Mr Dave let go of him, and stepped back the better to see his face.

"The big men?" he asked.

"They say the big ones."

This time Kasim seemed in earnest.

"You know what they say, son," said Mr Dave. "If you can't fight them, join them."

"Join the big ones? Are they recruiting?"

"All the time?" said Mr Dave. "You decide your own pay too, and write yourself as large a cheque as appeases your money-and power demons, and you will not have to work this late. It would be a real job for you."

"Uncle Dave, I have a real job," Kasim said. "It would be a respectable one too, but for the pay, if you would let me do it my own way."

"Your way? Look at the mess you have started. Now I must call up favours from my friends at the station. Have you any idea what it will cost?"

"Just leave it to me, Uncle Dave."

"This is not a job for you, son."

"Are you saying I am not talented?"

"I have been witnessing the talent you talk about for how long now? Days, weeks, months, years? All I see is a good, well-meaning man break his nuts on stage, night after night, and it breaks my heart."

"Don't worry about me, Uncle Dave," said Kasim. "King'oo nuts can take a pounding. I'm sorry for your heart."

"In that case," Mr Dave pointed behind him.

The patrons were about to start hurling chairs and tables.

"Go end it," he said.

"No problem, Uncle Dave."

Kasim started to leave, then turned to the barman and ordered a coke.

"On Uncle Dave," he said.

The barman hesitated. He glanced at Mr Dave. Mr Dave shrugged. The barman gave Kasim a bottle of coke. They watched him take a sip, thank Mr Dave with a nod, and carry the bottle back on stage. He took his time finishing the coke, while men shoved one another, threw punches and women yelled for help. Then he picked up the microphone, cranked it up.

"Cease," he yelled.

The pushing and shoving stopped. The room went suddenly quiet. Some sat, others waited to see what he would come up with.

"Come on people," he said. "You have all been here before. Now grow up and be men about it. Watch your wallet next time."

They looked at one another. Was that all? They shook their manes and were about to resume warring, but Kasim did not give them a chance.

"You and you and you," he pointed at random. "Return the wallets you took from the gentleman to your right. And you back there, yes, you with goats' ears, take your filthy hand off his girl's behind. And you pay back the beer you stole from the drunk next to you. And you with

171

the big belly, return the coat you are wearing under your coat."

Some wallets reappeared under the tables and seats, along with car keys and house keys and phones. The chaos quietly subsided. Women smiled, men laughed and shook hands.

They were good people, most of them, most of the time. Faces that he knew from *Uncle Dave's* and from clubs around town. Men who would not award him for his comedy, and sometimes hurled bottles and insults at him on stage, but in River Road they greeted him like a brother, recalled jokes he did not, and said he was the funniest joker in town.

Ghetto celebrity to his cousin Salim, ignorant praise from people with the sense of humour of an old Beetle. Kasim was fine with it. Much better than hustling down River Road anonymously like a failed politician that no one cared to remember.

"Money is only money," he informed his audience.

In through one pocket and out of the other. That was the nature of money. Hard to make, and easy to lose. But when it was gone, it was gone.

"Same as beer," he said to them. "You buy it here, drink it here, go shoot it at a wall at the back, and it too is gone. So, let us be men about it. Settle down and listen to me."

The room resumed being dead, just as fast as it had revived, oblivious to his jokes, and ignoring his presence on the stage.

Kasim was on his own. He turned to the bar for inspiration, Mr Dave shook his head at him and tapped on his watch. It was still the wishing hour. He had three quarters of an hour left before his wish could be granted.

He considered doing an improvisation of a drunk politician coming home late at night to find his wife at the door armed with an axe demanding all the titles to their three Mercedes, two Toyotas, one truck, four mansions and half the county land he stole. The last time Kasim did the joke, the club was full of big ones helping their politico friends celebrate the achievement of a self-awarded third salary increase in a year. When they heard the joke, they rose and tried to lynch Kasim. He escaped through back stage, and they broke chairs and bottles before storming out without paying bills. Months later, Kasim was still paying Mr Dave for the damage.

Remembering, Kasim decided against improvisation.

"Just this one before I let you go," he said to the audience. "What is red and green spinning at a hundred miles an hour?"

Men had gone back to sleep and women back to work inspecting their wallets. Then there was loud laughter from close to the stage.

"And you call yourself a comedian?" said pink lips.

"My clever sister," he said to the audience.

On such nights he was grateful for any target.

"Imagine this," he said to her. "Imagine you are a pushcart pilot flying down River Road pulling your old pushcart and …"

"I am a woman," she cut him short.

"Thirty per cent gender representation," he reminded her. "Anything a man can imagine a woman can imagine better."

"Let them imagine it," she waved her arm at the room. "They are your pushcart pullers turned big men."

"Don't be so righteous, my sister," Kasim said to her. "You were once a big man too."

She was once a Member of County Assembly for Gender Affairs, courtesy of the government mandate of thirty percent gender representation in government, and in all spheres of life. Then she discovered she had the same rights as a Member of Parliament and other elected politicians and she started wheeling and dealing in government tenders, and playing monopoly with county development funds. She was suddenly as arrogant and impudent as her male colleagues, and they resented it. They discreetly deployed county auditors, all of them men and none of them clean, to investigate her accounts and they caught her diverting funds meant for tampons for county schoolgirls. Careful not to make a precedence, her male colleagues spared her a prison term, and she went back to the only job at which she was ever any good, inspecting wallets at *Uncle Dave's*.

"Imagine this then," he said to the room. "You are hustling down River Road pulling your old pushcart, the old one because the new one has been repossessed by the Christian Prosperity Bank, the people who brought you salvation, and promised they would never do such an ungodly thing as take back your heavenly blessings, because they were patriots and Christians and God-loving and brothers, and all that crap; the crap they tell any fool that will believe. And now, because they came back for the same *mkokoteni*, the new God-given pushcart, the one that made you start going to church again on Sunday, made you a believer again, you now are back to pulling the old one with square wheels, the one you rented out to your cousin, the cousin who is also now looking for someone to eliminate you like you have eliminated his ambition of becoming a self-employed Kuyu man. Imagine that for a moment.

Then, as you try to understand what that means for you and your family, you get a phone call from a number you don't recognise. You ignore it and keep on pulling your square-wheeled pushcart. The phone rings again. You let it ring itself hoarse. You are too experienced to send money to a convict in prison in exchanged for a detailed map of the spot in Langata Cemetery where he buried the money from the robbery for which he is serving life. How many of us have received such a call? Hands up those who have."

Not a hand went up except his.

"Of course, we have," he said. "Did we send money?"

The hands stayed down including his. Pink lips snickered.

"Of course, you did," he said to her. "And you, you, and you all did. So, now you let the phone ring. You are yet to learn hard-life men behind bars have nothing but time on their hands. They will call you ten times a day, every day, until you give up and do as they tell you. Unless you block their numbers. But then you remember we have country friends and family who use borrowed phones to call asking for money. And we don't want them coming to look for us in the city, do we? Of course not, we don't want friends and neighbours realising we come from villages of hustlers and strugglers who cannot bury their dead."

The last remark was aimed at Mr Dave who sat calmly sipping his soda at the bar.

"So," Kasim continued. "you decide to answer the phone from that moment on. The very first call you receive is from a cousin you have not heard from for decades informing you that Onyango Kona, a cousin you have no memory of, has been lying dead at city mortuary since February while his family and friends try to raise money for his burial. They need your contribution too, and you better find some money quick, or your uncle will come to help you sell your pushcart."

He paused to let them take in the scenario, imagine being a hard-up, hard-life man with a crappy pushcart, and a dead cousin they did not remember. Not even bored wallet inspectors had time to waste on it.

His quarter hour was up, and the band was about to come toss him out of the back door. He grabbed his guitar, determined to play his closing number. The band leader already had the mike.

"I will be back," Kasim waved at the audience.

Ignoring the jeers, he swaggered to the bar and Mr Dave. The barman had a coke ready for him.

"I told some good ones tonight," he said, sipping hic coke. "Not a single titter the whole night. Are these really the big ones?"

"Probably," smiled Mr Dave.

"Why don't they laugh?"

There were many possibilities, but Mr Dave had no energy to deal with Kasim's mind. All he wanted was for the night to be over so he could go home and put his own demons to bed.

"But I was funny, wasn't I?"

Mr Dave nodded and made a gesture of *somehow*, which seemed to satisfy. He knew his clientele better. They did not come to his club for the comedy, or for the best curry in town, which was on the menu on the tables that no one ever opened. Their need for laughter was less important than their desire for validation, and for the courage to go home and face the other thirty percent gender mandate waiting at home with pick handles to discuss outstanding financial matters.

Kasim's job at *Uncle Dave's Curry And Comedy House* was not to heal souls, or make the world a better place for all. He was hired to keep customers awake and eating or drinking until they dropped under the tables, or they ran out of money, or they gathered enough courage to go home deal with their house dragons.

But Kasim would not accept that the club patrons did not care for his comedy, that a respectable number of patrons came solely for clandestine business meetings in the dark corners of the club with someone not their wife, and the rest also for the wine and the beer that Mr Dave sold for less than recommended price to keep them coming.

There was also a small, mournful clique that rarely drunk beer, and that Mr Dave suspected drunk from clear unlabeled bottles at the back of the urinal with the band. They sat apart from the rest of the patrons, listening to *Black Survivors* tell their tales of woe, the aments of their journeys from birth in national slums without any toilets or water, and their slog through national schools without any books or teachers to land in a city without any heart or soul. They were bitter and they were angry, as they sung of their struggle to survive a soulless city condemned to die by arbitrary curfews, and lockdowns, and whimsical protocols that devastated livelihoods, families, and nation. Theirs were hard memories full of pain and emotional destruction, rendered with a sincerity that got their fans jumping up and down on the stage to the thumping reggae beat with tears running down their eyes.

That was what Mr Dave liked to see, he said to Kasim, entertainers who moved patrons to tears. The *Black Survivors* did that every time.

"Uncle Dave," Kasim said, solemnly, "are you suggesting I recruit a gang of thugs, grow dreadlocks and call ourselves a reggae band?"

"I already have a reggae band," said Mr Dave.

The great irony was he was not a reggae fan and, but for Kasim's intervention, he would have replaced the band with a rhumba one from the Congo.

"I still don't like reggae," he said. "But this is business, and they are good boys. Normal young men, like you, Kasim, cursed with dreams that seek to be more than they can ever be."

Kasim empathised with them too, but they would never be like him. He had travelled farther than they had to get to where they all now were, and he still had miles to go and dreams to realise and he aimed to continue trekking. And he would never forgive them for calling him an impotent poet because he did not use his guitar as much.

"But I will take your advice, Uncle Dave," he said.

He would learn to play his guitar. But he would not join any sort of band."

He had never been a gang player not even at school.

Chapter 21

Kasim's grandfather, father, uncles, and men of his family line considered it a waste of resources to sell a cow to educate an ox. Caesar had to use his own resources to pay Kasim's school fees.

But educating Kasim would turn out to be an uphill battle for everyone involved. He tried hard, everyone tried hard and, at the end of it, Aunt Charity, who taught him to read and write, was about to agree with his father and grandfather and release him to the fate of countless other school dropouts. Then Caesar intervened again. If a donkey could be taught to pull a plow, he said, then no boy was unteachable.

"Some seeds have thicker skins," he said to Charity. "But they too germinate eventually, and in their own time."

They sent Kasim to Uncle Tivo's school, where they hoped he would learn to repair cars. Kasim found car engines equally uninteresting and spent his time playing practical jokes and telling stories while his friends got career education. When he graduated at the end of two-years, he could barely tell the difference between a spanner and a wrench. Uncle Tivo declined to award him with any kind of certificate, including the one for attendance.

Kasim was back in the real world, facing a bleak future, the future of a village thug, when Aunt Charity found him in the company of old dropouts and notorious market thieves and brought him home. Caesar was disappointed, but he pulled strings and soon had Kasim in government employment as a trainee customs officer.

After two years of training, and a failed attempt to place him in any position of responsibility, the customs department dispatched Kasim to a remote border post where no goods officially crossed the border, and where they thought he could do no harm to the government's revenue collection system.

One side of the border was Fahari territory, and the other was Afari country, related peoples that, when not trading in illegal imports, feuded over cattle, grazing rights and water rights and the true position of the border between their two countries. Often, the arguments led to a friendly exchange of gunfire across the unmarked border with the customs house, the only building in the no man's land between the two distant countries, as the target marker.

Days were hot and dusty, the nights cold and dusty, food and water scarce and law and order irrelevant. There was little to do for a customs officer but get out of bed at sunrise, eat boiled goat meat, sit in an oven-hot customs office for eight hours, wait for sunset, eat boiled goat meat, go to sleep and do it all again the following day.

Tired of sitting for hours in a hot office with just the flies and the dust for company, Kasim relieved the boredom by walking about the village talking to anyone who would listen, in a language they did not understand, and entertaining them with stories about Nairobi. He sang, danced, clowned, and joked about things of which his hosts had no concept, and in a language they did not understand. It was good for him, and it kept him sane, but after some time, the old men wearied of humouring him and left him to his madness.

Women and children avoided him altogether. Young men, the warriors with Kalashnikovs and belts of ammunition over their shoulders, wanted him to stop demanding custom duty for the goods they brought across the border.

From time to time, the warriors exchanged gunfire with their Fahari friends from across the border with the customs house, the only permanent structure in no man's land, as target marker.

The standard procedure, as prescribed in the civil service manual for survival in hostile areas, was to crawl under the desk and stay put until hostilities ceased. But

Kasim quickly realised hostilities could take a long time, sometimes as long as a day and a night of sporadic gunfire that had no aim or purpose other than to annoy the other side.

To prolong the annoyance, gunmen would fire two bullets, go about their business for a while, come back, fire two more, go to lunch, and siesta, come back fire again and go take a nap, or sleep, and start over the next day. But, when they got serious, they crossed the border and shot at anything that moved, except cattle.

Women screamed, children ran scared, cattle stampeded, and dust obscured the customs house, where Kasim crouched under the desk as instructed while bullets smacked the roof and the walls and, now and then, entered through the door and left through the window. It did not take him long to realise if he hid there long enough one of the bullets would eventually find him.

He wrote an urgent appeal to Aunt Charity explaining the precarious nature of his job, how unfit he was for it, and how remorseful he was. He begged her to plead with Caesar to have him transferred back to the city to do what he was born to do, to restart his life and discover his true calling. The letter was never answered.

Kasim was determined not to die from heatstroke, or bullets to the head, and he promptly wooed a Fahari woman and started learning Afari, her language. He figured, if he spoke Afari and married Fahari, both sides would consider him kin and stop shooting at each other through his office windows.

Halima was a graduate of *Mount Kulal University* and had been the previous customs officer's girlfriend until the day he rose from his safe place under his desk as the last bullet of the day was passing through one window and out the other and took most of his right ear with it. He packed his things and left that same night, striking out across the desert on foot, never to be seen or heard of again.

When Kasim took over the post, he inherited the girlfriend, and hundreds of dusty, sun-bleached books, most of them hard cover tomes, stacked like bricks along the walls to provide extra protection against bullets. He could not find anyone to tell him how the books got there, hundreds of miles from the nearest bookshop, or what his predecessor intended to do with such a diverse collection of knowledge of philosophy, history, politics, literature, and gastronomy. All that his girlfriend said to Kasim when she handed him the keys to the office was the books belonged to the *University of Maralal*. She was still mourning his disappearance and could not articulate anything that concerned him.

But, thanks to him, Kasim had enough books and magazines to keep him occupied under the desk for years. Among them was a collection of *Teach Yourself* books and instructional books such on how to build and sustain a biogas unit with dung from a single cow. Kasim focused his attention on learning what he could immediately use when he was freed from his exile. He started on *Teach Yourself Italian*.

He grabbed the book and dove under the desk with the first shot, and read aloud until the chaos subsided. Often he could not remember anything he had read, but it kept fear away. Between the pages, he worried the parties would storm the office, flush him out and make him disappear.

He got so used to the routine he sometimes fell asleep under the desk to be woken by the silence after the mayhem. Perhaps out of respect for the fool who had seen it fit to build a customs office in the middle of no-mans-land, the warriors did not attack the building. They had no grudge with the occupants. It just happened to be in the way of gunfire meant for someplace else.

Being lost and ending up someplace else was not unique to AK 47 bullets. It had happened to the books too, Kasim learned from his Fahari fiancée who was still mourning her vanished fiancée, better known as *the other one*,.

The other one, as everyone called Kasim's predecessor, was a good man, loving and caring, who had not chosen to come to Taeyang but made the most of it when he got there. He was calm and easy going and everyone liked him. Hardly ever in his office, he spent most of his time acquainting himself with life around the post, chatting up the wheeler-dealers, the brokers, and the smugglers on both sides of the border. He did not interfere with their cross-border business. Traders passed by his office in the evenings dropping presents and thank you gifts and donations for poor slum children in Nairobi.

Sounding forlorn and nostalgic, his mourning girlfriend finally answered the nagging question of how the treasure trove of books meant for *University of Maralal* ended up hundreds of miles north at a makeshift public library inside a besieged customs office in the no-man's land between two friendly nations with feuding communities on either side.

A long time ago, when she was a school-going kid, a truckload of books, enough Kasim guessed to stock a bookshop, landed at Taeyang, and were stashed in the only government establishment there was.

And, just like that, a customs office became a library, and the customs officer who had no clue how to, became a librarian. No explanation was offered, and none was required. Taeyang, like its counterpart Taeying across the border, had so little to do with the customs office it would not have noticed if they woke up one morning to find it gone without a trace. But, from then on, a mobile library truck stopped by every six months to replenish the stock and replace books that had in the meantime wandered off in the desert with their readers and, like their readers, never returned.

An unemployed *University of Lodwar* graduate volunteered to watch over the books, and dust them from time to time, and in time somehow turned the idle customs office into some sort of a library. People dropped in to look at the books, admired them and, from time to time, picked one to go read, or light a fire with. Sometimes they returned what was left of the books, or not, and it did not matter for the books kept on coming.

Kasim found out later what had really happened. Someone he met at the unofficial civil servants' club on River Road, told him Uncle Gove had dispatched a truckload of books to the new *Maralal University* in Maralal Town, but the delivery team of driver and loader could not read a map, and the books ended up hundreds of miles farther north, having driven through Maralal Town at night. The driver only realised his blunder on the way back to Nairobi when he stopped for petrol at a station in Maralal Town. He blamed it on his loader, who blamed it on the dispatcher, who blamed the chief librarian for not telling him the *University of Maralal* was in Maralal Town; never mind that everyone had *gps* and all claimed to know how it worked.

To cover up for the potentially fatally expensive error, the dispatcher, who happened to be the man Kasim met at the unofficial civil servants' club in River Road, changed the delivery label to read the *University of Maralal Desert Campus* and made everyone happy. From then on, books kept on coming to Taeyang customs post, some of them to be rerouted to the librarian's own used books shop in Lodwar, and the rest to wander off in the desert or across the border with readers, or stay to be shredded by passing bullets.

Then aid money ran out and Uncle Gove resulted to belt tightening. With no money to fuel the mobile library truck, it was the end of desert deliveries. Taeyang residents were left with a customs office that housed a library with enough *do-it-yourself* knowledge to irrigate the desert, produce own biogas from one cow's dung, and harness the sun, but no tools do it with.

Soon after, the volunteer librarian got tired of volunteering, borrowed half of the library, and took it back to Lodwar to expand his used books business. The rest of the books, those that his borrowers admitted finding too tedious and pointless to read, remained at the customs office in Taeyang. That was where Kasim found Tolstoy, Shakespeare, Robespierre, Max and Engels and dozens more, stranded in a bullet-riddled office after his predecessor absconded.

He was wallowing in *Teach Yourself Russian*, having given up on teaching himself Portuguese, Turkish, Icelandic, Lithuanian and Irish, all of them languages spoken in countries he would visit someday; when a new kind of bullet smacked through the metal door, leaving a whole large enough for a hyena to walk through, and scattering blown out book pages all over the office. It exited out of the back wall leaving a similar sized hole in the masonry.

'Who will fix that now?' Kasim thought even as bullets continued to hammer on the walls and whistle through the windows. Uncle Gove was unlikely to send a mason from Nairobi, unless perhaps the entire office was blown to dust and there was a need to build another one. Thinking of which, Kasim ducked lower under the desk and covered his head with the hard cover copy of Shakespeare's complete works.

When calm returned, he taped a cardboard sheet over the hole in the door, paid boys to plug the hole in the masonry with cow dung, and started to teach himself Nepalese for no reason.

Later in the day, during the afternoon lull, he called on the warring parties to mediate peace.

"Why?" they asked him.

He remembered an old man telling him the Fahari and the Afari were kin and had been throwing rocks, shooting arrows, and firing guns at one another since the beginning of time.

He had not considered that when embarking on his peace mission, and now he had to think on his feet.

"War is bad," her said. "Especially for women."

The elders looked at one another.

"And children and other living things," he added.

They smiled, and informed him women and children knew what to do when war broke out. They got the hell out of the way.

"The cattle?" he tried. "They don't like war either."

The old men smiled again and pointed out that cattle too knew what to do when the first shot was fired. They also got the hell out of the way.

"And so should you," they said.

With that, Kasim's peace mission fizzled out, returned to where it had originated under the customs desk and stayed there.

"Would you, at least, ask your boys not to shoot at one another through my office windows?" he pleaded.

That they could do, the elders agreed. But they also reminded him, it was his customs office that was in the way of their bullets; an ancient route much by bullets travelled. Chinese AK 47 bullets had trouble going round houses.

Kasim finally understood why *the other one's* peace missions had failed. It had nothing to do with anarchic disdain for distant governments, or for Kasim's vexing demands that the young men pay customs duty for the bullets they fired across the border at each other. This was their country, their way, and their life. Take it or leave it. Kasim took it. He did what women and children, and cattle did. He went and crawled back in his safe place with Shakespeare, Tolstoy, and Karl Max.

Then, one hot and dusty, flyblown afternoon, when no bullets were flying and the way of life seemed normal, a naked man walked in the customs office wearing nothing but an AK 47 over one shoulder and a large leather sack over the other shoulder. He dropped the sack on Kasim's desk and sat his bare backside next to it. He leaned over the table, smelling of sweat and guns, and pointed at the sack.

"What is in it?" Kasim asked.

He answered in Fahari.

Under the tutorage of the old man who smiled at his joke, Kasim had learned phrases like, *no tobacco, no cigarette, no wife* and *no I don't want to marry your daughter.* None of them were any part of what the man with the gun said.

He reached out and carefully, pulled the sack to him, and opened it. It was full of glass-like stones.

"What is this?" he asked. "Diamond?"

The man rubbed his thumb and index fingers together. That was the same in Kamba, Kisii and Kikuyu. But what was Kasim supposed to do about it? He rose to go fetch the old man. The man cocked his rifle. That too was the same in any language. Kasim sat back down.

The man pointed at the office safe. The safe normally held dust and old office files. But just that morning the paymaster had delivered the payroll for Taeyang government departments. Salaries for the clinical officers, livestock officers, and anti-stock-theft patrols were also in the customs' safe awaiting paying out.

The naked man pointed his gun at Kasim and motioned at the safe. Kasim took the key out of the desk drawer and opened the safe. He took out the payroll and handed it to the naked man. The man open one pay envelope and counted the money. He emptied his sack on the desk, swept all the pay envelopes in it, and walked back across the border. That was Kasim's one and only dealing with a real cross-border businessman, and an incredibly honest, smuggler.

Two weeks later police from Lodwar came and took him back for questioning. They found his story of a naked holdup with AK 47 amusing, and even more so when he said it was not a joke. Why leave the stones when Kasim had already handed over the payroll?

"He was an honest man," Kasim told them.

"An honest bandit?" They never heard of such a being.

"Businessman," he said.

"And you, what were you?" They asked.

The question stopped Kasim with a jolt. What was he? And what was he, north of the Turkana desert, explaining commonsense to officers who never heard of it, men who never spent a day and a night under a desk fearing for their lives. What was he? He was not even a real customs officer. What was he really?

"What I am?" he said to them, "is a man."

He blew up his chest, straightened his back

"A comedian," he said. "Standup comedian."

They seemed disappointed. They would have preferred to deal with a really big criminal. A drugs smuggler, human trafficker, or international arms dealer.

"So, to you this is all a joke?"

"Hilarious," he said. "Very funny."

"We will see how funny in court when you face seven years in prison," they said disappointed.

They kept him in a cell for a fortnight, feeding him whenever they remembered to, then they sent him to Nairobi for two more weeks of grilling, before setting him free. Somewhere along the way, all references to the naked man and his leather bag, and the precious stones, had gone missing, vanished from the report books, and Kasim freed for lack of sufficient evidence. Caesar had no sympathy for him. The fact that he was suspected of theft of government property was enough for Caesar to finally give up on Kasim. But not Aunt Charity.

Chapter 22

The time for ritual mourning was over. The meetings had turned solemn, and appropriately unhappy, since Aunt Eva ordered King'oo men to raise half the cost of burying Caesar. They were yet to do so, and she was tempted to believe, as their wives said, they would not give a bean more than they had already given. But she did not give up torturing them.

She sat with her four sisters next to Aunt Charity, the donations basket by her feet waiting for them to prove their wives wrong. A path was cleared for them to file past the basket handing in their donation so the sisters could witness and measure their love for Caesar.

"We need money," she said to them. "Not words or tears."

She ordered Sam to tell them in a language they understood.

"We need money," Sam said, speaking to the men's corner. "You know what that means."

There were quiet moans. The air got chillier.

"The budget keeps growing," he told them. "As we speak, the mortuary fees are growing exponentially."

"Speak Kikamba," Aunt Kamene said.

"Heavier," he said. "The fees are getting heavier every day."

"How heavier?" someone asked.

"Very," he said. "And now I see that the casket will cost us …"

While he consulted his clipboard, Aunt Eva raised a different issue.

"There was no funeral notice in the papers today."

"Or the radio," said Aunt Kamene. "Who is in charge of notices?"

"Here we go again," Kasim whispered to Roger before slowly rising. "I will go see them tomorrow, find out what happened."

He started to sit back down.

"Have you paid?" she asked him.

"What?"

"You heard me, Kasim."

"Have I paid?" he said. "We agreed I'll take the money when we raise it."

"What is wrong with your head?" Salim asked him. "Do you know how much time you have wasted? Why didn't you tell us you had no money to pay for it?"

"I did."

"You did not."

"I tried to."

Roger watched bemused, as the exchange heated up and Sam stepped in.

"Looking at the budget," Uncle Sam referred to his clipboard, "We have two days of radio and one day of newspapers left. We need Uncle Richard in this. There is no other way."

The room was quiet. Everyone but the aunts avoided eye contact. Men shrunk into their seats trying to seem insignificant.

"Who has the balls?" asked Uncle Tivo in Kamba.

Roger turned to Salim.

"Who is Uncle Richard?"

"Someone you don't want to know," said Salim.

"What is he to you people?"

Before Kasim could start explaining Uncle Richard, his mother called his name.

"No, mother," he said, "don't ask me to go back. Uncle Richard offered his pickup."

At the mention of pickup, Aunt Charity broke out in loud sobs.

"We rejected it?" Aunt Eva said to her. "So, what is the problem."

Charity was twelve, and she could fix her father's shirt buttons and repair tears in her school uniform, when

Kamene was too busy taking mangoes to the market and Eva was breaking boys' hearts.

Caesar sat in the yard, his hat on his head and his walking stick at hand, looking like he wanted to go, but was too distracted to get up and go, or could not decide where to go. It happened on weekends when he was free and did not know what do with his day.

Then they heard a choir in the distance sing *God Be With You Till We Meet Again*. She sang along, while he sat still and forlorn, as the singing approached. Then the procession passed by the front gate, and she put down her sewing and followed him to the gate. The casket was on a one-donkey wagon decorated with bougainvillea and banana leaves, and in the choir was Kioko, a boy she knew from school.

When the procession had passed, Caesar remembered where he had to go and put his hat back on his head. He followed the procession down the road and Charity went back to the house.

He was sad and tired when he returned late in the day looking crushed. He went to his place under the mango tree and sat watching the sun set and thinking of what he had seen. Charity found him in despair, fighting to hold back tears.

He had worked with the dead man at finance ministry for many years, until he was hounded out of office for refusing to join in the looting of public funds. Then he was barred from being employed in any organisation in which the government had a say and he descended into depression, alcohol, and suicide.

"To think that a man works so hard," Caesar said, his voice broken, "Works so hard for so long, and so selflessly, for his people and country, only to be maligned by greedy politicians and driven out of office and sent to his final resting place on a donkey wagon. A donkey wagon."

The disgrace, the shame of it, was worse than the death.

"Dad," she said, wiping her own tears. "You will not go to your final resting place on a donkey wagon. You will go riding on a big, black Mercedes like before. A big, black Mercedes car like the one you drove us in."

He looked up at her, smiled sadly and touched her hand. Then he rose and went to check on his mango trees.

Chapter 23

Sam's train was off the tracks again, the driver demoralised and his henchmen, the motley gang of funeral planners picked to make Caesar's last ride trouble-free were cowering in their shells for fear of Hurricane Eva.

The burden of Charity's promise to Caesar was now firmly on Salim's shoulders and it did not matter to anyone how it got there. Meanwhile Kasim, the one who helped offloaded it on Salim, was desperately scrambling for ways to lighten it before Salim buckled under and all hell broke loose.

He sought out people he remembered owing him money, or favours, begging them to pay back what they owed him or lend him money. They pleaded corona induced poverty, like everyone else in the city, and begged for more time. Club managers patted him on the back and suggested he come again when the corona woes were really over, the economy back on its feet, and he was a real comedian. Salim was more disappointed than Kasim.

"What about your Indian uncle?" he asked, on the point of giving up.

"Leave Uncle Dave out of this," Kasim said.

"And you call him uncle why?"

"Sometimes he calls me son," said Kasim. "He is old enough to be my father."

"He is not King'oo."

"And if he were he would not be from Kathiani."

"King'oo come from Kathiani."

"How often have I heard you wish you were from another planet?"

"That is different," Salim said, as they entered Bombay Club car park.

The Manager, also of Indian and not King'oo, descent was less subtle. He would not advance Kasim lunch money against his stage appearances, if he were dying from hunger.

Kasim's shows almost always ended with broken bottles on stage and patrons howling for his blood.

"How do I get my money back?" another club owner asked Kasim.

"You always get your money back," Kasim told them.

"What if you move to Kapenguria?" another asked.

"To do what in Kapenguria?"

"I don't know," he said. "You comedians are a strange lot. The last one got drunk and was run over by a bus he was boarding?"

"I don't get that drunk."

"What if the bus driver were drunk?"

"In that case," Kasim indicated Salim. "This is my cousin Salim. Salim is the best lawyer in the country. He will guarantee you get every cent of my life insurance pay out."

"What?" Salim said startled. "I want no part of this. Leave me out of it."

"He was about to consider it," Kasim said of the manager.

"This is a waste of time," Salim rose "Don't you see what he is doing?"

Kasim turned to the manager, watching them quietly with a smile on his face.

"Saying *no* in too many words?" he asked him.

The man nodded. All the club managers, it turned out, had as little faith in comedians as the comedians' own families. Kasim started for the door.

"Never, never, never give up," he said, as they battled heavy city traffic.

Seeing how desperate he was getting, Salim let him alone. They had visited all the clubs Kasim was certain would be a sure source of help. In all of them, he had asked for *harambee* donations first and, when that bore no fruit, requested a lone against future earnings. Now they were back in Nairobi traffic jams with apparently no place left to turn to and Salim was getting weary.

"I know a place," Kasim said.

Half an hour later, he parked the Beetle behind Kijabe Street and led Salim on a perilous dash through four lanes of traffic, across an overgrown roundabout with half-naked men basking on the grass, across another four lanes of fast traffic to the western end of Kirinyaga Road.

"New Grogan Road," he said.

"Kirinyaga Road," Salim pointed at the road sign.

"We prefer New Grogan Road," he said.

"You and who else?"

"You will see," Kasim said.

Like the new old normal, there was little new about New Grogan Road. A rugged, potholed stretch of old, and dilapidated buildings, the road was the traditional home to auto garages, spare parts stores, repair shops, machine shops, chop shops, print shops, and documents reproduction shops that printed forgeries more authentic than the government issued one.

The pavements were crowded with hawkers looking for counterfeits to sell on main street, and bargain seekers after smuggled European products to re-label and export back to Europe as locally made products. Pickpockets and muggers too plied their businesses in open sight, and beggars and destitute were everywhere.

A man lying on the pavement looking dead, suddenly sat bolt upright startling Salim. He nodded at Kasim, as they walked round him, laughed at Salim, and lay back down to sleep, or to die, or whatever he had been trying to do. Several paces on, another man was on his knees confessing to a lamppost.

"Former high court judge," Kasim said as they passed him. "Fired for extreme corruption."

People stopped to listen to the judge's confession, laughed, and walked away shaking their heads.

"I don't remember him," Salim said.

"Before your time," said Kasim.

"And you know him how?"

"River Road."

"How?"

"There are no secrets here."

A man talking to a parked car stopped to great Kasim, shake his hand, and call him brother. Then, ignoring Salim, he continued conversing with the car.

New Grogan Road throbbed with life. A kilometre long stretch of raw, hard life, so potent the city officials did not know which laws applied or did not apply to whatever went on there.

Kasim demonstrated his familiarity by leading Salim through a gauntlet of aggressive working women, unfriendly peddlers and hustlers of every kind offering him services he did not need or want, while ignoring Kasim.

"The suit," Kasim said. "Shouldn't have brought it here."

Kasim was in usual artist's rags, recycled Kelvin Kline jeans, well-worn and properly rugged, old Jordan sneakers, a white Lakers' shirt, and a black leather vest all from the recycling market. He had donned a black knit cap over his shaggy hair just before leaving the car, to enhance his claim to belonging.

"Dead giveaway," he said of Salim's lawyer suit. "Does not belong here.

"Again, why are we here?" Salim asked uneasily.

"You will see," Kasim said.

A young woman quarrelling with her image in a shop window saw their reflection in the window and yelled at them.

"Who are you laughing at," she said. "I was a queen before corona."

They ignored her. The old normal had brought back a wild mix of sanity and insanity, and other anomalies that would baffle and enrage honest human for generations. Grocers had given up selling and turned to farming. Teachers turned to fishers and doctors were now preachers, beekeepers were homeopathic healers, and bar owners were their own best customers and bank robbers were now money lenders.

They were nearly half-way down Kirinyaga Road, and Salim's still did not know where they were going and just a slight notion of why.

"We are there," Kasim said, entering a dark, greasy door between two repair shops.

The door opened into a dark passage leading to a stuffy flight of stairs rising into more darkness. They paused to acclimatise and, when their eyes got used to the gloom, started up the stairs. They climbed through a fog of smells, of diesel, old motor oil, cigarette smoke, human sweat, and urine. Salim was breathless by the time they reached the first landing.

To the right and left of the landing were four greasy, metal doors, two on each side, secured with steel bars and heavy padlocks. Signs on the doors indicated they belonged to the two repair shops on either side of the entrance downstairs.

The stairs continued upwards past more landings with heavy steel doors, some of them padlocked, others ajar, getting a whiff of *bhang* now and then, the aroma of burning *ugali,* a baby's cry behind a heavily padlocked steel door, loud music on one landing and deathly silence on the next. Salim had never imagined so many locks, on so many doors, outside of a maximum-security prison. It was disorientating.

"What do they do here?" he wondered when they paused to rest their lungs and legs.

"Everything," Kasim said to him.

Then he started on upwards, and Salim followed, passing more steel doors, not all of them padlocked, and hearing music, laughter, and stranger sounds from some of them.

The staircase got brighter as they approached the top landing. The light from the skylight lit an unlocked door marked *RENT A THUG.*

Salim stopped short.

"Who wants to hire a thug?" he asked Kasim.

"Anyone," said Kasim. "Politicians who hate competition, businessmen who can't stand competition and anyone who cannot compete with his father-in-law."

"How did you find this place?" Salim asked.

"Come, on Salim, don't tell me you have never imagined shrinking the competition."

"I really don't know you, Kasim," Salim said, disturbed.

They started off again, passed a door that said - *National ID Sold Here*, and another *Genuine Passports All Countries*.

The heaviest steel door was at the top landing. It looked as formidable as a bank vault, with a large combination lock and a wheel to swing it open, but it was wide open. Behind it was a heavy mahogany door that was closed. The sign above the door said *Double Donge Finance*. Four scowling giants in black suites, two on either side of the steel door, watched Kasim and Salim come panting up the last steps.

"What?" one of them asked Salim.

"Donge," Kasim said.

The man frisked them before letting them through. Inside the mahogany door was an office to put Salim's to shame. A dark desk in the middle of the room, black leather visitors' chairs arranged opposite the manager's throne-like seat, and a white wall-to-wall carpet that seemed to adjust to every step.

On the throne was a small man in a track suit and sneakers. But just in case anyone was tempted to mistake him for an office boy sitting in for the boss, he wore what seemed like a kilo of gold chains round his neck and a gold ring on every finger of the hand holding a phone to his ear.

"Ah, there you are," he yelled at them. "Kasim the Komedian himself and in person."

"Double Donge, my man," said Kasim, just as enthusiastic. "I tried to call you, but you were busy."

"I have called you many times, but you have not picked," he said, "I was about to call you for the last time, before renting a thug to come find you. But now you are here."

"Must be telepathy," said Kasim.

"Whatever it is, you are here now," he dropped the phone back on the table. "Come in and sit, sit. Your friend too, sit."

At the far end of the desk sat an Asian man in a light grey silk suit and a white tie. The wall behind him was lined with heavy safes with combination locks like of which Salim had only seen inside a bank strongroom. Leaning on a safe door was a huge baseball bat, and on the desk, within arm's reach of the man on the throne, was an AK 47. Salim thought to back out, but the small man was eyeing him as was his turbaned friend. Then Kasim stepped forward hand extended. The man ignored the offered hand and indicated they sit down.

They sat across the desk from him, on red, leather seats so soft that, like the carpet, they seemed to adjust to the sitter's shape and weight.

There was an uncomfortable moment after they had sat down, and it appeared the two had said all they had to say. Donge eyed them silently, looking from one to the other, then sighed and addressed Kasim.

"Where is my car?" he asked.

"*Jua kali,*" said Kasim, without the slightest hesitation.

Donge smiling turned to his turbaned visitor.

"Do you know this clown?" he asked. "Calls himself Triple K?"

Without waiting for an answer, he turned back to Kasim.

"When do I get my car, or my money?"

Kasim was expecting that one too.

"Soon as fixed," he said.

Donge turned and looked out of the window and across the river to the blocks of high-rise apartments he was rumoured to own. The wind blowing into the office from across the river was fresh with just a trace of leather and sandalwood and a hint of cologne. Salim guessed they were too high up for the smell of sewage from the river between to get to them.

The small man had a bemused smile in his eyes when he turned from the window and reached across the desk for Salim's hand, startling him.

"Donge is my name," he said. "What is yours?"

"Salim," said Salim, giving him the hand.

They shook hands, looking in each other's eyes for sincerity. The sincerity Salim saw in Donge's eyes was unsettling. The man was soulless.

"What can I do for you, Salim?" he asked.

"I am with him," Salim gestured at Kasim.

"So?" Donge turned to Kasim. "Where is my money?"

Kasim smiled the practiced, disarming smile Uncle Rich called a village fool's shield. It did not work with Donge either.

"You don't have my money," he said, faking despair.

"To tell you the truth …"

"Stop," Donge raised a hand. "You know what happens in court when you start with the truth?"

"Prison," said Kasim. "Everyone in Grogan Road knows that. But the fact is …"

"The fact is you don't have my money."

"Actually, I am here …"

"Without my money."

"Well, I am …"

"Here without my money." The gold chains clinked when he banged his fist on the table.

Donge was short and lean and as hard as an ancient acacia. Like the scrappy, puny street boys from the garbage pits of Mitaboni market that invaded Kathiani market on Saturday to bully school boys many times bigger. For once,

Kasim was lost for words, and that worried Salim. He had begun to believe Donge's gangster image was bogus, like the office, the gold cains and AK 47. All just for show.

"What are you doing here without my money?" he heard the man say. "No more bull, just straight up truth."

While Kasim thought how to proceed without bull, the man turned to the turbaned gentleman who sat watching through hooded eyes, his face passive.

"This one had his car for collateral," Donge said to him. "An old Beetle my wife loved."

"Where is my wife's Beetle?" he turned to Kasim. "You haven't sold it, have you?"

"I still have it," said Kasim.

"And my money too," said Donge.

Kasim, struggling to keep a straight face, fumbled for an explanation.

"As I was about to say …" he started.

Donge turned to Salim.

"Do you have my money?" he asked.

"No," Salim was quick to say.

"Then what are you doing here?"

Salim had been wondering the same thing since they walked in, and the man started demanding money from Kasim.

"He brought me here," he said.

"Salim is my cousin," Kasim said. "A famous lawyer."

"So?" said Donge.

"Just saying, in case you … ever need one."

"I am not a criminal lawyer," Salim reminded Kasim.

Kasim, about to spin a mitigating tale, stopped worried. He looked from Salim to Donge and back.

"For what would I need a criminal lawyer?" Donge asked him.

Salim realised that was the wrong thing to say to such a man in such a place.

"I don't know," he said. "I am just a conveyance lawyer if you ever need one. That is all I meant."

"And you still have not told me why you are here," said Donge.

Salim turned to Kasim.

"I think we should now disappear," he said.

"I can help you with that," Donge said to him. "Have my boys dump your bodies in the river and send your lawyer suit to *mitumba* women for recycling. But that would not get my money back, would it?"

Salim was quick to shake his head.

"You are here to sell me your corona story," Donge said to him. "Admit it."

Salim shook his head, wondering why the man was talking to him at all. He was there by the accident of being cousin to a moron who could not tell when a game was way out of his league.

"All right" said the man. "I am listening. Sell it to me."

He obviously had heard enough of corona laments to last his lifetime. From bankers who believed it was real, to people who never had a job in their lives, people who had had nothing all their lives, and street beggars who claimed to have lost it all to corona.

"No corona story to sell," Kasim said, with a smile.

"So why are you here?" He was still addressing Salim.

"To borrow money," Salim said, to get it over with.

"Who wants to borrow money?" Donge asked, looking from one to the other. "The lawyer or the comedian?"

Kasim hesitating. Salim pointed at him.

"Tell him, Kasim," he said. "It was your idea to come here."

"My grandfather died," Kasim said. "I need to borrow money for his funeral."

"You want to what?" Donge turned to the Asian. "Did you hear that, Roy? The joker wants to borrow more money."

The Indian smiled, shook his head bemused. Salim realised it was turning out to be another of Kasim's unbelievably bad ideas.

"I don't have to be here," he started to rise.

"You are here now; so, sit down," the man ordered.

"I only accompanied him."

"Sit down."

Salim sat. Donge rose, walked to an open wall safe, took a ledger and turned the pages. He counted ten pages, dropped the book on the desk in mock despair.

"Your record," he said.

Kasim and he had been in business for a long time. Salim could not help asking how long.

"Ask him," Donge said, busy adding up figures.

Kasim shrugged at Salim, smiled embarrassed.

"Now," Donge looked up from his calculator. "Interest and all, you owe me a Mercedes."

He turned to Salim.

"Do you own a Mercedes?"

Salim quickly shook his head.

"Didn't look like it," Donge pushed the paper with his calculations across to Kasim.

Kasim glanced at the total, shook his head, and laughed.

"And he laughs," Donge said to the Indian visitor. "He thinks it is funny."

The visitor smiled, shook his head at Kasim.

"There is also an inconvenience fee," said Donge. "Late fee too if we wait long enough. And if I have to pay *Hire a Thug* to find you, there will be collection fees too. And, if I send my own men to look for you, there will be pain to pay. Are we clear?"

"Clear as day," Kasim said, suddenly serious and business-like.

"You have seven days," Donge pointed at the door.

"What about today's loan?" Kasim said worried.

"Get out, before I call security."

Salim hastily rose and made for the door. Kasim rose slowly, stunned by the turn of events, glanced at the piece of paper in his hands.

"Seven days?" he said to himself, turned and was about to say something to Donge, then the Indian stirred.

"*Club Bombay*," he said, suddenly.

Kasim stopped and turned, startled.

"Kasim the Komedian," said the Indian. "Three Ks for Kuyu, Kisii and Kamba."

"You have seen my performance?" Kasim asked him.

"Not bad," he said. "But your Indian jokes? Very not funny."

"Which Indian jokes?"

"All of them. Not funny. Not at all funny."

"Comedy isn't about funny," Kasim said, approaching to set him straight.

To laugh at something as nebulas as life, he explained, one had to see, hear, feel, and understand life. Kasim's mission as a comedian was to light it up, shine a spotlight on it so bright and real the blind could see it and the deaf hear it.

"Make everyone see the mess they live in, this dung hill you call life, and the crap that comes at them from the blind spots in their minds."

An uncomfortable silence. Salim started to say something, Kasim stopped him with a raised hand, then looked from the Indian to Donge and back.

"That is all I do," he said.

"And you make a living doing that?" Donge was more puzzled than cynical.

"Some people care about the meaning of life.

Donge turned to the Indian for confirmation, the man nodded.

"Something I always wanted to ask," Kasim said to Donge. "Are you from Mitaboni?"

"Do I look like a Kamba to you?" He was not offended, just curious.

"Just wondered," said Kasim.

Salim was wondering where all that came from, what purpose it was supposed to serve in their mission, and why

Kasim was still talking when they had been dismissed and permitted to leave.

Donge and his visitor looked at each other and, no doubt, wondered the same thing. Donge shrugged like – *See what I have to deal with.* The Singh shook his head in sympathy and turned to Kasim.

"So, what are you really?" he asked. "A prophet?"

Kasim laughed.

"Let me ask you something," he said. "And don't be offended. Have you ordered your malaria condom?"

"What?" Donge interjected.

"Uncle Gove's next big thing," Kasim said to him. "Head-to-toe anti-mosquito body armour already in production at *jua kali* sweatshops in Dandora. You will soon be wearing mosquito net suits, ties, mask, gloves, socks, shoes, and underwear, whether you like it or not. That is what the people you elected have been working on. How to scare you of dying from malaria that you do exactly as what they say; lock yourselves down and wait for relief food from Europe."

"What is wrong with your head?" the Indian asked him.

"Are you really that crazy?" Donge asked him.

"You, my friend, will tell me when you stand ten feet from your best friend drinking beer through a straw."

"In my world," the Indian said, to Donge, "This crazy fool would be in prison for the crazy things he says. Prison, or long dead, or worse."

"Worse how?" Kasim asked him.

"Nyayo House?"

"Nyayo House?" Kasim said. "Don't you know your history?

The Singh turned to Donge. What was the fool talking about now? Salim groaned when the fool started to answer him.

"Truth, like history, is fixed," Kasim said. You cannot shift it with lies and fabrications and propaganda. Or as my hard-life brothers say, you don't fool us with your *parapaganda*."

"Is that so?" the Singh said, his inscrutable face breaking in a chilling smile.

Then Kasim suddenly remembered where he had seen those hooded eyes on a blue turbaned face. In the sea of turbans that he had failed to impress at *Mister Singh's* laugh-in club. He did not laugh again until they were safely out of the office, the door shut behind them.

"Seven days?" he said to Salim, "Who does he think I am?"

"You will find out when his *Rent A Thug* thugs catch up with you," said Salim.

Then they realised Donge's gate thugs could hear them and hurried down the stairs.

"What goes on behind these other doors?" Salim could not help asking.

"This is what they call a multi-purpose development. I thought you'd figure that out. People live here too."

"All armed?"

"Best is not to ask."

"But the AK 47?" Salim asked as they passed the *Rent A Thug* landing. "Is it real?"

"Donge never fired it in my presence, but the bullet holes in the walls are real."

Salim stopped, speechless.

"Happened before my time," Kasim said, to reassure him. "What I heard was that a crew of River Road thugs posed as clients then demanded to see inside his saves. He told them to go to hell, they pulled knives and *pangas*. Donge reached under the desk, came out with an AK 47, and shot them dead."

"How many?"

"Six or sixty, depending on who you hear it from. Police came, took them away, and that was that.'"

"Again, how did you find this place?"

"I told you."

"Looking for somethings else like what?"

"Something I never found, so give it a rest."

Salim could not walk fast enough to get out of there. The stairs and the steel doors seemed to have grown in number since he climbed past them on his way up.

They rushed from landing to landing, past more steel doors, and had to stop to catch a breath outside a door with the sound of a tortured woman coming from inside.

"Ten floors without a single lift?" he moaned. "What sort of hell is this?"

"Oh, there is a lift," Kasim suddenly remember. "But it belongs to Donge."

"He owns the only lift in the building?"

"The building too."

Salim started off down the steps.

"And while we are on the subject," he said. "Don't take me along when you visit such places."

"I like your company," said Kasim.

"What would my clients think if they saw me come out of such a den?"

"They would understand. They know bishops and politicians die in brothels too."

"Just don't take me along, okay. And don't expect me to defend you pro bono when you are arrested."

"Okay," Kasim said. "No more *New Grogan Road* for you."

"*Kirinyaga Road.*"

"*New Grogan Road*," Kasim said. "Better ring, more history, more life."

"How long have you been coming here?"

"I was born there," Kasim said. "Stollen by a King'oo and smuggled to Kathiani. Like me, the people here are real."

"How much interest do they charge you?"

"Let me just say that Donge Doubler is not his real name."

"Two hundred percent? Are you that stupid?"

"I would say not."

"Yes, you are."

"Okay, a little maybe," Kasim said, calmly to cool his anger. "Now that we have cleared all that, and still don't have money for a hearse, why not stop by Uncle Richard's again find out if he has seen the light."

Salim was too angry to speak.

"He will tell us to bugger off, but we are passing that way, anyway and, as Caesar always said, the secret to success was to never give up."

They were not passing close to Uncle Richard's, but Kasim drove there anyway and predictably, Uncle Richard was not home, and Aunt Gwyneth offered them cake which Kasim readily accepted.

"Wait here," she said going to fetch it.

Had Uncle Richard been a true King'oo man, he would have built her mansion on his father's land. She would have been better off surrounded by pesky relatives than alone in the big mansion with a husband who was never there.

She went to clan functions without him, to meet and talk to his people, only to be mobbed by his female relatives demanding to know why she had not dragged him along. Then there were Richard's aunts, grandmothers and cousins wondering out aloud what he saw in her.

The worst were the hordes of nephews and nieces, and jobless school leavers begging her to make her husband find them jobs in the city. They were qualified accountants, managers, engineers, and internet technicians, who had not been employed since graduating from college. And then there were the unremorseful dropouts looking for housework, gardening, car washing, gatekeeping, anything that paid money.

From time to time, she met someone who claimed to be Uncle Richard's uncle wanting to know what she and her husband thought he ate in his mud hut while they ate rice and chapati in their palace in the city.

Kasim was turning the car when she brought them the cake.

"Will you be at the funeral?" Kasim asked her.

"If Richard comes," she said. "You know I can't drive; and I expect his driver will be busy ferrying the clan back and forth.

"Salim and me will drive you," Kasim offered through a mouthful of cake.

"In this car?" she laughed.

"In Salim's Mercedes."

She saw the look Salim gave him and again laughed.

"Let us just hope Richard comes," she said.

Salim did not hold much hope of that ever happening, but he had not held much hope of Aunt Eva coming from America just to bury Caesar either.

"You want to know something else?" Kasim said as they got out of the car at the club. "The real secret of success is to always think ahead."

"You do the talking then," Salim said to him.

Uncle Richard was still trying to qualify for the championship. From what they had observed, he preferred brute force to gently persuasion in dealing with the ball. His peers had given up trying to talk him out of it. Uncle Richard was starting to realise he would never qualify, and he was not in the mood for begging relatives.

"Don't you two have anything better to do?" he asked them.

They were already doing it, Kasim informed. They were burying Caesar.

"So, what are you doing here?"

The question was directed at Salim. Kasim talked too much and said too little, and Uncle Rich preferred talking to someone he halfway understood.

"We are looking for a hearse," said Salim.

"Does this look like a funeral home?"

"We were just passing," said Kasim, "and we thought we'd say hallo."

"Hallo," he said. "Now, bugger off."

When they did not, he looked up. Salim decided to explain. He had reported the generous offer of the pickup, and everyone was very grateful. But now their thick-headed aunts wanted a Mercedes hearse.

Uncle Richard stared, ran it through his mind seeking to understand it.

"Apart from the pope," he finally asked them, "how many people do you know who were driven to their graves in a Mercedes?"

Kasim tried to remember, but Salim just shrugged. He had seen a lot of Mercedes hearses on television, but they were all funerals of kings and presidents, and mafia godfathers, and crazy rich people like that, and Caesar was not one of them, and it did not pay to disagree with Uncle Richard on it. Besides, Uncle Rich and he were on the same side of the debate on the issue of a Mercedes funeral with a donkey cart budget.

"Uncle Richard," he said, evenly, "No one will listen to me, when I tell them how hard this is for me. Aunt Eva says I am a fraud, an ambulance chaser, and a quack. Maybe, if you came and talked to her, she would see reason and stop sending us here."

"Listen," Uncle Richard's voice hardened. "The pickup is all you get from me. Go tell her that."

"Uncle Rich," Kasim tried, humbling himself close to grovelling, "I mean Uncle Richard. Your pickup is great for a normal funeral. But this is Caesar we are talking about, your grandfather Caesar, the great Fiscal Caesar, a man known all over the world for his charisma and integrity. This time your pickup will not do. We need to borrow money for a real hearse, a Mercedes hearse."

"From whom?" his eyes narrowed.

They looked at each other.

"A joker and an ambulance chaser," he said to them. "Who would lend you two any money?"

"A rich and generous uncle?" Kasim said.

He was touched, as much as all wealthy and powerful men are receiving such sycophantic dross from desperate relatives. He turned to the one whose words he could trust.

"A loan to pay how?" he asked Salim. "Another end of month?"

Salim turned and walked away.

"Where is your crappy, old Mercedes?" Uncle Richard called after him.

Salim stopped and looked back, his hackles bristling.

"It is two years old," he said, walking back. "And it is not crappy. If it would make you feel better, the dealer repossessed it."

"Too bad," said Uncle Richard. "I was going to suggest you sell it to another fool and spend the money on your Mercedes hearse."

Salim swallowed the insult and promised himself to never ever talk to him again after Caesar's funeral.

"So, how much money do you want?" asked Uncle Richard.

"Hundred thousand," Salim said the first figure that came to mind.

"Rupee?" asked Uncle Richard.

Salim was tempted to repay the contempt by saying dollars but refrained.

"Shillings will do," he said.

"Go to your bank," said Uncle Richard.

"They need collateral," Salim reminded. "Why I came to you."

"You still have the Beetle?"

"Kasim has it."

Uncle Richard glanced at Kasim and back.

"What is wrong with you people?" he said to them. "The lawyer doesn't pay for my wife's car, sells it to a comedian and then both of you come back to me for money. Who do you think I am? Bugger off!"

Salim walked away, but Kasim lingered.

"I have a job now, Uncle Rich," he said.

That got him attention. Salim stopped to see how Uncle Richard would take it.

"What do you do?" Uncle Richard asked.

"Manage," he said. "I help run the club, and I make people laugh. I am a comedian."

"The same thing you did before?"

"Differently."

"You are not funny."

"Uncle Dave thinks I am."

"Uncle Dave?"

"You do not know Uncle Dave. He is Indian."

"Indian?"

"From River Road. He owns *Uncle Dave's Curry and Comedy House.* You must pay us a visit for the best curry in town. Uncle Dave's."

"An Indian?" Uncle Richard, still struggling to understand it. "Why do you call him your uncle?"

"He is rich and generous."

Uncle Richard finally saw through that trick, and his eyes narrowed.

"Not as rich and generous as you, Uncle Rich," Kasim said. "But he is nice, friendly, and kind. You must come meet him"

"Does he play golf?"

"He works."

Salim stepped back to avoid blood splatter.

"Tell him to come see me," said Uncle Richard.

Salim withdrew, slowly walked away.

"Uncle Dave?" Uncle Richard, eying Kasim as an imbecile, shook his head.

"It is his real name," Kasim assured. "Davindranath Siewriter Hydrabad or something like that, in Indian. We call him Uncle Dave."

"We?"

"You have to come to the club," Kasim said. and bring Aunt Gwyneth. Meet Uncle Dave, enjoy the greatest curry outside India and see me perform."

"Perform?" Uncle Richard scoffed. "First go ask your mother what tribe your father was. An Indian uncle? What do you do for him?"

"Assistant manager," Kasim said, with some pride. "Please don't laugh, Uncle Richard. I am serious."

"Assistant Manager? Go back to school and learn a real trade. Now bugger off."

"Thank you for that advice, Uncle Richard, I will consider going back to school but, in the meantime, what about the loan?"

"What loan?"

"To bury Caesar."

"I said bugger off."

Kasim was still laughing about it when he got to Salim.

"Another thing," Uncle Richard called after them.

They stopped, and looked back startled. He was hunched over the ball, the club raring to whack it to oblivion somewhere far away.

"A shoe horse is not a horse that sells shoes," he said to them. "Now bugger off."

He was addressing the ball. They looked at each other puzzled where that came from.

"The man needs help," said Kasim.

"What did you tell him?" asked Salim.

"Me?"

"He must know that I know what a shoe horse is."

"So do I."

"Really?"

"Uncle Dave must have riled him, or he is losing his mind," Kasim said. "Having more money than the entire clan and nothing to do but beat white balls all day must be depressing."

They watched him swing the club and send the ball down the fairway wobbling out of control. Kasim could not help laughing aloud. Uncle Richard turned at the sound, saw them watching.

"Bugger off," he yelled.

This time they did.

"And life goes on," Kasim said when they got back to the car. "You have to lighten up some time, Salim."

"Tell me again the secret of life?" Salim said, sitting at the traffic light waiting for the policeman to wake up and let them through.

"The secret of life is," Kasim said. "Never, never, never give up."

"Tell me you learn that from fans at your joke clubs."

"Comedy, not joke clubs," Kasim laughed. "There is a difference."

He gathered a lot of nuggets, some of them real wisdom, from drunks and wallet inspectors in the clubs, and from street girls and muggers on River Road, but he could not call any of it learning.

"I get it from books," he said.

"Books as in ... real books?"

"I can still read, you know."

"Really?"

Before Kasim could confirm, the policeman jealously guarding the intersection grudgingly waved them through and Salim forgot his question.

Chapter 24

Black Survivors were in recess by the urinals at the back of the club, smoking weed, drinking clear liquids from unlabeled bottles, and disagreeing on everything, but especially politics.

Rumours said the *National Nightclubs Owners' Association* would nominate Mr Dave as their candidate for president, and some band members had problems with that. Apart from his ancestry being foreign, a small jigger that they had learned to live with, Mr Dave was a club owner not a politician, or a descendant of a political clan, or a member of a political cartel for which they would be obliged to vote.

Other band members thought they should forget tradition affiliations and vote for him in exchange for a pay raise. But then that would be straight forward prostitution not business or politics. They were poets and prophets not flatterers or bootlickers. They rowed over opposed political ideas, and almost came to blows over them. Finally, they agreed the descent and respectable action was to lay down their instruments, march up to Mr Dave's office and demand a pay raise.

Those still sober enough understood that was the weed talking. Smoking weed, drinking unlabeled concoctions, and holding political discussions anywhere within the club grounds were forbidden. Mr Dave turned a blind eye, because they did it quietly, and peacefully, out by the men's toilets and he sympathised for what they had been through.

He was River Road born, Grogan Road bred, and Nairobian through and through, and nothing fazed him. His grandfather, landed on African soil from India, conscripted by the British to build the Uganda Railway. When the railway was completed, he set up the first spice shop in the city. With the help of family, friends and other connections, the business became the major importer of Indian goods.

Mr Dave learned the business from helping at family shops on weekends and after school. While still in high school, he opened a bicycle repair shop, and several newspapers stands. By the time he was of age and out of school, he owned a coffee house, and was ready to venture in restaurants, bars, and night clubs. His clubs gained fame for inclusivity and innovations, but were also notorious for their bar brawls, armed holdups, and police raids. Mr Dave had spent much of his time shuttling between the licensing offices and police headquarters, and putting out fires to avoid being shut down by city authorities.

There was none of that sort of stress at the comedy house. All Mr Dave had to do was keep an eye on the staff and the patrons to prevent situations getting out of hand. But, with Kasim on the stage, there was enough to keep him awake.

The old normal was back. The club was packed with fat old men with bundles of money to burn, and pretty, young women eager to light it for them. Mr Dave's part was to provide room, drinks, waiters, atmosphere, and the ashtrays. Patrons came in droves. The wheelers-dealers, and their government tenders handling cartels, all out enjoying their equal rights to happiness and pursuit of happiness. The old scenario of the hyena partying with the gazelle. A sight that no one thought they would ever see again.

Another wishing hour at *Uncle Dave's Curry and Comedy House*. Any man not dead drunk was wishing he had heeded his mother's advice, and married the pretty girl next door that never went to high school, left her in the country to tend to the pigeon peas, and look after the children, and simplified his life and lightened his manly burdens. But any woman inspecting a miserable wallet wished she had stayed in school and become a nurse as her mother insisted.

And Kasim was wishing they would all listen to him, and let him lighten their hearts with laughter.

"*Jaamboo*," he yelled in the microphone. "Remember me? Kasim the Komedian? Three 'K' for half Kuyu, half

Kisii and half Kamba? Remember? Yes, the one who can't count, but tells jokes and, whenever you have the time, you laugh and lift his spirits too."

He felt a storm of aggression from minds too foggy with beer to turn it into words. But now he had an audience.

Imagine yourself now pulling this same old, crapped out pushcart down the road loaded with hate, and bitterness, and broken dreams, and old beer bottles, and rusty old iron, and old shoes, and discarded household junk, and all the shit that you sell for a living, because that is what your life has come down to, and life is not easy for a hard-working man. Life is always hard for hard-working hard-life men. Always running and hiding from the big, fat, corrupt, county policeman. Always hustling and always hungry. Always hungry and always angry."

Wallet inspectors had paused to listen.

"Do you know the madman you see walking down the road with a sack on his shoulders and talking to himself is not mad at all? He is just another pushcart puller driven to desperation by the city government's demands for a hawking license. Think about that. He must have a county license and a city license, and enroll in the roadside scavengers' union, and pay his union dues and his income tax too. A license to pick up the empty water bottles and garbage you toss out of the windows of your big cars as you drive by. A license to clean your mess so he can trade it for food. And to pay his taxes like a good citizen. Which is more than you good people ever do for old Uncle Gove."

At the bar, Mr Dave buried his head in his hands and groaned. It was never a good sign when Kasim started on one of his rants. Those in the audience sober enough to care wondered at what point the secret police would crawl from under the tables and chairs to escort the fool to the dungeons.

"And then," Kasim raged on, "as if that is not tough enough to give you swine flu, bird flu, cow flu, fake flu, or whatever scares you to death, your corrupt as hell Uncle Gove decrees that you must wear a mosquito suit, and be vaccinated against mosquitos, or else be isolated in a cattle boma in Tsavo."

Pink lips went back to work, unbuckling her companion's belt, unzipping his trousers, and reaching inside his underwear. She felt around for a moment, got frustrated and was about to give up.

"Under the rock on the left," Kasim said to her.

"Mind your business," she said.

But she did as he suggested and came up with nothing. She zipped the man's trousers, buckled his belt. Kasim gave her the thumbs up, she showed him her middle finger. Whatever else was said about hard-life women, they worked as hard for money as the hard-life men they took it from. And they were more thorough than wives when it came to frisking a sleeping man for hidden money. They knew the lengths to which desperate men went to hide money they did not want found.

"You," Kasim said to a man emerging from a stupor. "Your trousers gate is open."

Several men looked down at their zippers.

"Not, you," Kasim said. "The one next to you."

They looked at one another's zippers.

"Go home, Kasim," they said when they saw the foolishness.

Black Survivors, were coming back fortified, fully charged with the weed, and whatever was in the clear unlabeled bottles they drank from, and they were ready to reclaim the stage.

"Kasim's time is up," announced the band leader.

Some audience cheered.

"Not before I sing my closing number," said Kasim.

"The fat policeman song?" said the band leader. "We'll sing it for you. Go home and rest, Kasim."

"Kasim go home," the audience chanted.

"I have a new song for you."

217

"Go home, Kasim."

Two of them dragged him to the exit and tossed him out. A third one threw his guitar after him.

"I will be back," he yelled through the door.

It was a cool moonlit night, the air heavy with the intoxicating aroma of flowering shrubs. The kind of night that inspired club novices into imagining they could be safe creeping under the kiss-me-quick bushes with wallet inspectors.

Kasim wound his way through the bushes to the parking at the front of the club. His Beetle was parked next to Mr Dave's Mercedes in the space reserved for assistant manager. He crawled in the driver's seat, reached under the seat for the key, inserted it, turned. Not a whimper from the engine. He turned it again, and again. Then he crawled out, went to the back, and opened the engine cover.

Using his telephone light to see by, he jiggled the wires, pulling and pushing, trying to remember how he saw the mechanics do it. He explored with a screwdriver, looking for something to loosen or tighten.

"*Ero!*" a voice said suddenly behind him.

He turned and rose banging his head on the engine cover. A security guard loomed over him club in hand.

"I have no cigarettes today," he said to the guard.

"I have cigarettes today," said the man.

He unbuttoned his greatcoat, unzipped the jacket beneath it, reached under his sweater to his shirt pocket and came out with a packet of cigarettes. He offered one to Kasim.

"Dunhill?" Kasim said, looking at it suspiciously, "Where did you get these?"

"Shop," he said.

"I have never seen these in a Kibera kiosks."

"I live in Kawangware."

Again, the man's hand dove inside his greatcoat, jacket, and sweater and came out with a red and gold lighter. Kasim took it from him and examined.

"Dunhill," he said, lighting the cigarettes. "*Ero*, how much do they pay you here?"

"How much do they pay you?" asked the guard.

"Not this much," he said, still admiring the lighter. "Would you like to swap jobs?"

The man snatched back the lighter.

"Why do you tell stupid jokes about Kikuyu?" he asked.

"Apart from the money? I like to see them laugh."

"Laugh at Kikuyu people?"

"Kikuyu is a language," Kasim started to educate him. "Like Kikamba, Kimeru, Kiswahili, Kimaasai. People who speak Kikuyu I prefer to call Kuyu. Like Kamba, Meru, Swahili … you get the idea."

"Why do you tell jokes about them?" the man insisted.

"I joke about everyone and everything. Are you a Kuyu man?"

"No?"

"Then you can't understand why."

The man hesitated.

"Ero," he said, "the day you make fun of Pokomo will be the day you die."

"Pokomo?"

The guard walked away leaving him to remember where he heard the name.

He was sitting on the rear bumper, contemplating his next move when the band stormed out of the club contemplating life without money or respect and having an angry fight about it. They tossed their equipment in the van and continued their angry exchange.

From what was said, Kasim gathered they had acted upon a plan the drummer had suggested behind the urinal, and laid down their instruments, marched up to Mr Dave and demanded a pay raise in exchange for their votes. Where upon Mr Dave had sacked them. They were now unemployed, proving yet again that, in the words of their Guru Bob Marley, Babylon made the rules.

Six, good, young men, gifted to play instruments and sing and dance, though hardly any of the customers noticed or cared about that, fired for demanding respect. Six good votes wasted for lack of tact and wisdom.

Sensing a common fate, Kasim sidled up and let known that he too was not happy with the setup at *Uncle Dave's Curry and Comedy* and was considering quitting. They ignored him. He let slip he had a weekly gig coming up at *Hard Life* club in River Road. They ignored it. The manager was looking for a band. They ignored that too. He could put in a good word for them with the manager at *Hard Life*. They were too pissed off with one another and with Mr Dave to hear Kasim.

Good, normal men who had lost faith in politics and God. Good men whose rights were battered and mangled, turned upside down and inside out, leaving them in spiritual and physical wilderness at the mercy of universal predators. How could they ever salvage their humanity out of the ashes of such nightmare?

"They can, Kasim, they can, and they will. Believe me they will."

He believed in the power of the human spirit. But the band boys would have to believe it too and work at it. All the same they would have faith-bending stories to tell their children and grandchildren, of the things they had seen and heard. They were there, when hell yawned and swallowed love and compassion, and goodness and beauty, and destroyed knowledge, and wisdom, and reason, and trust and anything that was good.

They were there, when kings and presidents, politicians and intellectuals, gods and demigods, demons and spirits questioned humanities right to exist, reproduce and live and hope, and rewrote the laws of nature and man, decreed who would eat and who would hunger, who would live and who would die. They were there when self-declared, sane, and incorruptible holy men, teachers, and leaders were lured with promises of wealth, impunity, and immortality to worship at the devil's temple.

"Uncle Dave," Kasim said awed, "I did not know you were a poet too."

"All men are poets," Mr Dave said to him. "When they glean the truth and speak it to themselves and to others, especially to those who cannot, or will not see, hear or believe it."

The *Black Survivors* had done that. They had seen the devil awaken, heard what he had to say, seen what he had done before retreating to his lair leaving it to greedy leaders and corrupt politicians to complete his mission. It had made the boys angry when they realised how close they had come to annihilation. So angry that, by the third act of the nights show, they were bouncing off the walls to the delight of their worshipping mournful clique, and the end-month crowds, and playing medleys of protest songs that drove audiences mad.

They changed to *Black Survivors* from *Sunshine Boys* when they weathered the curfews and the lockdowns, and the masks and social distancing, and all the chaos, mayhem and fear that went with the corona scare. They still had most of their faculties intact, but they were forever marked, traumatized by how fast, how easily, their lives were taken out of their control, eviscerated, and used to fuel white leaders' imperial dreams and black leaders' greed.

Kasim thought they were on the same side, if not of the same kind. They had survived corona and come out smiling, if differently insane, and disgruntled. It was the band boys that encouraged him to think protest thoughts. He was one with them,, though they would not own up to being on his side. Their lyrics oozed anger and defiance, protested injustice and political brutality, the exploitation of the ignorant and the innocent. The kind of protest-fire Kasim had tried to catch in song and poetry out in the desert, crouching under a desk surrounded by books from great writers, while AK 47 bullets whizzed over his head.

To the band he was still an ignorant country boy, though most of him came from Machakos, a spitting distance from the city, while some of the band boys came from parts so remote and far away they had no fixed names. When he informed the band leader that he had lived and worked in those distant parts and learned things the band boys would never know, the band leader advised him to go back there and find a real job. His protest poetry was common, his songs bushbuck-barks, and had no meaning or purpose, and it embarrassed those on his side and offended the rest.

"If I were chief of police," the band leader had said, "you would spend the rest of your life wading in two feet of sewage at *Nyayo House.*"

"*Nyayo House?*" Kasim tried laughing it off. "Get your history right, my brother. Those dungeons closed before we were born."

"Is that what they told you?"

It was the band leader's turn to laugh at the shadow of doubt that crossed his face. His contemptuous laugh was disturbing, but King'oo men did not worry about contempt for more than a moment or two. The very next night he was back on stage protesting in his own way, and offending without regard to race, tribe, politics, religion, or wealth. Telling jokes about people; rich people, poor people, policemen, politician and their praise-singers, and any type of people that happed to be in the audience.

Now he watched the band load the equipment in their van and get in.

"Brother," he said to the leader, "give me a lift to Kibera?"

"Van is full," said the man, still angry.

"No, it is not," Kasim pointed at a space between the drummer and the base player.

The band leader snorted, hopped in the front seat, and slammed the door.

"Guys," Kasim pleaded through the open window, "I am a hustler too."

"We are not hustlers," they yelled back.

"Is that what they told you?" Kasim said with a laugh.

As the van started away, the band leader leaned out of the window and showed him both middle fingers. Kasim shrugged and went back to his car. The band had tried again to exhort a raise from Mr Dave, and had been sacked again.

"Good boys indeed," Kasim thought, watching them drive away. "We'll see how far that gets you."

He crawled back in his car. reclined his seat, closed his eyes, and reflected on what the band leader had said about being chief of police. Not worrying about it, just thinking about it. King'oo men did not dwell on disturbing thoughts for long either and, in no time, he was asleep.

Mr Dave found him slumped over the wheel, when the club closed in the wee hours of the morning, and banged on the roof of the Beetle.

"Kasim," he called. "Are you all right?"

Kasim sat up, yawned, and lowered the window.

"Just resting my eyes, Uncle Dave," he said.

"Go home then. The club is closed."

The parking had emptied while Kasim rested his eyes. The watchmen had retreated into the shadows to sleep, chew *khat* or whatever they did when there were no sleeping cars to watch.

"Uncle Dave," he said. "How much do you pay your watchmen?"

"A tad less than I pay comedians," said Mr Dave.

"How then do they afford gold cigarette lighters?"

Mr Dave admitted being surprised to hear about it, but he guessed they managed it like everyone else with vices that outstripped resources. They worked day and night to afford it. They watched cars at the club by night, and washed cars somewhere in the city during the day. There was no day or night for anyone with a mission.

"They hustle continuously," Mr Dave said. "That is how most people afford anything."

"Are you saying I should be a hustler too?" Kasim asked.

"You already are, Kasim," said Mr Dave. "You are just in the wrong hustle."

"I don't hustle, I entertain," Kasim said. "Explain to me how you pay a watchman just a tad less than you pay me, the one who brings customers with cars for him to watch?"

"I can't pay you more money than you bring in," Mr Dave explained. "Minus costs and expenses, of course."

"I understand that, Uncle Dave, but I do more than put on an act. I sing, I dance, tell stories. I entertain, educate, and loosen your customers fists and wallets."

"I only pay to make them laugh," said Mr Dave. "And you are not exactly good at it. Go home now, Kasim. Your jokes need a lot of work."

"I'm on it, Uncle Dave."

"I know you are on it, Kasim. I worry about you."

"No need to, I have it all figured."

"Figured how?"

"Right now, I am the greatest comedian in Nairobi. I have gigs here, gigs in Westlands, in River Road, Lavington, and that means I am a great comedian."

"A comedy king who is always broke."

"Everyone is a little broke, Uncle Dave. Everything is a little broke in this town too. Even trees, Uncle Dave. If it is not the branch it is the root. If not the arm, it is the leg, or the mind or the heart. We must make choices on that too, on what to let break, or the whole thing gets broken. I chose wisdom over riches, art over wealth, for a reason."

"Which was?"

He waited while Kasim remembered.

"Making people laugh," he said. "Seeing people happy."

"And then?"

224

"It may not seem much, Uncle Dave, but it is a calling, and I know where it is taking me."

"At this rate, will you ever get there?"

"I'll get there."

"Does it lead to a real job."

"Uncle Dave, this job is real."

"So you keep telling me. As real as rain."

"Rain may be cold ..."

"And miserable."

"But there is no harvest without rain."

"I have heard that many times too."

"So, why do you keep telling me about a real job?"

"You are not a comedian, Kasim," Mr Dave said. "What comic tries to annoy the patrons and the only club that will hire him?"

"*Club Bombay* loves me too."

"So much they are hiring thugs to assassinate you?"

"For real?"

"On stage to improve attendance," said Mr Dave.

"Clever idea," said Kasim. "Let us do it here instead. Make sure the thugs fail, and then ..."

"That will not work here, Kasim," Mr Dave said, with a tired smile. "You forget who comes here regularly. Just go find another job, okay?"

"Are you firing me?"

"When was the last time you stepped in the office?"

"Before I went on stage."

"Your office, the assistant manager's office?"

"That one?" he shook his head. "You know I am allergic to offices, Uncle Dave. In my last office, I had people shooting through my windows."

"In the middle of cattle wars," said Mr Dave. "You are in the city now, Kasim, no one shoots through nightclub windows unless they are crazy."

That was no comfort. Even Mr Dave knew there were enough guns and enough crazy people in the city to start a cattle war with no cattle involved. But that was not the point. Kasim got panic attacks, the constant urge to duck under the desk when someone coughed outside the office window.

"Paranoia," said Mr Dave. "You need help for that too. You can't go on like this."

"Are you firing me?"

"I fired you months ago, Kasim. I don't understand how you are still here."

"You keep paying me."

"You keep getting on stage," said Mr Dave. "And I can't find another comedian in this town who animates the audience the way you do."

"You are auditioning my job?" Kasim was flabbergasted, "Uncle Dave?"

"Don't start, Kasim," Mr Dave said wearily. "Okay, I didn't mean to tell you, but last week I auditioned a dozen hopefuls."

"For my job?"

"And, you know what? One would-be comedy king confessed he was not a comedian at all, but a male stripper and international gigolo with connections in Europe, America, and India. An all-round hustler, pimp, entertainer, and, above all, businessman. His biggest talent was getting working girls and boys to do whatever his clients demanded of them. He offered to reinvent *Uncle Dave's Curry And Comedy House* as a male and female strip club with live shows on stage and private ones in luxury tents at the back."

"Uncle Dave," Kasim said, "I love this club as it is, even with its boring audiences that do not know when or how to laugh. Sometimes I wish we had a sign over the stage that said - *now laugh!*"

"That is a silly idea."

Kasim thought about it.

"You are right, Uncle Dave," he said. "They have so many problems now they forget how to laugh. I wonder where they buried the corona billions. They did not spend it all here at the club, did they?"

"Bill's billions?" Mr Dave said, with a wry smile. "You must stop saying such things, Kasim. They might think you are serious."

"But I am, Uncle Dave."

"It is not funny."

"Not anymore," agreed Kasim.

Instead of sleeping the sleep of the rich, the new billionaires spent nights hunting for places to hide their billions. Having stuffed the sofas, the mattresses, and the pillows, and filled up the holes under the beds there was still so much of it left to hide that some of them gave up. They demanded a change in law to permit them to keep, and legally bank, their loot.

"Do you know how much money is a billion?" Kasim said. "The big, fat, corrupt ones wrestle that demon every night after they leave here. They carry the numbers everywhere they go; try to fit them all in their heads. You can be happy you don't lie awake night after night fearing uncle Gove will realise what you have done and come take it all away. I tell you, life with stollen billions is not funny."

"But you laugh at it every night."

"I don't know what else to do or think anymore."

Mr Dave patted him on the back.

"You will think something," he said. "But not tonight. Go home and sleep."

"I don't sleep anymore."

"I forget," Mr Dave started away. "You stay up to watch the world go to hell. Go have a good watch."

"See you tonight," Kasim called after him.

"Tonight, is Monday," Mr Dave opened his car door.

"Tomorrow night? The day after? Next week? Next year? You can't stop me, you know."

"I know, Kasim, I know."

"I was born to make people laugh!"

"So, you say."

227

Kasim crawled back inside his Beetle and curled up in the driver's seat. An hour later, the phone rang. It was Salim.

"Have you found a hearse?" he asked.

"You have to stop waking me so early, Salim," Kasim said. "I work nights."

"The Mercedes?"

"They were all round me a moment ago. The last one just left. What can I do for you?"

Salim was quiet, trying to understand him. Then he remembered there was no way of understanding Kasim.

"Be here on time," he said and hung up.

Kasim stepped out of the car, stretched, and yawned. The watchmen were over by the gate.

"*Ero*," he called.

They glanced his way, continued talking.

"Give us a push," he said to them.

They took their time finishing their cigarettes and walking over.

Chapter 25

The mechanics first instinct was to remove the engine, replace the piston rings, gaskets, clutch plate, starter motor and anything else they could think of. That would stop the dark smoke and the loss of power, and fix the aches and pains and whatever else was wrong with the Beetle. But first they wanted a down payment, a little advance, for they had not eaten all day and they were starving.

Kasim explained that all the Beetle needed was a carburetor, fuel system service, and respect from mechanics. But they could not do all that on empty stomachs, they said and started walking away. He called them back, offered to advance them a joke, and pay with money later. Then, without waiting for consensus, he told them of an ox team that died from hunger because it refused to be hitched up to fetch feed on an empty stomach. The mechanics did not find that joke funny. They needed food not laughter. Kasim suggested they start on empty stomachs and wait for Salim to wake up.

Salim had slept from his office to *Kajicho's International Garage*. He was still asleep in the passenger seat as the mechanics made their demand. When they saw him in the car, mouth open and snoring, they got started on the Beetle. Salim was an upright man, they said. Kasim left them at it and went to explore the yard. Moments later he was back waking Salim.

"I have an idea," he said, leaning in at the window.

"Keep it," said Salim.

"It could solve your problem."

"I have no problem."

"All right then," he went away.

Salim sighed and closed his eyes. After a moment, he opened them, stepped out of the car. He followed Kasim to the only tree in the yard, an old acacia, gnarled, almost leafless and about to die. Under the tree was an old Mercedes under repair. The owner was inside reading a newspaper. He looked up when Salim joined Kasim walking round the car inspecting it.

"What do you think?" Kasim asked.

"How?" Salim asked.

"Use your imagination, man."

"Aunt Eva will never go for it."

"It is a Mercedes."

"And it is mine," said the man with the paper.

"Would you rent it out?"

"Do I look like a taxi driver?" he said to them. "*Potea!* Get lost."

They did as ordered and went exploring the yard looking for other possibilities. Their Beetle was ready when they got back half an hour later. The head mechanics gave Kasim the bill but kept the car keys. Kasim laughed when he saw the itemised costs.

"Plugs, point, condenser and … look at this bill," he tried handing it to Salim.

Salim declined to take it. He had no money and did not have to explain himself to the mechanics. They knew it was now Kasim's car. Kajicho, the head *jua kali,* who had taken care of the Beetle for Salim knew it was no longer Salim's problem and had stopped dealing with Kasim.

"The car drove here," Kasim said to the mechanics. "You did not have to do all that work. I could have done it myself."

The mechanics were not impressed. He owed the garage money for repair works dating back months. The mechanics wanted it all and they wanted it now.

"Sadly, I have no cash today," Kasim said. "But I can pay you with jokes."

They went wild, swore they would undo their repair work. They would drop the engine, break it apart, see how he put it together. Then they would torch his car and lynch him. Then, and only then, would they accept payment in jokes.

"You can't burn my car," Kasim said, still smiling. "You would all be hanged."

They armed themselves with spanners and monkey wrenches, to prove they were serious, and sent one of them with a jerrycan to fetch petrol for torching the Beetle. Kasim pulled a machete from under the driver's seat and dared them to torch his car.

It was about to escalate. Then Kajicho called for patience. Arson and murder would not fill any empty stomachs, but would attract attention to their place of work. As they all knew, policemen sniffing about a *jua kali* garage always ended badly for mechanics and garage owners. He suggested they detain the car, until Kasim came back with the payment.

They were about to agree to that simple solution, then Salim objected. He had a lunch date and an appointment at his office, and the Beetle was his only transport for today. Kajicho had to step in again and negotiated a different deal for him. Salim would pay them ten percent over the bill in two weeks-time if they let him take the car.

"Starve now, eat more later?" Kasim said to them.

They handed the car keys to Salim, and he gave the keys to Kasim. They quarreled all the way to the Panafric. The hotel parking was full when Kasim drove up.

"She is already here," he said pointing.

The Mercedes was ten times bigger than Salim's.

"You never told me she was loaded," Kasim said.

"I don't tell you everything," Salim got out. "I will call if I need you."

He hurried up the steps and Kasim drove off. Valley Road was jammed solid, a river of stalled traffic running from city center and along Ngong Road to the hills. Town bound bus and *matatu* drivers watched helplessly as angry passengers got out and walked. Kasim changed his mind about going down to River Road and joined the out-of-town traffic crawling up Valley Road.

He was past the City Mortuary heading up Ngong Road when a new signboard by the roadside caught his eye. He doubled back along the service road, and drove into the *Used Cars and Hearses* display yard. Inside the yard was another sign advertising quality and affordable caskets. He drove past the place every day, to and from work, and it was the first time he saw it.

"I thought you sold cars," he said to the salesman. "What is this about caskets and hearses?"

"Two businesses, same family, same money," said the man. "Car business went down, moved to the back. Death business went up, moved in front. What may I sell you?"

Kasim, for once outpaced, was speechless.

"Anything funeral?" the man said. "Hearses, coffins, wreaths, tents, chairs, mourners, eulogies, you name it, we sell it. Or lease it if you prefer. What is your desire?"

"A Mercedes," Kasim said.

"That would be at the back," said the man. "But they don't sell European cars."

"A Mercedes hearse?"

"This way, please," said the man.

"I said a Mercedes hearse," said Kasim.

"And I said this way please."

Moments later Kasim was urgently trying to get Salim on the phone. He tried several times, getting the same message. Not available, try again later. He was back in the Beetle resting his eyes when Salim called back an hour later.

"You will not believe what I found," Kasim said. "Yes, I am looking at it right now. No, it is not going anywhere, it is ours, but there is a slight problem. It is in great demand. We need to pay now or someone else may get it. Now, as in the next two hours. Tomorrow?"

He turned to the manager.

"Deposit," said the manager.

"They have to have a deposit," Kasim said.

He turned to the manager.

"How much is the deposit?"

"Where do you want to go?"

"Kathiani."

"Near Machakos?"

The man scribbled on his clipboard.

"When?" he asked.

"When do we need it?" Kasim asked Salim.

There was deep silence. Kasim waited for so long the manager pushed his clipboard aside.

"Don't worry, happens all the time," he said, whipping out a calculator. He worked it out and showed it to Kasim.

"For now," he said. "Final cost when you know burial date. Deposit will be ten percent."

"Where do you people think money comes from?" Kasim asked him.

"The bank."

"I'm not a bank robber."

"Petrol is extra," the man said. "Look, the vehicle came in yesterday from Germany. Yours will be the first body to ride in it if you book for tomorrow."

"Salim," Kasim said to him. "They want too much. Call Aunt Eva."

Aunt Eva was on a break from the clan. She had taken Roger to Maasai Mara to show him how real crocodiles handled real wildebeests.

"Kasim," Salim said. "Seriously now, and just between the two of us, are you sure you have absolutely no money stashed away under a rock somewhere?"

"Not a cent."

"What really happened to the Lodwar payroll?"

"Like I told you, as I told the police, the naked man took the money. And the police stole the diamonds."

"Honestly?"

"Ask them."

Salim hung up. The manager watched Kasim suspiciously.

"Long ago," Kasim said to him. "Another world."

The man shrugged. He had to go for lunch. Kasim called Salim again.

"Wait," Salim sounded irritated. "I'm thinking."

"The man wants to go for lunch," said Kasim.

"He can go, but don't let the hearse out of your sight."

Salim was back in his office, gazing out of the window at the distant chimney stacks spewing smoke and cement dust at Athi River cement factories. He rose, walked to the window, and looked down at the busy city street full of people going about their businesses. People who were also likely as overwhelmed, and trapped in existences that demanded challenging decisions.

He paced the office talking to himself, counting his problems on his fingers, and blaming them all on the state of the economy, on the president, on the people who, according to Kasim who knew such things, started it all with a hoax and a plot to impoverish, subjugate and take over control of the world and of mankind. People who sought to benefit from the misery of people like himself.

He knew blaming corona or mosquitos was one thing, and doing something about it was another. One had to decide whether to wait for divine intervention, or bury his dead, deal with the living, and face the consequences. Death waited for no man. Life could not go on endlessly without change in momentum, direction, or purpose.

"Wednesday, Thursday, Friday, then ..." He thought out aloud. "Gigiri and Karen, then ... two weeks before that comes due, there is ..."

He picked up the office phone.

"Catherine?" he called. "Would you bring me the Clients' Accounts file, please? The cheque book too."

He hung up, picked up his phone.

"Kasim, pick me up from my office now."

He opened the safe and took out a bundle of money. He counted it out aloud.

"Not enough," he said to himself.

He tossed it back inside, locked the safe. His Secretary walked in, dropped the clients' file on his desk and started to withdraw.

"One moment, Catherine."

She stopped, turned, and waited, hand on door handle. She saw him reopen the safe, take out the bundle of money and start to count.

"Mister King'oo, you are not," she said horrified.

"Yes, Mrs Kilonzo, I am borrowing from Clients' Accounts?"

"That is so wrong," she said.

"Do you want to pay your rent?"

He held out the money. She hesitated.

"We could go to prison for this."

"Not you, I could go to prison. Do you want to pay your rent or not?"

She took the money.

"Now," he said, picking up the cheque book. "Go down to the bank and withdraw this for me."

She nearly fainted when she saw the amount.

"No questions," he warned.

She was back with the money before Kasim arrived. An hour later they were at the *Used Cars and Hearses* yard.

"We are here to book my Mercedes hearse."

The Mercedes Hearse was gone.

"Why?" was all Kasim could think of asking.

"I told you it was in great demand," the manager said to them.

Someone had come in, shortly after Kasim left, and booked it.

"That hearse is mine," Kasim said. "I saw it first."

"They paid first."

Salim jumped in to explain they had to have the Mercedes. They needed it for Friday, but he would pay for the days until then to secure the booking.

"That is difficult," said the manager. "What do I tell them?"

"Easy," Kasim said to him. "Park it inside one of the garages I saw at the back, tell them it went for major service, and offer them the Volvo at a reduced rate."

The salesman was tempted. He checked the booking records.

"Come back early tomorrow morning," he said. "I will see what I can do."

Salim did not sleep much that night. Between the excitement of having found Aunt Charity's hearse, and the dread of what could follow when the clients' money he had borrowed became due, he tossed and turned all night long. Then Kasim was late picking him up, they got stuck in morning traffic and they did not get to *Used Cars and Hearses* yard until half past nine.

Aunt Charity's Mercedes hearse was gone.

"How?" Kasim yelled.

"We agreed first thing in the morning," the manager said. "It is now nearly ten. The vehicle must be halfway to Naivasha by now."

It was transporting a body to Kampala. But not to worry, it was due back the following day.

Salim glanced at his watch.

"Let's go," he said to Kasim, and dashed out of the office.

He was behind the wheel, with the engine running, when Kasim caught up. He made a gravel-spitting turn out of the gate and out of the yard and sped up Ngong Road. Kasim restrained his curiosity until they turned off Gong Road and were on the way to Nakuru.

"So, where are we going?" he asked.

"I stole clients' money," said Salim. "I will not go to prison for nothing."

"This is a getaway? Let me out here, please."

"You are coming with me," Salim said. "It is your fault we were late."

The Beetle flew along Limuru Road, through the mist and fog, to Kijabe and the treacherous escarpment road.

"Remember I am innocent when we get caught."

"Keep quiet, I must concentrate."

He hung on to the wheel hardly breathing, and Kasim hung onto his seat, as the car took the bends at a pace it was not used to in the city. The slightest mistake, one turn of the wheel too far left, would send them plummeting to the bottom of the escarpment. The tension in the car was unbearable.

"How far do you intend to run," Kasim tried to break the tension.

Salim's whole being was concentrated on guiding the Beetle down the winding road. Heavy trailers driving in the opposite direction flashed warning lights at the Beetle, as it leap-frogged slow-moving container haulers at hair-raising speed. They were almost at the bottom of the escarpment when the fog lifted.

"There," Salim said pointing. "There is where we are going."

Through the gaps in the traffic, they saw the town of Maai Mahiu way down basking in the Rift Valley sun. A black hearse was speeding through towards Naivasha.

They caught up with it on a bumpy stretch a mile past Maai Mahiu, moving carefully trying to dodge the potholes. Salim overtook and flagged it down.

"You drive like a maniac," Kasim said, waiting for the hearse to stop.

"Thank you," said Salim.

They walked back to the stopped hearse.

"What now?" asked Kasim.

"Now Aunt Charity gets her wish," Salim said.

The hearse driver and his loader were waiting outside the vehicle.

"You drove," Kasim said. "I will handle this."

"Don't screw it up."

"*Jambo*, Onyango," Kasim said to one of the men.

"Kamau," the man said.

"You are not Onyango the driver?"

"Kamau," said the man.

Kasim turned to the other man.

"Then you are Onyango the driver."

"Mogaka."

"The office gave your names as ..." Kasim searched his pockets. "Where did I put that note?"

He turned to Salim. Salim left it to him. He stopped and offered handshakes instead.

"My name is Kasim. Kasim the Komedian. You have heard of me I am sure. The greatest comic in town. No? Let me tell you a joke and you decide. A Catholic pastor died in a bus crash and ..."

"Priest," said the loader.

"All right, a priest," said Kasim.

"He was Catholic, so priest, not pastor."

"I got it," said Kasim. "You would think they went to the same place when they died, wouldn't you?"

"Some go to limbo."

"And some go to hell too," said Kasim. "Do you want to hear the joke or not?"

The man was about to say something else, but the driver gestured him to wait.

"Finding a lengthy line at the door," Kasim said, "The priest used his good name, and that of his bishop, to sneak in through a side entrance reserved for saints and angels, and repentant politicians. A security guard who had last seen him at the back of the line with other favour-seekers asked him how he got in so fast.

"By bus," said the priest.

The hearse driver, his loader and Salim, missed the joke. Kasim laughed anyway, and admitted it was too cerebral for tired minds. He often had to explain the word *cerebral* at the *Hard Life Club*, but not here. The driver was impatient to know why they stopped him.

"This hearse is booked to go to Mombasa," Salim said to him. "To bury the minister who died in the helicopter crash."

"Crash?"

"Minister for …."

"Roads?"

"That one," Kasim took over.

"It can't be," said the driver. "The court stopped his burial until they decide which wife will bury him."

"The former minister then," Kasim tried.

But that one was from the loader's home village, and he had seen him on television the day before handing out mosquito net masks.

"The thing is," Salim said, to stop wasting time, "this vehicle must return to Nairobi right away."

The driver took out his phone and, before they could stop him, hit the speed dial. He listened. They waited. He listened and they waited. It took him several attempts to realise they were in a network dead zone. They were too close to the escarpment for telephone networks to find them. They waited for the driver to decide what to do.

"What about the Ugandan?" he asked them.

"There are pickups at Maai Mahiu," Salim said, removing a bundle of cash from his pocket, making sure they saw it.

"Your boss said to give you this," he started counting. "How much will it cost?"

They looked at the money in his hands, at one another and back at Maai Mahiu a mile away.

"I will give you a lift back for the pickup," said Salim.

The loader took the driver aside. The wind was blowing towards Kasim, and Salim and the hearse crew's whispered exchange turned out to be not so private.

"*Omwami*," they heard him say. "That is a lot of money."

The driver scratched his chin thoughtfully.

"*Omwami*," he said. "What if we get caught?"

"How?" the loader asked.

Driver scratched his head and thought harder.

"My daughters could go back to school," he said.

They thought about it for a moment longer. Meanwhile, cars, buses, and trucks zooming by oblivious to potholes had Salim fearing one would lose control and plow into them.

"What do we tell the Ugandans?" the loader asked the driver.

"We tell them the hearse broke down on the escarpment. We left it to follow us after the repairs. They must be past Naivasha by now."

Having heard enough, Kasim turned to Salim.

"What if Caesar's funeral is not on Friday?"

"One problem at a time."

They approached the hearse crew.

"What do you say?" asked Salim.

"It is a long way to Kampala on a pickup."

"It is," Kasim agreed. "You will need money for petrol. And for food and accommodation. And a little extra for fun."

"Here, take it all," Salim handed the money to the driver. "Now take the Ugandan out and we'll go find him a pickup."

The driver counted the money, as the loader opened the door to roll the casket out.

"*Omwami*, wait," said the driver.

He was frowning down the road to Naivasha at a white vehicle charging up the road shimmering in the mirage.

"That looks like …" he started.

"Trouble?" Kasim asked him.

"Big trouble," he said to his loader. "Push it back, push it back and close the door."

The loader waited and watched the car approach until it was almost on top of them, then closed the door. Four hefty men in black suits pile out of the white car and came forward.

"What is the problem?" one asked.

"We had a flat tyre," the driver said. "They stopped to help."

Kasim took the bundle of money back from him and handed it to Salim.

"I think you should take over from here" he said walking back to the Beetle.

"So close," Salim heard the driver say to himself getting back behind the wheel. "*Omwami,* let us go."

The Ugandans watched intrigued as Salim followed Kasim to the Beetle and they drove off.

Through the rear view, Salim saw the loader hop in the hearse with one of the men in black.

Chapter 26

The committee was in dismay, the meeting despondent, when they heard how close Salim had come to securing them their hearse, the Mercedes one that everyone now wanted. Had he succeeded, it would have been a miracle come true, the ray of hope over turbulent King'oo sky that got darker by the day.

Uncle Sam was clearing his throat, and staring at his clipboard with nothing to say. Salim stared down at the floor, broken. He had cried out in despair when Kasim reported the *Used Cars and Hearses* manager had phoned to say their magic hearse, which he had booked and paid for, had broken down somewhere near Jinja and had to be brought back on a truck.

by disappointment. Everyone else tried not to put any more pressure on them by looking at any of them. Now there was a hush over the gathering. Then, Uncle Sam said what was in everyone's mind. Their train had derailed again.

"Again?" Roger shook his head confounded.

"Relax, Roger," Salim said to him. "King'oo trains derail many times before they go anywhere."

"No need to worry, Roger," Kasim whispered. "We are off the rails more often that we are on, but we get there."

Uncle Sam had a pained look on his face.

"We must rethink the Mercedes hearse," he said.

He was addressing the men's corner, to be on the safe side, but they too would not look him in the eye. Their opinion seemed to be to let the fool who first thought of it rethink it on her own.

Kasim was the only one who understood Aunt Charity would never rethink her promise to Caesar.

As a young school boy, Kasim carried messages between Aunt Charity and young Pastor Kioko. Often they had no envelopes, for Kasim was trusted not to read the letters, but he had read the one from Kioko promising to wait forever if Charity would promise to one day be his wife. Kasim had also read her reply telling him she could not promise such a thing, for then she would have to keep her word, and who knew about tomorrow? Now tomorrow was here, and no one had any idea what to do with it.

Those not with Aunt Charity in staring at their hands in their laps stared harshly back at Uncle Sam. He was the chairman, the leader of the clan for the duration of the funeral. It was his duty to make decisions and solve everyone's problem.

"Any suggestions then?" Uncle Sam turned to the clansmen.

He was facing the men's corner still. No guts to face the women's army, Uncle Tivo grumbled taking out his phone. Everyone ignored him when he started talking aloud into the phone. Only Roger seemed interested in the old man's angry phone calls.

"I gave him that old thing," Kasim whispered to him. "He used to bug me to use my phone."

"Who does he call?"

"Everyone from his long-dead army comrades to the President. When he is really upset, he phones God."

"He must run up quite a bill," said Roger

"The phone has no sim card," Kasim revealed.

Roger laughed out aloud, startling everyone. He coughed apologetically. Aunt Eva, looking from Roger to Uncle Tivo and Kasim, shook her head.

"Is he ever sober?" she asked aloud.

"Ask him," said Aunt Mutheu. "He is your uncle."

"He is your father," said Aunt Eva. "And I say he is always drunk."

"So was your father."

"My father was not disgusting."

"How would you know? You abandoned him and went off to America to find a husband."

"I did not abandon my father."

"Where were you, when he wandered in the market lost and we had to find him and bring him home on a wheelbarrow?"

"Ladies, please," Roger pleaded.

"You keep quiet, Roger," Aunt Eva ordered him.

"Speak, Roger," said Sam's wife. "In Caesar's house men speak."

Someone guffawed.

"Ladies, please," Roger tried again.

"Roger, shut up!" Aunt Eva barked

Roger joined the men in staring at the floor with his hands between his knees.

"You have your own husband," Aunt Eva said to the other woman. "Let him speak."

"Sam?" Aunt Wavinya called.

Sam was in his place, stealing furtive glances at the women's side.

"What?" he asked.

"Speak."

"Speak? What do you want me to say?"

"This is Mzee Mophat's house. Here men also speak."

"Roger," Aunt Eva said harshly, "are you just going to sit there and listen to them talk to me like that?"

Roger, as confused about the exchange as other men were, rose and walked out. The room held its breath. Aunt Eva was as startled as the rest of the aunts.

Salim was the next to rise.

"Where are you going?" she asked him.

"To drink water," he said, heading for the kitchen.

Kasim rose too. The aunts glared.

"Toilet," he said following Salim through the kitchen, out of the back door and round to the front. Roger was walking about the yard talking to himself when Salim caught up with him.

"Is it true you are a lawyer?" he asked.

"I don't do divorce," Salim said.

"Something is wrong with this whole scene," Roger said. "This is not what I expected."

"Relax, Roger," Kasim said to him. "This is how we do things here. After all the crisis and the chaos, and the ego trips, everyone defaults to King'oo. Take a seat and enjoy the ride."

"King'oo is normal," Salim took out a packet of cigarettes. "King'oo we can all live with. Cigarette?"

Roger hesitated, then he made up his mind and took one. They lit up.

"All will be well in the end, Roger," Salim told him.

Then Aunt Eva's voice sliced the evening air like a machete.

"Roger?"

She stood by the door, hands on hips.

"Yes, dear?" Roger said.

"You don't smoke," she said.

He gave back the cigarette and put his hands in his pockets. She shook her head and went back inside.

"She made me quit," he said, watching them light up.

"Not an entirely sad thing," said Salim.

"Your aunt is ..." words failed him.

"The giant battle-axe," Kasim said. "Welcome to the family."

"You know," he said, "you boys say that to me. Everyone else wants money."

"To tell you the truth, Roger, I too want money," Kasim said.

Roger smiled uncertainly. He had visited times before and every time was like the first. He had to negotiate a landmine of cultural mayhem with people he barely understood. They smiled, they laughed, hurled words like spears without restraint, then went back to laughing and being family. He could not tell when anyone was serious about what they said, and it worried him.

"Relax, Roger," Kasim said to him. "Salim and me know you don't have any money. Why else would you still be married to the battle-axe?"

Caesar's daughters have a reputation, Salim revealed. As kids they sang – *'Teacher, teacher have a question. What is big, what is beautiful, what is as last week's muthokoi?"*

"Answer," Kasim said, "Caesar's daughter! But it was granite not *muthokoi.*"

"*Muthokoi,*" said Salim. "You didn't know granite then. *Muthokoi* was the hardest thing we knew. We got a lot of beatings over that song."

Kasim turned to Roger, and explained why Eva married him. King'oo women could not stand King'oo men, so they married outsiders or swore off men altogether and joined convents. Growing up with King'oo boys made it an easy choice. Likewise, King'oo men sought out women who never heard of them.

One King'oo woman had married a Chinese man who, tired of eating King'oo *muthokoi,* and unable to teach her to cook Chinese *muthokoi* fled back to China. One of Caesar's daughters was married to an American man and the others were married to men of unclear origins and dubious occupations.

Several foreign husbands had died of suspect causes, indigestion, and despair among them, while others had quietly divorced the clan and absconded without a fuss. Those who stuck it out got domesticated and adopted King'oo code of never finding any situation too bad to make worse.

Roger nodded, uncertain where he stood in all that. Seeing the confusion on his face, Kasim slapped him on the shoulder and laughed.

"It is all right, Roger," he said. "You will survive. Salim and me will see to it that you do. Salim?"

Salim was preoccupied, thinking of the hearse he had so recklessly promised Aunt Charity.

"I have an idea," Kasim said to him. "I will tell you what it is and, you don't have to say a word, just think about it until tomorrow then …"

"I can't think anymore," Salim said.

"You are not alone."

"Why can't King'oo be sane and uncomplicated like other people?"

Other clans would have had sheep mowing grass on Caesar's grave by now.

Chapter 27

The years of caring for everyone, and her father, had left her with the serene appearance of a grey-haired sage, one who listened a lot and said little, spoke only when necessary, and only that which was true and essential. When she suddenly broke down and wept, there was a panic. Some wanted to run away and hide. Others wanted to wail and rend their clothes in grief, but most agonized, for they did not know what to do or feel.

It was so overwhelming. No one dared wrap arms round her and tell her all would be well. How could it be? How could anything ever be well again when Caesar was dead? Only Caesar could make it all well, make everything right again, but Caesar was dead. And she had promised him a golden chariot.

A group of old men and women went aside to see what they could do about it. They respected Charity for remaining by Caesar's side until he died, for watching over Caesar while he faded away and eventually died. They had to do something for her. But, after beating their brains for a bit, they concluded there was no way round a Mercedes hearse that was not there.

They chose several of the kindest, most compassionate of her friends, they who understood what it meant to give a promise to a dying parent and be unable to keep it. Some of them had made similar promises, only to realise later they could not fulfil their promises. Some had promised to bury their relatives on their ancestral land, only to realise later that the land belonged to another family. Some had promised never to leave their King'oo husbands, a promise no King'oo woman should ever give to a dying parent and were still living the nightmare. They had promised all manner of things, but no one ever had done anything as reckless as Charity had. And yet they all agreed, aside from the men, that it was the easiest promise to keep. All that was needed was money, and a Mercedes.

They returned to the meeting and admitted failure to find a resolution. Aunt Eva tried convincing Aunt Charity the clan would understand if she did not keep a foolish promise made by a foolish child at the height of innocence. Even Caesar would understand.

When it was the old men's turn, none of them had anything to say. Most had no idea what a Mercedes hearse looked like, having never seen one, but some were seduced by the thought of a daughter promising her father something so large it would take a whole clan to make it happen. They were heard to mutter that a daughter like her was worth a dozen King'oo sons.

When it was Kasim's turn, his suggestion, like most of his ideas was facile, and most thought as foolish as any he ever had.

"Borrow Uncle Richard's Mercedes," he suggested. "Secure the casket to the roof of the car and bring it home."

The all looked at one another, not certain what that meant, and Salim waited for Hurricane Eva to break a stool on Kasim's head. Kasim was ready to duck. All eyes were on her. Aunt Eva was silent for a full moment considering it. Then, calmly, she turned to Aunt Charity.

"Would that do?" she asked her.

Aunt Charity stared in space. Eva turned to Uncle Sam. Uncle Sam busied himself with his papers, and everyone else tried to look insignificant.

"Any more suggestions?" she asked them.

No one else had a suggestion. That was normal for such an occasion. She knew if she gave them time to come up with a different proposal, she would be in Kathiani till Christmas.

"It is a Mercedes," she said to them.

No one said a word. She would have to decide on her own. Kasim's proposal, as daft as it sounded, was all they had and, if adopted, it would fulfil the spirit of Aunt

Charity's promise to Caesar without leaving everyone financially broken and destitute.

They saw her reach for her phone to call Uncle Richard, the only person who could scuttle that plan. Salim politely suggested she do so outside, away from their hearing, but then, again, that was not the King'oo woman's way.

"*Kwani*, you think I fear him?" she said to Salim. "Is he God?"

She would do it right there with everyone watching and listening so they may learn something. She searched in her bag for the phone, so deliberately slowly that Salim hoped she was having second thoughts. Then she found it, smiled to show she was not afraid and speed-dialled Uncle Richard's number.

It was on speaker, and they all heard it ring and ring. While waiting for it to be picked up, she glared round the room, at the cowards who thought she dared not call the ogre that had made them wash their feet before crossing his threshold.

"Is he God?" she asked them.

Uncle Tivo laughed, the sad laugh of a man witnessing a woman make a fool of herself and everyone else. She scowled at him, but he was past the age when a woman's anger could move him. He had seen them grow up, go their diverse ways, and come back home pregnant and more rebellious, and harder to tame than a herd of scorpions.

"Is he God?" he laughed quietly. "Let him tell us."

The rest looked away from her to avoid being called upon to answer any question of that nature. All they knew about him was that Uncle Richard made them take off their shoes and wash their feet before entering his house. On that score alone, yes, maybe he was. Then Uncle Richard's voice boomed out so loud it was startling.

"What!" he said.

"Muya wa King'oo," Aunt Eva said calling him by the name in her class register. "Stop talking like you have a firebrand up your backside and tell me why you are not here."

It was suddenly quiet in the room. The unknown cousins sniffling in the dark corners to earn their dinner paused to see what would happen. All eyes were on Aunt Charity, waiting to see how she took it. Those expecting her to break down in tears, and those hoping for a long overdue clash between her and Aunt Eva, were disappointed. Aunt Charity did not flinch, or glance at her sister, that would have been sufficient, but she sat as still as a sculpture chiselled out of pain and suffering.

"I want you here this evening, without fail," Aunt Eva said to Uncle Richard.

"Where is here," they heard him ask.

"What do you mean where? When was the last time you visited your dying uncle?"

"He never told me he was dying."

"Next time he will tell you," she said. "His home is where you left it. I want you here, this evening. This evening. With your Mercedes not pickup."

She hung up and looked round, dared anyone to have an opinion. All eyes were away the second she snapped her phone shut. Salim was tempted to yell "I told you so!" but he dared not break the tension.

Only Uncle Tivo dared break the silence.

"So," he said, "does he come, or does he not come?"

"He will come," she said to everyone and no one. "He will come."

No one believed her. The rest looked away when she scanned their faces for contradiction. The danger with Eva was that no one was ever sure what she expected of them. They tried to make it look like it did not matter to them whether Uncle Richard came or not.

"He will come," she said again.

Still, no one believed it. She did not know Uncle Richard the way they did. They knew him from the tumultuous encounters they had with him; when they tried to borrow money for school fees, hospital bills, or for clan get-togethers to plan a united front against poverty. Their encounters with him, when they went to plead with his wife to persuade her husband to use his enormous wealth and influence to get jobs for their children, were terrifying. They did not know anyone who ever got a job, money, or anything from Uncle Richard.

They waited for Sam to get over his mauling and get the meeting back on track. Hopefully, they would figure how to survive the storm and navigate the issue of the Mercedes funeral before they died of Eva fatigue.

Aunt Eva could not know Richard as someone that anyone could turn to for anything. She remembered him as a barefoot boy who could not remove jiggers from his own feet, and how Caesar made her wash and debug him, and dig all those disgusting jiggers from his feet. For that alone, she was entitled to more than a lifetime of gratitude from him. He owed her a nephew's reverence and a son's devotion; the same things she expected from every pupil who ever passed through her classroom, as well as every parent whose child she taught to read and write. The way she saw it, she educated the whole of Kambaland not just the King'oo clan.

Still, she did not know Uncle Richard. He was a boy looking to go to University when she left for America. Then he had gone to one University, and then to another, and not just any University, not the dusty goat pens in every village and town in the country that they now called Universities. Uncle Richard had gone to Europe and to America and some said to China too and returned with many degrees and a wife who did not speak a word of Kamba and who made them take off their shoes and wash their feet, before stepping inside her house. Her house, not his house. Not their son's house, but her house. How many clans had a son like that?

"He will come," she said yet again.

She did not know Richard the way they did.

Chapter 28

Salim could not wait for Uncle Richard to fail to show up. The way Hurricane Eva operated, and the clan thought, the problem would end up with him whether he volunteered or not. Uncle Sam was drowning in the familiar King'oo failure to grasp the concept of fundraising, and Kasim was plotting his own path to greatness in comedian.

Salim got Kasim to drive him to Uncle Richard's house to make his desperate move, an insane, and potentially fatal, mistake that Salim suspected Aunt Eva had only approved to demonstrate her disdain for King'oo men and Salim.

Uncle Richard had ordered them never to go to his house uninvited, but he was not at the club, and Caesar was dead, so the order was redundant.

Salim tapped on the dashboard impatiently waiting for the security guard to make up his mind whether to let them in. The silence in the car, the aura of hopelessness they had brought with them from Kathiani, irritated him. He reached for the radio and found a gaping hole where the radio used to be.

"What happened to the radio?" he asked exasperated.

"Did you just notice?" Kasim said laughing. "The radio was ripped out months ago on River Road. The side mirrors too. I use stick-on mirrors now, Chinese invention, genius. I take them with me when I go on stage. I have ordered a stick-on radio with speakers I can carry in my coat pocket. Amazing what Chinese technology can come up with these days."

Salim was staring at him mouth open in disbelieve.

"Are you ever serious?" he asked

"You can listen to my phone," he said. "If it is noise that you need."

Salim pressed the car horn again.

I know I'll live to regret this," he said as they waited for the gate to open.

Kasim did not ask regret what. They had done so many regrettable things in the past few days there would be an awful lot more to regret, if they lived through Hurricane Eva. And much more if he let Salim confront Uncle Richard in the mood he was in.

"Just let me do the talking," he said.

The security guard finally came out, leaned in at the window.

"*Sema?*"

"Say what?" Kasim said. "You know us by now. Open the gate."

The guard stepped back startled, considered, and went back inside.

"See?" Kasim said. "It works already."

Then the guard returned looking worried and asked whether *mzee* was expecting them.

"We are here to see *mama* not *mzee*," said Kasim.

"Mama you can see," he said relieved. "No problem, you may enter."

What he did not tell them was that Uncle Richard was at the front yard by the garages in his pajamas and dressing gown washing his original German-made Mercedes while his driver stood watching.

"The man needs help," Kasim observed.

"The best help we can give Uncle Richard is to stay away from him" said Salim.

"Jambo," Kasim greeted the driver.

The driver decided not to know them. They had not believed it when he told them Uncle Richard washed his own car. In an attack of solidarity, after he saw them flee out of the golf club with his employer after them, the driver had told them how an over-zealous gardener who thought to show initiative by washing his bosses original German-made BMW had ended up on clutches.

"No jokes today, okay?" Salim warned.

"Leave it to me," said Kasim.

The dogs were barking from their kennel behind the garage. Emboldened, he raised his voice and called out.

"Uncle Richard," he said cheerfully, "we come to lend a hand."

He was about to pick up a duster. Uncle Richard turned and stubbed him with a terrifying look.

"Touch this car, and it will be the last car you ever touch," said Uncle Richard.

Kasim quickly dropped the duster and stepped back from the car.

"Good morning, Uncle Richard," Salim said, not to be a part of what just happened.

"What do you want?" Uncle Richard asked him.

Their relationship was different. No jokes, no fawning, no kinship, no business; nothing but cold encounters they often left unconcluded. Humans whose paths crossed from time to time for no good reason.

"Your sisters sent us again," said Salim.

"Did you tell them what I told you last time?"

"To grow up?" Kasim had to charge in. "We did but, Uncle Rich, you know how old they are. Old women can't grow up."

"So, why are you here?" Uncle Richard asked him.

Certain it would make no difference now, Salim let Kasim speak. Uncle Richard dropped his sponge in the special car shampoo he had sent for from Germany and listened to Kasim tell him about the night meetings, how many people turned up and how they all missed him and wished he were there too. He heard how most of them had no money to donate, or ended up eating more than they donated, so that in the end it would have been better if they did not come at all. All of it was stuff Uncle Richard had heard before.

Then Kasim told him how hard everyone tried to persuade Aunt Charity to forget her promise to her dad and accept Uncle Richard's generously offered pick up, which under the circumstances even Mzee Mophat would understand. But, failing to make her change her mind, the clan had decided to plead with Uncle Richard, their most prominent clansman, to lend them his Mercedes for one day so they could all help keep Aunt Charity's promise to her father.

When Kasim finished his speech, delivered with the solemnity of a badly staged tragedy, Uncle Richard, dropped the duster, picked up the towel, and dried his hands.

"And how do you propose to transport a corpse in my Mercedes?" he asked, fetching his car keys from the ignition.

"Passenger seat," Kasim said. "Like he used to sit when he was in government."

Uncle Richard unlocked the trunk. He lifted the lid, leaving the keys dangling from the lock. He reached inside for his golf bag, leaned it on the rear bumper, still speaking calmly asked which of the two fools standing in front of him came up with the brilliant idea of using his Mercedes as a hearse.

"The two of you, or just yourself?" he asked Kasim.

"Both of us," said Kasim.

"Just you," said Salim.

"With your support," said Kasim.

Salim suddenly realised he had been right about having to live to regret coming.

Uncle Richard reached out for the biggest club in the bag. He weighed it in his hands, put it back and picked a heavier one. Salim turned and ran.

From his place at the gate, the security guard saw the visitors scramble into their car with his employer after them wielding a golf club. Salim frantically turned the ignition, as Uncle Richard approached weighing the golf club.

"Lock the door!" he yelled. "Lock the door!"

They locked the doors, wound up the windows. He was struggling to get the engine started when Uncle

Richard's club exploded on the roof of the Beetle, and it all stopped being funny to Kasim.

"Not the car," Kasim yelled. "Not my car."

Uncle Richard hammered the roof once more, realised it hurt the club more than the car, and went after the headlights.

"Drive," Kasim screamed at Salim. "Drive."

Uncle Richard took a swing at the windscreen and missed, as the engine suddenly came to life and the Beetle shot away in reverse. He followed, whacking it again, and again, as it sped towards the closed gate. Kasim watching scared, saw the gate come at them fast, while the guard stood mesmerised. He rolled down the window, stuck his head out and yelled.

"Open the gate! Open the gate!"

Salim braked hard and the Beetle screeched to a stop a meter short of smashing into the closed gate. Kasim jumped out and run to open the gate. The guard took a swing at him with his club. They tussled, fought for the club. Kasim wrestled it from the guard and hurled into the bushes. The guard ran for his club. Kasim threw the gate open, jumped back in the Beetle and it sped out of the gate.

"Uncle Rich needs help," he said when they were safely away and back on Riverside Drive. "He is a lunatic."

Salim was still shaken, and he did not say a word all the way to Kathiani.

Aunt Eva was at the front door with Aunt Nyiva when the Beetle rattled back with a smashed windshield and broken headlights. Kasim dodged them by going round to the kitchen to look for food and Salim tried to force his way in the front door.

"What happened?" Aunt Eva asked barring his way.

"You know what happened," he said to her.

"Uncle Richard? Why?"

"I told you it would not work."

He stepped round her into the house. The house was still in mourning. No surprise as Caesar was still above ground and no idea when he would be under it. Auntie Charity sat by herself on a sofa, looking inconsolable. Her women seemed to have given up and gone to find something real to worry about. Sam was somewhere recovering from the strain of trying to push another King'oo train out of a King'oo station.

Salim sat down next to Aunt Charity.

"As you know, Aunt Charity," Salim said, taking her hand, "your brother is a madman."

"I told you," said Uncle Tivo.

"We all knew that," Aunt Eva said, stepping inside. "What did he say?"

Kasim came through the kitchen door chewing on something and sat next to Roger and the only person who was not distraught. Kasim wondered out loud if anyone had reminded Tivo why they were there.

"What did Richard say?" Aunt Eva remained at the door waiting for answers.

Salim and Kasim exchange glances. Salim turned to Aunt Eva, paused to frame his answer the safest he could.

"Kasim told him what you wanted to do with his Mercedes," he said. "You have seen what he did to Salim's. That is what would have happened to us had we been outside the car."

Kasim suddenly rose.

"I go drink some water."

"Sit down!" Aunt Eva said. "What did your uncle say?"

"Not even a bugger off," he said.

Aunt Eva waited.

"He just went for Salim's car and beat the crap out of it."

"Your car," Salim corrected.

"Who has the title?"

"Still your car," said Salim. "And you still owe for it."

"Beat the car how?" Aunt Eva wanted to know.

"With a golf club," said Salim.

Kasim sat down. Uncle Tivo patted him reassuringly.

"I told you there were no men in King'oo house," Aunt Eva said to Aunt Charity. "Now we'll have to use the pickup you rejected."

Salim felt Aunt Charity wince and swallow back a sob. The cruelty of King'oo women was confounding. He laid a hand on her shoulder and spoke to her gently.

"Don't worry, Aunt Charity," he said. "I will get you what you want."

"From where?" asked Aunt Eva.

"What does it matter? I will get her a hearse."

"A Mercedes as promised," said Kasim.

"I will believe it, when I see it," Aunt Eva said.

Kasim rose and went to the kitchen. Aunt Charity, lightening up a little, placed her hand on Salim's shoulder, patting it. He took her hand, pressed it in his. He did not know what else to say. He rose and followed Kasim through the kitchen to the back of the house. Kasim was on the back porch, sitting on the step with a plate of *muthokoi*. He looked up when Salim sat next to him.

"You know what you have done?" he said. "You have promised a sick and grieving woman the moon."

"Not I," said Salim. "We have five days to do it, so stop eating and let's get going."

"May I come with you, gentlemen?"

They turned to find Roger standing behind them.

"I have cleared it with the old battle-axe," he said. "Or rather she has ordered me to keep an eye on you boys."

"Spy on us?"

"I don't know exactly what I am expected to do," he said, "But I have to come along."

"Did she give you gas money?" Kasim asked.

"I have my own money," he said.

"Why didn't you say so?" Kasim set the plate aside. "Of course, you come with us from now on. Give us tips on how you do it in America."

Two hours later they were stuck in city traffic asking each other where they were going.

"In America," Roger said, to break the tension, "we would stuff the old guy in an oven and scatter his ashes over the nearest corn field."

Kasim turned to him. He was folded in the passenger seat looking pitiably uncomfortable.

"You have to come up with more useful ideas than that, Roger."

The Beetle turned off Parklands Road, down a potholed lane, and into a compound with an old colonial building tucked under ancient jacaranda and flame trees. The Jacaranda was in bloom and the gravel parking speckled with purple petals. A small board by the entrance said it was the Rotary Club met there every Wednesday night.

There were several big cars in the parking. As Roger uncoiled himself from the back seat, an Asian man came out of the building and headed for the parking. Salim intercept him before he got to his car.

"Mister D'Souza," he said, "I was coming to see you."

"Salim," said the man. "You should have called. I have a meeting in town in a few minutes."

"Just came by to introduce Roger," said Salim, as Roger extracted himself from the Beetle and stretched, towering over them.

"Roger Culpepper," he offered his hand.

"Roger is my … what are you, Roger?" Salim asked.

"Married to your aunt. What does that make me?"

"Related," said Kasim.

"I thought so," Roger laughed.

"My cousin, Kasim, you know?" Salim said.

"The comedian?" said Mr D'Souza.

"The very same," said Kasim. "You have heard me at *Club Bombay.*"

"Once," said Mr D'Souza.

"The grey beards there don't get me at all," Kasim said. "You don't think I am unfunny, do you?"

"The jokes about Indian shopkeepers, those are very not funny."

"I have funnier ones," said Kasim. "Would you like to hear the one about a Kikuyu who hanged himself with a *kamba* and blamed it on a Kamba?"

"No thanks," said Mr D'Souza.

"What about how many Maasai *morani* it takes to castrate a cow?"

"Not today, thank you," Mr D'Souza turned to Salim. "What can I do for you, gentlemen?"

"Roger is from America," Salim said. "He has never been to Africa before, and I'd like to show him around Nairobi on Friday. But, as you know, this city is full of potholes and, as you see, he is a big man, too tall for my limousine. So, I was just thinking …"

"You'd like to borrow mine. When?"

"Friday?"

"You can have the Volvo. Friday only."

"I was thinking more like …"

"My Mercedes? Even my wife does not drive my Mercedes. Only Maria is allowed that."

"It's a mighty fine car," said Roger.

D'Souza looked from one to the other.

"Haven't you got an important date on Friday?"

"Maria's exhibition," said Salim.

"He is dating my daughter," Mr D'Souza said to Roger. "I am looking forward to meeting my in-laws, but he is not so keen."

"I am very keen, sir, but the timing …"

"I understand," said Mr D'Souza. "Funerals can't wait."

"I will come pick her up, when I'm finished with Roger," Salim said.

"Six o'clock sharp?"

"On the dot."

Mr D'Souza got in his Mercedes, started the engine, and turned to Kasim.

"Mosquito suits?" he said flabbergasted.

"Coming soon to a shop near you."

"Really? Where do you get such absurdity?"

"Reading."

"Reading what? I read a lot, and so does Salim, and I have not heard of such a thing. Have you heard, Salim?"

"All the time from him."

Mr D'Souza shook his head, reversed, and was about to drive off.

"Mr D'Souza, sir," Kasim stepped up to the car window. "Is this a real club?"

"It is," said Mr D'Souza.

"Do they do standup?"

"Stand up how?"

"Comedy?"

"Not that kind of a club," said Mr D'Souza.

Kasim stepped back and they watched him drive away.

"Salim," Roger said, watching the car drive out. "You are good. Real smooth. I'm impressed."

"My idea," Kasim reminded them.

"But are you really going to take that nice gentleman to meet the rest of you? Really?"

"No choice," said Salim. "But that is for later. Now we must think how to fit a casket in his Mercedes without scratching Mr D'Souza's car."

"Start thinking," Kasim said to Roger.

Roger crawled in through the passenger door to the back seat, where not much thinking was possible, and sat crouched down, his head touching the roof of the Beetle. Salim was in the driver's seat. Soon they were battling the midday traffic on Uhuru Highway.

"Boys, I'm very impressed," Roger could not get over it. "Very impressed. You are the most wicked boys I have ever met. If I had sons …"

"Eva would turn them to girls," said Kasim.

There was an uncomfortable silence.

"No offence, Uncle Roger," Kasim plowed on, "but, if you had sons, I think she would eat them alive."

Salim turned to Roger.

"Why do you talk to this idiot?" he asked.

"I find Kasim very refreshing."

"Then take him to America and save my life."

"You will clear it with the battle axe?"

"I have known Kasim all my life, and know him to be nothing but exhausting."

"Interesting?"

"We shared a desk through primary school and the most interesting thing he did was hide my pencils when we were about to start a written test. Aunt Rachel got tired of punishing him for it and moved me to the back of the class where there were even worse bullies."

"Which I sorted out for you," said Kasim.

"And made me their enemies for life. Even today I can't help avoiding them."

The car hit a pothole, Roger's head hit the roof and Kasim apologized, explained why he had to sit in the back folded in two. Kasim needed to sit in the co-driver's seat next to the window in case a big, fat, corrupt, traffic policeman got chatty.

Chapter 29

Roger's head was still sore when they got back that evening. There was a bigger crowd than usual, crammed in the living room and overflowing into the back patio and garden. Sam sat next to Uncle Tivo looking more miserable than Salim had ever seen him, listening to reminiscences and improvised eulogies from some who knew Caesar well, and some who did not know him at all but knew of the good things they had heard said about him.

He perked up when he saw Salim and gestured him back outside. They ended up under Caesar's favourite mango tree away from the rest.

"The funeral home called," he said, glancing over his shoulder. "We must move Caesar from there. Their power supply has been out for a week and now their standby diesel power generator has died."

Salim leaned on the tree exhausted.

"Has Aunt Eva been informed?" he asked.

"Would you do that for me?"

"Do what?" Kasim had walked up unnoticed.

"The funeral home has had no electricity for a week," Salim informed him.

"You didn't know?" said Kasim. "The whole town has been on emergency generators."

"Would you inform Aunt Eva?"

"I would," Kasim said. "But we all know what she would say. So, why don't we bury Caesar tonight?"

"Are you crazy?" said Sam.

"Or take him to Nairobi mortuary," said Kasim.

"And who pays?" asked Salim. "You?"

"The Americans."

Sam and Salim looked at each other. They had not considered the financial implications until now.

"You will tell them too?" asked Salim.

"She does not believe anything I say," said Kasim. "Uncle Sam should tell her."

"She will expect me to pay for it," Sam turned to Salim pleading.

"Don't even look at me," Salim said to them. "My landlord is hiring thugs to evict me."

"All right," Kasim said, feigning stress. "I'll tell her then."

"With your suggestion to bury him in the morning?"

"That was a joke. Everyone knows I have no money."

Sam and Salim looked at each other. Salim shrugged.

"I better do it myself," said Sam.

Fatuous speeches were still on when they went back inside. One person was praising Caesar for this, another for that, and another for how much value he put on the youth and their education. Caesar had arranged bursaries and scholarships for deserving students and used his own money to pay fees for blockheads like Kasim, whose own fathers likened educating them to chucking buckets of water in a blocked toilet when all it did was spread the mess.

When Caesar was the director of education, he went to schools all over the country educating teachers and students about available government bursaries, scholarships, and school development funds. He expected Kathiani teachers who had hard-headed King'oo boys in their classes to turn them to model students or change careers.

Years later, when King'oo men met in beer dens, friends remember their school days as the good old days. They laughed at the memory of desperate teachers trying to change them. Most of them had dropped out of primary school harder than they went in, ready for the rock quarries, the cement and salt mines and the sand pits of Kitui. Through no fault of their teachers, a sizable number had made it to secondary schools, and a few had gone on to University. All that would never have happened without Caesar.

Realising the praise-singing and reminisces could go on all night, Salim approached Uncle Sam and made his plea. He had to go back to Nairobi before it got too late.

"The hearse?" asked Uncle Sam.

"Got it."

"Mercedes?"

"As promised."

Uncle Sam was so excited he interrupted the speeches to make an announcement. Salim retreated to his seat by Roger.

"As of today," Uncle Sam said to the gathering, "our train is back on tracks."

His train being back on tracks, to most people, meant that the casket had been found, the gravediggers contracted, and Salim had found the hearse. They would have to pay for all those things, but everyone was happy the hearse was a Mercedes. All except Aunt Eva.

"How much?" she asked.

"How much?" Uncle Sam turned to Salim.

"My life and soul," he mumbled.

Still, she heard it, as old teachers heard every mumbled excuse for missed homework.

"How much is that worth?" she asked him.

"Still under negotiation," Salim said.

"I'll have to see the hearse first," she said.

"Sure, Aunt Eva," he said. "You will."

"I very much doubt it," she said to herself. "You can't twist me round your finger like you do these people, Salim. Psychology, sociology, philosophy, I have read them all. What have you read?"

"Law," he said.

"You are an ambulance chaser, Salim. What law is that?"

Salim turned to Roger in dismay.

Can't help you there, son, Roger's look seemed to say.

"Let it go, Salim," Kasim said, from the corner of his mouth. "She will run you over again and again."

Salim sighed and went back to looking down at his shoes. They had walked from Kathiani where, when the Beetle packed up, they left it with Kasim's ex-polytechnic mates and walked kilometres to get to Caesar's house and be humiliated like errant schoolboys. This was the last clan funeral Salim would ever go to.

"Do as Kasim does," Roger whispered. "Just let it be."

But Salim was not Kasim. He rose and stormed out.

"Salim!" Aunt Eva yelled. "Come back here right now. Salim!"

"Just a few more days," Kasim said, joining him for a cigarette. "Then we'll all go back to being normal."

"Normal?"

"King'oo normal."

They smoked silently for some minutes, finished their cigarettes, and went back inside. The clan was still figuring the passenger manifest now that Sam's train was back on the tracks.

"Photographer?" Aunt Kamene asked. "Kasim?"

"What photographer?" he said.

"Taken care of that too," Salim said.

Aunt Eva had been watching them since they came back with the news of the Mercedes hearse being found."

"Salim," she said. "The hearse, where is it?"

"Somewhere safe," he said. "Does it matter where it is? It will be here when necessary."

"I will not pay for something I can't see."

"You don't trust me?"

"I don't trust any man with my money."

"Not even your husband?"

Aunt Eva turned to Roger.

"Tell them, Roger."

Roger walked out of the room. He was pacing the garden distracted when Kasim caught up with him.

"Not true," he said unasked. "Not that I need her money, but I see the pattern."

She had an axe to grind with King'oo menfolk. That Roger knew. Especially due to their claim of having gotten to the place of creation before Adam and cornered the pick of manhood long before Adam rose from the mud of creation. Roger knew, because she talked about it. She would do anything to see King'oo men change. See them grow up, admit their incompetence in every sphere of human endeavor, get out of the way and let women rule.

"I would not lie to you, Roger," Kasim said, "but King'oo are the chosen people."

"Chosen by …?"

"The chooser," Kasim said. "We have everything a man could want. Land, water, and productive women who know how to make it produce. Women who love us most of the time and keep silent the rest of the time. What more could a man want?"

Roger glanced at Salim. Salim was staring at the dust on his shoes. He heard, without listening, how according to Kasim, King'oo men were the bravest and their women the hottest and most educated. Their honey beer was the strongest and most potent, their men the most pugnacious and their women the most educated. King'oo sired the first woman teacher in the country the first woman doctor, the first woman bus driver and the first woman policeman. All of them women of substance sired by King'oo men. There was no doubt in anyone's mind anymore, but that the first woman President would be King'oo.

"Hurricane Eva?" wondered Roger.

"Rumour has it she is coming back to take care of Aunt Charity and the clan. And to vie for the presidency."

Roger turned to Salim. Salim begged out of it.

"You people are …" Roger had to stop and think. "Very special."

"I told you," said Kasim. "We are a clan of super Kamba. But that is old women's talk. Let us talk men talk. Two years ago, a ninety-year-old King'oo man was dumped by his wife of seventy years for finally being too much for her. She could not keep up with his King'oo demands for conjugal rights, so she packed up her old dresses and *lesos* and went back to her people. She was not a King'oo woman, or she would have known how to deal with him. It took the clan months of night meetings to persuade him to give up demanding back the bride price. Uncle Sam got tired of hosting that dispute and ordered them to relocate to *Garden Square Bar and Restaurant* in town."

The story went from bar to bar through Kathiani, across the valley and over the hills to Sultan Hamud where a Chinese correspondent for the Wuhan Journal picked it up and it ended up in Moscow, Berlin, Paris, Rome, and London. From there it was gobbled up by the internet, went viral, and the old man was suddenly a star. He got letters of sympathy and solidarity from similarly suffering men round the world; and from women in the same situation, he was in. So many letters came at him that he had to hire a young man to read them, translate and burn any from women over fifty.

"Serious?" asked Roger.

"Seriously," said Kasim. "He got offers of love and marriage from countries I never heard of before. He got one from a woman of a European country that must remain unnamed to protect national pride, which topped them all. It read, *Is it true you are ninety-years old and still partying? Hell, I will marry you myself. Our men thirty years younger fall asleep on the job. Where in Kenya is Kathiani? Is it hard to find?*"

Roger turned to Salim, uncertain whether to believe.

"Is he pulling my leg?"

"This time, Roger, I don't know," Salim said. "I don't keep track of such things. Come, we must go back inside."

The meeting was nearly over. Salim stood by while Sam tackled Aunt Eva over the cost and logistics of moving Caesar to Nairobi.

"I knew that funeral home was fake the moment I walked in," she said, turning to Salim. "Why on earth would you preserve Caesar's body in a warehouse?"

"That is where we always keep bodies before burial," Sam answered for him. "This has never happened before."

"All right then," she said to him. "Go do what you have to do. I'll hold you responsible."

Then she walked away.

"So, who pays?" asked Salim.

"You and I, my guess," said Sam.

"I don't have money," Salim said.

"Don't worry. I will stick it in the budget and, when the Americans have paid their half, worry about the rest later."

Salim had stopped worrying about any new hurdles that cropped up in the crises-ridden process of burying Caesar. He rounded up Kasim and a handful of cousins and took them away from the rest. The problem was simple but delicate, he said to them. It was how to turn a borrowed Mercedes into a hearse good enough to fool Aunt Eva. He heard a snicker and looked behind.

"You don't have to be here, Roger," he said.

"I won't tell," said Roger. "I promise."

"And keep your American ideas to yourself," Kasim said to him.

Not that many people in Kathiani understood American. Most of the cousins at the meeting were *jua kali,* tree-shade mechanics, ex-students of Uncle Tivo. The rest were a motley gang of masons, builders, and artisans of every kind. Of those, Salim could only use the car mechanics, the metal workers, and spray painters.

"Before anyone makes a stupid suggestion," Kasim warned them, "the Mercedes has to be returned to the owner by sunset."

"Without a scratch," Salim added.

Heads nodded. Then there was a disturbing silence. Cousins wracked their brains.

271

"I could build it a rack," one offered.

"Without a scratch?"

"That is hard."

They thought some more.

"What if we made him sit in the back seat?" another asked.

"Who sit in the back seat?" Salim asked.

"Mzee Mophat."

"Do you know why we are here?"

"You know," Roger said. "That is not the worst idea."

"Roger," said Kasim, "here in Kathiani, dead people do not sit."

"In that case," someone else said, "why not shove him in the boot?"

These were the educated minds of the clan. Some of them thought that was a worthwhile contribution. There were other suggestions, none of them Roger's, and they all melted away when Salim reminded the contributors the Mercedes had to be return to the owner in its original condition by Friday night. While they mulled over it, Salim engaged Kasim to help figure how to keep his girlfriend from finding out he intended to use her father's car as a hearse. Also, that he had no intention of taking her along. He could just see Aunt Eva's reaction.

"Who is this?" she would ask with her imperious stare.

"My girlfriend."

"Girlfriend?"

"Fiancé."

"Now you have to go marry a foreigner? What is wrong with King'oo men?"

Salim could not let that happen.

Chapter 30

Day Light Club was tucked away in a quiet corner of River Road among similarly dilapidated buildings waiting for the old men to die so their heirs could sell them to developers with even less imagination and be turned to brothels.

It was once a lively *Day And Night Club*, but it had lost pretentions to glamour at about the same time the alley on which it stood lost its name sign to scrap metal recyclers. Then the roof caved in, some said due to corona, and when it came to repairing it the name above the entrance had faded so the sign writer could only make out *Day Light Club*. The patrons did not mind the name change if the beer remained cheap and the meat was well roasted.

At lunchtime, the place was full of well-fed, men in long sleeved shirts, with gold cufflinks, and English-made neckties with gold clips. The jackets were at work back in the office, hanging on office chairs so bosses looking in could see the owners were not too far away.

"Did you hear the one about the jacket that asked for a raise?" Kasim asked them. "And the jacket owner said, 'You are fired'."

Someone got it and laughed. The club was popular with civil servants looking for cheap beer and lunch. Some of them understood their jobs were a joke too and laughed a lot about it. A government accountant with no money to count since Uncle Gove did not have money to count, an auditor with nothing to audit since financial records disappeared overnight, and roads inspectors with no roads to inspect, since contractors vanished as soon as they received their initialisation fee. Normal civil servants who understood their mandate was to be in the office from eight to five, give or take a day or two, and laughed at his jokes, enjoyed a slow lunch and beer then went back to their offices to pick up their jackets and go home. Smart ones brought their jackets along, so they did not have to go back to the office and could enjoy their slow beer and jeer at

Kasim until it was time to go back to the thirty-percent gender mandate waiting at home.

"How many civil servants does it take to change a nappy?" he asked them.

He liked to stir them out of the smugness of a job they did not have to do.

"Anyone?" he asked them.

They had gone back to their conversations. It was at times like these that Kasim missed the booing wallet inspector. Wallet inspectors, like vampires, slept days and worked nights to avoid revealing daylight.

"I tell you," he said to his audience." The answer is zero. Civil servants do not change nappies."

"Who says?" someone yelled.

"Thirty percent," another said.

They laughed.

"Now, here comes the hard one," Kasim said. "How many civil servants does it take to change a light bulb?"

There was a snicker and a half of a *booo*.

"This is more serious than you think," he said. "How many?"

"Zero?" someone guessed.

"Correct," Kasim said. "Give the man a beer; the manager will pay."

That got some laughs.

"How many here have ordered mosquito suits and ties?"

No one seemed to know what he was talking about.

"Hurry up and kit up; it is the next mandate they roll out. If they did not get you with the last one, they will get you with this one. You will all be wearing mosquito net suits, ties, socks, shoes, and masks. Else you will not be paid. Uncle Gove is serious this time. Suit up or pack up."

The room was uncomfortably still.

"Cheer up," he said, with a laugh. "You have *Big Donge Finance* down on New Grogan Road. A nice and friendly Kuyu shark, who does not care jabbed or not, and only breaks your fingers, one at a time, if you fail to repay on time. I see some of you have already met him."

He paused, saw the suppressed desperation on some faces, and shifted gears.

"But that is for tomorrow," he said. "For now, drink and make merry and tell me how many of you it takes to change a light bulb."

"Civil servants do not change light bulbs," one had the courage to admit it.

Uncle Gove paid for outside technicians, preferably someone connected to a big one, to change bulbs in offices, and in the streets and in civil servant housing at least once a month. That was how Uncle Gove created employment for the youth and kept tax money circulating to show he cared for the taxpayers and their taxes.

Not a single laugh.

"How many civil servants do we have here today?" he asked. "Hands up."

Not a single hand went up.

"Good," he said. "I would hate to offend anyone here present. Do you ever wonder why we call them civil servants? Have you been to a government office lately? I was in one yesterday. The tall, tall one with few windows and lifts that sometimes work? You know the one I mean. I would not have gone at all, but for someone who owed me money and kept telling me Uncle Gove did not pay salaries to servants refusing to take their medicine. Which I just now learn from your headshakes is not true.

So, after walking up and down for ever looking for the right floor, I went to the reception desk for help. Where I should have started, as someone now tells me. There is a milelong line at the desk. All I need is a number, so I go to the head of the line to ask. Excuse me, I start ..."

"*Join the line,*" mimicking a grumpy civil servant.

"I'd like to ..." I try again.

"*Join the line,*" he says it a little louder in case I am deaf.

"But I just want to ..."

"I said join the line!"

"I just want to know what floor I'm on!"

"Join … the … line!" That was final.

So, if you are a humble, law abiding citizen like all of us here present, you line up behind a big, fat, corrupt policeman, who also has to behave like a humble, law abiding citizen for a change, something they don't teach at training college, all because the busy civil servant has just informed him this is not police headquarters where a big, fat, corrupt policeman can jump any line at will. And he happens to have eaten beans for lunch and you, a humble citizen are gasping for air until you get back to the front.

"Have you seen the arrows?" Asks the civil servant.

"Yes," you say, "yes, but …"

"Follow the arrows," he orders.

You try to tell him the arrows point up and down, tell you which way is up or down.

"They don't say which floor I'm on," you plead.

"Next!" Calls the busy civil servant.

"We should call them civil masters," Kasim said. "Yes, master, civil master, here's the kickback you ordered. When can I get my driving license now?"

The room was incredibly quiet.

"I see I touch a live wire," Kasim said. "Believe me, I wasn't talking about you. But here is one to cheer you up. How many Uncle Gove's men, does it take to change a toilet roll?"

A charged silence.

"How many?"

Not a smile, not even an embarrassed one. He could have done with that, anything to show they were still with him, alive and thinking.

"I'll give you a hint," he ploughed recklessly on. "One deputy president, two prime ministers, six to eight Governors, Cabinet Secretaries, two Assistant Ministers, a Permanent Secretary … the whole government and one old toilet cleaner. Do you want to know why?"

Now there were furtive glances behind, faces silently asking one another where the shadows were, the ones supposed to come out of the woodwork and cart the fool away.

"Come on, you must know the answer to that one." Kasim said. "We are all civil servants here. Club owner, manager, barman, cooks, waiters, we all live to serve the big ones in big Mercedes cars."

The silence got deeper, colder. An old man, in a ragged security guard's uniform, and wielding a baseball bat, stepped up on the stage, walked up to Kasim and whispered in his ear. Kasim nodded, smiled, patted him on the back and sent him back outside to guard the sleeping cars. Then he turned to the audience.

"Ladies and gentlemen," he announced. "I have just been reminded this is the Alternative Civil Servant Club's end-of-week celebration lunch. I would like to apologise to you all for telling the funny truth at such a serious time. I have also been asked to inform you that the manager has ordered a round of drinks for all of you good people. Uncle Gove will pay for the drinks with buckets of *wananchi's* sweat."

The old man came running back with a reinforcement of two other old men in different uniforms.

"I have to go now," he said to the house. "Good day civil masters, you unfortunate lot. I love you all. And I will be back!"

He let the old security guards drag him out by the sleeve.

"Kasim," the first guard said when they got him to his car, "Do you have a death wish?"

"A Mercedes funeral," said Kasim. "Can you men grant it?"

The men walked away shaking their heads. They were a retired police sergeant, a former big one's driver, and the only cop Kasim knew that laughed at his corrupt policeman jokes.

Kasim sat in his car for a bit deciding where to go next. It was too early to go home pick the extra locks the landlord slapped on his door whenever rent was late. He decided to head for *Hard Life* club to pass time, trading tales of woe with his hard life brothers. He had enough money for two beers for himself and a bottle of chang'aa for his brothers, so he was safe.

A cheer went up when they saw him walk in and, before he sat down, he had a beer in front of him. The place was quiet, subdued, funereal. The club band was fired for going the *Black Survivors* route, demanding a pay raise in exchange for votes. Just as well the *Black Survivors* had gone back, and apologised to Mr Dave when they sobered up.

"I keep telling you boys," Kasim said to his hard-life friends. "You don't mess with money people. The big ones pay for the wind you so recklessly break."

To demonstrate his disdain for the big ones and their money, one of them, a legendary street maize roaster, broke wind. No apology offered, none expected.

"Tell us a joke," they said to Kasim.

Kasim obliged, told a joke and then another and another. His beer ran out and they invited him to share from their clear unlabeled bottles. One thing led to several, and he woke up on the pavement in an unfamiliar back alley with a stranger seated next to him stroking his hand, and telling him he would be all right. He could not recall leaving Hard Life Club, or how he ended up in a garbage strewn back street with a strange man holding his hand.

"Concussion," the man said. "You hit your head on the pavement, but you will be fine."

He had a lean, happy face, sharp features, and a well-groomed beard, vaguely familiar.

"It is just a bump," he said. "I have seen worse."

Kasim's confusion was slowly turning to panic. The man laughed

"I am a nurse," he explained. "A hospital nurse."

To Kasim, that made as much sense as nonsense. He was certain he was not in a hospital. He could smell the rot from an overflowing garbage bin, see the ragged old man rummaging it for food and the three cats and a dog doing the same.

"Who are you," he asked.

"You don't remember me?" the man said, with a laugh. "You were about to give me a lift home to Kibra. Gerry."

"Gerry who?"

"I live in Kibra too."

"Then why are we here?" Kasim asked.

"You annoyed Solo. A giant with big, hairy arms and a gold chain round his neck. You don't remember him? He is the bouncer and he tossed you out."

Now Kasim remembered flying head-first through a black door into darkness.

"That is not like me," he said. "To pick a fight with someone bigger."

According to Gerry, Solo was a lover, not a fighter. Solo owned *The Roosters Club* up on Museum Hill before corona. He was a sharp dresser, big cars and always in company of well-dressed younger men. Then came corona protocols, mandates, curfews and lockdowns, the whole madness, and it became impossible to run a night club with all that and social distancing. Solo lost everything including wife and children. He got a bouncer's job at a one of the clubs he used to own.

"He is a nice guy really," Gerry said.

Quiet, soft spoken, and he never hit anyone that Gerry heard of.

"He hit me," Kasim reminded.

"You called him a loser. At least you implied he was one when you welcomed him to the billion-miles-long trail of losers left behind by Queen Corona."

"That is not like me," Kasim said. "I owe him an apology. Do you have his number?"

"Why would I have his number?"

"He is your friend."

"Solo is everyone's friend."

Kasim was searching in his pockets for his phone. He found his wallet, uninspected, and his car and house keys too, but no phone.

"Did he take my phone?" he asked Gerry.

"Solo can buy you a hundred phones," Gerry said, with a laugh. "Your phone is at the bar charging. I will get it for you."

The backstreet was coming to life, the street people out in search of sustenance. Down the alley, two market women set up business serving food in old newspapers. A man in greasy, ragged trousers went from bin to bin collecting bottles and tossing them in the sack on his back. Close by, a drunk lay in the road and no one bothered him.

Kasim's watch had stopped when he landed on the pavement, but the city was awake and on the move. Telling by traffic noise, and the smell of despair filtering in from the main street, it was his time to head home. Gerry was gone for so long Kasim wondered if he would ever see his phone again.

His phone was ringing when Gerry brought it to him. It was Salim on the phone, and he was not happy.

"I have called dozens of times," he said. "Where are you?"

Kasim looked around. Last he looked he was on stage at *Hard Life* on River Road encouraging hard up, thirsty, weary, angry, and nearly suicidal handcart pilots to find strength to go back to work and go on living.

"*Hard Life* closes at midnight," Salim reminded. "That was six hours ago."

Kasim turned to Gerry.

"Where is this?" he asked him.

"*Club Casablanca*," said Gerry. "It does not look much from the back."

"I don't remember it."

"Solo hit you very hard," said Gerry. "You told him a joke he did not like."

"*Casablanca*," Kasim said to Salim.

"What are you doing in a gay bar?"

"A gay bar?"

"Changed ownership and patronage months ago. Don't you read newspapers?"

He looked at the man by his side. Then he remembered him, the only man who laughed at his jokes and bought him Mojitos.

"Gay as in …?"

"Gay," Salim said.

"That explains everything," said Kasim. "No one laughed at my jokes."

"No one ever laughs at your jokes," said Salim.

"Gerry does," Gerry said aloud so Salim would hear him. "He is hilarious, Kasim is. I could have died laughing."

There was an uncertain silence on the phone.

"Who is Gerry?" Salim sounded concerned.

"Nobody," said Kasim.

"Nobody?" Gerry protested. "I am nobody now, after all the drinks I bought you and saved your life. Nobody? I am so offended."

"Nobody you know," Kasim said, to make amends. "He is no one you would know."

Gerry was again holding his hand. He pulled it away.

"What is going on, Kasim?" Salim asked.

"I will explain later. What's up?"

"Where is my car?"

"You mean my car?"

"You have not paid a cent. Where is it?"

"Your car needs a new battery, among other things."

"Where is it?"

"It is with me."

"Bring it to my office."

"I told you the battery was dead."

"I want it here by four," Salim said and hung up.

"Who was that?" Gerry asked.

"The man who owned my car."

"Does that mean you don't give me a lift to Kibra?"

"I don't have a lift to Kibra."

Kasim had forgotten about the car battery. Gerry sagged with disappointment. Had he known Kasim was such a loser, he would have left with the boys of the band who were his next-door neighbours.

"Would you like to hear a joke about the Martian who hitched a spaceship ride to Pluto and woke up in Kibra?"

Gerry shook his head.

"Then I must tell you the one about the big, fat, corrupt Martian highway policeman who crash-landed in Kibra and thought he had died and gone to hell?"

"You should not make fun of poor people," Gerry said.

"I live in Kibra," Kasim said. "You live in Kibra too. Are we poor people? I know I am not. We may not have a big house, a big car or big money, but we are working men and, if we keep at it, we will one day achieve the dream of all Kibrans and get out of the place. All Kibrans want to live with running water and working sewage. Poor is for politicians who fake empathy, to get votes, and for conmen raising money for poor kids in Kibra."

"The joke?" Gerry said.

"First a call."

Kasim called Salim's mechanic to tell him where to pick up the Beetle. Kasim would fetch it from the garage later in the day.

"The joke?" Gerry could not wait.

"The joke is Martians have no concept of poor. Poor does not exist in Mars, where everyone is a Martian, and there is no other way of describing a Martian. So, when the big, fat, corrupt Martian policeman's patrol car crash-lands in Kibra, he sees earthlings, not poor people. Some Kibrans might disagree but that is my story. I like to annoy people who believe politicians are God-chosen to labour for us, think for us, and make life better for us all."

"Why are they here then?" Gerry asked.

"To make us work for them, and their wives and children. To pay for their palatial homes, big cars, and extravagant lifestyles. Your sweat and mine pay for all of it."

Gerry glanced over his shoulder.

"You are not funny anymore," he said rising abruptly. "I have to go now."

"I have to go too," Kasim rose. "Take the same bus; I will pay your fare."

They walked down the alley together.

"What do you do?" he asked.

"Me?" Gerry said. "I used to work for an abortion clinic. They closed it down, never to reopen."

"They have better ways to do that now," Kasim told him. "Inoculate baby girls against pregnancies, castrate baby boys at birth and the problem is solved."

"How do you know?"

"I know."

"How?"

"This is River Road, isn't it? The back side of it anyway."

One did not need a university degree to figure things out on River Road. One just had to be King'oo, or similar. A natural-born cynic. And a man.

Chapter 31

The night meetings got longer, people dropped out, others dropped in, and no night was like the other. When Sam's trains went off the tracks there would be a sudden outbreak of grief at the back of the women's side, weeping and wailing and upsetting the program so much that Aunt Eva had to order them to keep quiet or find another venue.

Anecdotes were told about Caesar memories shared, and speeches made praising him. One person remembered him for this, another for that, but most talked of how much value he put on the youth and education. Caesar arranged bursaries and scholarships for their children inside the country and abroad and never wanted anything in return. Caesar's emphasis on educating girls changed the traditional clan view of girls as family wealth. Most girls could read and write as well as boys, and sometimes better than boys. Girls could be teachers.

Most King'oo boys, on the other hand, were like King'oo men hard as nails on the outside and just as rusty on the inside. It was impossible to make them do anything they hated doing and school was at the top of that list.

Uncle Richard was one of the few boys who defied destiny. He was good in everything, except discipline, leading to rumours he was only half King'oo, and the wrong half at that. Had his mother not died so early, she would have had a tough time explaining the other half.

Caesar loved Richard for proving him right, for demonstrating that, driven with whips and canes, a King'oo boy could be as successful as any of the dozens of men he had helped rise to prominence throughout the country. Moreover, thanks to Caesar, King'oo boys who had opted for the rock quarries at an early age were harder than Caesar to any of their sons dreaming of following them into the quarries. Some were heard to threaten their sons with death if they did not get the best marks in school and follow in Uncle Richard's footsteps.

"No son of mine will be a *nyangau* like his father," they were heard to say. "If I ever catch any of them in a sand pit, I will bury him in it."

In his late years, Caesar had sold his property to pay fees for poor students, some of whose claim to King'oo blood could not be verified, as King'oo propensity to proliferation was legendary. The clan claimed to have sired half of Kambaland, a boast that was given some credence by the fact that half of Kambaland seemed to have turned up to mourn Caesar's passing.

Tired of hearing old relics sing Caesar's praise, Aunt Eva called for a younger man, a beneficiary of such Caesar's love of education, to speak for the youth. One aunt caused a stir by picking Kasim. Aunt Eva promptly called out Kasim's name, reminding everyone that Caesar used his own money to pay school fees for Kasim's education when his own father likened it to trying to unblock a blocked toilet by pouring good honey beer in it.

People looked at one another. Did she know Kasim at all? Salim and Sam exchanged worried looks. Salim leaned over, begging Kasim not to do it.

"It is a trap," he whispered.

Whatever Kasim said, Hurricane Eva would crash him with it.

"Why not Salim?" asked Aunt Charity. "He is better read."

"And he is a lawyer," added Aunt Kamene.

"I am better read than Kasim too," said Aunt Eva, "and I rarely understand anything Salim says. And then I don't believe a word of it."

She turned to Salim's mother.

"Do you?"

"Can he speak without a book?" someone else asked.

Every time they asked Salim to speak, he started writing his speech.

"We have no time for that," they said.

"Kasim," Aunt Eva decided, "you will speak for the King'oo gathered here today. Who speaks for the rest? You Musau will speak for your people and Ndambuki … where is Ndambuki?"

"He went home."

"Why?"

"He said he had no time to waste waiting for King'oo train to get started. His son will fetch him when his turn comes."

"Kasim?"

Kasim promptly stepped up.

"Do you know what to say?" Aunt Eva asked him.

He turned to face the majority, cleared his throat, and started talking.

"Friends," he said, "Clansmen and women, friends of friends and others, lend me your ears. We come to bury Caesar, not to praise him."

Aunt Eva grabbed a stool. Salim leaped between them and received the stool on his head instead, knocking him out cold. Women wailed, as men watched stunned, and Kasim calmly returned to his place. Sam called for a bowl of water to throw on Salim's head. Aunt Kamene pressed a wet towel to Salim's head.

When calm was restored and Salim, still groggy, seated next to Roger and Kasim in the quiet men's corner Roger was speechless.

"I am fine, Roger," Salim said to him.

"Why take life too seriously?" Kasim said. "By the end of the week, Caesar will be happily in the ground, Aunt Eva will be busy forgetting she was ever a King'oo, and Roger will be glad he was never one of us either."

"I am not?" Roger asked startled.

"Only if you insist."

"I do insist."

"Then watch out for the dragon woman in a black. She hates us."

Roger thumped him on the shoulder.

"I love this guy," he said to Salim

"Take him to America and make my life safer."

The bump was still visible when Salim and Kasim arrived at Uncle Richard's house. Uncle Richard was not in, but his wife was, and she had big slices of cake for them as usual.

"What happened to your head?" she asked of the bump on Salim's forehead.

"He walked into a stool," said Kasim.

She smiled. She knew enough King'oo not to pursue it farther. But her husband, when they caught up with him, did not mind pursuing what he called King'oo shenanigans, absurdities, and abnormalities.

"What happed to your head?" he asked.

"Aunt Eva," said Salim.

"When will your mothers learn to be mothers?" asked Uncle Richard.

"My fault," Kasim said.

"Thank you," said Salim.

"You should have known she would hit me with a stool."

"You should have known better than to spout your ignorance in her presence."

"Enough," said Uncle Richard. "State your business and bugger off. Go discuss your King'oo foolishness somewhere else. Why are you here?"

"The aunts insist you attend," Salim said. "They have determined you were the greatest beneficiary of Caesar's generosity, and you must therefore ..."

"Who says?" Uncle Richard asked him. "But for Caesar, your mother would be fetching water for the neighbours as a house girl. You, Kasim, would be driving a donkey, harvesting sand in riverbeds, and you Salim ... what would you be?"

"Nothing," Salim said to save time.

"But *Ungle* ...," Kasim started to protest.

"Uncle," Uncle Richard said emphatically. "When will you learn to speak properly. All the money Caesar wasted sending you people to school!"

"But Uncle, your sisters …"

"My sisters?" His grip tightened on the club.

"They are not as educated as you are."

"Except Aunt Eva," said Salim. "They feel that …" Salim hesitated. Kasim took over.

"Women don't understand like men do," he said.

Even Salim was startled by the approach.

"What are you trying to say?" asked Uncle Richard.

"They need you there, Uncle Rich."

"Richard."

"They can't do anything without you."

"That is what husbands are for," he said. "Go tell them that. I have my own wife to deal with. Let their husbands deal with them."

"But Uncle Richard," Salim said, "This is not about your sisters. This is about Caesar; burying Caesar with dignity."

"A Mercedes funeral?" bellowed Uncle Richard. "You are not getting a cent from me to bury a man who, but for his arrogance, could have been a billionaire when he died. Go, now, or I have you arrested for trespassing."

"But *Ungle* Rich," said Kasim. "We signed in at the gate."

"The guard told you I was here?"

"We already knew where you were."

"I told you boys not to bother my wife."

"We only spoke to your guard."

"My security guard? How does he know my whereabouts?"

Kasim hesitated, turned to Salim.

"We guessed," said Salim.

"Based on?"

"Guesswork," said Kasim.

"Guessed based on guesswork?" Uncle Richard fixed him with a flabbergasted stare. "Where did you go to school?"

"For heaven's sake, Uncle Richard," Salim burst out. "What does it matter how we found you? You are always here. We are here now, and you are here and ..." he sighed, weary.

"The aunts sent us," said Kasim.

"I don't care anymore why we came here," Salim said. "Your Mzee Mophat, Grandfather Caesar, the man who sent you to Cambridge on a full scholarship, is dead. The aunts would like you to be there to help them give him a decent burial. We have delivered this message repeatedly, and again. I swear this is the last time I am doing this. What you do now is up to you. I am not coming back here again ever, whatever the aunts say. Come, Kasim, let us go. Don't waste any more time on him."

He started off, leaving them astonished.

"You, Salim," Uncle Richard bellowed. "Come back here, right now."

Salim kept on walking.

"Salim? Don't walk away from me."

Salim walked on.

"So, you think you are world-class lawyer now?"

Then he realised Kasim was still with him.

"What are you doing here?"

"*Ungle* Rich," he started.

"Uncle Richard," he corrected.

"Uncle Richard, Salim is having an awfully tough time with Caesar's funeral. They want him to shoulder the whole burden."

Seeing the hard look on Uncle Richard's face, he added quickly, -

"But his behaviour towards you is deplorable."

"Really?"

"Inexcusable."

"When did you realise this?"

"Always, but …"

Kasim had played peacemaker between them from time to time, when they let him, starting from when Uncle Richard sold his wife's old Beetle to Salim. But that was about Salim giving out money, not the other way round. It never happened before that Salim needed money from Uncle Richard.

"Go," Uncle Richard said to Kasim. "Follow your pig-headed brother."

"Cousin."

"Whatever. Next time I see you at my club you will both leave on wheelbarrows. Now, bugger off."

Then Salim surprised them by walking back purposefully and facing Uncle Richard.

"Uncle Richard," he said, "I did not mean to disrespect you."

Uncle Richard glared at him, waiting for the apology, but that was all that Salim had come back to say. Kasim could see it was not enough for Uncle Richard.

"Uncle Richard," he said as gently as he could, "That is the apology."

Uncle Richard looked from one to the other and shook his head disappointed.

"It hurts to think we share blood," he said.

"Aunt Eva says the same about you, Uncle Richard," said Kasim, thoughtlessly.

His grip tightened on the club.

"That is not why we are here," Salim said quickly.

"Why are you here?"

Salim hesitated. They were there to borrow money, but the direction their conversation had taken from the start now made it more of a begging mission.

"I see," said Uncle Richard. "You still need my Mercedes for your funeral."

"We have got that sorted out," Salim said.

Uncle Richard's eyes narrowed. He turned to Kasim. He could trust Kasim to blurt out the truth.

"Almost," said Kasim.

"The aunts would like to see you, or your donation, at the next fundraising meeting," said Salim.

"Did you tell them I was busy?"

"We did," Kasim said.

Then he launched into how hard it was to make the aunts understand how their Richard was too busy to bother with Caesar's funeral. And how Salim was tired of being shunted between them and Uncle Richard in a family dispute that no one could win.

"They say you never take their calls," Salim said.

"And listen to them tell me about pigeon peas? The bumper harvest they would have had this year, if I had sent them money to till, plant, weed and harvest?"

"They have other issues too," Salim said, to make his day worse. "Why don't you call and tell them that I too have better things to do and to stop sending me to you? We all know your position on Caesar's funeral, but they will not quit sending me to you until they hear it from you. Just one call to tell them never again to send me to you."

Uncle Richard studied his face for impudence, saw that he was fed up and sincere, and after thinking about it for a second, took out his phone, dialed and listened. He put the phone on speaker for Salim's sake, and stood glaring at him while they waited. The phone rang several times while he tapped the ground with his golf club. He was about to hang up when a woman answered.

"Hallo," she said, with the unique King'oo aunts' accent. "Who are you?"

"Who are you?" Uncle Richard asked her back.

"Wayua," she said.

"Wayua, this is Richard," he said. "What do you mean Richard who?"

He listened to her count them; there was one who bought eggs to sell in the market, one who fetched water for her from *siranga* on his donkey wagon, and another who bought her *nzuu* to go sell in Nairobi.

"Listen, woman," he said, now furious. "I do not eat pigeon peas, and have no interest whatsoever in pigeon peas. Tell your sisters to stop sending me stupid boys. Yes, Salim and Kasim. Stop sending them to me."

"Richard?" she said doubtfully. "Richard King'oo? The one who …?

"Made you all wash your feet before stepping in my house," he said and hung up.

"There," he said to Salim. "I have called them. Don't let me see you here again"

Salim walked silently away. Kasim lingered hoping to salvage the situation as he sometimes was able to.

"*Un*gle Richard," he started.

"Uncle Richard!" he yelled, leaving him standing alone.

Kasim shrugged and followed Salim.

"Why do you do it?" Salim asked him when he caught up. "Calling him *Ungle*. Why?"

"If I did not do it, we would still be there hearing how bad our mothers were. Good that we did not bring Roger along. This could have been embarrassing."

The aunts were feuding again when Salim and Kasim got to the meeting that evening, and it seemed not even Sam had time for his report. Old gripes had resurfaced igniting unpleasant exchanges, a twisted nostalgic return to the old days when their shouting filled the big house and Caesar was there to curb their excesses.

Next to Eva, Aunt Kamene was the loudest even then. Pushy and fearless, she did not give way to anyone.

"See where that got you," Aunt Eva now said to her. "You are as old as your mother, and you are not half her age."

"Don't start on me, Eva," she said. "I spent an entire day in the market fighting mean, cold-hearted women like you."

"Selling *mitumba*?"

"Selling second, third and fourth-hand garments," she said. "Yes, recycling dead people's clothes."

"The rags I throw in dustbins in America," Aunt Eva said.

"The rags you throw away feed me and my children and pay school fees."

"You are proud selling dead people's underwear?"

"Doing what it takes for my children. What do you do for them?"

"I'm not your husband."

"Then leave me alone before I tell you what we think and say about you when you are not here."

That silenced Aunt Eva. She sat back with a hurt look on her face. Then she noticed Salim. She did not have to ask him. Salim was overwhelmed. He had failure written all over him. She looked for Kasim instead. He was never anything but himself.

"Kasim?" she asked him. "What did he say?"

"He said to bugger off," said Kasim.

By now everyone understood what that meant. She took out her phone and called Uncle Richard. Without any introduction, she told him where in his body he could go to park his pickup. Her father was not a beggar to travel his final mile on the back of a rusty, old bucket.

"Eva?" said Uncle Richard. "Is that you?"

"Aunt Eva," she said.

"I was told you were against the whole crazy idea of a Mercedes funeral on a donkey wagon budget."

"Who told you that? Salim?"

Salim looked up in panic. Kasim pretended he was not there.

"Is it true?"

"Caesar's last wish?" she said.

"Caesar's last wish? From what I gather, he died in his sleep."

"You may gather all you want, but get Caesar a descent hearse, you hear. And pay for it!"

She hung up, mumbled to herself, looking about for someone to assail. They avoided her eyes. She took out her phone.

"Bugger off?" she yelled at Uncle Richard. "What sort of language is that to use on children."

"Aunt Eva, those boys know worse, and not from me," he said. "Ask them."

"I want you here tomorrow," she said. "With a Mercedes hearse."

She hung up glared round. The old men looked at one another, silently impressed. None dared voice his opinion except Uncle Tivo.

"Huh," he said. "I told you Caesar's women were men."

Aunt Eva shot him a devastating look. Uncle Tivo was immune to it.

Chapter 32

The old men were not as excited as Eva had hoped they would be if she offered to meet them halfway with her donations. Halfway? They cried out.

"Why?" they asked.

"He is your brother," she said to them.

She said it in Kikamba, their language, but the old men needed someone to translate. Salim buried his face when Kasim volunteered to do it.

"It is your duty to bury your brother," Kasim said to the old men.

They already knew that. Caesar was dead. They had to bury him. What they wanted Kasim to explain was the halfway deal.

Kasim gave them the condensed version leaving out the bits that would have had them burning to lynch her. He told them Eva had to get back at them for all the wrongs they had done to their women. And for making her change her return flights and pay more for it. In clan-speak, it sounded much worse.

The old men knew some of that already, and suspected more. But ordering them to raise half of the burial costs for Caesar was outrageous. They buried their heads in their hands in woe and groaned, sighed, and despaired. That was not how Caesar's funeral was supposed to go.

Before Eva came to usurp Sam's throne, everyone donated what he could, whatever he had. The clan understood, and the clan was grateful for it. This being ordered what, or how much, to contribute was alien, and not King'oo at all, and had to be from her foreign mother's side. Caesar was King'oo through and through. Caesar would have buried himself rather than be humiliated.

The men's corner went into mourning, but not for Caesar. Caesar was able. Caesar was a man. This time they mourned for their traditions, their way of life, their manhood. If only Caesar were here to tame his women.

"Stop moaning like beggars," Aunt Kamene said to them. "Go home now and fetch the money."

"From where?" they asked. "Our wives are here too. Ask them if we have money."

"Even goats know King'oo men hide money from their wives," another woman said.

The old men had to turn to Kasim again, this time with a hypothetical question. How many goats would each have to sell to pay for half of Caesar's funeral? He gave it to them straight.

"Very many goats," he said to them.

They had voted with Kasim's father in the debate on whether to sell a cow to educate an ox. But for Caesar, their sons would never have gone to school either.

"Let him learn to herd goats like our boys," they had said.

Now Kasim had the pleasure of seeing the squirm as he informed them they could not raise enough money to bury Caesar. Not if they sold their *shambas*, their wives and their grandchildren too. He watched them wilt, sink deeper in their despair.

"Woe," they cried, "we are finished."

He heard one grumble and say if they had known how Caesar's burial would turn out they would have gone on long journeys until after the funeral. They had heard rumours that a government big one had visited Charity in the middle of the night, and offered to pay for Caesar's funeral if she let them change the postmortem report and cause of death on his death certificate. It angered them that she had turned down the only chance Caesar had of getting a state funeral.

The man was dead, was he not? They argued away from Aunt Charities hearing. What did it matter what lie anyone told about him? It was not like he would rise from the grave and contradict them, was it? And here they were being pressured by his daughters to sell their chickens, pigeon peas, goats, and bicycles to pay for his burial. What kind of funeral was that?

Kasim was on their side in that argument, but Salim, again thinking like a lawyer, found it disgusting, immoral, criminal and, and, and ….

"I don't know," Kasim had to interrupt him, "But if you lived in the deepest, darkest corner of a city slum where wealth, health and justice never get to, you might give it a fair thought."

"Is that where you live?" Salim asked. "In the slum where justice never reaches?"

"Besides the point," said Kasim. "But you should see how smartphones, fridges, televisions, and *piki-piki* have flooded the place since muggings, stabbings, malaria, cholera, old age, and murder officially quit causing death. A woman whose family perished in a suspicious fire is now a landlord at Joska, and her kids attend a private school."

Uncle Tivo stirred, and slowly emerged from the *chang'aa* fog he had brought back from Musau's Bar and off-licence.

"Talk, talk, talk," he said aloud. "That is all you know to do."

He was never far away even when it seemed he was.

"You worry too much," he said to men's corner. "Always complaining about wives, money, children, and government."

That was all losers' politics, their biggest mistake, their cause of failure as men. Worry made them impotent, made it impossible for them to think, decisions. Uncle Tivo did not worry, he was a man of action.

"Now I tell you what you will do," he said to them. "You, Kimeu, go sell your plough oxen. All four of them."

"*Atsi*," Kimeu sat up alarmed. "Sell my bulls? Will you pull my plough for me?"

"You have a wife and children," said Uncle Tivo. "Let them do that. Wasn't that why you married her, and had them? And you Musau …"

He turned to the next one.

"And you, Musau," he said to his friend the brewer. "Go bring all the money I spent in your bar last month."

"*Atsi!*" said Mzee Musau, outraged.

"You Mzee Kiribiti," Uncle Tivo said to the next one, "Go sell your Kathiani plot to Kilonzo. He has been begging you to do so for years. And you Karafuu ..."

"I will not sell my shop to bury Caesar," Karafuu rose to leave. "If Caesar wanted to be buried inside a Mercedes, he would have bought one for himself. Caesar was not a bloodsucker like some people here. Caesar was a man."

"Sit down," Eva ordered. "No one leaves this house without donating."

He hesitated, thought about it, and sat down.

"As it was," she said for those not aware of the true situation, "Caesar left an empty granary. Not even money for his own coffin."

The room stopped breathing. Now it was not just the old men that worried. They looked at one another, at the floor, at the ceiling and anywhere her eyes were not. What did she mean Caesar had no money? Was Caesar not the minister for finance for all those years? Was he not the President's own right-hand man with the keys to the national treasury? Was there any granary larger than the government's own treasury?

Mzee Karafuu grumbled. If he had suspected this was how Caesar's burial would be, he would have closed his shop and gone to visit his old friends in Nanyuki Town until after the funeral.

"And you?" Aunt Eva asked Uncle Tivo. "What will you sell?"

"What can I sell?" he said to her. "Everyone knows I wasted it all sending you to America."

Karafuu sat down next to him. He too had sold a cow for that lost cause. A Solidarity of losers. He had also sold something towards Uncle Richard's overseas education too. Caesar made them do things, including dig pit latrines for schools, and some of those things had yielded nothing. Few of the children they sacrificed for came back to Kathiani to buy them a soda at Musau's bar.

Salim finally decided he had donated enough time to the clan and informed Uncle Sam he would not be available for any chores during the following day's meeting. He had handed in his reports and his assignments were up to date. Kasim would be there if anything involving them both came up.

Kasim rose to protest.

"Sit down," Aunt Eva ordered.

She turned to Salim, waited for an explanation.

"I have a date," he said it to Uncle Sam.

She gave him a penetrating look.

"With a girl," he hastened to add.

"How come you don't bring her with you to the meetings," she asked him. "Is she one-eyed? Where is she from?"

"Seychelles," he said, boldly.

"What is wrong with you King'oo men?" she asked him. "Now you have to go and marry a woman from India?"

"Seychelles is not India," he said, avoiding her eyes. "Not that it matters. And we are dating not getting married. Not yet, and not that it matters."

"Not yet?" she said. "Why don't you all go marry Chinese women and leave King'oo women to run this country?"

"Just a date, Aunt Eva," he said. "A date."

"There are reasons goats don't marry gazelles."

"Meaning?"

"Go think about it."

He was tempted to remind her that her mother was a foreign woman too, but he checked himself. That would earn him a lifetime of stools on the head.

"Aunt Eva," he said instead, "You are married to an American man."

"A man worth ten King'oo men."

"*Atsi!*" someone grumbled. "What is wrong with this woman?"

Sam escaped back in his clipboard as, with all King'oo men's eyes now on Roger, Kasim told him what his wife had said. Roger heard the old men's minds grind gears trying to understand what she meant by that. A foreign man worth ten King'oo men? They eyed Roger, weighed him.

"That lizard worth ten of us?" Salim heard one say to the other in Kikamba. "Worth ten of us?"

"Not in this land," said the one sitting next to him.

Roger, feeling the sudden chill she had stirred against him, ducked his head between his shoulders and lay low, studiously examining his wedding band, fearing he would be challenged to step outside and prove Eva wrong. He remained that way, eyes on his ring, until he felt the tension begin to dissipate as Eva unveiled more problems for the old men to worry about.

"You realise she will get you killed here, don't you?" Kasim whispered.

"Am afraid so," Roger whispered back.

"Look needy and harmless," Kasim advised. "That is how men survive here."

"I try, Kasim, I try," said Roger. "Here, there, and everywhere, I try."

Aunt Eva caught the tail end of the exchange, saw Roger's bemused smile, and called out.

"Roger, I told you to stay away from those two."

Kasim shrunk back, tried to squeeze away from Roger, but there was nowhere to go. The seat was overloaded with cousins and grand cousins and neighbours and people he had not known had anything to do with Caesar. Salim sat on the edge of the armrest uncertain what to do next. Whether to sneak out and go or stay and face the hurricane.

Uncle Tivo leaned over and spoke to Roger in Kikamba. Roger turned to Salim.

"You don't want to know," Salim said.

"Why not?" Roger asked.

Salim turned to Kasim.

"Tell him," he said.

Interpreting Uncle Tivo was Kasim's business.

"He wants to know if she was the best woman you could find in America."

Roger smiled, the worried, patient smile he had to learn since his arrival.

"Salim?" Uncle Sam called.

They were waiting for his report. Salim rose and Kasim took his seat.

"Tell me," Roger said. "How are we really related?"

"Your wife and my mother are brothers," said Kasim.

"Brothers, huh?" he said, catching on. "And which one of these brothers is your mother?"

"The big one with a beard."

Roger looked about, saw no woman with a beard.

"Just kidding," said Kasim. "My mother is not here today. But she's every pound as formidable as your wife."

Roger, taking it all too seriously, worried.

"We can have Uncle Richard's pickup," Salim reported. "On condition Aunt Eva is responsible for any damage and we return it with a full tank of petrol."

"What do you mean we?" asked Aunt Eva. "You offered to take care of the hearse."

"Aunty, I did not promise to pay for it."

"We heard you," said Aunt Wavinya. "Even Kasim heard you. Kasim?"

Kasim looked up from chatting with Roger, saw the stern look on her face, nodded. It was always safer to agree.

"How much have we raised?" Aunt Eva asked Sam.

"Little" said Sam.

"How little?"

"Less than half of the budget."

"I always said there were no men in King'oo clan," she said.

"Aunt Eva," said Salim, "this is only our third or fourth real planning meeting."

She turned to Sam.

"What does he mean real? Were all the other meetings you told me about imaginary?"

"Uncle Tivo forbade us to make any real decisions without you."

"Forbade you?"

"He thought you would undo everything we did," said Kasim.

She turned to Uncle Tivo. He was on the phone with his imaginary friend.

"All right, then," she said to Sam. "Before we go any further, let us see what you men can do. Where is the *chondo*? Bring the basket here."

Aunt Kamene handed her a huge woven bag, large enough to carry a goat. She placed it by her feet.

"Salim," she said, "Show them what to do."

"Why me?" he said startled.

"You are the most educated."

"No, I'm not," he said. "Uncle Richard is."

"Apart from you, Aunt Eva," Kasim said.

"You are next in line," she said to him. "Salim, let us see your money now."

Salim took out his wallet, saw how little there was and paused to calculate how much he needed to survive for the next two days. They saw the uncertain look on his face. Suddenly, some men started plotting their escape routes.

"Go lock the gate," she said to one of the women. "No one leaves before this bag is full."

Salim took out his money, covering it with his hand so no one could see the amount, and dropped it in the bag.

"Five hundred?" Aunt Kamene announced looking in the bag.

"Only five hundred?" said Aunt Eva. "You are a lawyer; you can do better than that. More money, Salim, more money."

"That is all I have for now," he said. "More to follow."

"Write a cheque."

"I don't carry cheques."

"I want to see more money from you tomorrow," she said. "Who is next? You with the torn jacket. Take out all the money you brought for *harambee* and bring it here."

The man bolted from the meeting.

"I said to lock the gate." said Aunt Eva. "Someone go guard the gate."

"Kwani, how much petrol does Uncle Richard's pickup drink?" Uncle Tivo asked aloud.

He knew about cars, and what Salim had given was enough to fuel any kind of pickup from Nairobi to Kathiani and back. What Uncle Tivo was yet to realise was that the pickup was no longer an acceptable hearse of choice.

"Quiet," Aunt Eva said to him. "I want to see your money too. One by one starting with the young men. Maina?"

As the men started to file past Aunt Eva dropping their contributions in the basket, Uncle Tivo turned to Roger and spoke to him in Kikamba.

"What does the old guy want now?" Roger asked Kasim.

"He wants to know if it is true that money grows on trees in America?"

"He too is kidding, right?"

"One never knows with him."

"Who is he really?"

Before he could answer, Aunt Eva called his name.

"Now the torture begins," he said to Roger. "Watch."

"Kasim!" Aunt Kamene said. "Bring the money you make in bars?"

Kasim rose, adjusted his belt, and clowned his way to the aunts. Uncle Tivo turned to Roger, spoke to him in Kikamba. Then he nudged the boy by his side to translate.

"He says," said the boy, "Uncle Tivo says there is reason goats do not with gazelles marry."

"Meaning?"

The boy shrugged. Roger turned to the old man, then back to the boy and back at the old man.

"What do you mean by that?" he asked. "I know you speak English."

The old man smiled and winked.

"Kasim?" Aunt Eva asked, "Where is your money?"

"That was for Salim and me," said Kasim.

"Salim?" Aunt Eva asked. "Is that true?"

Salim shrugged, nodded. Always safer to agree.

"More money from you two tomorrow," she said.

She looked in the bag, did a quick count and threw up her hands in despair. At this rate she would never get to go back home.

"Just enough for a donkey wagon," she said to them.

The aunts did not know what to make of that statement. They turned to Aunt Charity. Aunt Charity had withdrawn to her quiet place in her mind. She had nursed Caesar through his sickness. Now it was their turn to take care of him.

Chapter 33

Salim was driving, Kasim in the passenger seat and Roger was folded in the back seat as usual. He had found a way of sitting sideways, with his back against the side and his feet on the seat, so that his legs did not get as numb.

"Why don't we use your Mercedes?" he finally asked.

"It is a sports car," Salim said. "Not what anyone has in mind for a hearse."

"I meant for running about town."

"Garage."

"How long does it take?"

"Let it be, Roger. It is not available."

Roger let it be. But not for long. Moments later, he reopened the case wondering why people who did not possess bicycles were so mad about Mercedes.

Salim advised him to follow Kasim's example and take a nap. That was what passengers did in Nairobi traffic to save emotional energy. Otherwise, they went raving mad and picked fights with street venders.

They were descending Museum Hill, one inch at a time, and the smell of car brakes and overheating engines wafted through the windows. There was little a driver could do but hate the government and the governors, and wish politicians and their henchmen all manner of misfortunes.

For veteran traffic survivors like Kasim it was time to take a nap and dream, to build castles and to plan what to do when they were big men and got away with lying, stealing, murder, and all the crap that big ones got away with. Kasim was yet to reach the big-as-governor part and he was dreaming of the day he would be River Road's comedy king and teach the city to laugh at all traffic jams and related nonsense would fade away.

He was woken by a sudden grinding of brakes as a decrepit old lorry pulled up beside the Beetle. The driver was a hefty man with a dark aura and mean disposition. He looked down at the Beetle with customary truck driver sneer and, when their eyes met, snarled at Kasim.

"We buy junk," he said.

"Not selling," said Kasim.

On the back of the truck was a beaten-up Mercedes.

"How much is the scrap on your back?" Kasim asked.

"Not selling," said the man.

"What do you do with it?"

"Scrap."

"*Jikos* and *karais?*"

"Whatever."

"Braziers and basins," Kasim translated for Roger's benefit.

Then he had an idea.

"Where are you taking it?"

"What is it to you?" said the driver.

"Sounds like they stole it," Kasim said to Salim.

"I want to buy it," he said to the driver.

"Not for sale."

"Rent it then," Kasim said.

"Are you crazy?"

The lights changed.

"Follow that truck," Kasim said.

"Why?"

"Just follow. Go."

Salim glanced at Roger. Roger nodded and gestured at the traffic that was now flowing again. He could not endure another discussion between Kasim and a traffic policeman. Their exchanges had so far ended up with him having to contribute to the policeman's salary. And, when Roger offered to pay the bribe as soon as the policeman flagged them down and save time, Kasim would not hear of it. That was not how it worked. Kasim had to first lament the criminally low wages paid policemen by the big ones who paid themselves more than God's own salary. And then, after Kasim and the policeman had had a good laugh and bonded, Roger had to contribute to help the 'poor, underpaid, fat, corrupt policeman feed himself and his family.'

"That is how it is done," Kasim explained.

The truck led them down Uhuru Highway to Nairobi West then through to South 'C' and across Mombasa Road to South 'B' and through to a world Kasim had not known existed. They followed it along a road that was yet to be a road, dodged potholes large enough to swallow a car and waded through sludge from broken sewage lines, and went through craters filled with green slime from the last rains.

They came to a yard with a high stone wall, topped with razor wire. There was no name on the steel gate or anything to say what the place was. Just a large notice declaring it private property not for sale. The lorry stopped at the gate and honked.

"Stolen," Kasim guessed. "This is where they chop them. They come in new, leave as loads of spares."

The gate slid back and when it was fully open, the lorry drove in. The last thing the driver did before driving in was flip them his middle finger. Then the gate slid back shut.

"What now?" asked Salim.

"We go back," said Roger.

"Scared?"

"Just tired."

"All right," Salim was tired of looking at junk.

They drove on to find a place to turn and entered surreal landscape of mounds of rusting car bodies; of grease-covered mechanics and ragged old men hauling cartloads of junk to recycling yards. There were piles of scrapped cars everywhere, the clanging of hammers, the buzz of metal grinders. Thick black smoke rose from heaps of burning tyres and paint cans. The smells assaulted the senses.

Salim entered the first yard without a stone wall or steel gate. He found turning space and was about to drive out when Roger yelled out.

"Wait," he said. "I think I see something."

307

Kasim opened the door, stepped out and without a word let him out. Before Salim could say a word, he was off into the graveyard of junked old cars soon to be basins and braziers. Kasim got back in the car, leaned his seat back and tried to sleep. They waited.

"Do you think it is safe to let Roger go out on his own like that?" Salim asked.

"He has got to grow up some time," said Kasim.

They waited, Salim getting more nervous by the minute while Roger scoured the *jua kali* yard fascinated by the number and variety of stacked up old junk. The garage owner tried to stop him getting on top of stacked car bodies for a bird's-eye view of the yard. Roger told him not to worry; he had scaled more precarious heights in his earlier life as a marine.

The garage owner went in search of the people who brought him. Salim was squatting by the Beetle watching a mechanic tighten the shocks while Kasim slept inside the car.

"Come quick," he said to Salim. "Your old man is behaving like a small boy."

Roger had descended from the junk pile by the time they got to him and was sitting in an old Ford Taunus fooling with the dashboard playing with the controls.

"My grandpa had one of these," he said excited. "Look at these dials. Isn't this a beauty?"

"Was," said Salim, pointing out the torn back seat with its rusty springs and rotten-through floorboard. "And it smells like the mechanics used it as a urinal."

Roger sniffed the air, nodded, and got out. He headed for an old Dodge sedan sitting on blocks.

"Stop snooping about," Salim said to him. "The man thinks you want to steal his junk."

Roger waved him away. His phone rang. It was Mr D'Souza with unwelcome news. His wife insisted on having the Mercedes on Friday, but Salim could borrow the Volvo.

"Thank you, sir," Salim said, his spirit crumbling. "The Volvo will do fine. Thank you for letting me have it. See you Friday then."

He snapped the phone shut, dropped it in his pocket and walked silently back to the Beetle. He got inside and slammed the door so hard he startled the mechanics and woke up Kasim.

"What's up?" Kasim asked.

"Mister D'Souza," he said.

"I knew it was too good to be true," Kasim tried to go back to sleep.

Roger leaned in through the window.

"What's up, Salim?"

He had seen the defeated way Salim walked back to the car after the phone call. Salim was too angry to speak.

"Back to the drawing board, Uncle Roger," Kasim said.

"Oh," said Roger.

He went back to scouring the yard, leaving them under a cloud of despair. Salim turned to Kasim, spoke to him earnestly.

"Don't you sometimes wish you were the only child of the only child of an only child?" he asked.

Kasim was trying to understand the question when Roger's face reappeared at the window.

"Just got an idea, boys," he said. "Come with me."

They hesitated. Kasim got out of the car first. Then they follow Roger through the mountains of junk, with the garage owner following, till they came to an old station wagon with a dented roof and missing windows. The vehicle's body was in good condition, otherwise. They could see that the interior was large enough for a casket, but it was still a junk, and not a Mercedes, and they did not see Roger's point.

"Now look," he took out a Mercedes badge from his pocket and held it to the hood of the car.

"Mercedes," he said to them.

They looked at each other and walked away.

"Stop snooping in a *jua kali* yard, Roger," Salim said. "You might find something you should not."

Kasim took over watching the mechanics while Salim dozed in the car. He was woken by a sudden crash, and sound of falling cars. Then silence. The mechanics stopped work.

"Where is he?" Salim heard one say.

"Underneath," someone said.

Suddenly everyone was running and shouting. Salim scrambled out of the car to find the mountain of piled up junk had toppled over, and Roger was not in sight.

"Roger?" he called in panic.

"Roger!" Kasim yelled. "Roger."

They got to the fallen heap of junk and tried to see under it.

"Uncle Roger?" called Kasim.

There was a terrifying silence. They imagined a mangled body, broken bones, bloody rags; and how to tell Aunt Eva they killed her husband.

There were faint movements behind the fallen cars.

"Roger?" Kasim called.

"I'm all right, boys" Roger said. "Don't panic; I'm fine."

He rose from behind the pile of rusty cars and waved.

"All is good," he said, with a smile. "I'm fine."

The mechanics looked at him, at one another, at their boss, and went back to work. Salim walked back to the Beetle and lay down in the passenger seat totally exhausted by the sudden realisation of the awful responsibility they had assumed taking Roger along? Kasim would have to explain that.

"Salim," Roger called

Salim tried to ignore him. After a moment, Roger tapped on the window.

"What?"

"You have to see this."

Salim took his time getting out of the Beetle. Garage owner watched him follow Roger back to the junk heap and followed them. Kasim joined them on the roof of a car to peer over the fence into the yard next door.

"What do you do, Roger?" he asked.

"I'm retired."

"What did you do?"

"Worked for a government agency."

"Is that why you snoop around?"

Roger laughed so hard he slipped and again fell in a hole in the junk pile. They left him to his plight, after making sure he was all right, and walked round to the next door *jua kali* yard. Salim followed Kasim through the junkyard to the Mercedes station wagon he had glimpsed through the scrap heaps.

A man in the driver's seat reading a newspaper stopped to watch them walk round the car discussing it. After arguing about it for a bit, Salim approached the driver.

"Is this your car?" he asked him.

The man nodded, turned a page.

"My name is Kasim," Kasim said, jumping in. "Maybe you heard of me. Kasim the Komedian?"

The man shook his head.

"I am also a film director," Kasim said. "This is Salim, my executive director."

Salim looked at him startled.

"I am making a commercial for Mercedes," Kasim said to the man. "I am looking for old models for it. They do not have to move, just look good. We will repaint it so that it looks new, film it and return it, and that is it."

The man looked from one to the other. Salim tried to look like an executive director.

"We pay for the bodywork," Kasim said. "And the rental fees, of course."

The man thought.

"You were going to repaint it anyway, no?" said Salim. "Now you do not have to. You will make money doing nothing."

The man considered. He took out his phone and talked to someone in Kalenjin. They seemed to argue, his voice getting louder, harsher. Finally, he hung up, turned to Salim.

"How much?"

"Ten."

"Fifteen."

"Deal."

They shook on it.

"Thursday?" asked Salim.

"I'll be in Eldoret for a funeral. When I come back."

"We could start tomorrow," said Kasim.

He could not trust anyone to work on the Mercedes in his absence.

"I understand," Kasim said. "But we could start on it, tomorrow, and you are back Tuesday and if you are not happy, we put it back to the condition it was in. You lose nothing. What do you say?"

The man looked from one to the other.

"How about we give you twenty thousand for the day?" Kasim asked him. "Six to six."

"My business card," Salim gave him.

He glances at the card, relaxed.

"Your car will be in good hands," Salim said. "I'll drive it myself."

Man thought about it.

"Twenty plus petrol?" Salim said. "For one day."

"Forty plus petrol," said the owner.

"Twenty-five?" said Kasim.

"Thirty-five?"

"Deal," Kasim said and offered to shake hands.

Salim turned on him startled. The man smiled and shook hands, just as Roger arrived on the scene breathless.

"This is not the one I meant," he said. "But it is in better shape. Is it big enough for the casket?"

"Casket?" asked the owner.

Kasim turned to Roger.

"Roger, that question was not helpful."

"So, I see."

They walked away without another word to the owner. Roger led them an old Mercedes under repair at the back of the yard.

"This is the one I meant."

They examine it from every side. The body needed paint, wheels were buried in grass and mud, and it had not moved for a long time. Salim forced the door open. The upholstery was in fair shape, dashboard intact. Finding the key in the lock, he turned it. The dashboard lit up, but no sound from the engine.

"This thing is very old," he said.

"Does it have to be new?" asked Roger.

Salim opened the hood. A gaping hole where the engine used to be.

"An engine would help," he said.

Roger left them to think about it and went in search of adventure. The garage owner found them discussing possibilities.

"That is a special one," he said.

"Special how?" Salim asked him, seeing as it was no more than a shell.

"It belongs to Kimeu King'ei."

"Kimeu the thief?" asked Kasim.

"You know him?" Salim asked surprised.

"My business to know such people," said Kasim. "He was a politician, retired after involvement in the worst corruption scandals on record."

Collaborating with a cabal of big ones and international criminals, he had orchestrated major infrastructure investment frauds involving French and American companies that gobbled up billions of dollars of public funds leaving the country trillions of dollars in debt it could never pay. The courts were full of related cases waiting for an incorruptible justice system.

The garage owner revealed the man had a company that sold restored old cars on the internet.

"Probably stolen," Salim said.

"This one has been sitting here for two years," said the garage owner. "Waiting for parts from South Africa."

"Probably stolen," said Salim.

"How long will it take to restore it?" Kasim asked.

"When the parts are all here, a month," he said. "To make the body like new, one week. I have a body crew from Kisumu that can rebuild a car body so it looks better than new. But to make it drive like new ... depends."

"Three days to make it new," Kasim said to Salim.

"Just the body work," said the garage owner. "What are you looking for?"

"For something like this," said Kasim.

"You will not find it in this country."

They started to leave, remembered Roger.

"Roger?"

"I have other cars," the owner said.

"Another day," said Salim. "Uncle Roger!"

Roger caught up with them at the gate.

"How come you are so comfortable in junk yards, Roger," Kasim asked him.

"My grandfather was a collector," he said. "He collected junk, sold it for a living."

"Seriously?" asked Kasim.

"The only trade he knew," Roger said. "Did well too. A big house, a truck, a wife, six kids, food on the table ... talking of which, I am very hungry."

"Me too," said Salim. "Let us go find something to eat."

"*Nyama Choma?*" asked Roger.

"We eat other things too in this country, Roger," Salim said. "But if you prefer *choma* ... we go for *nyama choma.*"

Along the city's eastern bypass was a stretch of roadside meat roasting shacks built on the road reserve, so that smoke and sight of roasting meat would tempt travellers to stop. Once the stopped, they were in meat eaters' paradise.

On the opposite side of the road carwash stands, timber yards and hardware stores competed for space steps away from speeding traffic.

Chapter 34

The band was hurdled round a three-and-half-legged table in the corner mulling the meaning of life without money, while eyeing the patrons, wishing one of them would notice and send over some drinks.

It was the wishing hour at the *Hard Life Club* too. Any man not dead drunk was wishing he had listened to his mother, married her choice of wife, left wife with her in the country to mind the *shamba* and the children, and uncomplicated his own life.

And any woman at the club not on duty as a wallet inspector was wishing she had stayed in school, gone to nursing college as her mother said and married a doctor and lived happily ever after.

And Kasim was wishing they would stop ignoring his presence on stage and let him ease their pain. It happened every time the band left him the stage and the audience had to listen to him. It turned unfriendly and they wondered what he was doing on stage. He had to keep reminding them who he was, and that they had no choice but laugh at his jokes because the management was paying for them.

"*Haalloo?*" he yelled in the mike. "Remember me? Kasim the Komedian. I tell jokes and, whenever you have the time, you laugh and forget your troubles. Remember? Kasim the Komedian?"

"With three K for Kuyu, Kisi and Kamba?" asked a familiar voice.

"Correct," he said. "Half Kuyu, half Kisi, half Kamba."

Then he saw who had spoken. He had not noticed his pink-haired nemesis lurking in a dark corner with the king of the pushcart pullers they called the Godfather.

"What are you doing here?" he asked her.

"Not your business," she said.

Kasim could not imagine her trying to inspect the wallet of the Godfather, a man who started out as a street

316

thug, made a fortune pushing handcarts across the city trafficking in hot house-hold items, and who now had two hired thugs for bodyguards.

"Greet the Godfather for me," Kasim said to her.

"Go away," said the Godfather.

"All in due time," Kasim said. "But first imagine this …"

"You are not funny," said Godfather.

"Neither are you, Godfather, so shut up and let me work."

The man smiled tolerantly and went about his business. They knew each other from way back when he was a clueless street hustler, and Kasim was a clueless roadside mechanic. Then he became bank robber, and Kasim a comedian. Now, in River Road, he was a banker and Kasim a joker.

The most intriguing manifestation of the new old normal was how men who had owned nothing before, and were happy, now owned cars and houses, and real estates, and were still happy. Men who had no money or career ambitions before, and were unhappy, now had political careers and were *shilingi* billionaires from selling air and imaginary medical supplies to the government, but they were still unhappy. And weed-happy *matatu* bus drivers were back at work doing what they did best, enlivening the city transportation system with wild, driving antics and devil-may-care attitude.

And the hustler bank robber, had deployed all his street skills and become a loan shark owning fleets of pushcarts across the city that he rented out to unemployed youth. His *Hard-Life Loans,* an off-the-records shylock operation, loaned money exclusively to pushcart pullers. His head office was at the darkest table of the darkest corner of *Hard Life Bar* and only registered members of the pushcart fraternity dared approach.

"Godfather," Kasim called from the permitted distance. "Mosquito net suits will be the next massive thing.

Socks, underwear, ties, and masks to match. Get in on it before the Chinese do. You will be a billionaire."

"I am already a billionaire," said Godfather.

"Then you will be God," Kasim said.

Godfather thought about it, smiled, and gestured to the barman.

"Give Kasim a beer," he said. "And make him, pay for it.

The barman looked from him to Kasim.

"What are you waiting for?" said Kasim. "You heard the man."

The barman dug a bottle out of the fridge, opened and dumped it on the counter in front of Kasim.

"You know where to send the bill," Kasim said to him.

The man gave a tentative nod, glanced at Godfather, and nodded again.

"After I leave," Kasim walked away back to the stage sucking on his bottle.

The audience had naturally forgotten about him.

"Tell me, brother," he said to one of them. "Why do you pull a pushcart?"

"Why not?" said the man.

"It is a push cart."

"My push cart."

"Push cart! Also known as a hand cart. Which you do not pull with your foot."

"Who says?"

"I will get back to you," Kasim turned to another pushcart puller.

"Excuse me, brother …"

"No beer, no questions," the man waved him away.

"All right," he said in the mike. "Who knows what is red and green at a hundred miles an hour?"

"Traffic lights," someone guessed.

"A pushcart pilot with his *mkokoteni* on fire," said another.

"*Booring*," said pink lips.

"Wrong," he said to her. "Anyone else?"

There was uncertain silence.

"Okay," he said. "Here is an easier one. Imagine this - you have just parked your *mkokoteni* handcart for the night and you step inside some dive much worse than this one on River Road for a drink and a bit of sanity, because life on the street is full of madness, as we, all hard-life men, know, and you have not had your first shot of cane spirit to lift you up. So, you rush in here for a quick slug of the stuff the barman keeps in unlabeled bottles under the counter, and which he assures you is not *chang'aa*, and you down one or two.

Then, just as the fog begins to clear and your life fades back in focus, the phone rings and you get a call from Cousin Francina telling you Onyango died.

"Onyango Kona Kona is dead?" you ask.

"Very dead," she says.

"When?" you ask.

"February," she says.

"How?" you ask, "because, just this morning, he phoned to borrow money to bet on European football games."

"No," she says, "that can't be him."

Because she just got off the phone with another cousin, one you also do not remember, who informed her the clan expects everyone to send money for the funeral?"

Kasim paused to see how his audience was taking it. Yarns about funerals, clans, cousins, money, and football in the same breath kicked off all manner of emotions.

"Of course," Kasim said, to ease their pain, "you do not believe Cousin Francina, whom you have never met or heard of before. You are not that stupid. You are a city man. You have been had before, by pretty women and some bad men, some of them armed with machetes. And you have also received calls from strange female voices threatening to tell your wife where you were drinking, the day you lied to her you were in Eldoret transporting sacks

319

of potatoes for a client from Mogotio. Remember that one? They ordered you to send money by phone, or else your wife would see pictures of you in a lodging room with a mega-bottom barmaid."

He got loud guffaw from the back of the room.

"Did you send the money?" he asked in that direction.

More laughter, genuine laughter.

"No need to answer that one," he said. "We all know it never happened. But just to be certain Kona Kona is not dead, you take a day off your hard-life hustle and trek to the Mortuary. You slip the mortuary attendant his customary inducement, enough *chai* for himself and his boss, and he takes you on a tour of storage freezers, body bags and shelves pulling out body after body for you to see that none of them is your cousin. You begin to believe you have been telephone-fooled, again. Then you get to the last freezer and the body at the very bottom of the pile turns out to be that of Onyango Kona Kona, frozen solid and dead. So, now you begin to wonder who it was that you sent money to bet on Man-U against Man-C hoping for a share of the millions he promised he would win. Still, you cannot be sure Cousin Kona Kona is not playing another trick on you, so how do you tell this time he is really dead?"

There was dead silence in the club. The band rose to reclaim the stage, but all the eyes and ears were still on Kasim.

"How do you tell?" he repeated. "I give you a hint. Ochieng is a Kuyu."

"Ochieng a Kikuyu?" laughed his pink haired wallet inspector.

She was as obstinate as a waste dump dog.

"How?" she insisted.

"His mother says so."

"Why?" she asked.

"Because his father went fishing," Kasim said to her.

"She had a Kikuyu boyfriend?"

"What does it matter who she had? Ochieng is dead. How do you tell the Kuyu called Ochieng is dead, not faking it?"

"You ask him," she said.

"Anyone else?" Kasim asked.

"*Boooring!*" she said.

"You shut up."

"No, you shut up," she said in her usual calm voice.

Uncle Tivo would have said she was as hard as the hair on a street dog's nuts.

"King'ori," Kasim called to the barman, "why do you let in wallet inspectors who have never been to school?"

The barman waved him away. He was as tired of Kasim as he was of the wallet inspectors

"Hands up any woman who has ever seen the inside of a classroom," Kasim said.

The first bottle to fly at his head was from a woman offended by his remarks. The next one was from a man who blamed him for the breakup with his girlfriend. The third came from someone with no reason to hurt Kasim other than he made a lot of noise while all he wanted to do was sleep.

"Go home," Kasim told him.

"Go home yourself," he yelled back.

He threw a neighbour's cigarette lighter starting a brawl that quickly spread to include men who had just woken up with their heads on the wrong bosom and realised there was no purpose to life. They directed their resentment at Kasim raining bottles, glasses, and shoes at him.

Kasim dodged the missiles, taunted the throwers, and refused to be forced off his stage by a bunch of drunken pushcart pilots. It was getting ugly, with some of them about to start tossing chairs at him. Then the bandleader, the barman and the security guard bundled Kasim out of the back entrance.

"I will be back," he yelled when he heard them bolt the door.

He stood, momentarily lost, looked one way then the other trying to orientate himself. He had been ejected from the back doors of so many River Road clubs he was familiar with the eerie backstreet lighting, when it worked, the smell of urine, the rotting garbage, overflowing rubbish bins, and the air of impending doom.

The Beetle was parked under the only streetlight that worked, coming on, then went off, then on again in an ominous manner. A famished figure in a ragged security guard's uniform, sat on the car's rear bumper. He scrambled to his feet when he saw Kasim and saluted.

"*Jambo*, boss," he greeted.

"*Jambo*," said Kasim.

The man was one of a growing number of freelance security guards that roamed the streets at night in discarded police uniforms and armed with clubs as big as axe handles demanding protection money for parked cars.

He watched Kasim open the car door and stow his guitar in the back seat. Kasim imagined he was deciding whether to clobber him or try another approach.

"Everything is fine with your car, boss," he said, going for another approach. "There were street boys stealing your headlights and I chased them away."

"Thank you," said Kasim.

While he figured his next move, Kasim got in the driver's seat, reached under the seat for the key, inserted it, and turned. Not a sound from the engine. He turned it again, and again, no sound.

He crawled back out, opened the engine compartment, inspected the wires, pulled, and pushed them to no avail. He probed with a screwdriver, looking for something to loosen or tighten as he saw roadside mechanics do as they tried to help restart his car.

"Sell me this crap and buy a car," they said, when they failed to get it going again.

"Do you know anything about car engines?" he asked the man with the club.

"Me?" the man said startled.

Kasim met all sorts of stray life in the backstreets of River Road. From scruffy felines to scrawny canines; from disgruntled garbage men with university degrees in waste management, to barmen with business management diplomas; from plumbers with degrees in water engineering, to psychiatrists operating backstreet drug .dens; from jua *kali* mechanics with university degrees in electrical engineering, to discharged policemen with an axe to grind. One never knew with River Road.

He was about to get back in the car, take a nap and wait for dawn, when the watchman turned thug and demanded money for guarding the car or else.

He was the same height as Kasim, but he was lighter than half Kasim's weight, which was not much to start with, and he probably had eaten less that day than Kasim, who had eaten nothing all day. And the club in his hands was too heavy to keep raised over his head. Seeing him for what he really was, - another hard-life brother in the throes of life -, Kasim burst out laughing.

"Did you see how I flew out of *Hard Life*?" he asked him. "I was ejected by an angry audience, an angry barman and an angry security guard. Without pay."

The man lowered his club. Again, seeing more of what he was, Kasim tried to help him.

"Can you play guitar?" he asked.

Again, one never knew with River Road.

"Me?" said the man.

He was about to walk away defeated.

"Do you have a cigarette?" he stopped to ask.

"Maybe."

Kasim searched in his pockets and came up with a crunched packet with a single cigarette in it.

"It is my last one," he informed, to show his spirit of brotherhood. "But you can have it."

The man took the cigarette gratefully, seemed to consider giving it back.

"Keep it," Kasim said. "Smoke it. Maybe it will make you feel better. I know how hard is the life of a hard-working, hard-life man."

The man was about to start away again.

"I tell you what," said Kasim. "I will tell you a joke and maybe it too will help you feel better."

He stopped, waited for it.

"There was this Martian man," Kasim said. "A real Martian man from …"

"Mars," said the watchman. "Where Martians are from."

Kasim paused to take that in. Never judge a man by his rags.

"But did you know Martians spoke marsai?" he said. "No, not maasai - marsai."

That he did not know.

"Good," Kasim said. "So, there was this Martian man, who spoke marsai and, no, he was not a politician."

Politicians were guilty of everything including of being from planet Senseless, the nearest planet to Mars out in outer space.

"What was he?" asked the street guard.

"Let us just say he was a big, fat, corrupt Martian policeman. I tell jokes about big, fat, corrupt policemen too. Everyone loves a big, fat, corrupt policeman joke. Except a big, fat corrupt policeman, of course. You know how they are in real life. After official duty, they put on their civilian clothes, arm themselves with a *rungu* as big as yours and go freelance. Then they stop you at the corner, ask you stupid questions, turn you upside down and shake out all your change. Then they … then they clobber you on the head with their *rungu* and threaten to shove it up your ass if you do not give them your bank card and pin number. Worse than career muggers. They could be career muggers, masquerading as police officers, but you never know with

River Road. You don't have a brother who is a big, fat, corrupt policeman, do you?"

The man hesitated.

"It is not your fault," Kasim said to him. "Not your fault at all. We all have skeletons under our beds that we know we did not put there. But, if you like, I can change that to a big, fat politician. People like a good joke about a politician too, a big, fat, corrupt politician, but I prefer a big, fat, corrupt policeman joke. So, this big, fat, corrupt, Martian traffic policeman is out on patrol, flagging down space cruisers and checking out driving licenses, doing freelance after-duty patrols, demanding bribes, and harassing space travellers. He gets excited, cruises too far from base, runs out of diesel for his space patrol car and crash-lands somewhere not far from where we are. Dazed, he crawls out of the vehicle, looks round and realizes he has never been here before.

"Where am I?" he asks in marsai to the first creature to come along.

The he realises the creature does not understand marsai and results to his automatic intragalactic digital translator.

"Kibra," says the man.

The Martian whips out his intragalactic smart phone, takes photographs of every creature and every object in sight, chicken, cats, dogs, goats, and sends the pictures back to Mars.

"Planet Kibra?" says his OCPD back on Mars. "Where in hell is that?"

The Martian cop turns to the Kibran.

"Where is Kibra?" he asks in marsai.

"Did you know Martians looked just like us?" Kasim asked the man.

The man shook his head, beginning to feel uneasy.

"So, the Martian asks the Kibran where Kibra is."

"Here," answers the Kibran.

"They are not highly intelligent," the space cop reports back to his commander in Mars. "What do I do now?"

"Send your coordinates," says mission control. "Our systems are down, but we'll get you out of there as soon as they are up again."

He sends his position and waits. Shortly after, he gets a call from Maritias. Did you know the capital of Mars was Maritias?"

"Like the island?"

"The Indian Ocean one?" Kasim shook his head. "That one is Mauritius. How come you know so much?"

It seemed every hard-lifer Kasim met, man or woman, uptown or down, up River Road or down River Road, had been to school and stayed long enough to learn something. School was supposed to safeguard them from the curse of a hard-life existence; get them well-paid, sweat-free, stress-free jobs; make them rich like politicians. Then they ended up on River Road feeling they had taken the slowest train to *Hard Life* only to encounter the realities of a hard-life existence.

"Anyway," he could see the street guard was getting restless. "Our Martian traffic cop is stuck in Kibra wondering what to do next. He gets a call from his people back in Mars. They have good and sad news for him, they say in Marsai. By the way, Marsai means 'Mars-says'. Anyway, our Martian police officer wants the good news first. The good news is they have located Kibra on the far, dark side of some planet, and according to their map of inter-galactic politics, Kibra is an informal settlement not a slum. They have locked onto the settlement with their space googler and sent out a rescue ship. The sad news is the rescue and retrieve spaceship will take seven years to find the planet and the settlement.

And that is that. The space cop is on his own in a strange place in space. Stuck for things to do, the hungry and homeless Martian policeman, gets a job as a traffic policeman and is assigned roundabout duties along Uhuru

Highway. He makes friends easy, and in no time, becomes a big, fat, corrupt city traffic policeman too. So big and bad that he is promoted to sergeant and assigned a larger roundabout.

So, now this big, fat, very corrupt, Martian police sergeant stops at a roadside tea kiosk for lunch and orders the only thing he can afford with his earthly traffic police sergeant salary, and his share of the bribe money. *Ugali* and sugarless, black tea. The waiter, also a big, fat, off-duty policeman, Kuyu not Martian, working to supplement his meagre policeman pay, asks him, "How hot?"

The big, fat Martian policeman turns to the customer sitting on his right, also a big, fat, underpaid policeman, Kalenjin not Martian, and dips a finger in his tea to see how hot it is …"

"This hot," said the street guard walking away.

"You should have told me you heard it before," Kasim called after him.

"You are not a good man," he said over his shoulder. "That is a joke about my people."

"You are Martian?"

The man kept on walking. Kasim finished tinkering with the engine, slammed the lid shut, slid behind the wheel, and turned the ignition. The engine clattered to life startling him. He coaxed it into first gear, flicked on the headlights switch, and was about to start off in a hurry in case the engine started having second thoughts, when he saw the road in front was still dark. He crawled out, leaving the engine running. He stepped in front of the car and stopped dismayed. There were two empty sockets where the headlamps used to be.

"There were street boys stealing your headlights and I chased them away."

Those were the words of his friendly street guard. Had he not been so busy empathising with him, Kasim would have heard what the man really said.

As he stood thinking what to do next, the engine died. It was suddenly disturbingly quiet then but for the faint music from inside the club. He rushed back in the car and tried to restart it. After a couple of turns on the ignition, he got out again and was about to open the engine cover again, when he remembered he knew less about car engines than about guitars.

A man who repaired cars under a tree by the roadside had offered to sell him a *new* used engine, and he was about to buy it, sight unseen, when Salim, whose car it still really was, asked him what sort of an engine he thought it really was.

"A new used engine?"

Only Kasim and roadside mechanics could understand such a thing. Another tree-shade mechanic had offered to swap his engine with a Toyota engine. He was also selling the transmission, and the chassis that went with the Toyota engine. Kasim would end up with a Toyota and a Beetle for the same low price.

"Sell me this crap and buy a car?" another mechanic offered.

Kasim heard it often from friendly *jua kali* mechanics who could not afford a bicycle.

They knew him by his car, the only saffron Beetle in town, and every *jua kali* mechanic wanted it. They also knew what ailed it and how to cure it, but would not do it without payment first. They were good men, most of them honest, and some of them over-educated for the job, but they were always hard up, and their solutions sometimes involved a little down payment and a lot of corner-cutting.

BOOK 3
What stops Kamba laughter faster than a bullet?

Chapter 35

Garages had closed for the day, the yards reverted to cemeteries for old vehicles. The Beetle stopped a hundred meters away and three men got out and walked back to *JK and Sons* garage. The gate was secured with a chain and padlocked on the inside. They had come prepared.

"Bolt cutter?" Salim asked.

"Roger," Kasim said.

"Shit!" said Roger.

He had left the bolt cutter in the Beetle. He started to go back for it.

"Wait," said Salim. "Someone is coming."

The night guard looked like a walking scarecrow in his dark coat over layers of sweaters and jackets. He approached the gate.

"What?" he said keeping his distance.

"We left our car here," said Kasim.

"It is closed."

"For repairs," said Kasim. "We are here to pick it up."

The man had two dogs on leashes, mongrels that did not know what they were expected to do. They whined instead of barking.

"Which car?" asked the night guard.

"We'll show you."

The security guard looked from one to the other. He lingered on Roger's face longest. Then he opened the gate. He followed them warily to the one-of-a-kind Mercedes.

"This one?" he said startled. "This one belongs to a man from my village?"

"Kiroboto," said Kasim. "We are also from Kitui."

They switched to Kikamba and Kasim concocted a story, laced with Kamba jokes that had the security guard laughing in no time. Along the way, Kasim let it out they did not really own the vehicle, but they needed it for a commercial and they had the garage owner's permission to borrow it for the weekend. The guard took out his phone.

"No, don't call your boss at home," Kasim said. "Bosses don't like that."

They had not really spoken to the owner, Kasim confessed. But all they wanted was to rent it for the shoot and return it by Friday night. They would hand the cash deposit to the guard and the rest when they brought back the car.

"Cash," Salim emphasized. "Real money and no questions asked."

The man stopped laughing. There and then Kasim had something for his next act.

"What stops Kamba laughter faster than a real bullet? Talk of real money."

The man thought about it.

"You are a funny man," he said in Kikamba.

"Will he sell it?" Roger asked Kasim.

"How much do you have?" Kasim asked him.

"I spent it all on gas."

"I see you have caught the King'oo disease of spending money you don't have," Salim said to him. "Welcome home."

The security guard suddenly remembered.

"This thing does not go," he said, still in Kikamba.

"We know," said Salim. "We will repair it, fix it, use it and return it."

"Why?"

"Why what?"

"Why repair it, fix it then return it?" he said. "The thing does not belong to me."

"We know," said Kasim. "And we are buying it from you."

"Buying?" Salim was startled.

"For the same price," said Kasim. "He does not want it back, and we don't have to return it."

"How much?" Salim asked the guard.

"I must think," he said. "Wait here."

He took his dogs and disappeared among the broken cars and heaps of junk. He was gone for a while. They began to worry. Fearing he had gone to phone the police, Salim suggested they leave right away. Kasim was already snickering at the idea of the guard calling the police to report a car theft at a junkyard.

He lifted an imaginary phone, held it to his ear.

"What colour is the car?" he mimicked the voice of a big, fat, corrupt policeman. *"Black? What make is it? What year? What year did you say?"*

"Sounds familiar," Roger said.

"You know how long it takes them to get to the scene of a murder?" Kasim asked him.

He lifted the imaginary phone again, held it to his ear.

"You say the man is dead? Murdered? So, what is the hurry."

When he came back, the guard confessed making a call, but not to the police. He had called to ask advice from a cousin who traded in stolen cars. He had a proposal of his own, a deal that only a Kikuyu or a Kamba from Kitui could think up at such a short notice.

"Sounds good to me," Salim said, when they heard it.

"Half down and the rest when we return, or don't return, the car," Kasim said. "Sounds good to me too."

"But how do we get it to the other garage?" Roger asked them.

"Mkokoteni," said the security guard. "This thing is as heavy as an empty beer gourd."

"That," Kasim said to Roger, "is the Kamba way of saying light as a feather."

The guard directed him to a *chang'aa* bar three *jua kali* plots down the way where he would find a dozen handcarts parked outside. The men who pushed were inside the bar taking a break.

While they waited for Kasim to return with a handcart, the guard tried to strike up a conversation. Salim was not good at chatting with security guards, and Roger did not understand Kikamba, and the guard gave up trying.

"What does he tell his boss?" Roger asked Salim.

Salim relayed the question.

"About this thing?" he said. "It was not here when I came on duty."

"How original," Roger could not help laughing.

"What else could he say?" said Salim. "That three armed and dangerous men scaled a barbed wire fence, overpowered him and his guard dogs, tied him up and stole a car with no engine or wheels?"

Kasim came back with a robust handcart and four reasonably sober men, and in half an hour their newly acquired Mercedes sat in another *jua kali* garage down the way, where the garage owner waited with a crew of body mechanics itching to get at it. They pushed it to a secluded repair shed at the back of the yard and let the body crew at it.

Chapter 36

Work had started at the garage when Salim returned early the following morning. The sun was dangling at the point of no return between the morning horizon and the zenith; metal clanged on metal, grinders wailed and spewed sparks, and the welding torches were zinging and flaming. The smell of hot metal, raw sewage and burning paint filled the air.

Kasim and Roger were already there, having left Kathiani at dawn to save Roger from having to lie about their mission. Salim found him shaking his head in awe as he watched Kasim do the only thing he learned at *Uncle Tivo's College of Car Mechanics*, - entertaining mechanics with crude jokes while they worked. The workshop was full of laughter and camaraderie.

Kasim had introduced himself as a former, potential *jua kali* engineer, now a famous entertainer, and urged the young men not to despair when their *jua kali* dreams did not go as dreamed, for there was hope in heaven for them too.

Salim saw the mechanics laugh, as they ripped the Mercedes with axes, hammers, chisels and metal files, tools he had never seen used on the Beetle, and worried.

"Relax," said the garage owner. "This is a Mercedes. Different tools for different jobs. If this were a restoration job, we would build a special shed over there. And then you would cry tears."

Then he took him by the shoulder and walked him away from the noise and mayhem, deeper into the yard past dozens of rusting shells, to a white Audi standing on its own.

"This one too is German," he said.

"It is not a Mercedes," Salim said.

"I will let you have it for the cost of repainting the Mercedes."

"We talked about it already," said Salim. "If it is not a Mercedes, I don't want to know about it."

"Why do you put yourself through so much pain to repair such an old thing?" he asked. "Just so you can say you have a Mercedes?"

"I have a Mercedes," said Salim.

"Another one? Which year?"

"Last year."

"We do accident repairs too."

"Stop wasting your time," Salim said. "I am a stubborn Kamba."

"You are a Kamba too?" He switched to Kikamba. "Then let us talk like men."

Kasim handed him his business card.

"You are a lawyer?"

"If you decide to buy land or property, call me," he said. "I have handled criminal cases too, but I found the lying too tiring."

He walked on. The man followed him, placed the hand back on his shoulder.

"What is your problem?"

"I have no problem," Salim said. "Yes, I have a problem, but it is not one you can solve."

He broke free from the hand. With the garage owner in tow, he scavenged in the yard looking at old engines. He found an old Beetle, lifted the engine cover.

"What about this one?" he asked.

"Irreparable," said the man.

"How much?"

"Don't you listen? The engine is beyond repair."

"How much?"

"Listen, if this vehicle were my daughter, I'd pay you ten cows to marry her. The engine is completely dead, as was her brain when she eloped with a fisherman from Masinga. Useless! *Bure!*"

"The engine or your daughter?"

"Both," said the man, now angry.

"How much?"

"You must be a very bad lawyer," he was getting tired trying to save Salim more pain. "The engine does not work, cannot work, will not work."

"Who said it had to?"

"You want a dead engine in a dead car?"

"You finally got it."

"*Ayee!* Don't you like money? What sort of Kamba are you?"

"A stubborn one."

"Which part of Kitui do you come from?" he asked.

"Kathiani."

"That is not Kitui."

"I did not say I was from Kitui."

"But yesterday your brother told me ..." he was pointing at Kasim.

"Did he also tell you the one about ..."

"The Kamba who hanged himself with a *kamba*," the man said. "Not funny. Are you the King'oo of Mzee Caesar Mophat?"

Salim was tempted to deny it, then thought it might help convince the man from wasting his time.

"There are no other King'oo from Kathiani," he said. "Let us talk about the engine."

"I heard your Caesar died," said the man. "Caesar paid for me to go to polytechnic."

Where, unlike Kasim, he had learned to repair cars. He had repaired all Caesar's cars when he was a government man.

"He paid for it every time too," he said. "Caesar was not King'oo. Caesar was a man."

Not even a King'oo woman could have put it better, Salim thought. Decent men seemed to say that a lot since he died. Caesar was not King'oo, Caesar was a man!

"His funeral is tomorrow," he said.

"I have another funeral tomorrow," the man said. "Musumali Nyundo. Did you know him?"

"Let us talk about this thing," Salim said.

He had a meeting in Kathiani in a couple of hours.

"I don't know what you intend to do with your Mercedes," the man said.

He paused, waited for Salim to confess his true motive for the car. Being King'oo, Salim had to have a devious plot for the Mercedes, otherwise he would not be wasting money on it. He was likely planning to patch it up, repaint it, throw in a hodge-podge of useless, old parts and features, and sell it to another brain-dead King'oo back in Kathiani.

"My business," said Salim. "Yours is to have it looking like new."

"Frankly, I don't care what you do with it," he said. "But this is a Beetle engine in case you have not noticed. There is no way you can fit this old thing inside of that hole."

"What thing?" Kasim asked. "Which hole?"

Kasim and Roger had caught up unnoticed. The garage owner was a little annoyed by their intrusion. It was hard enough talking to one King'oo. He read Kasim up and down and waited for Salim to explain.

"He is a comedian," said Salim. "And he is not my brother."

"Is he King'oo?" the man asked. "You people never cease to surprise."

"We never do the same thing the same way twice," said Kasim.

"Does your uncle still repair pots and pans?" the man asked him.

"My grandfather," Kasim said to Roger. "Our grandfather from … from some side of the family, was the pots and pans engineer. He worked for Uncle Tivo."

The man was looking at Roger puzzled. Kamba his age did not wear single gold rings in their ears. He greeted him in Kikamba. When Roger did not respond, he turned to Salim.

"Not King'oo," Salim said. "He is Caesar's son-in-law. His name is Roger."

"Hi," Roger greeted him.

The garage man nodded, uncertain how to respond, turned to Salim and for a moment sounded earnest. He could not count the old men in his family that he had unquestioningly called grandfather all his life. Not wishing to be side-tracked, Salim ignored that problem and turned to the one at hand.

"How much?" he asked.

"For this old thing?" he seemed to agonise over it and finally give up. "I give it to you; the engine for you is free. But labour will cost."

He picked up a dusty piece of paper carton from under the car, tore a piece from it and asked for a pen. No one had a pen. Remembering, he felt about on his head, found a ball point pen buried in the tangles of his hair at the back of his head and started writing.

"What is there to write?" Salim asked.

"One moment," he said, starting to add up the figures he had scribbled on the piece of carton.

The pen ran out of ink before the final figure. He tossed away pen and paper, picked up a burned matchstick and continued on his forearm. He held out his arm for Salim to read. One look at the figure and Kasim yelled like someone whacked his head with a tyre lever.

"What?" he cried.

"The best I can do," said the mechanic.

Salim picked up the torn carton on which the calculations had begun.

"Five kilo grease," he read aloud. "Ten litre oil? And Musau, Kilonzo and Katiku. Who are these people?"

"My assistants," he said with a shrug.

"*Makarau,*" Kasim translated. "The big, fat, corrupt policemen. Not their real names, but good enough for him."

They collected every Friday evening in the name of permits, licenses, and assorted illegal fees. The garage owner also had to pay yard rent daily to county hall thugs who claimed to own the land that belonged to the county.

"And for my boys you see waiting for you to make up your mind and give them something to work on."

His boys, the gang that did not get to work on the Mercedes, hovered around with hammers, metal files, blow torches, and spray guns waiting for the word to begin work on the Audi.

"We know the boys don't cost," said Kasim.

They were dropouts from technical high schools, and graduates of hard-life polytechnics, hoping to land jobs as motor vehicle mechanics after internship.

"Strike out the boys," Salim said.

Internship was how employers, including doctors, lawyers, and hotels, got desperate youth to work for them without pay. Labeled 'trainees', and sometimes provided with uniforms, they were no more than serfs.

"You can do better than this," he said waving the piece of paper at the garage owner

"That, or we take our free engine and go elsewhere."

The man burst out laughing.

"That is funnier than your Kamba with a *kamba* joke," he said to Kasim. "I have not finished giving you the engine for free and you already want to take it, and your business, somewhere else? If I was not one of you …"

"You are King'oo?" Salim was startled. "*Kwani* how many are we?"

"My cousin's brother-in-law is married to King'oo," he explained.

That made him King'oo too.

"Why then do you treat us like strangers?" Kasim asked him.

338

"Your King'oo sister has my cousin's brother-in-law living like a wet chicken on a perch in his own house."

"What do we have to do with that?" Kasim asked him. "If your men are not men enough …"

"All right," said the man with a change of tone. "You are now strangers to me. So, this is my offer, my final offer."

He scratched on his forearm with the matchstick.

"I would not give this price to my own father," he said, showing it to Salim. "My final, final offer, take it or leave it, and we are not negotiating it anymore."

Salim looked at the figure. It was higher than the first offer, and more than he could afford. Again, all due to Kasim's big mouth. Still, it was easier to live with than another session with Hurricane Eva. He offered the man a hand to shake.

"Put it in," he said.

The mechanic withdrew his outstretched hand.

"Put what in?" he asked.

"The engine."

"I did not say I could put it in anywhere," he said.

"At least try."

The man shook his head, and waved his arms in the air, and swore so loudly his assistants stopped working to watch.

"What are you stopping for?" he yelled at them. "I want that gearbox ready before three or you are all fired."

Then he turned to Salim and took his shoulder again and talked to him like an idiot son.

"Listen," he said.

"I am listening," said Salim.

"You King'oo don't listen well, so now listen," the man said. "The engine does not work, can't work, will not work."

"You already told me that," said Salim.

"It is dead, *kwisha*. It will never work again."

"Who said it had to?" Salim asked him again.

339

The man slowed down his protestation, took a step back and regarded Salim strangely. Salim smiled encouraging.

"You really want me to put a dead engine inside a dead car?" he asked.

"You finally get it."

The man thought, saw no problem with that, only a crazy possibility where before there was none. He nodded.

"All right," he said. "I can do that, but it will cost you. It will cost you a lot of money."

"How much?"

"I will not even ask why," he said. "But this will cost you a lot of money. More than the Audi would have cost you."

He found another burned matchstick on the ground and started scratching on his forearm.

Salim glanced at the figure, shook his hand, and left.

Chapter 37

Mrs Kilonzo brought in a tray, served Salim and his visitor then withdrew.

"Mister Ryan," Salim said, stirring his cup. "I will have your cheque ready by Tuesday."

"Which Tuesday?" asked the visitor.

"Next week," said Salim. "Trust me."

Mr Ryan was a descendant of old colonial farmers in Laikipia where his family grew wheat and raised cattle long before Salim's grandfather was born. That much Salim got at their first appointment, delivered in Kiswahili to be sure he got it all and understood there would be no racial nonsense between him and his client. He was Laikipian through and through, born and bred, and he knew politicians, government officials and other influential people on first name bases.

Having said that, he appreciated that Salim, though young for the job, came highly recommended. Caesar, the most upright man he had met in and outside the government, had sent him to Salim. Salim had not disappointed him once in years of standing for him in land and other business matters. Until now.

"I am sorry, Mister Ryan," Salim said to him. "But I have some problems with Caesar's burial, and it has nothing to do with inheritance, so office work has slowed down a bit. But ..."

"Why Tuesday?" asked the client. "You have my files, my money now, you have everything. I'd like my cheque now if you don't mind."

"I can write you a cheque now," Salim said. "But my partner has to countersign it and he is in Mombasa until Monday."

"Not good enough," Mr Ryan shook his head. "You promised Thursday, remember? Thursday is today, so, my cheque now."

The desk phone rang. The secretary picked it up, listened, handed it to Salim.

"The partner," she said.

"Hello?" said Salim. "I told mister D'Souza I'd be there at six o'clock. After the funeral. Yes, I understand. Six o'clock. I have cheques for you to sign. Mister Ryan is here with me now. Tuesday afternoon?"

He hung up. Mister Ryan rose. He was a big man, with a big, florid face, thick grey hair and sun-burned arms and legs.

"Mister Salim," he said, adjusting his shorts. "I will be very upset, if I don't get my cheque by Tuesday."

"This time Tuesday, you will have it. I promise."

"Good day, then," he rose, picked up his briefcase and walked out of the office.

As soon as he heard the exit door close behind him, Salim grabbed his phone and hit the speed dial.

"Maria," he said when she answered. "Disregard what I said a moment ago. I will be there to pick you up on Friday, as originally agreed. I will explain."

He had a knot in his stomach when he hung up. Since borrowing from his client accounts, Salim felt he was a thief waiting to be caught. He could continue to play the old game of borrowing from the left pocket to pay to the right pocket, but that would only delay the consequences.

He rose and walked to the window. There was a factory fire in industrial area, flames leaping in the sky and smoke billowing over surrounding areas. He could almost smell the poisons rising from burning rubber, plastic, paints, and chemicals smuggled into the country for manufacturing counterfeit products. It reminded him where he had left his partners in crime.

He took his jacket and pulled it on as he made for the door. Kasim was entertaining the mechanics and Roger was dozing inside the Audi that Salim rejected, when he got back to the garage.

"Ready for lunch, Roger?" Salim asked him.

"Ready since morning," Roger said, crawling out of the car.

He looked old, tired, and hungry.

"Soon as Kasim is done with his mechanics," Salim said.

"How many Maasai does it take to castrate a cow?" Kasim was asking the one greasing the front right bearing.

"How many?" asked the young man.

"Zero?" said Kasim.

"Who castrates it then?"

"Don't you have cows where you come from?" Kasim asked him.

"He is from Dandora," said his friends laughing.

"An easier one then," Kasim said to him. "How many wheels does a car have?"

"Four."

"Where did you go to school?" Kasim asked him.

"Dandora," his friends laughed at him.

"Let my boys work," the garage owner said to Kasim. "This lot swears milk comes from a Brookside delivery lorry."

"Doesn't it?" asked Kasim.

The young men laughed. The garage owner turned to Salim.

"Sell me your Beetle," he said. "I will trade you for …"

He looked round the yard.

"That Toyota," he pointed.

"No," said Salim.

"You did not look."

Salim was preoccupied with how he would pay for everything the funeral committee expected him to, so that they could bury Caesar and let him go back to his normal pains.

The Toyota was in a good condition going by what they had seen so far in all the junkyards and jua kali garages they had toured. A forty-year-old Toyota Crown in neon blue, with black and red upholstery and robust chrome fenders. It was the sort of thing that could interest a comedian.

"Talk to the comedian," he said to the garage owner.

"But the Beetle is yours, is it not?" asked the man.

"Talk to him," he said.

"I want your Beetle."

"Listen," Salim said wearily. "I did not come to trade scraps. The Mercedes must be ready tomorrow morning, remember?"

The man walked away disappointed. The grease boys working on the Beetle would have finished by then but for Kasim's interference.

"Kasim," Salim said impatiently, "Let the boys work. Roger is hungry, and so am I."

They stopped for lunch at a cool garden restaurant on their way back to Kathiani. Roger had a beer and they had orange juice while they waited for the goat ribs and *ugali*.

"Have you guys considered working together," Roger asked them. "On something other than funerals?"

"Me and him?" Kasim laughed. "In case you have not noticed, Salim has no sense of humour."

"Some other business perhaps?" said Roger

"Me and him?" Salim said. "In case you haven't noticed, Kasim never made it through high school?"

"I went," said Kasim.

"You dropped out."

"See what I mean?" Kasim said to Roger. "Who wants to work with someone like that?"

"I am sorry I asked," said Roger. "My brother and I were a bit like you two. When one rose, the other sat, when one ran, the other walked. It drove our father mad how we could not pull together. At least you talk to each other."

"He does not take my calls," Kasim said.

"He only calls me when he is in trouble," Salim said.

"Who else can I call?"

"He does not understand I have to be in courtrooms and land offices and wherever the clients are."

"Still, you do talk to each other," Roger said.

"When we must," Salim agreed. "But for Caesar's death he would be dodging me to avoid paying for my car."

"All he thinks of is money," Kasim said.

"See, you are talking now," said Roger. "So, did we, my brother and me, with our mother standing by with a stick. Dad, rarely had a say in that."

"Was he King'oo?" Kasim asked him.

"See," said Salim. "Never serious."

"My grandfather," Roger laughed. "He could have been King'oo."

He settled in Detroit, where Roger's father was born, and Roger's father worked in a car factory while his mother cleaned for white folk. After high school, Roger enlisted in the army to fight wars he did not care for but, in the process, he learned a great deal about people.

In times of stress people turned predator; lions, tigers, and bears, while others turned prey. Rabbits, deer, ducks, even chickens, sheep, and cattle. With the King'oo, his theories went out of the window. Rabbits had fangs, chickens had talons and worms had scorpion stings. All was mixed up. Nothing he learned before came close to what he learned since he married Eva.

"Tell me," he said. "Is your Aunt Eva really one of Charity's sisters or not?"

"I think so," said Kasim.

"You don't know?"

"I wasn't born."

He looked from Kasim to Salim. Salim looked away, stayed out of it. The two had formed a relationship and a way of exchanging information that would exhaust him.

"Same mother?" Roger asked Kasim.

"I think so," said Kasim.

"Same father?"

Kasim looked around, saw that no one was listening, but he lowered his voice all the same.

"Roger," he said. "You don't ask such questions here. Too many skeletons under too many beds. Man goes to the city looking for work, comes home for Christmas, and discovers he is a baby girl richer."

Roger turned to Salim.

"Caesar?" he asked.

"Let it go, Roger," Salim said. "A few people have gone mad trying to unravel King'oo bloodlines."

Bloodlines that stretched across the country to Wote, the origin of the original King'oo, and beyond. Some said all the way to Kwa-Zulu, and now to China.

"You have met our Chinese cousins," Kasim reminded.

"Kung Fu and Karate," Roger nodded.

He had his reservations about that too.

"You do not know the father or the mother," he said to them. "How can you tell there is blood there?"

"They say they are King'oo," Kasim said to him. "No one does that unless they are King'oo, or insane, in which case they are as good as King'oo."

"The way I understand it," Roger said, "no one, not even Caesar had any clue who their parents were."

"Roger," Kasim again explained, "Anyone admitting to being King'oo must be genuine, regardless of what his mother says. Now, leave it be, or lose your inheritance."

"Inheritance?" Roger asked surprised.

"Everything Caesar's, no matter how big or small, now belongs to everyone Caesar's by birth, marriage, adoption or by any kind of affiliation."

To be shared as the clan saw fit, regardless of need or justification.

Roger nodded thoughtfully. He reached deep into his head and reviewed the reservations he had regarding his wife's clan.

"As I understand it," he said, again thinking like a non-King'oo, and American, "What I have gathered from all the mayhem here is that Caesar died poor."

"Poor?" Kasim feigned outrage. "Who said that? How can a man have been poor and have so much love around him, so many grateful hearts and minds gathered to mourn his passing?"

"Without money?" said Roger.

"The name, Roger, the name," said Kasim. "The name is worth more than gold. There are people would pay to be King'oo."

"Why?"

"I told you already."

"When?"

"Let it be, Roger," Salim said, again trying to lay the issue to rest. "You will not understand King'oo in a lifetime of trying. I know, Roger; am one of them and I still don't. Only Kasim believes he does."

"All this hullabaloo to bury one man?" Roger pressed on. "You don't do anything in halves, do you?"

"Wait till the inheritance battles begin," Salim said to him. "Knives, machetes, pots, and pans, and no one is safe anymore. You have not seen anything yet, Roger. But you have nothing to fear. Hurricane Eva will whisk you away."

"Hurricane Eva?"

"I keep forgetting you are not one of us."

"I'm not?" Roger was startled.

"I mean you are one of *hers*."

That did not sound right either.

"I don't mean it in a bad way, Roger," Salim said. "but your wife, Aunt Eva, is the clan ogre. When we were little, parents would tell us to be good or Aunt Eva would come and take us to school. They called her *ngatunyi*, lioness. Fierce like a lion and as sensitive as a crocodile. Now, after abandoning her father for all these years, she thinks she can whip us back in line and decide how, when and who is going to bury Caesar. And with whose money. Poor Aunt Charity who sacrificed her life for him has no say in it at all.

"Except for the Mercedes funeral."

"Except that."

"Where did that crazy idea come from?"

"It is not as mad as it seems, Roger," Salim said. "In this country, the Mercedes symbol, that thing you stole from the garage, once meant more than the car. Before Prado, it was the emblem of quality, beauty, reliability, and power. It was a sign that a man had arrived in heaven on earth. Kings, presidents, and men of power believed in it. Today, the most mediocre politician, and wealthy man, is not contented unless he has more than three in his garage and a helicopter."

"Caesar?" asked Roger.

"Caesar had just one car," Salim said. "Then something terrible happened."

Aunt Charity told it to Salim one Sunday afternoon when he was visiting from boarding school and Caesar had gone to the market to visit with the old men and to 'shorten the evening' as he used to say.

She was in a reminiscent mood, not sad, just not happy as she told him how, after school, she and her sisters played round the mango trees, climbed the pepper trees like boys and jumped down on the roof of their father's old car, much to his dismay.

Then, one day, she came home from school to find six boys from Uncle Mativo's Polytechnic loading the remains of the old car onto a donkey wagon.

"What are you doing to my father's car?" she asked the donkey wagon driver.

"Ask them," he said pointing at the boys.

"Your father's car?" said one of them, "this is not a car anymore. This is scrap."

Uncle Mativo and her father were under the pepper tree, with cups of tea, haggling over the price.

"We are going to cut and chop it up and hammer it," said the boy. "We are learning how to make braziers and basins out of old cars."

"But don't worry, little girl," said the donkey driver. "It will feel no pain."

She run to her father with tears in her eyes.

"You promised."

"I know, little mother," he said to her. "It hurts me too, but we can't afford to repair it now. Uncle Tivo has bought it for his students to learn from. God knows, we need the money."

"Don't cry now," said Uncle Tivo. "I will make something useful out of it for you. What would you like? A basin? Or a chapati pan? Chapati pan will remind you of your father's beloved car each time you cook chapati."

She ran in the house to cry. The image of the car in which her father drove them out on weekends to Magadi, Naivasha and Hell's Gate to experience the world outside Kathiani, being lifted so easily onto a donkey wagon to be taken away and cut to pieces by boys without compassion, had remained with Aunt Charity all her life.

Salim remembered how sad he was when she told him about it. But he could not have imagined it would lead to the predicament he was now in; sitting in traffic jam on Uhuru Highway, with hawkers hanging in the windows trying to sell him everything from nail clippers to car seats. It irritated him, but he understood they were doing what they had to do to survive.

Roger found it hard, but he finally let it go when the food came. He stared at the trays near shock. Salim realised the mistake he had made letting Kasim go to the kitchen to make the order. There was enough food to feed a gang of *jua kali* mechanics and their assistants. A feast of grilled ribs, fried meat, and blood sausages with an accompaniment of *ugali, sukuma wiki* and mugs of boiled goat's hoof soup.

Chapter 38

With two beers and a ton of tasty food in his belly, Roger was in high spirits, when they left the meat den. He talked nonstop about the things he saw along the way, the activities and the many informal businesses set up on the road reserve on both sides of the road. He was amazed at the number of bars, barbecue dens, metal workshops, repair garages, car washes, furniture shops and ...

"Casket!" he yelled at Salim.

Salim braked hard. With his mind focused on the hearse, Salim had forgotten he was also expected to deliver a casket.

He waited for a break in traffic, made a U-turn and drove back to the coffin workshop Roger had seen. It was a simple, wood structure with a sign that advertised funeral services at affordable prices, and caskets to fit all budgets. There was a coffin leaning on either side of the entrance and a vase of plastic flowers by each coffin.

The salesman stepped out to meet them the moment the Beetle stopped at the front, and he ushered them in a big, airy room with a beige-tiled floor and white walls and plastic ceilings. He herded them to the office corner and tried to sit them by a large, executive sales desk, with a vase of white plastic lilies next to a black telephone, and a large executive chair behind it. Facing the desk were four visitors' chairs.

No one went casket hunting on his own, he explained happily. Sometimes the funeral committee came along to be sure the size, the colour, the shape and handles were as specified by the clan and there were no kickbacks in price negotiation.

"So, what can I do for you, gentlemen?" he asked them.

"We are here for a casket," Salim said.

"So, I assumed," he said, laughing as he went round to his executive chair. He sat down picked up a thick, photocopied catalogue.

"Please do sit down."

Kasim sat down. Salim and Roger remained standing. He had to choose who to address.

"As you can see," he opened the catalogue to Kasim, "We have several modes here."

"Coffins have models?" Kasim asked.

"Types, makes, call them whatever," said the salesman. "We prefer mode, see? As in mode of travel to the other side."

"Do you have a black, four-wheel drive, hard *pondo*, nineteen twenty-one mode?" Kasim asked him. "That was when Caesar, the one we want to make travel in style, was born."

Salim and Roger looked at each other. It was going to be a hard sell, they thought. They drifted away, started browsing the showroom. The salesman was torn between going with them and dealing with Kasim.

"Apart from coffins?" Kasim asked him, "What else do you do here."

"Caskets," said the salesman.

"So, you just sit and wait for people to die then sell them modes?"

"We have a workshop at the back," he said rising. "Would you like to see it?"

He was halfway to Salim and Roger, before Kasim could respond.

"Can I show you anything, gentlemen?" he asked them.

"Not if this is all you have," said Salim.

"Step this way, please," the man led then through another door to a dark, windowless room at the back.

He flicked a light switch to reveal a showroom-cum-storage space with caskets of diverse types and shapes arranged around.

"We have several models of very affordable caskets here," he said. "Take this one, for example. It is light, roomy and within most people's budgets. And this other one here is our most affordable casket. We have sold hundreds, thousands of them in the last two weeks."

Salim and Roger looked at each other. The casket was vanished deep oak and looked decent enough for a Caesar to travell in. They felt its silk-smooth finish, tapped on the lid. They looked at each other puzzled. Roger took a step back and tapped on the last one they had considered. That one sounded solid, like an oak casket. They turned to the salesman. They did not need to ask.

"Paper, gentlemen," he said. "This one is made out of recycled paper," he said. "Pressed and reinforced so you cannot tell the difference by looking at it."

"A paper bag," Kasim said.

"You could say so, yes, it is, essentially, a paper bag. A large paper sack."

"People bury their people in paper bags?" Salim was awed.

"Sure," said the man.

"Why?" asked Salim, thinking like Aunt Eva would.

"With the cost of living being what it is today, one has to choose between the living and the dead."

"How?" asked Kasim. "Starve the living, feed the dead?"

Realising he was not going to make any business out of them, the salesman gave it to them straight.

"It depends on what you want to do with your loved one," he said. "If you want to frame them for future reference, we offer you our deluxe, Mahogany model for the modest price of a hundred-fifty thousand. But, if all you want is to bury them, stick them in the ground and be done with it, this ten-thousand casket is the perfect one for you."

"You know, gentlemen" Roger said to Salim and Kasim. "This makes a lot of sense. Ashes to ashes, dust to …"

"Roger!" they said together.

"Seriously, gentlemen," he said to them. "You know how the Mayas interred their dead kings?"

"We are not Mayas," they said together.

"Kikuyu?" asked the salesman. "Did you know Kikuyu did not bother with graves until the white man came insisting the get the bones out of site? They left their loved ones under a tree for the spirits to take and the hyenas to clean up afterwards. Many communities round the world just wrap the body in linen, animal skins, old newspapers or whatever is at hand, and bury it. Indians burn their dead for a clean, no fuss, send-off. A recycled paper casket is just one way of doing the same thing."

"What did I tell you boys?" said Roger.

"Roger," Salim said, "first, we are Kamba."

"I know, you are King'oo," Roger said. "You must go with the deluxe mahogany otherwise the other clans will consider you cheapskates. Hurricane Eva will love it. To go with the deluxe Mercedes hearse you are getting for her."

"Are you sure, Roger?" Kasim asked him. "About the cost?"

"Positive."

"A hundred-fifty?"

"I give a discount," said the salesman quickly. "Hundred-forty."

"Hundred-twenty," Kasim said.

"Thirty-five," said the salesman. "Final offer."

"Hold it right there," Kasim said. "How do we know it is not recycled."

"Recycled how?"

"Buried today, back in the showroom by morning?"

The salesman turned to Roger expecting clarification. Roger turned to Salim.

"Your call," he said.

"Hundred," said Salim. "Final offer."

"Credit card?" Roger had his card out.

"Roger, wait," Kasim and Salim said together.

The man grabbed the card and, while Roger smiled, and Salim and Kasim dithered, charged it, and had Roger sign it before they could stop him.

"Excellent choice," the salesman handed him the receipt. "Your receipt."

"How much is that?" Roger asked, handing it to Salim. "In real money?"

Salim and Kasim looked at it together, looked at each other and shrugged.

"For Caesar," Kasim said to Roger, "It is just right."

Salim gave the salesman instructions on where and when to have it delivered.

"King'oo," he said. "Mophat Caesar."

"Where have I heard this name?" the man said looking at the delivery note he had written. "Caesar?"

They were almost out of the door when it came back.

"Fiscal Caesar?" he called after them. "The money-man?"

They left the city feeling they had done something good that day. Accomplished something that would make Aunt Eva happy and make the clan proud.

Chapter 39

Uncle Sam's train had built up a decisive level of steam and there was no going back. No more raking over cold ashes and problems that had no solutions. Any plan not completed would be abandoned and anyone not on board left behind.

To any other clans' men, it would have been good news, but not for King'oo. There was no such thing as a smooth ride in their experiences and the clan was apprehensive. Sam's train had been on and off the rails so many times they did not believe it could remain on the rails long enough to get them to their destination.

Uncle Sam tried to assure them with optimistic reports that did not tell the whole truth. The fundraising had not hit its target, but as expected, they had raised enough to bury Caesar. That was the important thing, he told them.

He, like others who had stepped out boldly to support the course, did not expect to ever see the promised refund for money spent over and beyond their agreement.

In his final winding up report, he thanked everyone for their daily attendance, their support and cooperation, for their effort in contributing, for the sacrifices and for the good will and patience. He understood they all had personal challenges, hardships, and commitments, but, despite that, the clan had once again overcome its differences, its burdens, and challenges, and showed the world that, with goodwill and communal spirit, there was no problem that a King'oo could not overcome.

"You have not buried Caesar yet," Aunt Eva had to remind him. "You can save the self-praise for the eulogy."

"Ah, about the eulogy," Sam said. "As this is our last meeting, there is something I would like to run by you all to see if it meets with everyone's approval."

He shuffled his papers, cleared his throat.

"Who is in charge of flowers?" Aunt Eva interrupted to ask.

The gathering went silent. Uncle Sam had to repeat the question aloud for her.

"Who handles flowers? Aunt Kamene?"

"Why me?" said Aunt Kamene.

"You always take care of it."

"Will you cook for the visitors while I do that?"

"Aunt Wavinya?" Uncle Sam asked.

Aunt Wavinya sighed wearily. She had been running around alongside Aunt Kamene caring for and feeding everyone since the first meeting.

"I am too tired to do that now," she said. "And we have to cook for the funeral tomorrow,"

"Let everyone take care of her own wreath," Aunt Kamene said.

"We budgeted for flowers," said Aunt Eva. "Where is the money?

"Nothing," said the assistant treasurer.

"What do you mean nothing?"

"It was all in the same pot," he said. "We paid for this and for that and for this."

The donations, as everyone knew were erratic, and he had spent his own money not in the budget.

"Who had the accounts?" asked Aunt Eva. "Salim?"

"Not me," Salim said. "And not Kasim either, remember?"

He sat squashed between Uncle Tivo and Roger dead tired. The treasurer had excused himself to attend another burial in Meru.

"Where are the accounts?" Aunt Kamene demanded.

"Ladies, please," Uncle Sam said. "Tomorrow is the Friday we have all been waiting for. Can we talk about budgets tomorrow after the burial?"

"You talk," said Aunt Eva. "But I will want to know where every cent went."

Roger turned to Kasim.

"Any particular reason you bury people on Friday?"

"So that they don't mess our weekends," Kasim told him.

As usual, Roger turned to Salim for confirmation, but Salim was too tired.

While the aunts argued about donations, and Uncle Sam tried to calm them down, Uncle Tivo took out his phone and made a call.

"Put that away," Aunt Eva ordered him.

He went ahead to make his call, nonetheless, until Kasim tapped him on the shoulder and told him she meant him. He glanced at Aunt Eva, nodded, and put the phone away.

"We meet at eleven at the mortuary," Uncle Sam said, "Shall we have a viewing there?"

The question was directed at Aunt Charity. She shook her head.

"What about here, before the burial?"

Again, she shook her head. She did not want anyone to see Caesar as he was at the end. She wanted them to remember him as he was when they named him Caesar.

"That is that then," Sam said. "No viewing. The funeral service will be here at the graveside. Pastor Kioko has kindly offered to preside. We pick Mzee Mophat from the mortuary at ten and come straight back here. The hearse?"

Everyone turned to Salim.

"It will be there," he said.

"Ten o'clock?"

"Before ten."

"Promise?"

"Promise," he said. "The casket too."

"A decent casket," Aunt Eva said. "Else you will have to take it back and get another one."

"It is very decent," Kasim said. "Ask Roger."

Roger glanced at him, then at Salim and sighed. They had all agreed to wait until after the funeral, when it would be too late for her to make them take it back. Kasim had tossed him under Sam's train. Salim quickly dug up the delivery note and handed it to her.

"This is a delivery note," she said, holding it with the tips of her thumb and index finger. "Where is the receipt."

He made a show of searched his pockets. Kasim, too proud of what they had accomplished to let it keep, told her where it was.

"Roger has it."

That stopped her short. While she worked out the implications, Salim calculated the shortest distance out of the room.

"Why Roger?" she asked him.

"He was the eldest among us," Salim said, quickly to forestall Kasim's recklessness.

Roger had no choice but to give it over. She glanced at it, looked impressed by the cost, and smiled at Salim appreciatively.

"Salim King'oo, you surprise me yet again."

Then she saw to whose credit card the casket was charged.

"What?" she bellowed. "Roger? Salim? Whose idea was this? Kasim?"

"Mine," Roger owned up without the hesitation.

"Take it back," she said to Salim. "Take it back at once."

Kasim stepped in to remind her it was late, and Nairobi was miles away, and the coffin shop would have closed, and the casket delivered to the funeral home by the time they got there. And tomorrow would be too late for it too. They could not return the casket, shop for another one, pick Caesar up from the funeral home and bury him on the same day.

"First thing in the morning," she ordered. "I will not waste my money on a casket no one, not even Caesar, will ever see again."

"Waste your money?" Aunt Kamene leapt in. "How much do you think we *wasted* taking care of your father?"

"Keep out of this, Kamene," Aunt Eva ordered.

"You don't tell me what to do," Aunt Kamene said. "Who do you think you are?"

"I am not one of your market women."

"I am a market woman," Aunt Kamene said to her. "I am a mother too. What are you?"

Roger turned to Salim and Kasim by his side and apologised for trying to impress her on their behalf..

"Sorry, boys."

"Just goes to show how little an American man knows his King'oo wife," said Kasim, with a discreet laugh.

Roger smiled his perennial bemused small smile, as they like errant pupils waiting for punishment. Salim knew it would end up on his head all of it. She would never believe he and Kasim had not tricked Roger into paying for the most expensive casket in Nairobi and the entire world. True, Salim could have stopped Roger, if only he tried to, but he had been tasked with buying a casket without money. The only casket he could have afforded was the one up a tree, or the budget model, the paper bag one, and that would have probably earned him a death penalty.

He was ready for the bashing. Like a King'oo man, without a whimper. In a regrettable way, he had struck a blow for King'oo men, one for which he could never claim credit. Aunt Eva would find a way to get back at him and Kasim, but he knew it would be worse for Roger.

"Roger," he whispered, "Let me know when you get fed up with the old battle axe. You will be free before she can say hit the road jack."

Roger smiled his small smile and touched his shoulder.

"Will remember that," he said.

"Don't worry, Roger," Kasim added. "We King'oo are experts at marriage and divorce. The old women you see there? Every one of them has married, divorced, and married more than a dozen times. Most times to the same King'oo man, out of spite."

Roger glanced at the women's corner. The ladies in question were galloping in the direction of their eighties with blissfully bright eyes and smiling faces, teeth, or no teeth.

"And they would do it all again just to see a King'oo man suffer," said Kasim.

Roger turned to Salim for fact check.

"I had nothing to do with that," Salim said.

"So, when do you boys plan to get married?" Roger asked them.

"To King'oo women?" asked Salim.

"Are you kidding?" said Kasim.

Sam finally managed to get his evening train back on tracks and leave everyone positive and reasonably optimistic of the following the day's success. Aunt Kamene started serving *muthokoi*, and Salim and Kasim slipped out to go back to the city and keep eyes on their hearse.

Hammers were ringing, files grinding, blowtorches hissing, sparks flying when they got to the repair garage shortly after nine. The foreman had rigged up floodlights so his boys could work through the night, and they were working feverishly to deliver on their promise. They were due a bonus if they finish the job before sunrise.

Kasim left Salim with them and went off to work. Salim begun to worry as he went round assessing progress. He could not see how they could finish the bodywork and paint the car in one night.

"My boys can do miracles," the foreman told him.

He had poached them from a chop-shop in Kisumu, where they had routinely turned junk into saleable cars, and on occasion converted one type of a hot car into another for sale across the border in Uganda.

"This is nothing," said the foreman. "You will see. When they are done, this thing will look like new."

That did nothing to silence the little voice in Salim's head whispering that his life was over, finished and gone to hell. If the gamble he had taken did not pay off, He would have to run away from the clan and never come back, or spend the rest of his life in prison. He would have to take his own life, or have someone take it for him. He wished Kasim were there with him.

And he was so tired he was about to drop.

Chapter 40
What do you get when you chop a cop's head in four?

The *Black Survivors* were on their third or fourth break of the night, smoking weed, drinking from unlabeled bottles, and arguing politics by the open-air urinals behind the club. Inside the club, the comedian had taken over the stage, but was struggling to do the same with the audience.

"Any protocol billionaires in the house?" he asked from the stage.

The question hung in the air, on a cushion of alcohol fumes and cigarette and marijuana smoke, in a part of the club marked smoke-free zone, and it was about to drift out of the stage door, out sight and out of mind, to join the band by the urinal, when Kasim dragged it back in and refloated the question.

The old normal was back. The architects of doom, the engineers of the mayhem that knocked out, and all but killed the city forcing inhabitants to flee, had retreated to their castles to stir cauldrons of digits, cook up prophetic numbers forecasting famines and plagues, earthquakes and floods, and death and destruction, of biblical proportions next time.

Fun and laughter, the joy of being, the old hedonism and the love of life they tried to extinguish with whimsical protocols and laws excavated from the swamps of colonial tyranny, were back.

Once a week, the big, big ones and the small big one closed their official city offices early to, ostensibly, go hang out with their voters in their home villages and, with their presence and their money, to grace weddings, birthdays, funerals, church services and public toilet openings. A power-filled four-day weekend of tossing bundles of money out of car windows, at roadside gatherings to show they cared for the welfare of their people, that they were one with their mud-hut followers, despite living hundreds of miles away in palaces.

Their power-packed weekends begun Thursday night at *Uncle Dave's Curry and Comedy House* in the company of like-minded men who made them see that it was all right to be big and important and powerful and rich beyond any imagination or justification.

"Any protocol billionaires in the house?"

The audience looked at one another. They lowered their voices, and he heard one wonder whether the fool on stage realised what day of week it was.

"*Haalloo,*" Kasim greeted for the third time that night. "It is Thursday night at *Uncle Dave's Curry and Comedy House*. Kasim the Komedian, triple K and all that, is now in the house."

Thursday was the day Kasim got to tell them the truth. In ill-disguised satire, he told them what their voters said about them. But from time to time, lost and tired of beating about the bush, he also told them what the hard-life, mud-hut creatures that lined up in the rain to elected them now really thought about them.

"Hard-life men run this country," he said. "Not the fools they elect to pay themselves more money than God pays himself, to do nothing for them. Hard-life men are the men in this town. Next time you pass one pushing a load of scrap metal down the road, sweating buckets, and about to collapse and die from hunger, press your horn, wave, and let him know that you see and respect him for what he is."

The house was suddenly still. Kasim knew he had them. He repeated his question about protocols and billionaires.

"Where is this fool from?" He heard someone ask.

"Find out where he lives," one Big One said to his henchmen.

Thursday audience had been trying to get Kasim fired from the day he was hired. At some point along the way, Mr Dave bending under pressure had Kasim sign a disclaimer stating that his thought, actions, and utterances while on stage, or anywhere in the club's premises, were his own thought, actions, and utterances, and the club would not be held responsible for loss, damage, or injury, occasioned by his words or actions during his appearances at *Uncle Dave's Curry and Comedy House*. Notices were posted by the club entrance and copies place on tables inside the club and glued to washroom walls and lampposts at the parking.

Kasim had read the disclaimer with amusement, signed it, and happily gone back to offending the same men who wanted him fired.

"A simpler one," he said to them. "What do you get when you chop a big, fat, corrupt policeman's head in four?"

It was a deliberate provocation of an audience that disliked him from the day he made his debut at the club, and they realised he had no regard, or respect, for rank, class, office, race, tribe, gender, or political correctness.

"Come on guys, you pay their salaries, so you must know."

Mr Dave had he would be fired the moment he stepped over the business line; crossed the line between profit and loss.

"I understand you people," he said to his audience the evening he signed Mr Dave's disclaimer. "Some in this room have as much sense of humour as a council *askari*."

He got a good guffaw or two out of that one.

"But trying to get a self-employed, hard-working, hard-life citizen fired over a joke is not a joke. What kind of a conniving cold-hearted leader does such a thing? I voted for you all, and I promise I will never again vote for any of you."

The room was dead quiet.

"That was a joke," he said and laughed. "I would never vote for such a mob. Or for the thirty percent you tout to ensure peace at home."

The audience was now mostly awake, holding their breath. He could not clearly see what the special people at the reserved tables to the side and back of the room were up to, but he suspected they were awake too and paying attention.

"You still have to tell me what you get when you split a big, fat, corrupt policeman's head in four," he said to them.

Mr Dave buried his head in his hands and groaned.

"This is it," he said to himself. 'Disclaimer or no disclaimer, Kasim is history."

He uncovered his eyes, cast about for someone to send to put a stop to Kasim's madness.

The band was out for the third break of the night, hanging out by the urinals, drinking, and smoking whatever they had brought to kill the pain of Thursday night with the executive. Mr Dave did not have to supply the band with refreshments as part of their contract, but he still wished their leader would spare time at the bar with him and help control the comedian.

"Come on people," Kasim was saying. "You have been here before. You know what you get when you chop a cop's head in four."

At a side table close by the stage sat four hard faced men in dark suits and ties. Their table was the only one without a wallet inspector, a breach of tradition at *Uncle Dave's Curry and Comedy House,* and at first Kasim had assumed they were bodyguards. Then he saw that each had a bottle of whisky in front of him and guessed they were Ugandan businessmen on their way to Mombasa harbour to clear import goods. Or perhaps up-country thugs from Laikipia killing time before going out to raid a late-night comedy club like *Uncle Dave's.* He itched to ask which was which but had a feeling that would not end well.

"What do you get when you chop a big, fat, corrupt policeman's head in four?" he asked them instead.

They sat up startled.

"Are you asking us?" they seemed to ask. "Us?"

365

"What you get when you chop a cop's head in four?" he said. "Yes, gentlemen, I am asking you."

They looked at one another, mildly amused. One of them slowly rose and approached the stage. He beckoned. Kasim leaned over. The man whispered in his ear.

"Don't do that with us," he said.

"I can't do that with you," Kasim said in the microphone, feigning shock. "I hardly know you."

The club fell quiet. All eyes were on the men, as they looked at Kasim, looked at one another and again at Kasim.

"What do you get when you chop a big, fat, corrupt cop's head in four?" he asked them. "I'll give you a hint."

They stared at him in disbelieve.

"You don't get arrested," he said. "The law does not like big, fat, corrupt policemen either. Here is another hint. You do not get the death penalty, or even life in prison. Judges hate big, fat, corrupt policemen too. So, what do you get when you chop a cop's head in four?"

Mr Dave buried his head in his hands again. The silence deepened, the silence of impending doom. Kasim tossed his hands in the air, in mock despair.

"Think about it," he said, and picked up his time-worn box guitar leaning on a chair by the mike stand.

"I sing you a little song while you think about it," he said. "Give you a little inspiration."

He stepped on the chair, rested the guitar on his raised knee.

"It is my favourite big, fat policeman song. It is called 'The Song of The Big, Fat, Corrupt Policeman'. A simple, little, feel-good, fat-policeman song. Let us all sing it together now, all of us together, including fat women in trousers, thin men in makeup, and the four nice gentlemen in dark suits here at the front. All of us together now …

He strummed his guitar, so out of tune someone laughed aloud, but the laughter spread when he started to sin.

"I will never go to Uncle Dave's anymore, more, more
There is a big, fat, policeman in the hall, hall, hall
He grabs you by your balls
Asks you for your pass
Takes all in your purse
And kicks you in your ass
I will never go to Uncle Dave's anymore."

The audience was about to begin throwing missiles at him, and Mr Dave downed his soda and rose to go calm them down. Then he saw two of the men in dark suits get up and approached the stage. Kasim met them at the edge of the stage, leaned over and held out the microphone to one of them.

"Your name?" he asked.

"We just want to talk to you," the man brushed it aside.

"What about?" Kasim again held out the mike.

"Outside."

"Why?"

"Step down now, please."

"Why?"

"We just want to talk to you," said the second man.

"I am working. Later?"

"Now," said the man.

Kasim glanced at the other two at the table. One of them was picking *nyama choma* out of his teeth with a matchstick, the other was playing with the box of matches, their eyes hard, lips curled in cold smiles. Kasim realised he had had gone too far.

Mr Dave was watching from the bar. When their eyes met he turned and slipped inside his office.

"Don't go away," Kasim said to his audience. "I will be right back."

He led the men out of the stage door and round to the parking at the front. The parking lot was deserted. The watchmen were by the gate. One of the hard-faced men grabbed Kasim by his trousers belt and dragged him along.

"Is this a police mugging?" he asked them on recognising the grip.

"Shut up," one said, going through his pockets.

"I have never been mugged by policemen before."

"Shut up," the man said again.

"You are not policemen, are you?"

"Where is your car?" the man asked.

"It is not worth carjacking," Kasim said.

They hustled him to the parking. The watchmen were nowhere in sight. Starting to fear for his life, he raised his voice hoping to attract their attention.

"The car over there," he yelled, pointing.

"The junk?" asked the one doing all the asking.

"The Beetle," Kasim said aloud. "My Beetle."

"What do you do with all the money they pay you?"

"The club pays me with food and drinks."

"No need to shout," said the man holding him by the belt.

"The car belongs to my cousin, Salim" he said, dropping his voice, for he was beginning to sound ridiculous. "He sold it to me three months ago, but I have not paid him a cent, so strictly speaking the car is still his. You may take it, but it is not much use."

They stuffed his documents back in his jacket pocket and kept the money.

"You can't do that," he protested. "I need my rent."

"Shut up."

"I will report you to Uncle Dave."

"We don't work for Mr Dave."

"Whom do you work for? Uncle Gove?"

One laughed, the other slapped Kasim hard.

"I said to shut up."

"I'll scream," Kasim said.

They knocked him down, pinned him to the ground.

"Now scream," they said.

Then they went to work on him, with kicks and punches. Hearing his cries for help, the watchmen came running. When they saw who was screaming, and who was making him scream, they retreated to watch from a distance.

Mr Dave ran out of a side door and, worked his way to the parking following the sounds of thumps and groans. The hard faces were working Kasim over like they had a contract. Mr Dave stopped at a safe distance and cleared his throat. The watchmen melted back in the shadows.

"Is he a friend of yours?" one of the hard faces asked Mr Dave.

Mr Dave hesitated. Kasim was everyone's friend and no one's friend.

"Keep out of this then, Mr Dave," the man advised.

"The young man has a show to finish," said Mr Dave.

"Go away now, Mr Dave."

"Gentlemen, please," Mr Dave pleaded.

"You are interfering in police business."

"He means no harm."

"Get lost."

Mr Dave retreated. Shortly after, while the men were still working on Kasim, the Governor came out of the club with his underage girlfriend and got in his big, black car. The chief of police also came out with his underage girlfriend and got in a different big, black car. The other two hard-faced men got in the same car, one behind the wheel. The two men sorting Kasim jumped into another big black car and a motorcade of five big, black cars left the club at speed.

Mr Dave came back to help Kasim to his feet.

"What is wrong with your head, Kasim?" he asked.

"It rattles," he said shaking it. "Those policemen kick as hard as donkeys."

"Are you crazy telling sick jokes to the real big ones?"

"Real big ones?" Kasim tried to laugh. "Why didn't they say so. I would have told them the one about the Sergeant at Arms and the Speaker's wife."

The joke had Mr Dave falling off his office chair when he first heard it, but he was not certain it would go down well with the lawmakers.

"Have you heard the jokes they crack in the big house?"

"Next time then," Mr Dave said. "If we still have a license. I will really fire you if no one laughs. Now go home if you can still drive. Otherwise, there is a couch in my inner office."

"Uncle Dave," he laughed, despite the pain. "Not where you audition barmaids."

"Very funny, Kasim, very funny."

"Thanks, Uncle Dave, but I have a funeral tomorrow."

"It is tomorrow already," Mr Dave walked away shaking his head.

His religion said to be kind to all living creatures, but being kind to Kasim, as easy-going as he was, was wearing him out.

Kasim pulled himself together, limped across the parking to the Beetle and crawled inside. He had never been so tired after a gig. But then he had never been so thoroughly worked over by an unhappy audience. He should do that more often, he thought. Make them see, hear, and think. Make them laugh, cry, and get mad. Make them so mad they wanted to drag him outside and lynch him. That would be his new goal.

An audience did not have to laugh aloud, not immediately. The best jokes were not funny in the moment. Like the one about a chief who would not chair a clan council to avert a tribal war because it was his day of prayer. Then the warring parties torched everything, including the church while he was in it. Kasim would have to find a way of telling it so the men in dark suits who worked him over got it too.

He was woken up by the sound of the security guard tapping on the car window with his club.

"*Ero*," he said, his eyes closed. "No cigarette."

"I don't want your cigarette," said the man.

Kasim sat up, peered at the man.

"Do I detect hostility?" he asked.

"Stop telling stupid jokes about Maasai," said the man.

Kasim was tired of hearing people tell him what jokes not to tell. He was about to tell him to go to hell, then he realised the man was serious, was chewing *khat* and he was armed with a *rungu*.

"I have not told stupid jokes about Maasai today," he said.

"Stop it," said the man.

"Okay," he said. "No more stupid jokes about Maasai."

The security guard walked away without another word. Kasim settled down thinking, - *No Kikuyu jokes, no Maasai jokes, no Indian jokes, no fat policeman jokes ... what was wrong with everyone?*

Then the parking lot lights went out and he realised day had begun. The parking had emptied while he slept, and everyone had gone home. He turned the ignition key. The engine was dead. He closed his eyes and was about to drift back to sleep. Then he remembered what day it was and got out of the car. The watchmen were smoking by the gate.

"*Ero*," he called."

They glanced his way.

"See?" he heard one said to the others. They laughed and continued smoking.

"Ero," he called again. "Give us a push."

They took their time walking over. He had a feeling if Mr Dave did not call him Assistant Manager they would have worked him over too. They found him messing with the engine, trying to remember how he got it to work last time.

371

"*Ero*," they said, "what is the problem?"

"My car died."

"But we are not mechanics," one said.

"Brain surgeons, I know," he said, "but give me a push, anyway? Would you believe I wasted two years of my life at my uncle's polytechnic university learning to repair cars?"

"I wasted three trying to be an architect," one of them said.

"See what I mean? said Kasim.

"But I got my degree in architecture," said the man.

"See what I mean?"

"Seriously," said the watchman. "I have a degree in architecture."

"And is this being the best you can be?"

"I can't get a real job."

"So, you settle for being a club watchman? Have you considered applying for a job as a politician?"

"Be a politician?"

"It is easier than you think. And the pay is unbelievably good. You get to write yourself a check from the Central Bank, a cheque as big as you like, and you do not even have to work at all. We have Governors who can't govern, Senators who don't know what they are supposed to senate about and MPs who can't understand why they must attend parliament every day. It would be a job worthy of a graduate."

The guard was giving it a serious thinking.

"And when the voters get restless, you send the police to club them on the head and remind them who is chosen by God to lead them to the promised land."

The guard got a bewildered look on his face. Kasim laughed.

"No kidding," he said. "I don't doubt your degrees; I have one too, if only I could tell you what it was. But what are they good for? Politicians buy them by the barrow to qualify for leadership, without once setting foot at the university where you got yours. Your degree may be genuine, but who cares or trusts such crap anymore? Just give us a push, okay."

They hesitated. They had pushed his car too many times already, and all for free. When would he start paying them for it?

"Come on guys," he said, "I am one of you, a hustler, a working man. I give you my cigarettes."

He got in the car, let them think about it. They discussed it for a moment, argued a little, then they put their shoulders to the car. The car rolled forward leaving a trail of engine oil.

"Faster," he called out.

He released the clutch just before the gate and the engine coughed, spewed a cloud of thick, black smoke, hiccupped a couple of times then was silent. Kasim stepped out, raised the engine cover, touched the wires, twisted, and turned, tightened battery terminals, knocked on the distributor cup, then closed the cover.

"Once more," he said.

He helped them push the car back to the top of the parking then hopped back inside.

"A lot faster this time," he said.

They put their hearts in it and sent the car hurtling down the drive to the gate. Just before the gate, Kasim released the clutch and again the engine coughed out dark smoke, let out an encouraging roar for a second then died dead. He got out, tinkered with wires.

"One more time," he said.

Again, they pushed the car back to the top of the drive, sent it scuttling back to the gate. This time the engine did not utter a sound when he released the clutch. The security guards walked away without a word, leaving him to get himself out of the way of passing cars.

Chapter 41

Friday morning brought with it new challenges, new uncertainties, and dreads of the day ahead. It was a bright and sunny day, Salim discovered when he crawled out of the cab of the pickup that the foreman had said was the cleanest and safest place to lie down and rest.

Crows and marabous whirled in a blue sky over the garbage tip round the corner, the clang of hammers, the wailing of grinders and the smell of hot metal, burning rubber and wet paint in the air. A deceptively normal and promising day.

He followed the sound of hammers to the back of the shed. Then he stopped astonished. The boys from Kisumu had done it. They had, as promised, performed a miracle.

"What do you think now?" asked the foreman.

He was lost for words. The Mercedes had turned out, not as good as new, as they had promised, but it was better than he could have imagined. They were rolling it out of the repair shed, when Kasim arrived in a taxi.

"Is this ours?" he asked, staring in awe.

"They say so," Salim said.

Then he saw the black eye.

"I was mugged," Kasim explained. "Four big, fat policemen who did not like my jokes."

"And where is the Beetle?"

"*Uncle Dave's.* Kajicho will bring it before nine."

They watched the mechanics replace door handles, mouldings, and mirrors. Then they cleaned up the interior, patched up the upholstery with glue and leather from scrapped cars, and by the time they were done, the Mercedes still did not look like new, but it was good enough to sell. It needed two to three hours for the paint to dry.

Salim glanced at his watch. He had slept less than six hours in two days and the biggest challenge was yet to come.

"I must get some sleep," he said to Kasim. "Go to the funeral home see how things are there. We'll need everyone out of the way when we fetch Caesar."

Then Kasim remembered the taxi was still waiting. Salim gave him money to pay for it and reminded him they would have to account for it to Aunt Eva.

Kasim found the clan milling about the mortuary car park waiting for someone, for any member of the burial committee, to tell them why they were standing there with nothing to do when they could have been home doing their chores until Caesar arrived for burial. The bus Uncle Sam had hired to take them to the mortuary to accompany Caesar on his last journey home, was parked nearby waiting to take them back. When they saw Kasim arrive in a taxi they charged forward with questions.

"Why are you all here?" he asked them.

That was the first thing they wanted him to tell them.

"Where is Aunt Charity?" he asked next.

Aunt Charity was at home waiting for Uncle Richard to pick them up. Kasim refrained from asking them where they got the idea that Uncle Richard would go all the way to Kathiani to bring their aunts to pick up Caesar's corpse.

Then his mind screeched to a halt, and he remembered something vaguely suggested in the chaos of the night before at Aunt Charity's house when his mind was on his job. He was getting late, and Salim was waiting impatiently in the Beetle, when Aunt Eva ordered him to make sure Uncle Richard went to fetch Aunt Charity so she would be at the funeral home to escort Caesar home. The idea of Uncle Richard driving to Kathiani to do that was so preposterous Kasim had not given it a second thought. Until now.

With a sinking feeling, he took out his phone and called Uncle Richard. The phone rang three times before it was rejected. He called again with similar result. The fourth call provoked an angry bellow from Uncle Richard.

"What?"

"Hello, Uncle Richard," he said, as humbly as ever, "Kasim here. Kasim what? No, do not hang up; this is your nephew Kasim. I am not calling to borrow money or your Mercedes. We got a Mercedes hearse. It is about Aunt Charity. No, she is fine, but, you know, today is the funeral. Grandfather Mophat's funeral. No, we have not buried him yet. Yes, we got the pickup, yes, we raised money for the coffin too. But now Aunt Charity wants you to fetch her at home and drop her at the mortuary. It is at …"

"Do you know what time it is?" Uncle Ricard asked him.

"It is morning," said Kasim.

"Then, bugger off!" Uncle Richard said.

"It is … Hallo? Hallo?"

Uncle Richard had hung up. Kasim was in real bad trouble. Aunt Eva would murder him. Then he looked up and saw the people gathered round him waiting for directions.

"There has been a change of plan," he said to them. "You must all go back to Kathiani now. Caesar is already on the way there, and you better hurry or miss the burial."

That confused everyone, but it was better than standing round with nothing to do. They rushed to board *Uncle Sam's Express* and others to go find own transport back. When the last one had cleared the gate, Kasim hopped in the taxi back to the garage.

Salim was supervising the mechanics rigging a carrier on top of the Mercedes. Two boys were painting the tyres black, cleaning and replacing the chrome wheel caps.

"Well?" he said to Kasim.

"Done."

"Aunt Charity?"

"She'll be fine."

Salim was baffled by the reply but, knowing Kasim, decided to let it be. Taxi driver called out of the window for his fare.

"You keep an eye on our Mercedes," Salim said to Kasim. "Make sure they do not sell it."

He took out the camera, which had been residing in the grove compartment ever since he got it, and hopped in the taxi. The mortuary was almost deserted when he alighted from the taxi. Aunt Charity and Roger sat in Uncle Richard's chauffeur-driven Volvo while Aunt Eva tried to find out where everyone had gone.

"Flowers?" he asked her.

"I will get the flowers but ... but where are the rest?"

"They will be here when you come back," he said. "You go get the flowers."

His phone rang. Kasim was in a panic. There were policemen at the garage.

"What do they want?"

Kasim did not know.

"Have they talked to you?" Salim asked him.

Then, realising everyone was listening, he changed the story.

"Where is the photographer," he asked. "What are you doing about it? Do not panic. Where are you calling from? What happened to your phone?"

He was in a call box across the road. He was out of credit as the men in dark suits had taken all his money the night before. The policemen at the garage had not talked to him yet.

"We have a big problem," he said. "They have our night security guard."

They had dragged the night security guard out of the back of the police car and were hustling him to the Mercedes.

"One moment," Salim said.

"They'll be here any minute," he said to Aunt Eva. "Why don't you go get the flowers while we wait?"

Aunt Eva did not like being told what to do by Salim, but she had a tiresome, long night with her sisters, and could no longer deal with the deviousness of King'oo men.

She hesitantly went back to the car with Aunt Charity. Roger smiled and winked at Salim as the Volvo drove off.

Salim's phone was still on.

"Stay away from them," he said to Kasim. Do not say a word, before I get there."

He turned to a young man standing with his arms folded over his chest.

"Who are you?" he asked.

When a King'oo man got a call from a relative asking how he was, the first instinct was to lie. Telling the truth, owning up to being alive and well and in good health, and happy, risked being promptly invited to rush home and help pick pigeon peas, dig a pit latrine, or build a chicken house. Or send money for the purpose. The young man could see he was not in danger of any of that.

"I'm your cousin," he confessed. "Kiluki, son of Musau wa Kamene. Aunt Kamene's daughter's son. You do not you know him; he never comes home. He drives a *matatu* bus from Makindu to Kangundo."

"I always said our mothers had too many children," Salim said.

He handed the young man the Nikon.

"What is this?" Kiluki asked.

"It is a camera. You are now the photographer. Take pictures."

"How?"

He looked through the lens.

"*Atsi.*"

Another young man took it from him and showed him how to hold it. Then he aimed it at the car park and took some shots. He changed shutter speed, took one more, and examined the camera closely.

"I see you know where to press," Salim said. "You are now our official photographer."

"No, I'm not," the man said.

"You will be paid."

"No, thanks," he seemed certain.

"Nikon F2," he said, intrigued by it. "I didn't know they still made them. Does it have film?"

"Of course," Salim said. "Tell me when it runs out."

"I am not with your party," the young man said. "I am with the cortege just leaving."

He gave the camera back to Kiluki and rushed to his car.

"Of course," Salim said to himself. "Too honest to be King'oo."

He looked round for someone he could hand that burden; someone he could trust not to disappear with the camera. There were young men around, all of them King'oo, and some of them he had not seen since the last funeral.

Then he saw the Chinese cousins, standing back away from the herd as usual, observing and conversing in their quiet, calm way. They were the only King'oo who could remain calm and composed inside King'oo hurricanes.

Salim approached them.

"Which is which?" he asked them.

"That joke is now very tired, Uncle Salim," one said.

"Just kidding," he said. "Kung Fu, right?"

"Karate."

"Then you must be ..." he said turning to the other one. "Kung Fu?"

"Karate," said the young man.

"Really?"

Karate was not lying. Knowing how Salim's King'oo blood flowed, he pulled out his identity card to prove which one he was. The card was genuine too, Salim noted, and handed him the camera.

"Take pictures," he said.

"Seriously," said the second young man, "I am Karate. He is Kung Fu."

"Why has he got your ID?"

"You can't tell us apart, who can?"

"Police?"

They laughed. They had been there, done that.

"One day I will figure you two out," he said to them.

Their sense of humour was unsettling. Very not King'oo.

One rumour said their mother was a King'oo woman who sold fruit and vegetable to Chinese railway builders at Sultan Hamud. No one could remember her name, but she was famous for learning to speak Chinese and for teaching Chinese rail builders Kiswahili and Kikamba. It was said that she and her Chinese supervisor boyfriend dumped the twins with the only family they knew would give them a home and migrated to South Kuria. Or was it to South Korea?

The other version, the one most favoured by King'oo women, was the twins' mother was a Chinese railway woman who had fallen for the charm and the wiles of a King'oo man and who, on realizing her folly, wanted nothing more to do with King'oo men. She had dumped the babies with their King'oo father and with her Chinese supervisor boyfriend, migrated to South Sudan. Or was it to South Korea? It was the boys' father who, true to King'oo men's lack of back-bone dumped the twins at Caesar's gate.

Caesar had them brought up King'oo, although many doubted they had King'oo blood in them. They were too polite, too quiet, too sane. Those were not King'oo traits at all. Not the King'oo way of being.

King'oo were royalty, everyone one a king. And like all kingdoms with multiple kings, most King'oo gathering were battle ground for egos. Everyone was his own general, captain and foot soldier, and no one could tell the other what to do, or why they were gathering. Bringing meetings to order needed heavy authority, but on occasion, Caesar had to have help from the police to control his people.

"We are not here to smell out witches," he said often. "We are not here to find out who stole whose goat and kid, who milked whose cow or who stole whose wife and children. Again, we are not here to know who sneaked in

380

his neighbour's house while he was away and fathered which child with which wife. Those issues you will sort out by yourselves when you go back home. We are here because we have a communal problem. A clan problem requiring sanity, unity, and seriousness of purpose. We are here to build a school. A place of learning for all the children of Kathiani, even those without fathers or mothers, whether or not they are King'oo."

Kung Fu and Karate did not miss clan functions, whether they were invited or not, and very often they were not invited. No one seemed to know exactly where they worked or lived. Some said they lived with Chinese relatives at Sultan Hamud. Some said they worked at cement factories in Athi River. Few remembered the boys' relation to the clan. Those who remembered them as boys had no reason to go find them. King'oo boys were expected to find their way home when the world overwhelmed them.

"Now, here is something you boys can do for your Grandfather Caesar," Salim said, handing them the camera.

They examined the camera, mumbling so that Salim did not understand what was said, then they laughed and broke into what Salim suspected was Chinese. Like everyone not a hundred percent King'oo, they laughed when they were baffled by the clan's antics.

"What did you say?" he had to ask.

"Nikon F2 very good," Kung Fu or Karate said, affecting a Kikuyu hustler's accent, the way Kasim did when he told bad Kuyu jokes. They had a unique feel for tongues, Salim could tell.

"Where did you learn Chinese?" he asked them.

"Mandarin," said Kung Fu. "We learned it on the train."

"From China?"

The normally placid faces broke in a smile.

"Uncle Salim," Kung Fu said. "This is not conversation."

He was a cook's assistant, for Chinese rail builders between Mombasa and Nairobi. His brother was a cleaner.

"Can you cook Chinese then?" Salim asked him.

"When the chef lets us," said Kung Fu. "Chapati, *ugali* and *muthokoi* too. *Mwaitu* taught us."

Aunt Charity had taught them things from when they were small.?"

Salim looked from one to the other, searched their faces for mischief. He could not tell them apart, but there was no old King'oo mischief in them. They had dropped out of school at the same stage other King'oo boys did, gone off to find themselves jobs, learned a language and learned to cook Chinese. That left no doubt in Salim's mind they were King'oo. There was not much a King'oo could not do when he set his mind on it.

"I want it back in one piece," he said of the camera.

"What about film?" asked Karate.

"Film?"

"Nikon F2 needs film," said Kung Fu.

"Who says?" Salim asked.

"Nikon."

Salim took back the camera, examined it, tried to open it, and realised he did not know how it.

"Are you sure?" he asked.

"I saw one at work," said Kung Fu.

"Show me," he said handing it back.

Kung Fu turned a knob, pulled and the camera back sprang open. He showed Salim the hollow inside.

"See," he said, "nothing inside. No digital."

"How did you know?"

Kung Fu smiled. At least they inherited something useful from that side of the family.

"They don't make these things anymore," said Karate.

It had not crossed Salim's mind that, like the owner, the camera would be generations out of style. Uncle Richard was probably not aware that, like his views, his camera was obsolete.

He took it back and looked at it. He had not really seen it until then. The camera was new, hardly used, smelling of leather and film dust. Uncle Rich had bought the best camera he could find, realised he was ungifted in photography and dropped it in his drawer.

"Can you use it?" Salim asked Karate.

"Without film the camera is crap," said Kung Fu.

Salim thought about it for a second and nodded.

"That figures," he said. "Trust Uncle Richard to gift me with a useless relic. But no matter; hang on to it. I will get you film."

"They don't make camera film anymore," said Karate.

"I said I will get you film," Salim said to them. "Just don't tell Aunt Eva about the film."

"If she asks me to take pictures?"

"Do whatever she says, but don't let her or anyone else know that there is no film in it."

The cousins looked at each other, smiled and said something in Chinese. All he caught was the word King'oo. Said in Chinese, it sounded complimentary. *King oh oh.*

"That's right," he said to them. "Original King'oo, that is me. I was *King oh oh* before you were born."

He was about to walk back to the taxi then remembered.

"When your Aunts get back tell them everyone has gone on ahead. Go with them."

"You want us to lie to Aunt Eva?" asked Kung Fu.

"We all do," he said. "Just don't let her catch you at it."

He hopped back in the taxi.

Chapter 42

The taxi driver was apprehensive, as the taxi rocked and rolled over the potholes and craters into the motor cars graveyard.

The place was known as the Valley of Thieves. It was where stolen cars went, and wanted thugs hid out in vast slums, abandoned garages and scrap metal dumps, and unwanted people disappeared without a trace. Police did not dare go there without good intelligence, and a definite target. Nor did innocent outsiders.

The taxi driver told Salim how, the first time he dropped a passenger to pick up his car, a garage owner had pounced on him and made him pay for repairs owed by the taxi's previous owner. The crazy mechanics were about to lynch him and burn his car when a police patrol chanced by and rescued him.

Then he saw a police car at the garage where he was to drop Salim, stopped abruptly and ordered him out of the taxi. He collected his fare and sped back to safety.

The garage was deserted but for the police officers searching the yard. The garage owner had left early, having made sure Salim's job was completed and received his payment. The boys he had left waiting for bonus were nowhere in sight. They would have done the sensible thing and disappeared deeper in the motor graveyard at the sight of a police car.

Kasim came out of hiding, when Salim stepped out of the taxi, and walked with him to the garage.

"What do we do?" he asked.

"Whatever they say," Salim said.

They were not the big, fat, corrupt policemen he joked about every night. One of them saw them approach and called out.

"Salim."

Kasim suddenly recognising the man and walked slower. He was a regular at *Uncle Dave's*, where he sat alone at the bar drinking whisky and scanning the room for wanted criminals. Salim recognised him too, from a different place and time.

"Inspector Odero," he said to him. "Still a cop?"

"Senior Inspector," said Odero. "Are you still a lawyer?"

"What else?"

"I catch bad boys and you set them free?"

"No, Inspector, the judge sets them free," said Salim. "I only speak for them. The law is crazy that way. But I do not do that anymore. I am in conveyance now. Why our paths do not cross anymore."

"What are you doing in the valley of thieves?"

"I brought a car for repairs," said Salim. "Where is everyone?"

"They scattered when they saw me coming. They see me here with the Flying Squad looking for car thieves."

Salim saw a face peek out of the back of the police car.

"Is that one of them?"

"Prime suspect," said Odero. "He has not told us much yet, but he will talk when we get him back to headquarters."

Salim had recognised the face, and he sought to change the subject.

"Did you know grandfather Mophat died?"

"Caesar died?

"We bury him today."

"Give my condolence to your family."

"Caesar left his Mercedes to Aunt Charity," Kasim spoke up. "Remember Aunt Charity?"

"I still remember the day she caught us smoking behind the school" said Odero. "My mother nearly killed me that day. Never smoked again."

"I had no such luck," Salim said.

There was nothing like a thorough beating to make a King'oo boy more stubborn.

"I wonder how many of you are in prison today," the inspector was serious.

"Perhaps more than are outside," joked Kasim.

Salim had watched dozens of them talk their way to guilty verdicts after he begged them to keep quiet and let him defend them. Then they had refused to pay his fee and promised to kill him when they came out of prison after serving their life sentences. But those were the easy cases.

Fresh from college, and full of passion for the career, Salim had taken on every ridiculous case the clan could come up with, most of them family related. The litigations often turned personal and exploded in fist fights with Salim in the middle. On occasions, irate judges ordered Salim and his clients locked up in the cells to cool down. The fights continued in the cells, but sometimes Salim was able to stop them and resolve the issues. A few times he had aggrieved parties withdraw their cases before the judge had them all brought back before him.

"You can't have the same lawyer for the defendant and the complainant," one judge said, reprimanding Salim.

"I know, your honour," said Salim. "But …"

"Why not?" both clients demanded. "We are King'oo."

As family, they split Salim's fee and ended up each owing him only half. He rarely received any of those halves.

"You are family," they said when he tried to collect. "How can you demand money from us?"

He had gone hoarse explaining it to habitual felons and their relatives that lawyers did it for money. But, as family, every King'oo lawbreaker, big or small, expected him to work *pro bono publico*. Most had no idea what the words meant, but they knew they did not have to pay him to defend them.

It was Caesar who set Salim straight, saving his life and sanity.

"When you work pro-bono for both sides who do you work for" he asked him. "Let them see that defending them is a job, a hard job, for which you had to go to school for many years. They cannot respect you if you don't make them pay. Make them pay so they think twice before bringing you chicken and goat lawsuits."

"But Caesar," said had Salim, "you know how hard it is to talk to them."

"Don't talk, tell them" Caesar said. "Tell them how the law works. Tell them I said to make them pay. It will not matter whether they come call me names at the gate on their way to church or back from the market. My brother has done it for years and it has not made me bleed."

"He was a man of wisdom your Caesar," the inspector said, when he heard of his advice. "But why did he leave this old thing to an old woman? It seems to me that this thing is more than enough trouble for a man."

"You know the way he was," Salim said.

Anything a boy could do, a girl could do twice as well. They said he planned to help women take over the government because men had failed. So men denounced him as traitor and kicked him out of the government."

"Didn't he resign."

"Exhibit A," Salim pointed at the Mercedes. "Now I have to repair it for her, with my own money, and I can't talk her out of it."

The Inspector looked at the car, at Salim's story. He knew and respected Caesar, the man who used his integrity and political clout to get him to police college. He also knew Teacher Charity, hard and soft at the same time, an angel with a book and a cane, a teacher and mother who alone had coaxed so many boys through school when their King'oo genes dictated otherwise. She was responsible for many boys graduating from Kathiani Primary School. Odero and Salim were just two of the many boys she had caned and scared to university. Inspector Odero was not Kamba but, in Caesar's school, everyone was King'oo.

"What happened to his face?" he asked of Kasim's black eye.

"Aunt Eva," said Kasim.

"King'oo have not stopped trying to kill one another?" he laughed. "How many have you killed so far?"

"We did not kill Caesar," Salim said.

"How old was he?"

"Everyone remember him being old when they were born."

The inspector remembered how, when his father, a policeman, could not raise the fees he dropped out of high school and got a job harvesting sand. Then one morning Caesar's driver came looking for him at home. What have you done now, his father asked him, why is the government looking for you? He had recognised Caesar's car and Caesar was government. The driver opened the door of the Mercedes and ordered Odero to get in.

"I was terrified when we drove to Caesar's house."

Caesar had invited him under his mango tree and offered him a cup of tea. He had heard Odero was the top male student in the county.

"Finish that cup of tea and come with me," he said.

The driver took them to Machakos where Caesar bought Odero school uniform and shoes.

"He asked what I wanted to be. I said a police officer. 'Come see me when you graduate,' he said to me. And so, I did. Caesar was a man."

"He was also a tyrant," Kasim said.

"He held your people together."

"With whips and tongue lashes," Kasim said. "He was everything a boy does not need when charting his own course. He made us study what he wanted, when he wanted, with no regard to interest or ability. I wanted to be an astronomer, a quantum physicist. A space engineer."

"And what are you?" asked the Inspector.

Kasim was about to say comedian.

"None of the above," he said, instead.

"When I was a child," the Inspector revealed, "I used to say I was King'oo. We had no like you in my family; just pastors and fishermen and businessmen and boring old men. No Caesars or Tivos or brawlers or anyone for a boy to take after."

"Then you should have married a King'oo," Salim said. "We have women who would have died for a police husband. Then you would have been one of us, and she would have demanded you take her as far away from us as possible."

"I'm married," Odero said.

"So are they," said Salim. "They will be your second, third or whatever number of wives you want them to be, as long as you take them away."

The inspector started to laugh, realised Salim was only half-joking, slapped him on the back and took his shoulder.

"I still remember how you thrashed me in class four," he said.

"You called me King Zero Zero."

"And for that you bullied me through primary school."

"We were kids."

"Don't worry, I cannot arrest you for it," said Odero.

"Had you been a King'oo, …" Salim started.

"I know, I would be a *chang'aa* brewer in Kathiani today."

"Or *chang'aa* drinker."

Their laughter was genuine. Then it was back to business.

"Not that I don't believe you," he said to Salim. "but step over here for a second."

Seeing them approach laughing in a friendly manner, the suspect concluded all was well again and he would soon be on his way home.

"Boss," he hailed Salim.

Salim looked through him. He lowered his voice and addressed Salim in Kamba.

"*Wakwitu*," he said. "*Si* you tell *affande* I am not the one."

Salim ignored him. Odero spoke Kikamba like a Kamba.

"Bring the suspect out here," he said.

They dragged him out of the car and shoved him forward. Kasim stayed in the background.

"Look up," the Inspector ordered. "Is this the man you sold the Mercedes?"

"I told you people," said the security guard, "I did not sell it, I rented it to him."

"To this man?" asked Odero sternly.

The watchman turned to Salim. Salim continued to look through him.

"He is not the one," he said. "Even the Mercedes is not the one. That one had no lights, or grill. It had nothing. It was a *mkebe*, an empty tin can."

He stopped, again looked from one to the other, realized he may have said too much. He had more to lose by telling too much.

"He is not the same," he said.

"You mean he was different yesterday?"

"Yes ... no, I mean he was a different man. Another man not him."

"Yes or no," said the Inspector. "No more stories."

"No."

"You are certain about that?"

"Even the Mercedes is not the one."

"You are certain?"

"It had no lights, no grill, no everything. It had nothing. I tell you it was a useless scrap car. I do not even know why you people are arresting me for giving it away.

"Giving it away? Last night you admitted selling it."

"Because of what your people were doing to me. Do you know officer, these people they grabbed me by my grenades, like this, and they pulled, and they twisted, and they squeezed, and they pulled until I screamed? I had to tell them something to let me go. I can hardly walk now. Let me go a little you see how I walk now."

He started walking away.

"Come back here," said the Inspector. "Back in the car."

They stuffed him back in the car. He started to rave and rant in Kamba.

"These people will kill me," he cried to Salim. "Tell them to let me go."

"*Kimya*!" ordered the policeman.

"Well, that is that then," Odero said to Salim. "I'm sorry about your Caesar."

"Come to the funeral."

"My wife's aunt passed away last week," Odero said. "Big, loud woman, member of the county assembly, former market woman and women's leaguer leader. Did you know her? I did not either, but my wife says I did. So, I must go to a stranger's burial instead of Caesar's. You know how these things are. I'll send my contribution."

He was staring at Kasim as he spoke.

"I know you?" he said to him.

"I don't think so," said Kasim.

"Are you not the fool that wants to chop a policeman's head in four?"

"You met my cousin?" Salim asked, before Kasim could deny it.

"Your cousin?"

"Kasim the Komedian."

"I should have guessed," the inspector was genuinely surprised. "Kasim the Komedian had to be King'oo. You have no idea how many police officers want to put their hands on this man. If he were not your cousin, I would deliver him to them right away. A night's stay inside a cell at the real police headquarters would do him a lot of good."

"Take him," Salim said. "He is not really my cousin."

"Really not?"

"He is joking," Kasim said quickly. "Don't joke like that, Salim. They nearly shot me over a joke."

"Then don't be making fun of our diligent police officers," said Salim. "Next time he makes such jokes, shoot him in the foot."

The inspector laughed, good natured, laid his hand on Kasim's shoulder in a half-friendly gesture.

"We don't do that sort of thing anymore," he said to him, "but there are other things we can do to you that are within the law and equally effective."

Listening in, the security guard worried.

"Boss," he pleaded with Salim. "Tell them I am not the one who sold you a stolen car."

A policeman slammed shut the boot. Inspector Odero and his men got in the car and drove off.

"If ever your paths cross again," Salim said to Kasim, exhausted. "Don't call me."

"You are better a lawyer than he is a cop."

"Just because you are not sitting in two feet of water in Nyayo House? Don't bet on it."

Uncle Richard's Volvo was just leaving the mortuary with Aunt Charity, Aunt Eva, Roger, and the Chinese cousins, when Salim's taxi arrived. He ducked his head under the dashboard until they were out of sight.

Kajicho the Mechanic arrived in the Beetle as he was paying for the taxi.

Chapter 43

Uncle Richard's Volvo, with Aunt Eva in the front passenger seat and Aunt Charity, Roger, Karate and Kung Fu squeezed in the back seat, overtook a rickety, old lorry clattering along Kangudo Road trailing a cloud of diesel smoke so thick only Roger saw the lorry and the black Mercedes on the back. He followed it with his eyes out of the window as they overtook it and, when he saw Kasim in the cab, smiled his mysterious smile. Aunt Eva following his gaze saw only the battered front of an old lorry.

Kasim had ducked under the dash the moment he saw the Volvo with Roger looking up at him from the back. Then the speeding Volvo was out of sight. The lorry chugged along until they were in the open plains with no houses nearby, then Kasim ordered the driver to stop.

"Why?" asked the driver.

"Because I say so."

He grumbled he had to be back before his uncle came back from Nanyuki. When Kasim ignored it, he drove for another three hundred metres, to make a point, before stopping. He needed to find a bush, he said, and ran behind one. He was gone for a while and came back in a mellow, more agreeable mood. They waited. Kasim grew restless.

"May I use your phone?" he asked the driver.

The driver did not own a phone. He kept losing them, so he had decided to do without phones.

"How can you work without a phone?" Kasim asked.

His uncle had a phone. His uncle went along on all delivery jobs to make sure they ended up at the right place, but had to go to a funeral in Nanyuki and, therefore, was the driver alone on this job. They waited. After an hour of waiting, he got agitated, wanted to know what they were waiting for. Kasim reminded him his job was to drive. They waited.

Kasim stepped down to have a cigarette and walked a little way away from the lorry. He smoked and paced the roadside as he anxiously watched the road behind. Time crawled by. The driver hopped down and ran back behind the bush, where Kasim observed him light a joint. He came back happier and ready to wait for as long as Kasim desired.

"When I get money," he said pointing, "I will buy all this land."

The joint had fired-up his ambitions.

"All this land needs is water," he said. "I will dig a well, and grow *bhangi*."

"*Bhang*?" Kasim asked startled.

"Cannabis," he said. "*Bhangi* is very profitable. Make you extraordinarily rich."

Kasim was about to dismiss the idea as a product of an overloaded mind, then he remembered toying with a similar idea long ago in an even drier land, but without the cannabis element.

Crouching under the desk at his customs office on the border, Kasim had a similar get-rich-quick brainwave after reading *Teach Yourself Water-Divining*. The clan elders, through his Fahari girlfriend had told him how cattle rustling was no longer profitable, and how, but for lack of water they would turn to farming and grow food instead. Kasim has seen how enterprising junior smugglers grew weed in tin cans irrigating it with cow piss.

With that in mind, Kasim crafted a divining stick out of the last branch of the last acacia tree in the village, and led the elders on a search for underground water. Starting from the village, they searched in ever-widening circles covering a large area of the desert around. The elders indulged him, out of boredom and respect, but, after two exhausting months of wandering in the open desert under a punishing sun, they had enough. They ordered him to stop wasting their time, or they would let their warriors shoot him as they had been itching to do ever since he started demanding duty for the goods they brought across the border.

Now listening to someone who did not sound like he had ever read a book, or sired any idea that was not fertilised with marijuana, Kasim wondered how much of the knowledge he gleaned from books while crouched under the desk with bullets whizzing overhead was ever of any use to anyone.

"What time is it now?" interrupted the driver.

Kasim showed him the time on his phone.

"Already?" he exclaimed. "I must be back before my uncle returns from Meru."

Kasim, noting how Nanyuki had changed to Meru in such a fleeting time, ignored him and stared down the road.

"I am hungry," said the driver.

Kasim's schoolmates at Uncle Tivo's school for *jua kali* mechanics were often caught stealing unripe mangoes, oranges, and lemons from the orchard after smoking weed.

"When do we eat?" asked the driver.

"When we get there," said Kasim.

Then he saw a flash of orange turn the corner, way down the road, and speed up towards them. The Beetle arrived minutes later with the coffin secured to the roof. Kasim helped Salim and Kajicho transfer the casket to the roof of the Mercedes on the lorry and lash it down. Kajicho got his money and drove the Beetle back to Nairobi.

"Is that the box?" the driver asked.

They looked at each other.

"Then what are we waiting for?" he said. "Let us go to Kathiani. I have never been to Kathiani. Is it a big place?"

The joint was ripening inside his head.

"I had a friend who worked in a bar in River Road," he said. "*Two Horn Bar.* Do you know it?"

Kasim and Salim looked at each other.

"Very big Kamba woman," he told them. "From Kathiani."

She was exceptionally beautiful and warm, but she wanted him to marry her, and she had a husband and four children who wanted to come live with him too, and his house was too small for so many people, and his uncle wanted him to marry a friend's daughter from Tharaka, and he was not sure he wanted to be married at all.

"And you thought you had issues," Kasim said to Salim.

"Do you think I should?" the driver asked them.

"Definitely do," said Kasim.

"Definitely not," said Salim.

They looked at each other again. The man agonised, rambled on talking to himself in different languages. Then he saw the alarm on their faces, and confessed he spoke five mother tongues. He could not explain how that came about, and they left him to it and went back their business.

"Is this the best you could find?" Salim asked, inspecting the lorry.

Kasim rubbed thumb and forefinger together. It was a matter of cost. Salim had said to keep the cost next to nothing.

"This thing will never make it up Mua Hills," he said.

"It will," said Kasim.

"My lorry can climb any hill," the driver reported. "Have you been to Maua? I took *khat* from Maua to Moyale in this lorry."

"See?" Kasim said to Salim. "Stop suffering. We'll make it."

They got in the lorry and, moments later were roaring past open fields dotted with stunted thorn trees. Hard men with ox ploughs fought to eke a living from hard cotton soil. Houses were scattered over the landscape, and along the road all the way to the hills. Among them were unplanned structures meant to be hotels, restaurants, and lodging houses when the road became a highway.

"Do you like *khat*?" the driver asked, reaching under his seat. "I have some here."

"Shut up and drive," Salim said to him.

"Not when you drive us," Kasim told him.

The driver stashed his *khat* back under his seat.

Salim's phone rang.

"Where are you?" asked Aunt Eva.

"We are … almost there," he said and hung up.

The phone rang again. He let it ring. She would kill him later. They were late beyond excusing, and she had not seen the hearse yet.

"It is a Mercedes," he said aloud.

"What?" Kasim asked.

"Nothing."

They drove in tense silence, the engine backfiring, spewing clouds of diesel smoke. The driver started grumbling, then talking to himself, when they started the slow climb to Mua Hills. He had not thought Kathiani was so far from Nairobi, and he had to be back before four for another delivery job. He pumped the gas pedal, pushed buttons, pulled levers, and talked to the lorry in Kuria. He rocked back and forth, his hands gripping the wheel as if he were in pain.

"What is it?" Salim asked him.

"The hills," he said.

"What about them?"

"So high"

"We have not reached the hills," Kasim said.

"Too high."

"How low would you like them to be?" Kasim asked him. "We know people who can make them flat."

"Really?"

He was sweating profusely, his shirt wet with sweat, and it was starting to stink in the cab. Salim tried to open the window and realised it was wound all the way down.

"Woi," the driver cried out suddenly. "We are now finished. We are completely finished. *Kwisha!"*

Up ahead was a police roadblock, two spiked steel contraptions laid across the road several metres apart, one on either side of the road, with room for vehicles to stop for inspection before maneuvering through. Salim turned to Kasim for explanation. Kasim had assured him there would be no police roadblocks on that road.

"What is this now?" he asked him.

Kasim had informed him that his big, fat, corrupt police friends at Machakos police station had informed him all police roadblocks in the county had been dismantled after the death of corona put an end to the graft bonanza. And now there ahead of them, so real a *ganja*-smoking lorry driver could see it, was a roadblock.

"I will take care of it," Kasim said. "I will take care of it."

There was no police car in sight. The government, in its wisdom, had stopped wasting money buying and maintaining police patrol vehicles and instead leased them from station chiefs for interesting amounts of money.

One such car, a decrepit, old Toyota, was parked by the side of the road under a thorn tree, while the officers had their lunch. They were gathered round a feast of *nyama choma* and *ugali* spread on newspaper over the engine cover.

As the lorry approached, one of them wiped his hands with a newspaper, tossed it in the bush and stepped out in the road with his arm raised. The lorry backfired, sending the rest ducking for cover, as the panicked driver stopped just short of driving over the metal spikes.

The police officer approached cautiously, rifle at the ready, peering in the cab to see the driver. The driver was ready to jump out and flee. Kasim grabbed his arm.

"Do you want to be shot?" he asked him.

The man was too scared to answer. Three more police officers finished their lunch, wiped their hands with newspapers, picked up their rifles and approached the lorry.

"Now we are dead," the driver said to himself. "Hyenas will eat our bones."

Salim's phone rang again. Again, he let it ring.

"This lorry," Salim asked. "It is not stolen, is it?"

"Not as far as I know," said Kasim.

He turned to the driver.

"Is it?"

"It belongs to my uncle," said the driver. "It is not stolen. *Haki, si ya wizi.* My uncle keeps everything here."

He rummaged through the glove compartment, came up with faded fuel receipts, burned fuses, smelly oil rags, a road license that was ten years expired, and a bundle of *khat.* He was about to jump out and run, but Kasim grabbed his hand and held him back. If he ran, the policemen would assume he was guilty and shoot him dead. Kasim and Salim would be left to explain the lorry, the Mercedes, and the casket, and why their driver tried to run away. That was if the police did not shoot them dead also.

"Calm down," he said to the driver. "Leave it to me."

They waited as the policemen cautiously advanced. Kasim was about to step down from the lorry, when he recognized one of the police officers. One of a group he offended at a club in Machakos with his big, fat, corrupt policeman joke. They had not worked him over that time, but he came close to spending a weekend in a police cell full of end-month muggers and their drunken victims.

"On second thoughts," he said to Salim, "you take care of it."

The policeman stepped up on the running board, his face filling the window, and looked inside.

"Jambo," he said, hitting them with the smell of roast meat and raw onions.

"Jambo," said Salim and Kasim together.

"What is this?" he asked them.

His hand moved to indicate the vehicle and the load on the back.

"A lorry," said the driver.

*"And that *thing* on top of it?"* he asked.

"I have nothing to do with that thing," said the driver. "That belongs to them two. Ask them."

"That is our thing," said Salim.

The police officer glanced from him to the driver, then up to the back of the lorry and the black Mercedes with a casket on top.

"Show me your license," he said to the driver.

"License?" said the driver.

"Driving license."

"But *Affande* ...?"

"Also, your road license, work ticket and ..."

"Work ticket?"

"This is not your lorry is it?"

"It is my uncle's lorry."

"Then he must have given you a work ticket," said the policeman. "Step down with you driving license, road license and whatever else you have."

"Officer, you know ..." the driver switched to Kikuyu.

"You don't have any, do you?" asked the policeman.

Lorry driver, desperate, turned to Salim.

"Officer," Salim said. "It is like this. We forgot those things at home. You see ... let me step down we talk."

He hopped out of the vehicle to find two armed policemen and a traffic inspector with a torn right ear checking out the lorry. They were shaking their heads and making tut-tut-tutting sound at the state of the tyres and the entire vehicle.

"And what is that thing up there?" asked the inspector.

"A car," Salim said.

"And the one on top of that?" he asked.

"A casket."

He turned to his men and smiled as if to say, "What did I tell you?"

"A casket," he said to Salim. "And where are you taking it?"

"For burial."

The Inspector motioned one of his men.

"Get up there," he said.

The man clambered on the lorry. He smelt paint, touched the car, and found the paint was not completely dry. Then he looked inside, saw the state of the seats and the floorboards.

"This is not a car," he said to the Inspector.

"Work in progress," Salim said in explanation.

"And the other thing?" the Inspector asked the man on the lorry.

"It is a coffin," he confirmed.

"Open it," said the Inspector.

"But officer …," Salim pleaded.

"Open it," the Inspector ordered his man.

While they waited, he turned to Salim and revealed how for many years he was stationed at border posts around the country, where he had routinely apprehended criminals trying to smuggle alcohol, cigarettes, drugs, guns, and live people inside coffins just like the one on top of the car on the lorry.

Salim had no comment to make. The Inspector felt his torn ear thoughtfully, realised the man on the lorry was not getting anywhere and again ordered him to open the casket.

"How?" his man tried lifting the lid, but it was screwed down.

"Go open it," the Inspector said to Salim.

"It is sealed," Salim said.

"Sealed why?"

"That is how caskets are transported."

"An old smuggler's trick," said the Inspector.

Then his constable discovered the viewing window. He slid it open, looked inside the coffin, yelped, and leaped off the lorry landing on top of startled colleagues.

"*Affande* there is someone in the box," he said, scrambling to his feet.

"I told you we were going to a funeral," Salim said to them.

"You and who else?" asked the Inspector.

"The others went ahead."

"*Affande*, the Volvo and pickup that passed earlier?" said one of his men. "He must be a big man."

"Very big," Salim agreed. "A government man. You heard of Caesar?"

"Caesar Mophat?" the eyes narrowed. "He was still alive?"

"Until a couple of weeks ago."

"This I must see."

He whipped off his hat and handed it to the constable. He reached for the top of the side of the lorry, grabbed it, stepped on the tyre, and hauled himself onto the lorry. He touched the Mercedes, smelt his fingers. Turning his attention to the casket, he tried lifting the lid, found it screwed tight. He peeked inside the coffin through the viewing window, saw the emaciated dead face inside and closed it.

He turned his attention to the car. He checked the tyres, the interior, and the registration; remarked how they were all incredibly old and useless. He hopped back down, received back his hat and baton. He straightened his jacket.

"The Kamba man who sent me to Taeyang to die, is really dead?"

Salim hesitated to answer. He could not remember where he heard the name Taeyang, but he was sure it was not in connection with anything good that Caesar did.

"The man was mad," the inspector said to his men. "He sent University books to a place that did not have a primary school. Taeyang!"

He said the name like a magic word.

"I read books that to this day I do not understand," he said to his men. "Caesar Mophat! What happened to him?"

"Caesar got very old," Salim said.

"Taeyang!" the Inspector said again wistfully. "Diamonds, green garnet, rubies, gold, dollars, rubles – everything came through Taeyang. My office in Taeyang! I came back richer than I ever dreamed. Richer than the hyenas that tried to get me fired from the customs department. If that casket were open, I would shake Caesar's hand and kiss his cheek."

Salim wished Kasim were present to hear this. The situation was turning out better than anyone could have imagined.

The Inspector drifted away for a moment, gently feeling his torn ear, and remembering. Then he came back to the present and held out his hand.

Salim reached out to shake his hand. He withdrew it.

"Permit," he said.

"What?" Salim was startled out of his wits.

"Burial permit."

Salim started searching his pockets. He broke out in a sweat when he realised he had placed the envelope with all the papers in the Beetle's glove compartment. He suppressed the rising panic with the thought that he could have Kajicho drive it back if the worst came to the worst. They were already hours behind schedule and his ulcers were waking up.

"Kasim?" he called out.

"Kasim?" said the Inspector.

"In the lorry," said Salim.

Everyone had forgotten about the two men in the cab. He had to call again before Kasim stepped out of the lorry, and nervously approached. Salim gestures to him. He searched his pockets, took out his wallet.

"The permit," said Salim.

"Permit?"

"The burial permit."

"Burial permit?"

"The one I gave to you."

"When?"

"When I gave it to you. Where is it?"

"Ah, that one?"

He searched in his pockets, with the inspector watching him suspiciously, searched every pocket and started over.

"Don't I know you?" asked the Inspector.

"No," he said.

"You are not the ...?"

"Permit?" Kasim turned to Salim.

"Burial permit," said Salim.

"One moment," Kasim walked back and stepped in the cab and closed the door.

"You are in serious trouble," he said to the driver.

"*Auwee!*" wailed the driver.

"How much money do you have?" Kasim asked him.

"Money? Me? Money?"

"Do you know the fine for carrying dead people without a permit?"

"You did not tell me there was dead people in the box."

"You did not ask," Kasim said. "Now go tell the *affande* you lost the burial permit."

"No one told me about it."

"Why didn't you ask?," said Kasim. "I will tell him you have no driver's license, no road license, nothing. You chew *khat* and smoke *bhangi*, don't you? I will tell him that too. He will search you and your lorry. You do not even have your uncle's permission to borrow this lorry, do you? I will tell him that too. He will arrest you for stealing it."

The lorry driver's mouth dropped open.

"How do you know all that?" he asked.

"I know everything," he said opening the door for him. "Go."

Ten minutes later, they were on the move again, the lorry groaning and grunting, wheezing, and coughing and farting and doing things that only incredibly old people and vehicles did. Salim's stomach pain got worse as he saw them take half an hour to cross the plains and start on the climb to Mua Hills, a distance the Beetle covered in ten minutes. They laboured up Mua Hills, a thick cloud of smoke in their wake. To the left was a wall of rocks rising to the top of the hill, and to the right a steep drop into a rocky ravine.

The air in the cab was charged. Everyone was angry, Salim at Kasim, Kasim at the driver, and the driver at Kasim, and at the big, fat, corrupt policemen who had taken all his money as well as Salim's and Kasim's to let them continue their journey.

"You did not tell me there was a dead man in the coffin," he grumbled.

"Shut up and drive," Salim ordered.

They were hours late. Kasim would find a way to save himself from the worst of Aunt Eva roasting as usual leaving Salim to face it alone. Salim was expected to act older, to know better. He was educated enough to know to value time, keep promises, eat well, and have a good night's sleep, things he had had no time to consider since the clan decided on a Mercedes hearse for Caesar. And it was all Kasim's fault. He started to say something to Kasim, thought the better of it and kept his peace.

"I will not say a word," he said, as to himself. "I will not yell or scream. But, if we are not there in an hour, I will …"

"Kill me," Kasim finished it for him. "Who was it forgot the burial permit in the Beetle?"

"Who was it hired this … disaster of a vehicle?"

"This can be mitigated."

"How?"

"I will think of a way."

They were quiet, fuming. Then the driver thought to make his point too.

"You did not tell me there was a dead man in the box," he said.

"Shut up!" they yelled at him.

He drove quietly for an hour and covered a mere five kilometres.

"I could walk faster," Salim said to himself aloud.

The driver started to explain that the lorry was not meant to carry cars and coffins up steep hills. They yelled him down.

405

They were nearing the top of the rise, the lorry backfiring, groaning, and wheezing, and it looked like they would make it. They sat with their fists clenched, hardly breath, willing the lorry up the hundred yards to the crest. Then the engine heaved a final sigh and gave up the struggle.

They looked at one another. The driver had terror in his eyes, Kasim a touch of amusement and Salim had fire in his belly and murder in his heart. He was about to die and go to hell, but he would not go alone. He swore to himself he would take everyone responsible for it from Aunt Eva to the debtors who owed him enough money to rent a decent lorry.

Then, just when it could not get any worse, it did. The lorry creaked, groaned, and made hellish sounds and started rolling backwards down the hill. The driver cried out in panic, stomped on the brakes, and managed to stop it moving. His passengers looked at each other, wondering whether to jump out of the lorry and run. Then there was a rusty screech under them, and the brakes groaned again, followed by the loud crack of the pads letting go. The lorry resumed its backwards roll raising more fear and panic in the cabin. The driver yelled out in tongues as he hung on to the wheel, eyes glued to the rearview mirror, and fought to keep the lorry on the road. If he made the slightest error with his steering, the lorry would veer off the road, drop over the edge into a dry riverbed, and they would all be killed.

Salim grabbed the hand brake lever and pulled hard. His action stopped the roll for a moment. They could feel the brake cables stretch and start to give way.

"Rocks," he yelled. "Quick, rocks behind the wheels."

Kasim leaped out, grabbed a rock from the roadside and placed it behind the rear wheel. Then the hand brake cables snapped with a loud crack. The wheel rolled over the rock and kept going. He picked a larger rock and dropped it behind the wheel. The lorry paused rolling. Salim leaped out of the cab and helped block all four tyres. The lorry stopped in the middle of the road and the driver leaped out of the cab. He was shaking all over.

A cloud of smoke exploded out of the engine when the driver opened the engine lid. Oil dripping from the engine flowed under the lorry and back down the road. Salim and Kasim watched in despair, as the driver tinkered with the engine, talked to himself, and swore he would never talk to, or do business, with another Kamba again ever. Kamba were bad, bad people.

"Shut up," Kasim could not take it anymore. "You are a Kamba yourself."

"A good Kamba," said the driver.

"A Kamba?" Salim asked Kasim. "What were all those other languages he spoke with himself."

"He is crazy," Kasim said. "And he has travelled."

He spoke five languages and could not tell for certain what he really was.

"And you hired him based on …?"

"Again, cost."

Salim pressed his stomach to stem the pain. It did not help.

"No one told me there was a dead man involved," said the driver.

"You promised this lorry could go up Mua Hills."

The driver appeared genuinely surprised.

"Are these the Mua Hills?" he said. "They look so small from Mombasa Road. There is no way this thing can go up this hill. Impossible! It can't be done."

They watched him begin to lose control.

"*Auweee, Ngai!*" he shifted to Kikuyu. "Why did I do this? Now everyone will know I am a bad man. They will say I am a thief. My uncle will fire me."

Watching and hearing him lose it in all his five mother tongues calmed Salim's own terrors. They were all three in the same crises; stuck in the middle of the road on a hill, with a body that should have been buried hours ago, and no clue what would happen next. All that remained to turn it into a national tragedy was for an overloaded *matatu* bus with faulty brakes and driven by a *khat* chewing maniac to come hurtling down the hill into their lorry.

"What now?" Salim asked, after the man stopped swearing.

"First we offload the Mercedes," the driver said.

Salim and Kasim were attentive.

"Then?" they asked together.

"Then you push it up the hill."

"Push what up the hill?" they asked.

"My lorry."

Salim sat down on the running board, exhausted, and tried to ignore his ulcers.

"There is no other way," the driver said to him.

"There is another way," Kasim said to him. "We tie a rope round your neck, and you pull this lorry to where we are going. That is one way. Do you want to hear the others?"

The look on their faces told him to *kimya!* He was in more trouble than he had been with the police.

"You pay me first?" he had to ask.

"I beat you up first?"

"And I beat you up second?" said Salim.

"You are the worst Kamba," he said.

He reverted to speaking to himself in tongues, moaning, groaning, and swearing to never talk to a Kamba, not even his mother, again. They let him be.

"Taeyang," Salim said. "I wondered where I heard the name."

"I told you about it."

"The Inspector at the roadblock was there too. He made so much money he wanted to open the casket and kiss Caesar for it."

"The Other One?" said Kasim. "Why didn't you tell me? I have a message from the fiancée he promised to send for."

"On the way back," said Salim. "How come he got away with it and you did not?"

"I was innocent," said Kasim. "You are the lawyer; you know how that works."

Then they heard a vehicle approaching fast from up the hill, from where an out-of-control *matatu* bus was likely to come, and they rose ready to leap out of the way. Uncle Richard's Volvo appeared speeding down the road towards them. Kasim stepped in the road and waved it down. The driver slowed down and stopped. Kasim stepped to the driver's window, and the driver suddenly accelerated and sped away down the road.

Salim sat back on the running board. This is it, he thought. I am finished, I am done, I will never go to another funeral again, never.

He would quit the clan, never talk to any of them. And he was tired and sleepy, and worried how he would ever undo the wrong he had done to Caesar, to Aunt Charity and everyone who worked so hard to give Caesar a fitting burial.

What would he say to his clients whose money had been swallowed up by this tragedy? His life was ruined beyond recovery. What would he say to Mr Ryan when he came for his money on Tuesday? Before long he was moaning and groaning along with the lorry driver.

Kasim left them at it, strolled up the road and disappearing over the crest of the hill.

"There goes a true King'oo," Salim said to the driver. "Another King'oo who does nothing but inflame my ulcers. Running away from a disaster of his own making."

The driver stopped wailing and resumed his attempt to revive the dead engine.

"You should have told me there was a dead man in the box."

"That is what coffins are for," said Salim.

"I would not have come."

"You would," Salim said.

"Not for so little money."

"How much do you make transporting stolen sand from Kitui to Nairobi?"

"Still, I would not have come."

"Just keep quiet," said Salim.

His phone was ringing. He let it ring. Then he remembered he had an office to run and took it. An honorable client was on the phone asking after his money.

"Today is not possible, sir," Salim said. "Not even tomorrow. I'm in Mombasa, sir."

The lorry driver glanced at him startled.

"I'll be away for a week," Salim said. "Yes, your client has paid up, all of it in the bank. All of it."

The lorry driver guffawed. Salim rose and walked away still on the phone.

"Monday? I will see what I can do about Monday. Your money will be there. *Mheshimiwa,* have I ever lied to you?"

The lorry driver, starting to fear for his own money went round to the driver's side, reached under the driver's seat for a tyre lever, and placed it within reach. Then he looked up the road and froze.

Kasim was coming back, and he was not alone. With him was a barefoot, old man and two donkeys each with two forty-litre plastic jerrycans on its back. It took them forever to reach Salim. Salim watched intrigued.

"Transport," Kasim said, answering unasked question.

"For what?" Salim asked.

"Five thousand," said Kasim. "And that is a fair price."

"Transport for what?" Salim asked again.

"For the hearse."

Salim was too tired to think like Kasim.

"Let us start again," he said.

He pointed at the man and the donkeys.

"What is this?"

"Tow truck," Kasim said.

Salim started breathing again. He looked at the donkeys and saw them in a new light.

"But how do you pay five thousand to rent two donkeys for fifteen minutes?" he asked.

"Five thousand each," Kasim said. "Buy not rent."

Salim glanced at the Water-Seller and, finding him grinning, turned back to Kasim.

"Did you explain to your donkey friend we just want to get up this hill, not run a water delivery business?"

Kasim turned to the donkey man and explained in Kamba. The smile vanished from the man's face. He turned his animals round and started back up the road.

"The man wants out of water delivery business," Kasim said.

"That is his problem," Salim said. "We rent, not buy."

"He can't use the donkeys to fetch water after we use them to carry a dead body."

"You did not explain," Salim yelled at him. "We want them to tow a car, not carry a dead body. What is wrong with your head?"

His phone rang. He picked it angrily, yelled at the caller.

"What? I am sorry, Maria, I thought you were someone else. A client who keeps bugging me. No, I do not owe him money. I am stuck in the bush, with my grandfather's corpse and two donkeys and three idiots … and there may just be more than one funeral tonight. No, I have not been drinking, and it is all your father's fault. If he had let me have his car …

"Is that what you wanted his Mercedes for?" she asked.

Salim panicked.

"To go to a funeral?" she asked him.

"Yes, no, it is complicated, Maria. But do not worry, just go on ahead. I will be there before your opening."

She hung up.

"How?" Kasim wondered.

"Not your business," he said. "How much are the donkeys, again?"

"Five thousand each."

"Why do you keep buying things I can't afford?"

Kasim yelled at the water-seller, waved him back.

Salim lost it then, kicking the lorry tyres and punching the air. They left him to it. The lorry driver returned to his tinkering with the engine, and Kasim tried to make a call, and realising his phone was still dead. The Water-Seller was appraising the lorry when Salim finally calmed down.

"Pay him," he said.

Kasim took a fat roll of notes he had stashed in his socks, a trick he learned from watching wallet inspectors work at *Uncle Dave's*. He counted it out and handed it to the Water Seller. The Water Seller recounted it.

"By the way," Kasim said to the lorry driver, "I told him you would sell him the lorry."

"What?" the driver jerked his head up, banged it on the engine lid.

"Three thousand," Kasim said, having fun.

"What?" the driver rubbing his head now really confused.

"Open the back," Kasim said.

Careful not to slip on the oil slick, they rigged the planks of wood they had used to push the Mercedes on board. Then, with the help of the water man and his donkeys, they gently rolled the Mercedes off the track and onto the road. It landed with a bump, they lost control, and it headed for the steep edge of the road. There were shouts and curses, as they scrambled to grab the front bumpers, door handles and window frames to stop it going over the edge. Then, just when it seemed disaster was inevitable, the Mercedes wheels caught on the rocks by the edge of the road and stopped.

They quickly hitched the donkeys to the bumper and pulled and pushed until finally it moved from the edge of the road back to the middle. No one said a word until the Mercedes was out of danger and safely back on the road.

"My money?" said the driver.

"I gave you an advance," Kasim reminded.

Which the bad police had taken from him, the driver reminded. Now he wanted the rest of the money. It was not his fault that Mua Hills were so high. It was not even the lorry's fault. Besides, they had not told him about the dead man. That was against his religion to transport dead people on a lorry used to carry building sand.

Kasim sat him on the bank and explained it to him. It was no one's fault but his lorry's. The agreement was for the lorry to carry an unspecified load from Nairobi to Kathiani. A task it had failed to do.

"What about the distance to here?" said the driver. "You must pay for that."

The load was not at its destination, Kasim reminded. The man offered to help them push the Mercedes to Kathiani for the full payment.

"You should have said that years ago," Salim said to him. "Now we have donkeys. You made us buy donkeys."

"You are very bad Kamba," the driver said. "I will never do business with you again."

He climbed in the cab, rolled back to the left of the road, stopped at the shoulder, turned the steering wheel in the opposite direction, released the brakes and let the lorry roll forward and down the hill.

All they had to do now was get their Mercedes up the hill. After that the road was flat for three kilometres to Caesar's final resting place.

Chapter 45

The mourners milled about, talking in hushed voices as they waited for Caesar. Caesar was hours late, no one seemed to know where he was, and Uncle Sam had called the mortuary and been informed Caesar had left with the same person who had checked him in. And Salim was not taking their calls and they suspected Kasim had forgotten to charge his phone since he was always charging it at the meetings.

Pastor Kioko paced the yard, a bible under his arm, muttering prayers and glancing now and then at his watch. The aunts were on the veranda watching soil fly out of the grave the boys were feverishly digging. The grave they had dug the day before was a waste of time because it was dug hurriedly and without Aunt Charity's knowledge. She was the only one who knew Caesar's last wishes, the most important of which was to be laid to rest under his favorite mango tree where he spent his last days.

"He is here, he is here," shouted the boy Sam had posted at the gate to warn them when Caesar arrived.

Uncle Sam rushed to the front yard, followed by Aunt Eva, the aunts and everyone who wanted to see Caesar's final return. Then they saw the gleaming mahogany casket atop a shiny black Mercedes pulled by two dusty, Kathiani donkeys and there was dead silence.

Uncle Sam's was not the only mouth wide open with astonishment, and Aunt Eva's not the only eyes about to pop out of their sockets from shock. Her whole being convulsed from despair, and she was about to collapse from the pain of defeat as she saw Caesar's funeral turn to a dismal joke, a family disaster, despite the time, the sweat, the money and all the emotional energy she had invested in trying to make it historic and memorable.

Only those who had not attended all the tumultuous night meetings could find any meaning to what they were looking at. Some were impressed by the sheer novelty of it.

Others were awed by the thought of a man who lived a simple life, so that others may live, going to his final resting place in such a manner. To them it was humbling and exceedingly fitting.

Aunt Eva saw it differently. She stomped up to the one person she had thought could make a difference, help her survive Sam's train wreak with her sanity intact, and demanded to know why.

"Mua Hills," Salim said. "Mua Hills."

His original plan was to offload the Mercedes from the lorry close to the house, push it home, plead a breakdown and be forgiven. But it was too late for worry now.

"Mua Hills," was all he could say now.

Everyone but Aunt Eva could understand his excuse. The hills were home to ancestral spirits that lived on the shims and nuts and bolts ripped from under old cars as they passed by. Stories were told, of eerie screams and agonised wailing issuing from the asphalt at night, and of cars rolling uphill by themselves when they were abandoned by the roadside after breakdowns.

Uncle Tivo could confirm that Caesar's own Mercedes was killed by Mua Hills.

"I warned him about them, but he never listened to me," said Uncle Tivo to Aunt Eva. "I told him, '*Mwana wa King'oo*, son of King'oo, buy a bottle of *chang'aa* and keep it under the car seat. Pour a little on the road for the spirits as you pass. That will keep the old spirits happy.' Do you think he believed me? Always coming and going, up and down, and everywhere with his car full of books."

If the ghosts in the hills could kill old cars, imagine what they did to the hearts of old donkeys.

"You, you and you," Kasim said to the boys admiring the Mercedes. "Take care of my donkeys."

"Whose donkeys are they?" they asked.

"I just told you. Do it now, quickly."

The animals had to be out of sight before Aunt Charity came out of the house.

"And whose car is this?" the boys had seen him behind the wheel when it arrived pulled by the donkeys.

"Mine," said Salim.

"Will you give us a ride?"

"Ask the driver."

"First take care of my donkeys," Kasim said to them, "then we'll see."

The donkeys were driven away just as Aunt Charity came out of the house supported by Pastor Kioko and two women. She stopped when she saw what had silenced everyone, stopped so abruptly the Pastor stumbled trying to prevent her from falling. She stood staring at the Mercedes with such intensity that Salim thought he would die from the pain in his stomach.

"He did it," he heard her say, quietly to herself. "Salim did it."

Aunt Eva was dumbstruck as she watched Aunt Charity walk unsteadily up to Salim, about to keel over from the tension, and embraced him. She hugged him, kissed him on the cheek, mussed his hair the way she used to do in class when he got it right, and kissed him again. Then she took Pastor Kioko's hand and let him walk her back inside.

Aunt Eva was speechless. She sauntered up to Salim, wagged a finger in his face.

"Don't think this is over," she said.

Then she followed Aunt Charity back to the house. Uncle Sam took over and the pall bearers heaved the Casket to their shoulders and carried it to the house.

"Now you owe me," Kasim said to Salim.

Salim was too relieved and too exhausted to hear him.

"Musau," he heard Uncle Tivo say to one of his grandsons, "I taught you to repair Mercedes too. Show me I did not waste my time. See what is wrong with that Mercedes."

The young man eagerly went for it.

"Don't you dare," Salim warned. "Go practice your *jua kali* skills on another car."

The boy held back, but the moment Salim was out of sight he lifted the engine cover and looked inside. He stood puzzled at the sight of a Beetle's engine lying askew inside a Mercedes, not welded, or bolted but attached with rope and wire. He tried to make sense out of it, wonder what magic made the car drive from Nairobi to Kathiani.

"Uncle Tivo," he called to the old man. "It is a Beetle."

"I taught you to repair a Beetle too, did I not?" said Uncle Tivo.

The young man nodded. Uncle Tivo had taught him that any car with an engine could be repaired, if it had parts that screwed, bolted, welded, or hammered together. But Salim's Mercedes was something else. To begin with, the Beetle engine lay upside down and sideways in the engine compartment. Secondly, other than the wires and ropes holding it in place, there was no way of attaching the Beetle engine to the rest of the car. It had no parts that could be screwed, bolted, welded, or hammered together. It was a problem with no intended solution, and was best left to the owner.

He could take out the engine, deconstruct it with an axe and monkey wrench, weld it to the transmission, toss in a battery and see what happened. But the sound of an axe chopping steel at a funeral would not be right.

"I can't repair this one here," he said to Uncle Tivo.

"Then I taught you car mechanics for nothing," Tivo concluded.

The casket was at the verandah, laid out on a long table covered with a white cloth. Charity and the aunts sat beside it singing with Pastor Kioko's choir, while Pastor Kioko and Uncle Sam held a private consultation at the end of the veranda. The rest were spread out in the yard in small groups trying to guess how much Caesar's casket cost.

Salim walked to the other end of the veranda, stood watching the furtive preparations around the grave. He felt a heavy wind bearing down on him from behind and saw Aunt Eva approaching, casting a shadow of doom over him. She wanted to know what happened along the way, why he was so late with Caesar, and what kind of hearse he thought that was?

"Aunt Eva," Salim said, politely but tiredly. "Caesar is here, and we are all here now, and that is all that matters. Whatever happened along the way is done, gone, finished, forgotten."

"Is that what you think?"

"Ask anyone," he said. "The moment Caesar is in the ground they will be off minding their shambas until the next one."

And he would be recuperating on another planet far away from all of them. She seemed to read his mind.

"You don't fool me, Salim," she said. "You will explain all of it later, beginning with the photographer."

"He is not here?" He managed to look surprised.

She pointed to a rugged youth with dreadlocks and scraggy beard, and no shoes.

"You call that a photographer?"

Everyone called him Cousin Deadhead. He was always high on something and unsteady on his feet. They watched him reel from group to group taking photographs. Salim could not imagine how the camera he handed Kung Fu ended up with Cousin Deadhead.

Aunt Eva saw the lost look..

"I thought so," she said. "Where is the real photographer? The one I paid for?"

Before he could start explaining, another cousin intruded with a more urgent problem. The gang of village hooligans, the idlers that Kasim had co-opted for the job stood round the grave, their mattocks and shovels held like weapons.

"Industrial action?" asked Aunt Eva.

"They are gravediggers, Aunt Eva," said Salim.

"From what I have seen here, death has become a lucrative industry."

From coffins on trees to space caskets, to disco trains with professional mourners and all. It was a wonder they got anyone buried.

"They say no one will be buried in their hole today unless you pay them first," their messenger said to Salim. "They were promised payment before burial."

"Promised by whom?"

The young man shrugged.

"Why don't you ask them?" Aunt Eva said, appearing to enjoy his exasperation.

The messenger started back, and Salim turned to the crowd, among whom were the burial committee members, all trying to avoid his eyes.

"Who promised the gravediggers' fees?" he asked them.

No one seemed to know.

"Who was supposed to pay the gravediggers?" he asked again.

There was prolonged silence. Then the messenger returned to whisper in his ear. Kasim had promised them Salim would pay them when the grave was ready. Then he went on to add someone gave the money to Uncle Tivo to give to Kasim. The last anyone saw of Uncle Tivo he was on his way to the *chang'aa* den at t Musikali Kombo's house.

"So, what are you going to do now, attorney?" asked Aunt Eva.

Short of sending the gravediggers after Tivo for their money, there was nothing Salim could do. He decided to let it rest until after the burial. If he could stall the gravediggers until Caesar was safely in his grave, then he would tell them where to find the one who took their money. And, knowing how King'oo minds worked, there would be blood.

"You go take the camera back from that fool," he said to the young man. "And tell the gravediggers I will bury them with Caesar, if they get in my way."

"I can't do that," said the young man worried. "You know those boys smoke *bhangi*."

"So?"

"They can do anything."

"I dare them to try."

"I also gave my word," said Aunt Eva.

"Then you pay them."

"What?" Aunt Eva suddenly flaring. "You dare talk to me like that, Salim King'oo? Do you know who I am?"

"Aunt Eva," said Kasim.

He had finally caught up after his detour through the kitchen to see what Aunt Kamene had saved up for him.

"Salim has not slept for a week," he said to Aunt Eva. "He is very tired."

"Who isn't tired?" she asked. "I have been here weeks and weeks trying to make sense of everything and everyone, and this is how you repay me?"

"I am sorry Aunt Eva," Kasim said. "Salim is sorry too, but he is tired and confused."

She noticed his black eye.

"What happened to your eye?" she asked him. "Did he do that to you? Are you two still fighting? What is wrong with King'oo men? When will you grow up?"

Aunt Charity alarmed by her angry voice rose from her sad place and approached accompanied by her retinue of old widows.

"I'm sorry, Aunt Eva," Salim said, when he saw them draw near. "I have not slept well for weeks, my shoe is torn, I am hungry, and I have no money left."

The old women overhearing him shook their heads tut-tutting. Aunt Kamene informed them Kasim was better than Salim at taking care of himself. Salim needed a wife.

"Come with me to the kitchen now," she said. "I don't want you dying from hunger at Caesar's funeral."

"Not now, Aunt Kamene," he said. "First I have to sort out this mess."

"Leave Kasim do that," she said. "Come with me."

"Stay," said Aunt Eva. "He will eat when he is finished."

"I know how hard you have tried, Salim," Aunt Charity said. "May God bless you and increase your energy."

"Amen," they said, and followed her back to their corner, leaving Salim feeling a bit more perky.

He sent another young man with a stern warning to the gravediggers. If they thought they could blackmail him, they should take their hole and bugger off. He would dig his own hole to bury Caesar in.

The young man was about to rush off, but Kasim intercepted him and brought him back.

"The gravediggers' strike?" Kasim said to Salim. "Leave it to me."

He let go of the young man and walked over to the gravediggers. Their leader was happy to see him, and to report they had done their job and were waiting for their pay. Kasim examined the grave, making a show of it by calling for setsquare and plumbline. He squatted to check the sides and corners with the instrument, rose and handed the instruments back.

"Good job," he said, offering cigarettes all round.

"Our pay?" asked the leader.

Kasim took him by the shoulder and led him aside.

"Listen, my brother," he said to him. "The way things stand eight now, someone will die here today, if we don't work together, you and me. You see all those old men there?"

The man nodded. He knew some, but not all of them. They had walked from miles over Iveti Hills and beyond. He had heard them moan how long Caesar's burial was taking. They want to bury Caesar as fast as possible and get back home before it got dark.

"You are King'oo too," Kasim said to him. "You know how angry King'oo men get when they do not get what they want. You don't want to see blood shed over an empty six-foot hole, do you?"

The man shook his head. But they needed money; he and his men needed money. They could not go home to their wives empty-handed after a whole day's work.

"I understand," said Kasim. "So, here is the deal. You take your men aside, over by that tree, and have them relax. Tell them your money is on the way. I will see that they get something to eat, for they must be very hungry. If your money is not here by the end of the day, you can take …"

He looked about.

"Those two donkeys," he pointed to the animals grazing over the fence where the boys had deposited them.

The man looked at the donkeys, looked at Kasim, looked at the donkeys. They were healthy, strong animals that could be put to work pulling a plough, ferrying goods, or fetching water from the river. They were worth more than the empty hole he and his men had just dug. But they were donkeys. How would one split two donkeys among five men?

"You went to school, didn't you?" Kasim said to him.

Caesar had seen to it that no King'oo was left behind. Every boy went to school, like it or not, and Aunt Charity and Aunt Eva scared them into learning how to read, write and count before some of them inevitably dropped out to dig graves.

"What is five by two?" Kasim tried.

"Two and a half," he said without hesitation.

"See? It is that simple."

That was all the math a King'oo boy needed to succeed in life. The kind of math questions every King'oo boy had to master to graduate. Fractions involving live animals were alien to him, but that was something they would have to work out among themselves.

"Whose donkeys are they?" he asked.

To a true King'oo, that should have been asked at the start of the negotiation.

423

"Would I give them to you if they were not mine?" Kasim said. "In front of all those witnesses?"

The gravedigger thought about it.

"Ask the boys playing over there," Kasim pointed. They will tell you the donkeys are mine."

Some King'oo were known to sell a house while the owner was asleep inside. He had his doubts, but he called his men over all the same.

"Two and half men for one donkey?" they turned to him. "How does that work?"

Kasim realised he should have left before it came to that. Now he was back in Kathiani primary school adding three mangoes and three oranges and getting six. Whack!

"Here is how," he said thinking back to his pushcart-pulling hard-life friends in River Road. "When luck deals you a donkey, you go into transport."

"What?"

He was wildly paraphrasing, but it was necessary.

"You put your resources together, buy a donkey wagon or two. Then you harness your two donkeys to your two wagons and put them to work carrying wood, water, building stones from the quarry, or whatever anyone will pay for. You save that money, buy two more donkeys and two more wagons, and add them to your fleet. Keep doing it until you own trailers, buses, *matatus* and cargo airplanes."

They looked at one another. Why hadn't they thought of that.

"What about today?" one asked.

"My wife will lock me out if I go home without money today," said another.

Kasim could not help with that problem. He left them to solve it by themselves and went back to Aunt Eva and Salim.

"Problem solved," he reported.

"What did you promise them this time?" Aunt Eva asked.

"Gave, not promised," he said. "I gave them a math problem to gnaw on until Caesar is buried. After that …"

"I can't believe we are related," Aunt Eva said disgusted.

"But we are Aunt Eva," he said with a big laugh.

"I will believe it when I see it," she said and left them.

They saw her stop to reprimand the photographer, take the camera from him, examine it, try to open it, give up and hand it back with more harsh words. The photographer rushed to Salim and Kasim.

"Aunt Eva wants to know how many films are inside this camera."

"Open it and count them," Kasim said.

"How?" trying to open the back.

"Don't you dare," Salim warned harshly. "If she asks again, tell Aunt Eva the camera is full of film. Go take pictures. I showed you how to do it, didn't I?

"I push this button."

"While looking through this hole here."

"How many."

"How many pictures?" Salim's irritation was beginning to take over.

"Ten thousand," Kasim said to the young man. "Go take pictures."

He hurried away.

"Are we sure there's a film in the camera?" Kasim wondered.

"Don't you start on me now," said Salim.

"I guess we will never know," Kasim said. "Until the film is developed."

By then Hurricane Eva would be gone and out of everyone's hair. Until then she was on Salim's case, and he was about to fall asleep on his feet. As Pastor Kioko begun gathering the mourners so that the ceremony could begin, Aunt Eva came back to reopen the case of the missing professional photographer.

"Is this the best you could find in the whole of Nairobi?"

She had been watching the young man rash about pointing the camera at every face that turned his way, without regard to relation, status, or relevance. She feared the family would end up with albums full of mugshots of chicken thieves, rogues, and madmen, and none of any person that mattered.

"Who pays for all this?" she demanded from Salim.

"I don't know," he said, sincerely.

It would take months to climb out of the dark hole she had had pushed him in with Caesar's funeral. He had betrayed trust, lied to his fiancé, and spent money entrusted to him by his clients all because of Caesar's funeral and Aunt Eva. He did not know if he could recover from that.

"Salim," she said, her voice hardening. "Other than I, you are the most educated person here. Who would know who pays for all this when you do not know it yourself?"

"Aunt Eva," he said, "I have tried, God knows."

"Where then is the photographer?"

He was tempted to repeat to her Uncle Richard's words when Salim called on him to contribute to hire a professional photographer.

"Photographer?" Uncle Richard had asked. "To photograph a dead man you are about to bury and forget? What did they teach you at college?"

"Uncle Richard," Salim had said, as wearily as now, "I am tired and hungry and ..."

"Don't they feed you at the wake?" Uncle Richard had asked.

"I also have not slept for a week," he had said. "You want to know why?"

"No!"

"Uncle Rich," Kasim had to step in and help. "The old women ... the aunts just need to see a camera at the funeral, and that is all. He does not have to be a photographer, but he must have a camera to be the camera man."

Uncle Richard had stared at him thoughtfully, confused that Kasim was for once serious and making sense. Then he had turned to the one who made most sense most of the time.

"Go back to my house," he had said to Salim. "Ask my wife to give you my Nikon camera."

"Thank you, Uncle Richard," Salim was overwhelmed. "That is one problem."

"Go find someone else to solve the other one."

"Thank you Uncle Rich ... I mean Uncle Richard," said Kasim.

"It is a Nikon F2," he told them.

"I have heard of it," Salim said.

"Best camera ever made," said Uncle Richard.

Salim nudged Kasim. It was his turn to grovel.

"Thank you, Uncle Rich," Kasim said, humbling himself. "Very kind of you Uncle Richard."

"You may keep it when you are done with it."

They looked at each other confounded.

"What is wrong with it?" Kasim could not help but ask.

"You don't want it?"

"We do, we do, but ..."

"We'll talk about how much you pay for it later," he said to them.

"We don't want to buy your camera," Salim said, struggling to stay calm. "You can keep your camera. We came for money to engage a photographer."

"A photographer to take photographs of a dead man," said Uncle Richard. "I got all that, but you don't get a bean from me until you pay what you owe for my wife's Beetle."

"I paid you for that," Salim said startled.

"When?"

"A long time ago."

"When?"

"You want the exact date?"

"Year will do."

"Uncle Richard," Kasim pleaded, "we are family."

"Have you got a receipt?" Uncle Richard had asked Salim.

"You know you did not give me one. I gave you the money, you gave me the logbook and the car keys. We are family, you said. You are my uncle. We are family."

"You know," Uncle Richard said to him. "For an attorney, you are very stupid."

He turned and walked away to the club house.

"On second thoughts ..." he said over his shoulder, "Bugger off; go buy your own camera."

"No, Uncle Rich," Kasim said quickly. "On second thoughts; we'll keep the Nikon."

"So, for what are you waiting? Go, get out of my face. Tell your aunts this is a members' club. Bugger off."

They did not report the encounter to the aunts verbatim, for fear of stoking family feuds and breaking broken hearts. Aside from Aunt Eva, all the aunts knew Uncle Richard and were not overly concerned about his ways. He had not attended a single funeral fundraiser since his return from decades of study and work abroad and the clan tried to saddle him with paying medical and funeral bills for a relative he had never seen. He had not been at a clan gathering or burial since then and was unlikely to come attend Caesar's burial.

"I want the real photographer here, before we begin," Aunt Eva said to Salim.

"He will be," said Kasim, too exhausted to care.

He had lost weeks of sleep, neglected his office work, gambled away his career and reputation, and all for what? So that Aunt Eva could afterwards take credit for single-handedly organizing Caesar's funeral? Prove yet again King'oo men were non-achievers?

"This is not the moment for despair," Kasim said watching her walk away. "What we need to do is find

428

someone who looks like a photographer and give him the job. But first we must recover the equipment from the idiot with our camera?"

"Your brother, or cousin, Kiluki."

"I told you I know no such relative," said Kasim.

They went looking for him. Everyone had seen the happy, young man with a camera, but no one remembered where or when.

"He was just there," they pointed vaguely.

"He went that way," one man said.

Kasim had to find someone not lost in the conspiracy of confusion to get some sense.

Choma place was an alter under an old flame tree near the fence where the old men had chosen and cleansed to host the farewell goat, the special barbeque goat for Caesar to remember them by. Traditionally, it would have been accompanied by copious amounts of honey beer, but Caesar would have frowned on such a sendoff.

Cousin Deadhead was now the grill master. Deemed too daft to be anything else in life, Deadhead was the person they turned to for meat-roasting duties at clan functions and family feasts. He had attended the same school as the other King'oo, and, unlike many of them, had stayed to finish his primary education, but he had ended up with less education than the dropouts.

Roger was there too sitting with the old men, having gained acceptance by clandestinely financing twenty liters of honey wine, which was clandestinely making rounds of the barbeque fire, one drinking horn at a time. None of the old men had seen or realised there was a photographer about.

"All right, Uncle Roger?" Kasim asked him.

"I have no idea what they are speaking, but … yes, all is right."

"Does the battle axe know what you all are up to?"

"What?"

"Making merry before your father-in-law is in the ground?"

"She will never hear of this."

"Don't be so sure."

Then Cousin Deadhead, impatient with the speed of the fire in the grill, tossed it a cup of paraffin to encourage it. The grill exploded in meter-high flames, the old men scrambled to safety, and a quick-thinking young man threw honey wine on the fire dousing it. There followed a moment of unbelieving confusion. The meat and those nearby were covered in ashes. Kasim ran up to make sure Roger was all right.

"Is there anything you people do right?" Roger asked

"You are still alive, aren't you?"

He was covered in ashes, but he was more amused than upset.

"Caesar's farewell feast will have to wait for another funeral," said Kasim. "Better go clean up before the battle axe sees you."

Uncle Tivo came back jollier than anyone had seen him all week. He wanted to know if the talking was over, and what everyone had said about Caesar. He hated windy replies, and waved them away. Then he saw Caesar lying on a table on the veranda and asked why he was not buried yet, and why the old men looked like they had crawled out of a warthog's hole.

Chapter 46

Pastor Kioko was a good pastor. Most of them thought so, though they did not say it. They felt for him as they saw him wrestle with his conscience as he read Aunt Eva's dissertation on Caesar's life. He should have been reading a meaningful, spiritually uplifting speech he read at every King'oo funeral, and which always left the clan happy. Aunt Eva's document belonged in an academic journal; one appropriately titled *The Traditional Burial Rites Of The King'oo Clan.* It went on and on, and for so long, that the Pastor had no clue what he was reading anymore. It seemed he was reading the life history of a man he had never met, a man not in the least resembling the Caesar he knew.

The Caesar that Pastor Kioko knew spoke no more than was necessary to express himself. He and Kioko had many thought-provoking discussions, social, philosophical, and theological ones, when Kioko as a young man came calling on Charity.

"So, you want to marry my daughter?" Caesar had asked him, the first time he revealed the nature of his friendship with Charity. "Do you own a house?"

"No," said Kioko. He was saving to build one.

"Do you own land to build a house?"

"No," he said, but he was saving to buy land.

"How much money do you have?"

Kioko hesitated. Everyone knew Caesar as an upright and reasonable man, a man who would spend his own money to buy school uniforms for neighbours' children. Kioko did not imagined Caesar would talk to him about money, knowing his humble background.

"So, you think my daughter wants to leave this house I built for her and her sisters to come live with you under a tree and eat grass like a gazelle?" Caesar asked him.

Kioko's will crumbled. He had known Caesar since he was a boy. He sat staring at the ground in despair.

"Kioko, my son," Caesar said to him, "There is no higher calling than preserving and nurturing the gifts you were born with, using them to uplift yourself and others. A trade, a profession, a real job. Telling people God loves them is not a profession. You can do that for free, in your free time."

Kioko had revealed he wanted to go to a theological college.

"Taking money from poor people telling them God loves them, is robbery," Caesar said to him. "Pastoring is a lazy and unscrupulous man's way of taking poor people's money while lying to yourself and to them that you do good for humanity. Go learn carpentry, masonry, or car mechanics."

Young Kioko took Caesar's advice and learned motor mechanics under Tivo. Then he went to Machakos and worked as a *jua kali* car mechanic, while he studied electrical wiring at the polytechnic.

When electricity returned to Kathiani, years later, he made a living wiring the town and surrounding farms. But his heart was in evangelism and his calling in saving souls.

He used his savings to go to Kilimambogo theological college from where he graduated as a pastor. He never took poor people's money, not even what they owed to the church for baptisms, weddings, and funerals. And from the wealthy, he took no more than was due to the church.

"King'oo is a disease," his father had said to discourage him from pursuing her. "You will never know peace."

That King'oo were a plague, Kioko found out for himself when he persisted in his quest for Charity's affections. He saw suitors come and go, all of them King'oo boys and men he thought had more to offer than he had, and it got worse when they grew older and tired of chasing after Charity, and went and got married, or did not, and settled down to being King'oo men, a famous plague.

And here he was reading an irrelevant story of the man who taught him integrity, written by someone who openly and publicly accused Kioko of greed and ill-will towards his estate and Charity's inheritance. It broke his heart.

Aunt Eva caught Salim's eye, gestured to his right. Kung Fu was leading Karate by the hand away from the graveside. Salim followed them. A short distance from the gathering, he found Karate weeping on his brother's shoulder.

"What now?" he heard Kung Fu say. "We agreed there would be none of that here today."

Karate nodded, even as sobs heaved his chest, and Salim heard him apologise for his weakness. He was cold and lonely, he said. He wished he could go embrace *mwaitu* and cry in her arms as he used to do. He wanted to hug and be hugged by her, to have her blow on his hurt heart and say that everything would be all right, just as she used to do. He wanted to be home with her, home where he had felt safe as a child, with the people who made him feel safe. But the aunts no longer lived here, and *nau* was dead and everyone was weary. How could anything ever be all right again?

Salim saw Kung Fu bend over his brother, whisper in his ear, lay a hand on his shoulder, pat it gently.

"Suck it up, bro," Salim heard him say. "Lock it up in here, in your heart, okay? You are a King'oo man. A true King'oo, not a Chinese cousin, okay? Now dry your eyes."

He gave him a handkerchief. Karate dried his eyes, took a deep breath, and steeled himself. Growing up King'oo was no different for them than for any other of Caesar's foster children. They got food, shelter, and loving care. Like all the other children, they were not allowed to call Charity *mwaitu*, mum, but by the time they went to nursery school, they spoke Kikamba like Kamba.

At school, Teacher Charity coaxed them from the back of the class, where they took refuge on their first day in nursery school. She held their hands through to primary school, then Eva took over and scared them to the top of the class.

That was where she left them when she left for America. With Eva gone, and Aunt Charity tied up with caring for Caesar, there was no one to push them through high school to University. They inevitably succumbed to the old King'oo boys' curse. The twins slid to the bottom of the class, returned to the back of the class, and eventually dropped out of high school, and went to work for the Chinese railway.

They turned, saw Salim watching them, and walked slowly back to the gathering. Salim went back to his place by Aunt Charity's side, whispered in her ear, then beckoned them. They hesitated, then approached, cautiously, their eyes on Aunt Eva. Salim nodded and she made room for them between herself and Aunt Charity. Aunt Charity placed her arms round their shoulders. A look of peace descended on them. Despite Caesar's absence all was well again.

Pastor Kioko read on. Stomachs grumble. Old men muttered unhappily and whispered about going for a walk down to Musikali Kombo's off-licence and returning when the talking was over. Pastor Kioko would have done the same too, if he had to sit through the dross he was reading. He started skipping every third paragraph to avoid a situation he saw often; mourners slipping away to water their throats, or their goats as they called it, and to deal with other issues, only to return for the funeral feast, some of them so drunk they had to be saved from falling in the grave. His plot worked for two pages of Caesar's imaginary history, then, just when he started to believe it would succeed, he felt a tap on the shoulder and turned to find Aunt Eva glaring at him.

"You missed three paragraphs," she said. "Go back."

He hesitated, lowered his voice.

"Is it really necessary to say this?" he asked her.

That imperial nod again. He was about to collapse from embarrassment. Now everyone who heard the exchange was eager to know what it was he considered unnecessary to read. When he did, no one liked it.

It was a blatant attack on all of them, rebuking them for their ingratitude towards Caesar, the man who sacrificed his family, his money, his career, and his health to eradicate ignorance and show them the way. A good and generous man, but for whose dedication to the clan, they would wallow in poverty, live in rat-infested shacks, and eat *Muthokoi* with no pigeon peas or salt.

Caesar built the first primary school in Kathiani, prevailed on the government to elevate Kathiani by building government offices to it easier for the clan to access government services.

It was Caesar who brought water and electricity to market centers, schools, and clinics, and to every home that could afford it. And he got them a post office, so they did not have to walk half a day to post a letter.

And how did the clan now honour Caesar? By pleading poverty and corona and donating empty words. Even the gravediggers, the boys he sent to school with his own money, were now demanding money, and threatening to fill his grave back if they were not paid before his burial.

Everyone turned to the gravediggers in dismay. Gravedigging used to be a communal duty. If they did an excellent job, dug an exceptionally good grave, they got money at the end of the day for beer to help dislodge the dust settled in their throats, and that was all. What was this now about paying them before Caesar was buried? The gathering turned to Aunt Eva. What was this about?

Aunt Eva turned to Salim.

"Kasim," Salim said to her. "He has sorted it out with them."

"How?" she asked, knowing Kasim had no money.

"I did not want to know," said Salim.

"Why are these boys after me then?" she asked.

Salim was at the end of his tether.

"Aunt Eva," he said. "Just leave me alone. Since this funeral started, I feel like a frog in a blender."

"A what?" she was utterly lost.

She looked round for someone to translate. The gravediggers were behind her waiting to be told who would give them their lunch money. They had already figured it would not be Aunt Eva, for she seemed to have forgotten, or to not care, who they were or why they were armed with picks and shovels. Salim had already said he had nothing to do with the grave digging and Kasim clearly had no money, and the deal he had made with their foreman had invalidated itself the moment they realised how hard it would be to divide two donkeys between the five or six of them.

"Aunt Eva," Salim said, calmly, "they want money for lunch."

"You will eat donkey," she said to them.

In Kikamba, it did not come out halfway decent. The young men did not expect such words from an old woman, a respected aunt and teacher. Uncle Tivo, whose language was out of bounds most of the time, way outside of the limits of decency, did not speak such words to them either. They were very unhappy.

"Aunt Eva," Salim tried on their behalf. "They don't eat donkey. No one eats donkey here."

She hit him with that hard, partly aggravated look she used in class when he did not grasp how x and y added up to something other than x and y. An orange and a banana did not add up to a mango, he had argued with her in class. He got a lot of whacking from women teachers for thinking and reasoning like that, like a King'oo man. When she left for America, he and all the other boys celebrated and prayed she would not return before they dropped out of school.

Then, during one of her tumultuous Christmas visits, she announced she had found the value of zero and it was equal to a King'oo man. A few learned old men died trying to find the formula that led her to such an outrageous conclusion. Most did not care, so long as she took her math with her back to America.

Now the gravediggers looked down at their dusty-red feet in embarrassment. Their leader raised his hand to speak. She ignored him. An uncomfortable silence followed. He turned to Uncle Sam. He had crept up to join the group, but was keeping a low profile to avoid committing himself to anymore expenses. It would not be the first time he was left holding the bag when the show was over and everyone had gone home except the caterers, the suppliers and the gravediggers waiting to be paid.

The head gravedigger had his hand up waiting to be allowed to speak and Aunt Eva was ignoring him, and Uncle Sam was not certain who was the custodian of the permission to let a gravedigger speak at a funeral. He turned to Aunt Eva. Before she could open her mouth, Uncle Tivo jumped in.

"This is a free country," he said. "Speak and speak loud so that even those who have no ears will hear."

"Thank you, Tivo," the man said, loud so that even those without ears could hear. "We are grateful to Mzee Mophat, Caesar, and his family for everything he did for us. It is true Caesar bought my first uniform when I started school. He bought many of us books too, even when our parents did not see any need to send us to school. But we were boys then, and our only responsibility was to go to school and learn. Now we are men, men with wives and children to feed and educate, and we have no jobs, no money, and no food."

Aunt Eva pointed at the giant pots of *muthokoi* bubbling away under the pepper trees and the gang of women sacrificing so that everyone present could be fed.

"Who do you think they are cooking for?" she asked him. "You will eat when everyone eats. Now go away, you are interrupting."

And that was that.

They lingered, grumbled, gripped their work tools. Their leader beckoned Salim aside and whispered in his ear. Salim went back to Aunt Eva.

"They always get beer money," he reported.

"Not from me," she assured.

Uncle Sam, overhearing, said he would take care of it. They were holding up his train. The longer it delayed, the more the uncertainty of reaching their destination any time soon. He had dealt with similar situations before. He knew how little it took to make such men happy. He took the head gravedigger aside and gave him enough money for two bottles of *chang'aa*. Enough to make them forget their personal issues and get back on board his train.

"Don't be too long," he warned.

"We will not be late," the man said, and beckoned his team.

They hurried away and Pastor Kioko resumed the eulogy, skipping a page here and there to speed up the process. Aunt Eva was too weary of King'oo slyness to bother asking him to slow down and start over.

Chapter 47

Sam's train was back on tracks and charging to final destination. Pastor Kioko, the engine driver picked for that final leg, had the hardest job of balancing between his conscience, and Aunt Eva's indignation, everyone else's wishes and the urgency to speed up the proceedings and finish Caesar's journey before darkness fell. Everyone saw how he suffered under the pressure of having to read Eva's decree and hoped it would all be over soon. Now and then he glanced at her to see how she was taking it, but he could not tell. She sat with her eyes closed, as if in great thought, or great pain, or hopefully prayer, and it was hard to tell which.

Ever since the Pastor could remember, Eva was at war with King'oo manhood, starting with the boys, ungrateful beneficiaries of Caesar's crusade to educate his people. To succeed in his mission to turn the clan into a super-educated society, Caesar had to start with King'oo women. He insisted girls get as much education as a teacher could push in their heads. Eva's eulogy was a testimony to his determination.

The eulogy, that she had worked on for a week, also read like a dissertation on the cultural practices of the King'oo men, their traditional moles, their gender beliefs, and the trials and tribulations of the King'oo girl child. Woven in it was the saga of a man of vision that had altered the lives of the women of a whole nation.

Pastor Kioko, a beneficialy of the gender bias, read the eulogy, painfully and haltingly trying to understand its purpose and why it had to be read at such a venue. From time to time, he glanced at Eva expecting her to allow him to stop, but she had her eyes closed.

Mourners stood about expecting to be told what the Pastor was reading and why. Those who had made it past Kathiani Secondary and Koma Rock High schools understood the words, especially the part about Caesar's dedication to the education of the whole of Kambaland. But some were hearing, for the first time, that all the beating they endured at the hands of the teachers was not a campaign against King'oo boys, but Caesar's way of ensuring they got sharp as razors and stayed that way. Now they could confirm what they had suspected all along – that the teachers were rewarded for the number of King'oo boys they whipped through to secondary school, and those that they scared to universities.

Some way into the thesis Pastor Kioko was reading, old timers called for stools and sat dozing. Some retreated to discuss business under the mango trees, and a few gave up and went home leaving their sons to fetch them when the speeches were over.

Aunt Charity had her reservations the moment Aunt Eva insisted on writing the eulogy. Now she sat rocking in her chair, praying for peace and patience. Other aunts who had strongly opposed the decision to let Aunt Eva write about Caesar without them were about to rise and protest. What had any of this to do with Caesar? Caesar was loved and loving. And now he was dead. And they were there to bury him. That was enough to say.

Aunt Eva remained stone-faced and above their suffering. It would not have been the first time a King'oo funeral erupted in a fight.

Aunt Charity signaled Pastor Kioko to speed it up, but the Pastor was going as fast as he could, and sweating profusely and starting to falter. He was hoarse, his throat dry, but he dared not stop.

Salim sent a boy to fetch him a glass of water. The Pastor would have liked to skip more paragraphs, jump to the last page, but he knew what would happen. Aunt Eva would accuse him of ruining her father's final moment, and hit him with her chair.

Among the few outsiders at the burial were two of Caesar's old colleagues who were in the government at the same time as Caesar when he declared war on impunity and vowed to reverse the tradition of decades of entrenched corruption.

It took him years of enduring insults and threats from colleagues, politicians, and fellow citizens, to see his dream of justice, fairness, and fiscal responsibility begin to take root in the Government. Years of uncertainty, worry and stress that took a heavy toll on family and health.

In the end, when it no longer seemed to matter, cynics and detractors lauded his determination and his tenacity. He had done something everyone thought impossible. He had sobered up greedy lawmakers, made them see the folly of perpetually raising their own income when the rest of the country languished in poverty. Something that respected political analysts had said would never happen. A country so long wallowing in greed could not run without corruption. A country where a man was a street hawker one day, member of parliament the next day, and a millionaire on the third day could not turn around, earn respect from its electorate.

His two colleagues had survived the nonsense of the politics of the day and were shocked by his abrupt resignation just when everyone thought he would be their next president. Now he was dead, and they had come to bury him, and were impressed by the fuss the clan made to bury a man they knew as a first-class organiser.

"Is this how you bury your dead?" one of them was heard to whisper.

"I am Kamba myself and I have never seen the like of this," said the colleague from over the hills in Makueni county.

Caesar's old driver overheard them, and he informed them, King'oo clan was Kamba and yet not Kamba. It was a special breed that most Kamba preferred not to leave well alone.

"Did you see the hearse?" he asked them.

They had stayed with the gravediggers and missed that part of the King'oo uniqueness. But the casket said everything. The King'oo revered their Caesar.

"Caesar came in a Mercedes," someone whispered to them.

A carriage drawn by two magnificent donkeys all the way from Nairobi. Just like in the bible. And Aunt Eva was the one who made it happen. Aunt Eva would have blown her top had she heard them, but she was busy instructing Pastor Kioko's on exactly how to deliver Caesar's eulogy.

"She is the big woman with a thatch hat on her head," another King'oo said to the visitors. "She is from America. Her husband is the beanpole sitting with boys."

They glanced at the old man seated between Kasim and Salim, talking in whispers with one eye on the woman they called Aunt Eva.

"How do you survive being married to her?" Kasim was asking Roger.

"My great, great grandfather grew on a sugar plantation in the Caribbean," Roger said with a smile. "I get the feeling our genes came from these parts."

"We are everywhere," said Kasim.

They heard a car arrive. Kasim and Salim looked at each other. Uncle Richard? was the unspoken question. They heard the car door open and close. They waited to see him storm the patio demanding why Aunt Eva summoned him, why so many men could not bury one old man without him. When he did not appear for some minutes, Kasim went to investigate.

There was a second black Mercedes parked next to theirs. A man in a grey suite and a white Panama hat was walking round inspecting their Mercedes.

"Caesar's burial is on the other side," Kasim said to him.

"I am not here for that," he said, his eyes on the car.

He knocked on the roof, kicked a tyre, peaked through the window. Kasim left him to it.

"Some fat guy in a Mercedes," Kasim whispered when he got back to Salim. "Says he is not here for the funeral."

"Who does he want?" Salim asked.

"I didn't ask him."

"What did he say?"

"I am not here for that."

Salim tried to ignore it. After a moment, he eased back out of the crowd and went round the house to the front. The man was not just fat; he was as large as Aunt Eva. He was standing back, one fist resting on his waist, right hand on his jaw, contemplating the hearse. He looked vaguely familiar; a fringe politician, or someone Salim might have run into when he was a defense lawyer.

"Can I help you?" he asked.

"Is this your car?" asked the man.

Salim hesitated.

"I have one just like it in a garage in Nairobi," man added.

Salim felt the cold arm of fate reach out to encircle him. What were the odds on Kimeu the Thief turning up at Caesar's funeral, when the whole country knew how the two spent their entire time in the administration playing cops and thieves? Caesar's home was not even on his way to Kitui where he was rumoured to have retired.

There could be just one explanation. Divine retribution. The watchman had cracked under interrogation. The Inspector knew where the stolen Mercedes had gone. To Caesar's funeral.

"We have a funeral," Salim tried to escape.

"Wait," said the man. "I want to buy this car."

Salim stopped, surprise turning to panic.

"I collect old cars," the man answered the question on Salim's mind.

Salim was about to plead busy funeral responsibilities, and leave that agony for later, but he remembered why and how the stollen Mercedes got to Caesar's house. And what it cost him to get it there.

How much?" he asked.

"How much do you take for it?"

"I am very busy right now," Salim dared not look him in the eye. "Come back tomorrow?"

That would give them time to make it disappear

"Tomorrow I am in Mombasa," the man said. "Today, or never."

Salim was tempted by never, but, again, he saw the image of Mr Ryan's livid face looming over his desk.

"How much are you offering?" he asked.

"A hundred thousand."

"Two-fifty."

"It's a junk."

"Vintage junk."

Noticing the shifty look, the man tried to find out who he was, what he did. Salim was about to say conveyance, then hesitated. Kasim would have been proud to say what he did.

"Are you a car salesman?"

Kasim would have had no problem being a car salesman from some bogus garage in town, and probably also sold him another car, sight unseen, into the bargain.. He should have let Kasim deal with it.

They heard the choir sing *Till We Meet Again* from the back of the house. Salim was one of the pallbearers, and Aunt Eva would be out looking for him any minute now.

"Come back in two hours," he said.

"I will be on my way to Mombasa. Hundred-fifty thousand, here and now. Final offer."

"As it is?"

"Caveats emptor," said the man. "I know the law concerning old cars. As is."

Kasim did quick mental calculations, realised it would clean the mess he left in the office. Caesar would have been disappointed by him, but he saw no other way out of it. It was for a compelling cause. Caesar would also understand that.

"The path you have chosen is a slippery one," he had said when Salim decided on a career at law, a career fraught with as many temptations to enrich oneself as the possibilities to end up in prison.

In his time in government Caesar had seen innocent gifts become habit, whet the greed, turn to conditions, and make honest administrators into graft monster.

"Strive to be honest," he had said. "Whether you work for demons or for angels, stay clean, walk tall, and be your own man."

Until recently, Salim was on the side of the angels, but that changed when a Mercedes hearse for Caesar became everyone's obsession. Salim wished he had Kasim handling the transaction. The deal would be faster and more natural coming from Kasim. Salim's hands would be relatively clean, and the resulting trouble easier to sort out in court.

Aunt Charity would be devastated if she knew low he had sunk. And Aunt Eva would hit him with a stool, when she found out he sold a stolen car back to the owner. His only consolation was Kasim and he had put a lot of man hours into the crime, not to mention the money, to get the Mercedes in the shape it was in. Besides, it was not like they had taken the car for own use or robbed an innocent man. The man from Masinga was a known thief, a corruption tzar until the government kicked him off the gravy train. He would have to prove he did not steal it himself. A car shell like that was unlikely to have proper papers, if any. It was only fair and just that Salim should get back his investment before returning the car to him.

"Two-twenty," he said to the man from Masinga. "Final offer."

"Two hundred," said the man.

"Cash?"

"Or cheque, if you prefer."

Salim considered. On the back seat of the car was a disposable camera.

"Is there film in the camera?" he asked.

The man was surprised there was a camera in his car. He glanced at it, shrugged. He had no idea how it got there.

"Two hundred, plus the camera?" Salim said.

"It is not my camera," said the man.

"It is in your car."

The man shrugged, went around to the back of the car, and sprang the boot open. Salim opened the car door, got the camera, and went around to the back. He watched the man unlock a briefcase filled with bundles of money.

"Cash," he said again.

The man handed him a bundle of cash.

"One hundred," he said.

Then he handed Salim another bundle.

"One hundred," he said. "Count it."

"No need to," Salim stuffed the money in his pockets.

"Keys?" the man held out his hand.

"Inside."

The man opened the door and looked inside. The key was in the ignition. He took it out.

"This key holder looks familiar," he said.

"They come with the model."

"Can you drive it to my house?"

"I have a funeral."

"Afterwards?"

Salim was again tempted. He could keep the money, make the car vanish and swear he had not seen the man at Caesar's funeral. There would a lot of witness to attest to it. So far, apart from Kasim, no one had seen him. In court, with Kasim's participation, it could be spun into a revenge suit against Fisco Caesar, the man who hounded him out of Finance. But that would be more trouble than it was worth.

"I can't," he said to the man from Masinga. "Send your driver to pick it up. The car is safe here, but it may need a push-start."

"Logbook?"

"Wait here," said Salim.

He rushed in the house. There was no on in the house. They were all outside by the grave. He opened a door into a narrow corridor he remembered from childhood. The only light came from a window at the end of the corridor. There were four doors in the corridor, two on each side. The first door, the one closest to the entrance was Caesar's. Caesar's room, he remembered from childhood too. Salim had come to see him there often when he was ailing. Next and on opposite side was the room Aunt Eva shared with one sister.

Aunt Charity's room was at the end of the corridor nearest the window. She had shared it with Aunt Kamene until Aunt Kamene left for Sultan Hamud.

Salim proceeded to Aunty Charity's bedroom, knocked politely like she had taught him. He knocked three times, then pushed the door, slowly and peeked inside. There was just one big bed in the room now, with a high mattress, a duvet, fat pillows and a mosquito net that hung from the ceiling. Family photos hung on the walls. On a bedside table, next to a table lamp with a blue-flowered shade, was a kerosene lamp and a well-worn Bible. An old, black, Kamba bible with gold letters and red edges.

He looked over his shoulder, before picking up the bible. Aunt Charity would be horrified if she caught him at it. He quickly took a bundle from his pocket, cut it in half, opened the bible, and placed the half in it. He closed the bible and placed it back on the bedside table, exactly where he found it. Then he hurried out of the room, down the corridor and out of the house by the kitchen door.

They were inspecting the grave again and clearing a path from the patio to Caesar's mango tree. Aunt Eva saw Salim arrive back and scowled. He had missed the most important paragraphs of her thesis on Caesar, and the praise singing, and speeches by people she had never met. He had a lot to answer for when the burial was over.

"Uncle Richard?" she asked him.

"Are you still waiting for him?" Uncle Sam asked her.

Then he thought he might as well tell her the last time Uncle Richard interacted with the clan was when he invited everyone to the opening of his grand mansion in Nairobi. He hired three big buses to ferry the clan from Kathiani to his house in Nairobi; to do away with facile excuses, and be certain they all came to see his majesty, and leave no doubt in anyone's mind.

He had his guests take off their shoes before stepping inside the house, but many were barefoot anyway, having never afforded shoes, and they had to bath their feet and step in a basin of disinfectant to be allowed inside.

Then uniformed servants ushered them through the foyer, along a corridor lined with gold-framed mirrors to the grand reception room, and out to the back garden where they were treated to a feast the like of which none of them had ever imagined.

Some people later said the buffet table was as long and wide as the road from Mitaboni to Kathiani, and that it sagged under the weight of roast meat, boiled meat, fried meat, and meat, meat, meat, and nothing but meat.

Others swore it was loaded with rice, chapati and chicken stew and beef stew and nothing else. And there were those who, having started from the desert end, saw an endless cake buffet the like of which no one thought possible, and did not need to look farther.

Uncle Tivo and his gang had refused to take off their shoes, found their way round the house through the garden to the party, and chanced upon the bar. It too was mile long and loaded with drinks the like of which they had never seen, or tasted before or after, and it was also all free. They tried to drink it all, and were high for days afterwards, and swore there was no food at the party for they did not see any.

The communal good memories eventually faded, overshadowed by Uncle Richard's indifference to the clan's demands on his time and money. All that anyone now remembered, some with humiliation, others with amusement, was having to line up like children and take off their shoes and wash their feet before entering his house.

"Like Uncle Tivo told you," Salim said to Aunt Eva. "Uncle Rich does not do funerals."

"We shall see about that," she said.

She had changed a little since she called him an ambulance chaser without any consideration for his feelings. She had lost a little weight, gained a few wrinkles and grown a little wearier, all of it curtesy of King'oo male obstinacy. The clan she left behind had moved on too, deeper into the jungle of futility, and she could never lure it back, if she cared.

"Aunt Eva," he said to change the subject. "Would you come to my wedding?"

He thought that might draw her out of her dire thoughts.

"To an Indian girl?" she asked.

"What does it matter where she is from?" he said, hackles rising. "Your own mother was from Puntland."

He saw her face change, as she turned and hit him with the withering, teacher's look, and she did not have to say a word for him to see he had crossed many lines. He quietly walked away.

He sidled up to Kasim and whispered.

"I sold our car."

He spoke in Kikamba, on account of Roger was standing next to him, then he surreptitiously handed Kasim the rest of the money in an envelope.

"On no account let the Hurricane get her hands on it," he whispered.

Kasim peeked in the envelope, seemed shocked. He had not set his eyes on such a hefty sum since his days as the government pay master at Taeyang. He turned to Salim for an explanation.

"Later," said Salim.

Roger witnessed the transaction without understanding a word of it, glimpsed the contents of the envelope, and wondered what the boys had been up to. When no one bothered to update him, he leaned over to whisper.

"What's up, Salim?" he asked.

"Not much, Uncle Roger," Salim said.

Uncle Roger? Roger swallowed back a laugh. Not that he expected to understand everything the two were up to, but it seemed this time they had something worrisome in their hands. At this stage of their journey together he did not to care to know what. It was enough they had pulled off the Mercedes funeral caper, created a one-of-a-kind hearse, and made everyone happy. Well, almost everyone. He still had the matter of the overpriced casket to explain to the battle axe when they got home. Until then, all was well with his world too.

Caesar's burial was progressing as expected, with close to half of Kambaland present, some weeping, others praying and others talking in the background, while Kiluki or Maluki, or whoever now had the camera, rushed about taking photographs and getting in everyone's way, and Roger looked on bewildered. Kasim, finally recovered, patted Roger on the shoulder.

"All right, Roger?" he asked.

"I don't know, Kasim," he said. "But I'm cool with it."

"If it's any help," Salim whispered, "there are crazier families in this country."

Roger laughed, then looked about self-consciously.

"I'll take your word for it," he whispered back. "I love this country."

"The people are great too," said Kasim. "Friendly, hospitable, and sane. It is just us King'oo. We hate doing things the boring, old way, no matter how much easier it would be."

"You must have figured that by now, married to a Hurricane," Salim added, and rushed to join the pallbearers.

Roger stifled a laugh, looked to see if anyone noticed. Aunt Eva was watching. She would wring it from him the moment the burial was over. Salim and Kasim were safe for as long as it took Pastor Kioko to do his duty.

As the casket was lowered in the grave, Salim looked up to find the man from Masinga standing on the patio armed with a baseball bat, surveying the gathering with a murderous look on his face.

Salim remembered successfully defending him in court when, as a Cabinet Secretary, he was accused of pulling a gun on a traffic police officer he thought disrespected him by not moving fast enough to clear stalled traffic for him as he rushed to State House for a Cabinet meeting. Salim got him off by arguing extreme provocation under great stress. It was nothing compared to the stress Salim now had him in.

"Ashes to ashes, dust to dust ..." Salim heard the Pastor say, as he hid in the crowd by the grave.

Wrestling with visions of permanent, physical disability, or worse, because of his actions, Salim remained hidden while the casket was lowered in the grave. Then he tossed a handful of soil after it, and went in search of Kasim. It was time for them to leave.

"Just a second," Kasim said.

He had one last chore to do before leaving. Salim watched him rush past the man from Masinga into the house. If anyone else noticed the man with the bat, they did not seem at all concerned. But Roger had been watching their movements since he realised they had stopped being open with him, and he was concerned..

"Everything all right?" he asked Salim.

"I'm cool, Roger, I'm cool," Salim said, though he appeared anything but cool.

He searched furtively round, ducked behind Roger, and crept to Uncle Tivo's side, startling him.

"Uncle Tivo," he said, "do you still have that old bicycle I used to borrow?"

"Yes," said Uncle Tivo, smelling a deal.

"May I rent it?" Salim asked.

"No," said Uncle Tivo.

"Why not, you used to let me ride it for free?"

"You were a school boy."

"May I buy it from you then?"

"No," again said Uncle Tivo.

Salim considered offering the price of a new bicycle but, as no money had been solicited, he knew that would be a fatal mistake. When Uncle Tivo was in a stubbornly, negative mood, only slyness could draw him out of it. Salim looked about, pointed.

"See those animals?" he said.

Uncle Tivo followed the pointing finger across the far fence to the tethered donkeys.

"I give them to you for the bicycle," Salim said.

"Where did you get them?" The first thing any King'oo would ask before considering any deal.

"I bought them," said Salim.

"How much?"

He would die from shock if Salim told him how much Kasim got him to pay for them.

"Much more than the bicycle is worth," he said.

Uncle Tivo looked him in the eye, nodded, looked again at the animals, nodded again, then reached for his phone. He wanted to know what the butcher would pay for them."

"No," Salim pushed the phone from his ear. "You can do that later, after the funeral goat. Just tell me where to find the bicycle."

Uncle Tivo returned his phone to his pocket and beckoned a boy.

"Kivindio," he said discreetly to the boy. "Take those bulls to my house. When they are safely in my *boma* ..."

"Bulls, grandfather?" asked the boy. "Which bulls?"

Everyone knew Uncle Tivo was short-sighted, among other things, and children sometimes made fun of it, but no adult dared challenge him.. Salim silenced the boy with a warning finger while Roger tried to understand what was going on.

"Those animals by the fence," Uncle Tivo said to the boy. "Here is the key to my *boma*. Lock it and bring me the key. Go now, go."

"Uncle Tivo, the bicycle?" Salim reminded.

The old man turned to him.

"Are those animals yours?"

"I told you they were."

"You did not steal them?"

"You know me, Uncle Tivo," Salim said to him. "I'm a man of law."

"So," again asked the old man. "Did you steal the animals or not?"

"No, Uncle Tivo, I did not steal the animals."

"Kivindio," Tivo said to the boy. "Show Salim where I keep my bicycle. Go now, go."

The grave was covered, red soil flying onto the mound by the spadefuls. Sweat turned to mud on the gravediggers faces and the aunts, Caesar's daughters, watched from the patio as a chapter of their lives ended.

"Roger," Salim asked. "Will you stay for the will?"

"The will? From what I've gathered, Caesar died penniless."

"You gathered that right, Roger, but you are probably the only one in the whole clan who believes it."

Had Caesar been one of the big, fat, corrupt government officials that Kasim loved to poke fun at, his remains would be lying at the morgue for decades while the clan fought over his ill-gotten wealth. Still, scores of King'oo men would need someone like Uncle Sam to talk them through it. Then they might understand how that was possible, and still may not believe it.

Kasim came out of the house, stepped round the man from Masinga and returned to the graveside.

"Are you leaving now?" Roger asked them.

"It is over, Roger," Salim said to him. "It is all over now. Your father-in-law is safely in the ground and there is no one to hassle you over bride price."

"The old geezer?" Roger asked pointing at Uncle Tivo.

"Uncle Tivo has no real claim to Hurricane Eva's bride price."

"Who says?" said Kasim.

"I know the law," said Salim.

"King'oo laws are different," Kasim said to Roger. "Ask any man here."

Roger was not convinced.

"Listen, Roger," Salim said to him, "I don't do divorces, but should you decide to dump the battle-axe, I can hook you up with the fastest *kamikaze* divorce lawyers in Nairobi."

"Really?" his bemused small smile was back.

Salim handed him a business card.

"Call me."

"Call us," said Kasim. "I can hook you up with the hottest Kamba ladies in town. And you don't have to marry them."

"And Roger," Salim said. "Don't wait for Caesar to die again for you to come to visit us, okay?"

"Will do," said Roger.

He was smiling again, the small, sad smile he had the first time he visited from America when the old men nicknamed him Small Smiles. He watched them sneak away from the gathering, duck through a barbed wire fence and out of sight in the *shambas*. Then he sighed and went looking for his wife.

Chapter 48

Uncle Tivo's house was smaller than Caesar's, but bigger than most houses in Kathiani. It was solidly built from quarry rock and roofed with heavy-gauge, corrugated red-oxide sheets from the days Uncle Tivo worked for a road construction company and such material came easily to him. The house sat on an overgrown five-acres among grevillea and flame trees and dozens of rusting shells of cannibalised cars and lorries.

Three barking mongrels met Salim and Kasim at the gate, made friends and followed them back to the house. Kivindio was driving the donkeys in the cowshed when they got to the house.

"What are they doing here?" Kasim asked confused. "I gave those donkeys to the gravediggers."

"They belong to Tivo now," Salim informed.

The boy shut and locked the *boma*, tugged at the lock to make sure it was locked, then led them to the back of the house. The garden behind Uncle Tivo's house was Eden in a junk yard. Mango and avocado trees sagged to the ground with fruit amid rusting scrap cars and abandoned construction machinery, all of them overgrown with weeds and bushes that spread right up to the walls of the house. Kivindio took them to where Uncle Tivo kept his bicycle. They stared dumbfounded when he pointed to the rusty, old thing, covered with cobwebs, hanging from the rafters.

"Kivindio," Salim had to know, "since you were born, have you seen your grandfather, or anyone else, ride this thing?"

The boy shook his head. Kasim gave him the job of getting it down, dusting away the cobwebs, rubbing away the rust and washing the bicycle with water. Then he was to inflate the tyres with the hand pump.

They left him to it and went to explore Tivo's garden. Kasim knew the place well having spent what seemed like half his life there learning to repair cars.

They picked their way through the orchard, their senses alive to the smell of blossoming fruit trees, jasmine bushes, and the buzzing of bees from hives hanging from the flame trees. At the end of the garden were two old sheds with rusty metal roofs made from split bitumen drums, partly hidden by rambling roses and bougainvillea hanging from the jacaranda and flame trees.

The first shed used to be the beginners' classroom, where novices were taught to cut out car roofs and side panels, and hammer them to sheets that could be made into almost anything. A sign on the door read – *Tivo Polytechnic, Department of Kitchen Appliances.*

"I wrote that sign," he said with pride. His first original joke.

That was where he should have learned to make pots and pans and farm implements out of old car bodies. He failed the promotion test for that department, and was about to be declared unteachable and expelled, but Caesar insistence he continue straight to the car repairs course.

The second shed was the car repair workshop. The sign on the door declared it - *Tivo University, School of Mechanical Engineering.*

"I wrote that one too," Kasim said with pride.

That was where he almost learned to be a *jua kali* mechanic, but instead wasted a career telling jokes while his peers honed theirs.

The double-door was intact, though the bottom hinges had rusted away leaving it leaning to one side and a wide gap on the other side. Through the gap they saw giant anvils with hoists dangling over them from beams under the roof. Everything was covered with dust, or choked by creepers that crept in through the broken door and windows.

Salim lifted the sagging end off the floor, dragged the door open, and they squeezed through the opening into the shed. The first thing he noticed was the hulking shape of a car covered with a huge tarp and weighed down by tons of dust and about to be buried under the creepers. The place reeked of old engine oil and diesel fuel.

The floor was covered with dried oil, grease, and dust. There was a pile of rusty wheel rims and old tyres by the wall. The workshop had not been used for a long time, but, thanks to King'oo trust in witchcraft, little seemed to have been disturbed. The light switches and wall sockets were intact, as were light bulbs hanging from the roof beams.

Kasim's old work bench was exactly where he left it, all those years ago, how he left it with a bucket of nuts, bolts and washers beside it, and an engine block on a hoist still hovering in the air above it. He rushed to the bench babbling about his days as a student of motor engineering, and telling how, had he but cared a little for the course, he would not need Kajicho or any other *jua kali* mechanic today.

While Kasim discovered all that, and talked excitedly about it, Salim went over to the covered vehicle, lifted a corner of the tarpaulin, and looked under it. He dropped it quickly when he saw what was under the tarp. Then he took a couple of deep breaths and looked again. He dropped the tarp and scratched his head thoughtfully.

Caesar had at one time instructed Salim to start court proceedings against Uncle Tivo for failure to pay for an old car he bought from him to teach his boys the basics of car repairing. Uncle Tivo had had admitted not paying for the car and, in mitigation, claimed it was an old junk that his students had cannibalised, stealing resalable parts, and the rest they had turned to *jikos and karais*, pots and pans. Caesar had not been serious about suing him anyway and asked Salim to drop the case.

And there it was now under a dusty tarpaulin, Caesar's old car, Mercedes XT100, sitting on the blocks where Uncle Tivo had abandoned it when he abruptly gave up trying to educate King'oo blockheads like Kasim. It was mind boggling how the car could have survived the hundreds of indifferent boys who had passed through the polytechnic on their way to unemployment and to Kajiado rock mines. Who would have imagined the vehicle would survive all Tivo's boys, and outlast its owner?

Salim peeled the tarpaulin all the way back and was in awe of what he saw. The body was intact safe for slight scratches and a few dents here and there. The headlights were undamaged, the windows whole and the door handles rust free. When he opened the car door a multitude of rats scrambled from inside the seats, leaped out of the door and windows scattering in all directions. The interior of the car was all torn up, covering hanging from the roof and sides.

He closed the door, went round, and lifted the engine cover. And there was the engine, the original one by the look of it, greasy and dirty and another nestling place for rats. More rats scrambled from the engine and scattered.

Kasim found him taking pictures with his camera.

"I don't remember this one," he said walking up.

"It was not here then," Salim said. "Caesar's."

He started dialing a number.

"And to think we went to all that trouble to …"

"History," Salim raised a hand to silence him.

"Mr D'Souza," he said into the phone, "Are you still interested in an XT100? I know where you can find one. I am looking at it right now. In excellent condition. How much? Your maximum offer? We'll talk."

He was walking on air when they went back to the boy and the bicycle.

"Before you go using our find to pay any bride price," Kasim said to him, "remember who led you to it?"

"You did not even know it was there," Salim reminded him.

The boy had finished the chores Kasim had given him and was waiting for his pay. Salim handed him the agreed payment.

"Go tell Uncle Tivo we'll get him for this," Kasim said. "Now go, *potea!*"

Moments later, they were riding down a dirt road, with their rickety bicycle about to fall apart under them. Salim was driving, Kasim riding pillion. The rear tyre deflated before they had covered five hundred metres. While Kasim pumped it, Salim tried to make a call and discovered there was no network. He checked with his watch, paced agitated.

"Don't panic," Kasim said. "Two more pumps and we are on Mombasa Road. It is all downhill from the next hill."

They could see Mombasa Road in the distance, trucks and buses speeding along, but it would be dark before they were halfway there. They heard a car approach and got ready to dump the bike and hitch a ride. They did not need to flag the car down. It screeched to a stop the moment the driver saw them, and the driver's door flew open.

"Run," yelled Salim, taking off into the bush.

Kasim saw the fat man spill out of the black Mercedes, baseball bat still in hand, and remembered where he had last seen that suit. He scrambled to his feet, hopped on the bicycle, and peddled furiously after Salim. By then Salim was yards away down a footpath that cut diagonally across and down the hillside away from the road.

"Salim!" he yelled, "Wait for me! Salim!"

Salim did not slacken pace, or look back, until he was at the bottom of the hill and completely out of breath. When he looked back, Kasim was coming helter-skelter downhill out of control and the fat man was waving his bat from the road at the top.

"That man …," he said, when he got to Salim.

"He wants the logbook," Salim said.

Kasim laughed till he had to stop for breath.

"Did he know about the engine?"

"He should by now. We better hurry or I miss my date."

He hopped back on the pillion seat.

Chapter 49

They were exhausted when they got to Mombasa Road, having ridden, pumped, then ridden and pumped, and finally pushed their bicycle for the last half kilometre.

Mombasa Road bus stops had a reputation of being not places to be waiting for a bus after dark. Career thugs, a lot of them King'oo, most of them young, some of them unemployed university graduates, rose from the asphalt and the roadside ditches and bushes, as soon as it got dark, and started collecting night tax from anyone stranded by the roadside.

Salim and Kasim sat at the bus stop for a while without speaking, exhausted by the race to beat the sunset to Mombasa Road. They saw overloaded buses and *matatu*s zoom by without stopping. They sat silently and waited for a long while, overwhelmed by what they had done that day. All Salim wanted was to do was go home and sleep the sleep of many nights.

"He never asked me what was wrong with my head," Kasim said suddenly said.

"Caesar?" asked Salim. "He never heard any of your jokes."

"But he knew," said Kasim. "Caesar knew we were on the same side, faced life head-on, without fear or compromise. We called them by different names, but you could say we fought the same hydra."

"Hydra?"

"It is in the dictionary," said Kasim. "Megalomania is in it too. So are avarice, arrogance, sadism, impunity …"

"Where is this leading?"

"I miss Caesar."

"Seriously, Kasim," Salim said, "he was the only one who never heard any of your lame jokes. Why don't you get a job like other people?"

"You have your law," Kasim said.

"I will not have any law if they realise what I have done. Raided clients' accounts to pay for a funeral I could not afford. Talking of which …"

He held out his hand.

"My money."

Kasim looked at the hand puzzled.

"The money I gave you by the graveside," Salim said.

"That money?" Kasim said. "Was that what it was meant for?"

"Where is it?" Salim suddenly panicked.

"I thought it was for Aunt Charity."

"What is wrong with your head?" Salim screamed. "I said to hang on to the money not to give it away, you incredibly foolish fool."

Kasim had never seen Salim so angry and desperate. He tried to apologise. Salim would not accept his apologies. His fiancée, his career, his face, his freedom, were down the toilet because of Kasim.

"Tomorrow I go back and get it," he promised. "She will understand."

"After you explain how we got it selling a stolen car?" Salim asked him.

"Perhaps not such a clever idea," he agreed. "I will make it up to you."

"How?"

"I'm an entertainer."

"Who doesn't have one intelligent joke in his head."

"There's nothing wrong with my jokes?"

"True there's nothing wrong with your jokes," Salim agreed, "which, by the way, are not your jokes, but there is everything wrong with your telling. You drop them on your audience like a bucket of shit and expect them to laugh?"

"But they do."

"Laugh at you, not at your jokes."

"You have never been there?"

"I have been to school," Salim said. "Read books I did not have to."

461

"So have I?"

He saw the look on Salim's face.

"Not in school," he admitted, "But I have read books I did not have to."

On his first dive under the customs desk to escape gunfire, he had found a stash of dogeared books stacked round the safe place for extra protection. He had soon also discovered what his predecessor had also found out before he abandoned his post. Books, no matter how thick and profound, were no protection against AK47 bullets. But books were a good refuge when mayhem broke out and naked terror rampaged through the post in the middle of the afternoon and there was nowhere to run. He had started reading.

Starting from books and authors he had never heard of, which was about everything and everyone, he read anything that came to hand. But the ones that interested him most were guide books and teach yourself books.

He grew used to crouching under the desk reading, and learning to live with the heat, the flies, and the dust. Sometimes he fell asleep under the desk only to be woken by the silence after the battle. He would then rise, dust himself up, straighten his tie, get back behind the desk and wait for dutiable goods to come across the border.

Then one day, at the bottom of his protective wall of books under the desk, he unearthed a book that would change his whole perspective. He read it from cover to cover, over the following months, and must have read it a hundred times, while crouching under the desk waiting for the shooting to end. The book was titled *Standup for Idiots*.

"An idiots' guide to standup," Salim said. "Any idiot could have told you that all a standup artist needs is one good joke. One original joke that makes them smile when he steps on stage."

"I have one," said Kasim.

"Not now," Salim rose to flag down a bus approaching at high speed.

The bus flew by without stopping, and they sat back down.

"How come you know so much?" Kasim asked.

"I told you I went to school."

"So did I. Okay, all right, I could have stayed a little longer."

"A lot longer," said Salim. "I am an attorney, so it is also my job to think logically. Think with me, for just a moment. What is red and green spinning at a hundred miles an hour? Which, by the way, is not your original joke but stolen."

"Borrowed."

"So you say," Salim agreed. "Red and green? Going at a hundred miles an hour? What could it be? What else but …"

"A frog in a blender?" they said together.

"Kindergarten jokes?" added Salim. "You must try harder, Kasim."

He rose to flag down an overloaded *Matatu* bus, and it surprised them by stopping. They squeezed in the front seat with the driver and the two front seat passengers. The driver, a bully Rasta with a huge head, a wild beard, bloodshot eyes, and a red, gold, and green cap that could not contain his Rasta braids, silently adjusted his position sitting sideways to accommodate them.

"What about the bicycle?" asked the conductor.

They looked at each other. They had forgotten Uncle Tivo's bike.

"Not ours," they said together.

"Wait," the conductor yelled at the driver.

He leaped out of the bus, looked round and seeing no one else about, heaved the bicycle onto the luggage carrier. Kasim and Salim looked at each other again.

"Why didn't I think of that," Kasim said. "We could have used it fare."

"Too late," the driver said with a deep chortle. "It is now our bicycle."

The conductor swung from the roof into the bus just as the driver released the brakes and the Matatu zoomed towards the distant city skyline. Salim's mood lifted when he realised there was a chance he would make it to Maria's show.

"I was wrong about you," Kasim said to him. "You do have a sense of humour."

"Thanks."

"We have to write jokes together."

"No," said Salim.

"All right then," he said. "I am on my own again."

"You always were on your own, Kasim. Didn't you realise it? No one can understand you; what you do, why you do it, who you really are, or where you are going. And your jokes are not funny, and they never were."

"No need to rub it in."

"I am trying to help you," said Salim. "I would like to see you win but ..."

"That is enough, thanks."

"Not that I don't appreciate you," Salim said. "You have come far, for someone with no clue of where he is headed."

Someone who left school with no idea what he had learned in school, or what he was supposed to do with it or with his life. Kasim had done well for a predestined sand harvester. Most importantly, he had not bugged Salim for cigarette money, or rent money, or a job, as many King'oo boys did. He suffered his world with a smile, taking his falls in his stride until they were too heavy to bear. Then he took Salim for a drink and unloaded the whole sack of demons on him.

Like many an artist, he needed something to take all his fears and worries and uncertainties away. To make the feeling of inadequacy and failure disappear. So he dropped all those things in Salim's hands and begged him to get rid of them. Salim tried to make him understand there was nothing wrong with him as a person or as a man. What he needed was a good woman, soft and cuddly, to lend a shoulder to cry on.

"I'm sure you meet them every night at your clubs," Salim said.

"I know women," he admitted to Salim. "But not the way you think."

"Get one of them to lend you her shoulders to cry on."

Kasim smiled, imagining a wallet inspector as someone on whose shoulder a man could cry. Wallet inspectors were good women in their own ways, kind to their husbands, children, and family, but they had no time to waste on men with no wallets to inspect.

"No girlfriends?"

"Not women friends."

"Not one?"

"None."

"*Mmm*, that is a big, sad thing," Salim said. "You know what happens to men without women."

"They sleep on tables at *Uncle Dave's*," he tried to laugh it off. "I spend nights trying to cheer them up, make them laugh and perhaps find love. Love themselves and love me too, from a distance, and go home love their real wives too. They throw bottles at me. You must come meet them."

"I have a woman," said Salim.

"After she dumps you."

"That is not funny."

"When she learns of the terrible things you have done to date? Let us see, in chronological order, you took your clients' money, stole a stranger's car, sold the car back to the stranger, lied to her, and lied to her father?"

Salim could not believe how, after all these years, Kasim could not be discreet, or remain serious for a moment. That was the Mophat sisters' biggest failure as teachers. They could not turn off the crazy long enough to teach Kasim how to add oranges to mangoes and get a universal number. Male teachers had tried to beat the comic out of him, but that too had failed.

"I have an idea," he said excited. "We work together you and I …"

"No way," Salim said.

"I will do all the heavy lifting."

"No way."

"Just hear me out," Kasim lowered his voice. "As my guardian angel, agent and legal adviser, you will take home five percent of every gig."

"Five percent?" Salim said startled. "Is that what you think my advice would be worth? This one is free – go get a real job, work hard like normal people, and stop wasting time with silly jokes. Besides, I am going to prison. How can we work together?"

"I will come with you?" said Kasim, half-serious.

"See what I mean," Salim shook his head. "No wonder your fans mug you."

"No wonder no one likes you," Kasim said to him.

"They want free things," Salim said. "Like you, they want free rides. Like you."

"Loosen up, man," Kasim lowered his voice, calm and serious. "Live life or die. That is the biggest joke I know. Did I tell you the one about the pastors who died in a *matatu* accident and went to heaven?"

"Stop," Salim said to him. "I don't want to hear it."

"I do," suddenly said the bus driver.

They turned surprised. It was clear he had smoked weed and washed it down with clear liquids from opaque soda bottles like the *Black Survivors*, and on top of it he was chewing *khat*, his cheeks stuffed with it, and that was already illegal for drivers of passenger vehicles.

"Tell me, bro," Kasim said to him. "How do you pass all those police roadblocks?"

"*Mullah*, brother, *Mullah*," said the driver.

Kasim did not have to ask what that meant, but Salim did.

"*Miraa?*" Salim asked.

"*Mullah,*" said Kasim, rubbing thumb and index finger together.

"Oh," said Salim. "That *mullah.*"

"The joke?" said the driver. "The pastors who died in *matatu* crash?"

"Oh, yes," Kasim said. "It was a *matatu* just like this one, driven by a man who chewed *khat* and smoked stuff and broke speed limits."

The driver was already laughing.

"The *matatu* was cheap, and the driver was the bishop's nephew, so the pastors hired him to take them to a revival meeting in Rift Valley. As the bus flew down the escarpment road, like a hyena with his tail on fire, the inevitable happened. The pastors suddenly found themselves in a dark and silent place they assumed was heaven. Those who hang on to life, arriving later, found themselves lining up at a door waiting to be allowed in.

"How did you get here?" asked the gatekeeper.

"We were on our way to a revival party then ..."

"Ah," the gatekeeper interrupted. "The party of liars, thieves, and hypocrites? That party is round the corner and down the stairs. You can't miss it there is a sign over the door spelt H-E-L-L"

By the time Kasim delivered the punchline, the driver was laughing so hard he was about to roll the bus and the passengers were hanging on to their seats terrified.

Kasim turned to Salim.

"And now?" he asked.

"*Khat,*" said Salim.

"Jealous."

"Weed?"

By then they had flown over Lukenya Plains, and zoomed past Athi River cement and meat factories without noticing, and were slowing down into the fog of the cement dust and the exhaust smoke from Friday evening's mega traffic jams. The standstill stretched for kilometres into the city, then it radiated in every direction to the suburbs and could last for days.

With the bus now solidly stuck in the jam, the driver reached across the other front seat passenger to take Kasim's hand.

"Speed Buster," he said. "Speedy or *Buster-Yo* for short."

"Kasim the Komedian," Kasim took the hand.

"Your friend is a loser," the drivers said to him. "A soul destroyer."

"Soul destroyer?" Salim started to protest.

"Quiet," the driver said, then turned to Kasim. "Follow your *jah-jah* spirit. Do not listen to a soul destroyer."

"Soul destroyer?" Salim pleaded. "Isn't that a bit harsh?"

"You keep quiet," the driver rose from his seat.

Kasim rose too, afraid the man would destroy Salim. The driver stopped him with a big hand, fingers sprayed to display the gold rings, and faced his passengers instead.

"Listen you all people," he said aloud. "This is my man Kasim. Kasim the Komedian. Hear that? Kasim the Komedian. Triple K for Kuyu, Kisi, Kamba. Raise your hand if you never heard of Triple K."

A few hands rose, tentatively.

"All of you step down," he said.

The hands dropped fast.

"Anyone who does not know Kasim the Komedian step down right now. I want you all off this bus now."

Salim and Kasim exchanged worried glances. The love fest was about to get out of hand.

"*Khat?*" wondered Salim.

"Weed," Kasim guessed.

"You see what you have started now?"

"Not my fault I am so popular."

"I see you on teevee," someone called from the back of the bus.

"Me too," Kasim said. "Very soon. In cinemas too."

"*Hard Life* bar," another said. "You make pushcart guys laugh. I love your big, fat, corrupt policemen jokes."

"Me too," said someone who looked like a real *mkokoteni* pilot. "I fall down laughing."

"I love you too, guys," said Kasim. "Hustlers, men with balls, real men. The future of this country."

"You are not funny," said a familiar female voice from the back.

She was painting her fingernails and did not look up as she spoke, but he knew who it was. His bogie woman, his torturer, his nemesis from everywhere.

"I know Kasim," she said to the other passengers and the driver. "He tells jokes to people who are not even listening."

Kasim's heckling wallet inspector was otherwise unrecognizable without her pink wig and fluorescent pink lipstick that glowed in the dark.

"Pink Sister," he said to her, "I did not recognise you without your red hair."

"Pink," she said, looking up. "And you are not funny. I see you at funny clubs every night where no one laughs. They hate you at *Ha-Ha Club*. Why do you come there?"

"Just to see my sisters lovely, red hair."

"It is pink, you fool."

She saw the look on the driver's face.

"Just joking," she said to him. "Kasim and I go a long way. Ask him."

Kasim was tempted to deny it and have her tossed out of the bus. But then she would take the next bus to town, show up at work and make it hell for him.

Before switching careers, she was a hardhat woman, the kind than never quit, harder to break than a monkey wrench and shoveling gravel ten floors up construction sites. Then she discovered wallets inspection and her fortunes changed.

"See you at work, sister," said Kasim. "I will have you falling down under the table laughing, and I mean it."

"You wish," she said.

"Thank you all, for your patience and kind words," he said to the rest. "Come to my shows, all of you, come see me perform. *Hard Life*, River Road on Mondays, and *Uncle Dave's* from Tuesday onwards. Look for me at *Club Bombay* too. They love me there sometimes. Also, at *Casablanca*."

"Tell us a joke," said a passenger.

"Here?"

He was not sure entertaining passengers in a stalled *matatu* was legal. Big, fat, corrupt traffic policemen were walking down the line of stopped traffic inspection driving licenses, checking tyre pressure, and snarling at passengers who laughed at them. He glanced at the driver.

"Tell a joke," the driver ordered.

"Tell the one about the big, fat, corrupt politician who finds the policeman he jailed for corruption guarding the gates of hell," said the wallet inspector. "That one is funny."

By the time the police officers arrived, one on either side of the *matatu*, checking the tyres, the side mirrors and driver's license, passenger were falling out of their seats laughing.

"Remember the name," Kasim said to his audience. "Kasim the Komedian. Or triple K for half Kuyu, half Kisi, half Kamba."

He sat down amid the laughter, turned to Salim with a smile on his face.

"Now?" he asked. "*Sasa?*"

"Which one of the three halves of you is Kamba?" Salim asked.

"All of them."

"You are crazy."

"And you are envious; admit it."

"Envious of you?"

"Of what I can do."

"Don't make me laugh."

"My job."

"I still don't understand why they like you?"

"You don't like me?"

"We are family."

Kasim shot to his feet.

"Listen, you all," he said to the passengers. "This man is Salim. He is my cousin Salim. Salim is the bravest lawyer in all of Nairobi."

Salim buried his face in his hands.

"If a big, fat, corrupt policeman arrests you for nothing, Salim is your lawyer. If a big, fat, corrupt politician steals your land or your wife, Salim is your man."

Salim groaned and buried his face in his hands. The last thing he needed in his life was a bus load of pro bono clients.

"He is cute," said the wallet inspector.

"Then call him. He is a very lonely man. He lives alone, in a big, lonely apartment in Westlands. And he is loaded."

"Phone number?" she asked.

Kasim rattled out the number.

"His fees are friendly, and he gives discount. He is family."

He sat down. Salim uncovered his face.

"Why?" he asked.

"I take twenty percent," Kasim said, with his never-fading smile. "Twenty-ninety split seems fair to me. Don't you agree?"

"You can't even count," said Salim.

Kasim laughed, slapped him on the back.

"Lighten up, man," he said. "Did you see anyone take down your number? The moment they step out of this bus it will be out-of-sight-out-of-mind. Ghetto celebrity, remember?"

Salim thought to ask where he got that happy, innocent smile, and how he learned to be who he turned out to be. He did not learn it from Hurricane Eva, Aunt Charity, or any teacher that Salim knew. Unfettered originality was not something they taught, or supported, at Kathiani Primary when he went there.

"How much does your in-law pay us?" he asked. "For our Mercedes?"

"You mean Uncle Tivo's Mercedes," said Salim.

"Our Mercedes," said Kasim.

The way he saw it, Uncle Tivo never paid Caesar for the Mercedes, which therefore, now belonged to Aunt Charity, whom they had just paid a lot of money, so the Mercedes rightfully belonged to them now, and they could sell it without any qualms. Besides, it was unlikely Uncle Tivo remembered it at all.

"Our Mercedes," he said. "See?"

That was the first thing Kasim had said to him that day, that Salim remembered, that made complete sense.

"Amazing," he said. "For someone who a minute ago could not work out five percent of a hundred."

"I keep telling you I went to school."

He had also figured that, if they gave Uncle Tivo enough money to keep him happy at the off license for some time, they could use his donkeys to tow the Mercedes out of his compound and down the road, load it onto a lorry and deliver it to Salim's father-in-law.

"Split the proceeds fifty-fifty," he said.

"Thirty-ninety," said Salim.

"If you like."

"You really can't count?"

"Anything to keep you out of prison, so we continue working together."

"I keep telling you we do not work together."

"But we are."

Again, Salim was amazed at Kasim's unique approach to dealing with serious situations; how he could so easily simplify the most daunting task by laughing and finding his way round it. For sure he did not learn that from Hurricane

Eva, or from Aunt Charity, or from Caesar; or from anyone who had ever tried to educate him. He could have learned it from Uncle Tivo, at *Tivo University, School of Mechanical Engineering,* but he confessed having been too busy entertaining fellow learners to learn anything himself. Nevertheless, whoever, however, and wherever, he learned it, Kasim had come out his own man, and a special kind of man too.

Chapter 50

Caesar was finally at rest place in his place of choice, in the shade of his mango tree, draped in six feet of rich King'oo earth lovingly heaped by family and friends and a grateful clan, and topped with bouquets and wreaths from forgotten friends and strangers.

The mourners relieved of their duty to the dead Caesar, and the need to look, act and sound sad and devastated, talked loudly, laughed, and mingled. Old friends and relatives, some who had not met since the last King'oo funeral, caught up with old news.

The gravediggers, redundant and irrelevant until the next funeral, had solved the math problem Kasim left them, how to share two donkeys among five or six men, and were by the far fence asking themselves what happened to their donkeys.

The barbecue fire disaster had been dealt with in the normal King'oo way, panic and pandemonium that sometimes produced the desired results, and most of the farewell goat had been rescued. Old men were tearing into the ribs and downing mugs of goat soup in readiness for the beer to follow. Rice and chapati and pigeon peas *muthokoi* they left to women and boys.

They were going for seconds when Uncle Tivo woke up from his *chang'aa* stupor, and saw that they were about to eat everything, and wondered aloud how long it would take before anyone got it in her head to wake him and feed him. They ignored him. His importance as the oldest King'oo at Caesar's burial had elapsed the moment Caesar's burial was over.

He struggled to his feet, still quite intoxicated, stormed to the front of the line, and demanded to know why with so many women around doing nothing he had to fetch his own food.

The women were busy feeding everyone else, but an aunt rushed to oblige. Aunt Eva shoved her aside, grabbed the serving spoon from her, faced Uncle Tivo across the serving table with pots of stew and roasted goat meat between them, and there was sudden silence. She was larger than any King'oo at the burial, or elsewhere in the clandom, and next to her Uncle Tivo was an anthill. Everyone saw that and waited to see what she would do to him.

Then Aunt Kamene, fearing Eva would brain old Tivo with the ladle, rushed forward ready to restrain her. Uncle Tivo was about to back down, turn around and go home.

"Wait," Eva ordered.

She took the largest plate on the table, piled it with roast meat, fried meat, and boiled meat and held it out to him.

"I have been told that is you eat here," she said. "No wonder you are all grumpy old men."

He hesitated, looked at the plate, then at the woman holding it out to him. The gestured was uncharacteristically generous of her, and he wondered why.

"For being there," she said.

"There?" he puzzled. "There where?"

She nodded in Roger's direction.

"*Roji?*" he was more confused.

"He values your friendship," she said.

"*Roji?*" he asked again.

She nodded and smiled. The smile worried him more than the overflowing plate and the strange words coming from her mouth. Words like *thank you Uncle Tivo, I really appreciated it, Uncle Tivo, and do let me know when you need more meat.* He stood undecided whether to stay or walk away all the way home. She waited.

Someone behind him yelled at him to take his meat and move along and stop holding the line. Aunt Eva shot the man with one of her manhood shrinking glances. Then she nodded at Tivo to take his plate and move along. Uncle Tivo, nearly sober now from the encounter, looked back and reminded the grumblers they had done what they came to do, bury Caesar, and they could now wait or go home.

"*Roji* is a good man," he said to Aunt Eva. "But he does not speak Kikamba."

The old men grumbled still. She shot them another look, warning them they would be there all night if they did not behave like men and be patient. That silenced them.

"*Roji* must speak our tongue," Tivo said to her.

She nodded to show she heard, even if she did not understand why or agree with it.

"Now tell me," she said to Tivo. "Salim and Kasim? Where are they?"

King'oo to the core, he made a big show of looking round for them.

"I don't see them here," he said.

"That is why I am asking you," she said.

He shrugged, picked up his walking stick. It took a moment of fumbling to realise he could not carry plate and stick back to his seat. He called a boy to help. Aunt Eva scared the boy away with one look, took the stick and the plate and carried them to his place by Roger's side. She waited until he settled down then handed him his walking stick.

"Teach your husband to speak Kikamba," he said in English, looking for a place to lay the stick.

She stopped astounded, her mind grappling with the how, when and where he could have learned so many words of another language. And especially why no one warned her drunken Tivo might have understood everything she said when she warned Roger from becoming too comfortable with King'oo males.

Uncle Tivo stowed his stick under his chair, looked up and found her waiting for an explanation.

"King'oo men speak Kikamba," he said to her.

"Hear that?" she said to Roger, a worrisome smile in her eyes, "You are a King'oo man now."

"How?" Roger asked, also worried.

"He will tell you."

476

"Now?" she turned to Tivo before handing him his plate. "Salim and Kasim. Where are they?"

Again, he shrugged and nodded to leave the plate on the free seat next to his.

"Roger?" she asked.

Like a true King'oo man, he made a big show of looking round for someone he knew was not there. Then he shrugged. She let it pass. She would find it out later, she said to them, placing Uncle Tivo's plate where he wanted it. Roger was yet to go fetch his own food, like other tame King'oo men. Tivo invited him to share his overloaded plate.

"What about Sam?" she asked them.

Sam had left as soon as the last wreath was on Caesar's grave. He was too mentally and emotionally drained to stay for the feast, but he came to bid Roger farewell and wish him and his wife a safe journey home. He had apologised for not finding time to go out for a drink with Roger and get to know him better. He hoped Roger would come back to visit and stay longer. Then he left without a word to anyone else, not even to Uncle Tivo who sat right there next to Roger. He had enough of King'oo people.

"He gave me his business card," Roger reported. "And said not to wait until another King'oo dies."

Eva nodded quietly, thoughtfully. First Richard not coming to her, and then failing to turn up at Caesar's funeral, and now Sam leaving without a word to her. More things she would probably only understand when she was back home where things made sense. She walked quietly away looking unusually disturbed.

Roger would have liked to find out what Uncle Tivo had done to make Eva friendly to him, but Tivo had moved on. King'oo men did not discuss important business in the presence of roast goat meat, he said. They ate, quietly and seriously like other men around them, and were full when they finished Uncle Tivo's plate. Aunt Eva sent a boy with mugs of hoof soup and, again, they wonder what was going on in her mind. They did not know whether to worry with her or rejoice.

"Now," Uncle Tivo said, while they waited for the soup to cool down. "Where is my bride price?"

He spoke in English throwing Roger into a panic, and desperately looking for someone to translate it from King'oo-speak. His guardian angels were gone, and his wife had abandoned him to his King'oo manhood.

"You are a King'oo man now," she had said.

He was no longer under her protection. Every man in King'oo land carried his own man cross. She had left him to it and gone to carry her woman cross.

She had found Aunt Kamene serving Pastor Kioko, the village chief, and Caesar's old government colleagues, now old and insignificant. She snatched the serving spoon from her, thrust it at a startled cousin, took Aunt Kamene's arm and dragged her away.

"Now tell me, my sister," she said, letting go her arm. "What do you people think about me, when I am not here?"

Aunt Kamene paused, disturbed by how shaky and insecure Eva suddenly seemed. Eva who was always the one to tell off anyone who did not like the way she was, her makeup, her dress, or her hairstyle. She was the last person Aunt Kamene would have expected to worry what people thought about her.

And now here she was at Caesar's funeral worried about what her sisters thought about her when she was not there. Kamene would have loved to stick it to her, make up hateful and nasty things, and watch her ego deflate and collapse. But she could not remember anyone thinking anything bad or untrue about Eva.

"Nothing," she said to her.

"What do they say?"

"Nothing."

"What about you? What do you think about me?"

"Nothing," said Kamene.

"I am your sister. You must tell me."

"You left your father to die alone."

"He had Charity."

"Poor little Charity who, because of it, did not get a husband and go live her life. And now she will die alone, like him, without anyone to care for her."

Eva's eyes clouded, her facelift sagged and, for the first time since her arrival, she looked her age, old and helpless.

"Now you understand why for us you don't exist," said Aunt Kamene. "For everyone here, Charity has no elder sister."

"But she does," Eva pleaded. "I am her elder sister."

The clouds in her eyes were about to turn to tears, slowly edging to the wrinkles at the edge of her eyelids.

"I am Charity's big sister," she sobbed. "I am her big sister."

She was about to fall apart. Kamene tried to take her in an embrace. Realising she could not get her arms all around her, she embraced one arm and held on until the sobs subsided. Then Eva wiped the tears, sighed, shrugged off Kamene's hand and looked about. Anyone witnessing the exchange would have believed she wept for Caesar.

Inside the house, an exhausted Aunt Charity sat alone on a sofa chatting with a handful of friends and relatives who had lingered to comfort her. Eva lumbered in and without a word to anyone sat beside her and took her hand.

"Charity," she said it loudly for everyone present to hear. "You have a big sister. I am your elder sister."

Charity was as startled as everyone else. Then she took Eva's other hand in hers, place it over her own heart and hugged it. They sat holding hands, for the next hour, as visitors came to say goodbye and wish Charity peace and comfort in her loss.

Pastor Kioko was the last to enter the living room. He stopped uncertainly on finding Eva by Charity's side holding her hand. He was about to turn and go back out when Charity beckoned. She indicated the place beside her on the sofa. He approached hesitantly, his hat in his hand, and sat down where indicated. She took the hat from him and placed it on the table. One by one, the others silently rose and walked out. Finally, Eva rose too and did the same, pausing at the door to look back and wonder. Then they were all alone.

The yard was nearly deserted, most of the mourners having gone home, when Pastor Kioko came out of the house, hat in hand, and walked to the gate with Aunt Charity by his side. They had both had a long, long day, and they were not so young anymore. They walked slowly to the gate, stood just outside the gate on the deserted road to town and saw the sun go down. She took his hand again.

"What would I have done without you?" she said.

"Everything," he said. "Everything. You were always the strongest. Caesar too would have been lost without you."

Then they were silent. She had explained why she could not promise marriage, and why she refrained from acknowledging most of the notes he sent with Kasim; the love declarations and promises of undying devotion. She had believed him, when he said he would wait for her however long it took her to be free to marry. But he had wanted assurance and that she could not give.

There was more to be said, but they did not know how. Not that it mattered anymore now, but words were not enough to say it all.

"Say it, anyway" she said to him.

"You gave your whole life for Caesar," he said. "Why did he let you do it?"

"He was my father," she said. "When he defied the clan, refused to take another woman for a wife after our mother died, he gave up his life for mine. I thought you understood. You would have done the same for your children. Given your life for theirs."

The Pastor sighed and nodded and sighed again.

"If only you had let me help," he said.

"You gave me strength, knowing that you were there."

He put on his hat, hesitated, moved to embrace her. She stepped back and offered her hand. There were guests about, she seemed to say. She did not want anyone remembering Caesar's funeral that way. He took her hand, shook it awkwardly.

"I will always be there for you," he said. "Always."

Then he walked away. She watched him go down the road to town, the way she had seen him walk ages ago, only this time he was slow, stooped, and despaired. The sight of it made her sad.

"Pastor?" she called.

He stopped and looked back.

"See you on Sunday," she said.

He smiled sadly, waved, and walked on.

Hours later, when the guests had left, Caesar's daughters said their private goodbyes. They did so with few words, succeeding to this time do it with no mention their father or their mother, or the funeral or anything that might bring back the tears. Weeks of sadness and sorrow, anguish and anger were now behind them. They were together again, like in the old days, when their father sat under the mango tree with his pipe, clucking his tongue at the words he heard hurled at one another and, yes, sometimes with a smile in his eyes.

Eva, always the quickest and the strongest, was the first to admit it was unlikely they would see days like these again. Caesar's burial, she confessed, had been so hard for her she had thought of leaving halfway through. She could not do it again, but she would one day come back home, and not in a coffin.

Aunt Charity doubted they would ever be together again, all of them in the same place, together like they had in the past weeks. None of them was as fast, as strong, as healthy, or as optimistic as she used to be. They were happy to be together again, in spirit if not in body, but none of them believed Eva would ever come back home to stay.

Then they retired to their old rooms to sleep away the exhaustion leaving Eva with Charity to say her goodbyes. Charity thanked her for coming, something that left them both startled and sad. Eva was not a visitor. She was family. She had her room there, in her father's house, the house in which she was born and grew up. She had an obligation to come to be there to bury her father.

"I want my room back," she said. "Keep it free."

Then she went back to the verandah where Roger sat feeling lost and lonely, like the first time he came to meet his father-in-law and found him deep in a political crisis. Charity left them making plans for their departure and followed the other sisters to bed.

In her bedroom, to which she felt a stranger since the day she woke to find Caesar dead in his, she changed and knelt to pray. She knelt for a long time looking for a fitting prayer, one that could express what was in her heart of hearts, the gratitude she felt for the chance to be with her sisters again, to experience their love and caring in a way she had never done before. She had prayed every day and night, prayed for herself and for anyone she could think of, prayed for strength and for peace of mind and heart. And all her prayers had been answered. All that was left now was to give thanks for everything, and she could not find the words, for her heart overflowed with such gratitude. She closed her eyes and prayed the simplest prayer she knew how..

"The Lord is my shepherd I shall lack nothing. He makes me to lie down in green pastures. He leads me beside the still waters. He protects me. Thank you, Lord, thank you, thank you, thank you."

Then she rose wearily and uncovered her bed. She took the pillow to fluff it and felt something heavy fall on her toes. She picked it up and held it to the light. She sat down on the bed and for a long moment her mind went numb trying to understand the bundle of money in her hands. She had prayed hard for ways and means in the last few weeks, prayed for just such a bundle to fall from heaven, money to make her last journey with Caesar lighter. This could not be the answer to those prayers. God would not wait so long to answer her prayer.

Then she thought who else could have placed it there, and decided she could not accept it. She would return it in the morning and tell him so. She placed the money on the bedside table, got in bed and reached for her bible. When she opened it, more money rained down on the bed all around her. She was terrified. No, she thought, this could not be him. Where would he get so much money without stealing? She lay awake for a long time not knowing what to think about it.

"Pastor, Pastor," she said in the end, "What have you done?"

It saddened her. He had her love and affection long before he had anything to give. It saddened her.

THE END

Made in the USA
Middletown, DE
03 May 2023

29540321R00275